JUNK MAIL

WILL SELF

PENGUIN BOOKS

PENGUIN BOOKS

Published by the Penguin Group
Penguin Books Ltd, 27 Wrights Lane, London W8 5TZ, England
Penguin Books USA Inc., 375 Hudson Street, New York, New York 10014, USA
Penguin Books Australia Ltd, Ringwood, Victoria, Australia
Penguin Books Canada Ltd, 10 Alcorn Avenue, Toronto, Ontario, Canada M4V 3B2
Penguin Books (NZ) Ltd, 182–190 Wairau Road, Auckland 10, New Zealand

Penguin Books Ltd, Registered Offices: Harmondsworth, Middlesex, England

This collection first published by Bloomsbury 1995
Published in Penguin Books 1996
1 3 5 7 9 10 8 6 4 2

Printed in England by Clays Ltd, St Ives plc

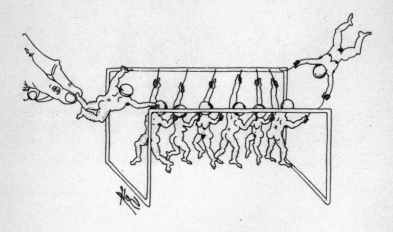

Contents

CONTENTS

Introduction and Acknowledgements

In 1991 I was living outside Oxford and broke. I was paranoid as well, convinced that tax inspectors were surveying the isolated house we lived in from a hide, cleverly constructed to look like an enormous poll-tax demand. In order to persuade officials in the council offices to leave us alone, I went into town shoeless, dressed in a donkey jacket fastened with tow rope, and bought them off with three crushed fivers and a show of imbecility (perhaps not altogether a show).

Together with an acquaintance, Phil Robson, an able and humane psychiatrist (not quite an oxymoron) who was then running the Chilton Clinic drug dependency unit in Headington, I conceived of writing a book on drugs that would bring in some cash.

Needless to say, nothing came of this meretricious undertaking. Phil and I couldn't really agree on anything much beyond what we didn't believe in; and as for a methodology, it chopped, changed and eventually disintegrated altogether.

Drug use and procrastination often go hand in tourniquet, so there seemed a certain justice in this. But further, I had been troubled by the idea of writing a book-length work exclusively on drugs for a number of reasons. First and foremost there was my very English dread of, as De Quincey put it, 'twitching away the decent drapery' and revealing personal scars and chancres to the eyes of the world. I knew damn well that a large part of what sold the treatment of the book to its potential publisher was the expectation that I would publicly grass on myself.

This in turn led to two further problems: the ever present possibility of harassment by the police; and an allied difficulty, the fact that unlike so many people who write on the subject I was not about to beat my tits and proclaim: 'I used to be a teenage werewolf, but I'm all right naooooo!' Or, as Lou Reed so succinctly puts it: 'Does anybody need another rock-and-roll singer, whose nose he says has led him straight to God?' And by the same token, does anybody need another piece of drug pornography, aimed at giving straights a hit on the blunt – yet tapering – pipe of chemical ecstasy?

And to admit to, or attempt to put forward, even remotely serious views on the politics of the subject would be asking for more opprobrium. There's something about sumptuary militancy that doesn't quite come off: 'March Now For More *Crème Brulée*!' is not a slogan calculated to win many conscientious supporters.

But the fact is that the Gordian knot of hypocrisy is now tied far too tight round 'drugs' for anyone to be able to cut it, unpick it, or do anything much but gnaw frustratedly at its hempen strands. At different places in the pieces assembled here on the subject, I quote Thomas Szasz, the veteran anti-psychiatrist: 'The so-called debate on drugs has become boring.' Quite so.

But anyway, when I came to assemble the material for this volume I saw that a large part of it was concerned with the culture of drugs, and that scattered throughout the various pieces were all the arguments and points of information that I would have wished to bring together in a book.

However, the bulk of the book is not about drugs, but rather represents the fruits of being prepared to do more or less what any editor asks me to do, having calculated the ratio of glibness to money that the commission represents. For the sad fact is that all too often the pieces I have written that have required all the labour of lifting an arse cheek and pooting it out have garnered more attention – and more importantly more money – than those I worked on for long periods and took seriously. The culmination of this tendency is the state-of-English-culture piece reproduced here, which I agonised over for a full month, and which then was published to resounding silence on all fronts.

It is characteristic of collections such as this for the author to preface them with some remarks on how things have changed since they were first written. However, in this case the pieces were written over only three or four years and not much seems to have invalidated them in terms of the march of time. Excepting, I suppose, that a chronic optimist would now view all that I had to say on the conflict in Northern Ireland a year ago as an irrelevance, given the advance of the peace process. I am not a chronic optimist.

What the tight, temporal grouping does evince, though, is the preoccupation I have had with various writers and thinkers over this period. Most notably William Burroughs, J. G. Ballard, Adam Phillips and Thomas Szasz. I make no apology for this, and hope that the reader experiences the cross-referencing of ideas that these preoccupations have engendered as a more or less acceptable curdling of the whole dish.

I would like to take this opportunity to thank all of those who have published my stuff over the years. My career as a cartoonist was aided and abetted by among others: Anna Coote, Julian Rothenstein, John Fordham, Marcel

Berlins, Vicky Hutchings and Cat Ledger. As a journalist I have tended to write for as many different publications as there are pieces in this volume, but there are some people I have maintained a continuing commissioning relationship with, and who have provoked some of the better writing I have done. In particular: Michael Watts, Andy Anthony, Tom Shone, Nick Lezard, Redmond O'Hanlon and Deborah Orr.

Thanks are also due to Shane Weller, Mary Tomlinson, Mathew De Abaitua and all at Bloomsbury who helped with the preparation of the manuscript.

But I think the last word on both drugs and journalism must go to an anonymous man in Boston who I had dinner with in May of this year, who looked at me long and dolefully over the rim of his Martini, before pronouncing: 'I've given up smoking marijuana – it makes me think too much about journalism.'

W.W.S.
Suffolk 1995

"My God, Carruthers . . . it's a rogue seminar . . .!"

PART ONE

ON DRUGS

Junk Mail

Last year having been a slap-up one for Burroughsians, it was almost too much to hope that the publication of the *Letters 1945--1959* would put any more flesh on the junk-atrophied bones of the notorious 'Hombre Invisible'. Besides, in the wake of media brouhaha surrounding David Cronenberg's *Naked Lunch* and Ted Morgan's exhaustive biography *Literary Outlaw*, how much more weight could the Burroughs myth really bear? Fortunately, the answer is: a lot.

The letters collected here by Oliver Harris have been re-edited from an expurgated edition long out of print. They are written principally to Allen Ginsberg, Burroughs's tireless friend, amanuensis, literary agent and all-round bum-chum, with short culs-de-sac heading off towards Jack Kerouac and Neal Cassady, the other corners of the Beat hotting circuit.

Harris has assembled these, together with a somewhat gee-whiz introduction and comprehensive notes, to form what may conceivably be Burroughs's best work of all. Burroughs was aware at the time of the centrality of his correspondence to his literary endeavour: 'Maybe,' he remarks to Allen Ginsberg at the core of this volume, 'the real novel is in letters to you.'

It is. The letters display all the sassiness, the marriage of Mandarin and slang, the shoot-from-the-hip aphorizing

3

of Burroughs's best prose, but decoupled from the rather portentous literary experimentation and attitudinizing that has marked his *oeuvre* since fame hit with the publication of *Naked Lunch*, shortly after the chronological end of this volume.

These letters are remarkable not least because, as their writer slowly acquires a sense of the possibility of having an input into mainstream culture, so the very cultural avant-garde of which he himself is the last great avatar fades into senselessness and irrelevance.

An omnivorous reader and perpetual student, Burroughs studded his correspondence with references both to the wilder shores of esoteric knowledge (his obsessions with Reich, Spengler and Korzybski), and, more surprisingly, to the orthodox canon of English literature: to Spenser and Dryden, Shakespeare and Pope. Burroughs quotes Pope – 'Willing to wound yet afraid to strike . . .' – in describing Bill Garver, the decrepit overcoat thief and addict-model for Bill Gains in *Junky*. And in this, his narced-out polymathy and propensity to envision grandiose universal schemas (the back-end of this volume is much preoccupied with the cancer/addiction/psychosis biopathy), Burroughs is more of an heir to De Quincey than a godfather to Frank Zappa.

The actual topography of the *Letters* includes all the muddled territories of Burroughs's best works. The journey begins within the sepia hinterland of New York, New Orleans and Mexico City that forms the backdrop for *Junky*. We then head south into Latin America, with our guide 'taking pictures, trying to get the bare dry mountains, the wind in the white dusty poplar trees, the sad little parks with statues of Generals and cupids'. It is this landscape, full of the 'stasis horrors', that gave Burroughs the material for *Queer*, his nostalgic *roman-à-clef*. But it was also in South America that he took yagé, or ayahuasca, and in a hallucinogenic trance 'called in' the mondial bazaar that would be the 'all cities, of all times and in all places' of *Naked Lunch*.

No wonder that, when Burroughs actually reached Tangier at the beginning of 1954, he was miserably disappointed: 'What's all this old Moslem culture shit?' he writes to Ginsberg with sublime incorrectness. 'One thing I have learned. I know what Arabs do all day and night. They sit around smoking cut weed and playing some silly card game.' But German efficiency in synthesizing opiates kept him there – he was soon heavily hooked on Eukodol, a particularly nasty hypnotic/analgesic morphine substitute – and Tangier gradually swam into view, its lineaments congruent with those of the other 'Cities of the Red Night'.

Part of the Burroughs mythology that he himself wilfully cultivated was the idea that *Naked Lunch* was written on junk. In the introduction to the Olympia Press edition (for a long time standard, and one which we now learn Allen Ginsberg objected to at the time), Burroughs wrote that he could 'barely remember' taking the notes that grew into the corpus of the book. In the *Letters* this confabulation is rectified. While the letters written during his pernicious Eukodol phase are relatively spare and constrained, after his revolutionary apomorphine treatment in London with Dr Arthur Dent (the founding editor of the *British Journal of Addiction*), they become lapidary, freighted with the almost hysterical material that made up the very best of his 'routines'.

When he was finally clean from junk, Burroughs was, in Hemingway's coinage, 'juiced'; and like Georges Simenon, another great high-speed typist, Burroughs felt the work 'coming almost like dictation'. For the Burroughsian these later letters from the Tangier period are the most satisfying. They contain almost verbatim several of the most important routines in *Naked Lunch*, including the 'Talking Asshole', 'Dr Benway's Interzone Clinic' and the genesis of 'A.J.', as well as providing far more effectively than Ted Morgan's biography the primary atmosphere out of which Burroughs distilled his great sense of millenarian miasma.

However, for committed non-Burroughsians these *Letters* are an even better investment. Whether it was drugs, homosexuality, gratuitous yuckiness, stylistic sloppiness or wilful obscurantism that in the past drove you away from the corpus of Burroughs's work, I can confidently predict that the spare wit of the letters alone may well draw you in at last.

Who else but Burroughs could write of London, a city he cordially detested: '[It] drags me like a sea anchor. I want to see bright blue sky with vultures in it. A vulture in London would be an Addams cartoon . . .' Quite so.

Independent on Sunday, August 1993

The Literary Monkey

William Burroughs's *Junky* is an oddity of a book. Ostensibly an account of heroin addiction in 1940s America, related in a deadpan style that owes much to the hard-boiled prose of Dashiell Hammett, it contains within its slender Trojan-horse narrative a veritable army of literary innovations. Cast in the form of a confession, *Junky* is as far from being a moral condemnation of heroin addiction as it is possible to imagine. Rather, it is an amoral discourse that inverts the practice of confessing, to reveal the impossibility of redemption in the modern world.

In order to counter possible objections – legalistic and otherwise – to publishing such a bald account of willed depravity, A. A. Wyn of Ace Books, Burroughs's original publisher, insisted that he append a prologue to the book which gave some explanation of how someone such as he, a Harvard graduate from a social-register family, came to be a junkie.

But despite the flimsy tales of adolescent delinquency and homosexuality, William Burroughs's prologue is remarkable for introducing a picture of sensual memory, linked to narcotics, that in every way echoes Thomas De Quincey's concept of the 'involute'. Burroughs writes, in his authorial guise as William Lee: 'My earliest memories are colored by a fear of nightmares. I was afraid to be alone, and afraid of the dark, and afraid to go to sleep because of dreams where

7

a supernatural horror seemed always on the point of taking shape.'

He hears a maid talking about how 'smoking opium brings sweet dreams' and resolves to smoke it himself when he grows up. When Burroughs begins his account of his actual heroin use, in the gloom and depression of wartime New York, this involute is recast. After his first shot of morphine, he experiences 'a strong feeling of fear. I had the feeling that some horrible image was just beyond the field of vision, moving, as I turned my head, so that I never quite saw it.'

The fear that adumbrates Lee's experience of junk is never directly named; instead, it is indicated by the way the narrative voice itself swims into the reader's consciousness, as if out of some indefinable darkness, an inchoate place where stories are begun but never completed. For *Junky* is a book not simply about heroin addiction, but really about the existential predicament of modern man in its broadest sense. It is no accident that one of the most commonly employed words in the text is 'subject', which Burroughs uses to distinguish his shadowy narrator from the 'object' or 'other'.

The bulk of the book is concerned with flat pronouncements about the nature of the heroin addict's life, his stratagems for obtaining money and drugs, his confrères and his sexual mores. In this area, Burroughs is masterful, never speaking with less than full authority. His opening apophthegm on the essential character of heroin addiction can serve as a model of all those that follow: 'Junk is not a kick. It is a way of life.'

But these plangent sections of philosophy are interspersed with a gallimaufry of grotesque characters and gobbets of demotic speech which bring the drug world to life beautifully. A hoodlum tells a story of how he beat a man to death, which ends with the memorable line: 'My girl was waiting out in the car. She called me – ha-ha-ha! – she called me – ha-ha-ha! – a cold-blooded killer.'

When Burroughs's narrator is trying to 'push tea' (deal marijuana), and the woman in whose apartment he keeps the stash has had enough, she expels him in this fashion: '"Take this and get out," she said. "You're both mother fuckers." She was half asleep. Her voice was matter-of-fact as if referring to actual incest.'

In other parts of the book, characters are summoned up by slender shards of sharp observation. Of one junkie: 'The cheek-bones were high and he looked Oriental. His ears stuck out at right angles from his asymmetrical skull.' Of another: 'He looked like one of those terracotta heads that you plant grass in. A peasant face, with peasant intuition, stupidity, shrewdness and malice.' And describing a psychiatrist who attempts to treat him, the narrator says: 'He had long legs and a heavy body shaped like a pear with the narrow end up. He smiled when he talked and his voice was whiny. He was not effeminate. He simply had none of whatever it is that makes a man a man.'

The story, such as it is, describes a line of great resistance, maintained by William Lee against a hostile world full of stool-pigeon junkies and short-count pushers; with 'the people', the Federal narcotics agents everywhere, waiting to pounce. From New York, he sets off on an odyssey that takes him via a sojourn at the Lexington 'drug farm', to New Orleans and, eventually, to Mexico City. Here the book ends, with Lee concluding that, just as he cannot divine what made him take up heroin in the first place, he has no idea why he has decided to give it up.

This is, of course, the logical conclusion. For in describing addiction as a way of life, Burroughs creates a synecdoche through which he can explore the being of man under late capitalism. His descriptions of the 'junk territories' of the cities his narrator inhabits are, in fact, depictions of urban alienation itself. And just as in these areas junk is 'a ghost in daylight on a crowded street', so his junkie characters, who are invariably described as 'invisible', 'dematerialized' and 'boneless', are, like the pseudonymous William Lee himself, the sentient residue left behind when the soul has been cooked up and injected into space.

Sunday Times, May 1993

New Crack City

A journalist friend of mine asks me to take her out on the street and show her some crack dealing in action. I can't understand why she needs my help. You only have to stand outside the main entrance to King's Cross for five minutes to start spotting the street people who are involved with drugs. King's Cross has always had a name for prostitution, and where there are brasses there's always smack; and nowadays if you're anywhere in London where there's smack, then there will be crack as well. The two go together like *foie gras* and toast.

Still, I suppose I can understand why my journalist friend needs me. The London street drug scene is as subject to the caste principle as any other part of English society; druggies identify one another by eye contact and little else. As Raymond Chandler once remarked: 'It's difficult to tell a well-controlled doper apart from a vegetarian bookkeeper.' All up and down the promenade outside King's Cross, druggies are making eye contact with one another. There are Italians – they're principally interested in smack – and a contingent of young black men hanging out with white prostitutes. These men are pimps as well as being crack dealers.

We watch the scene: dealers carry rocks of crack or tiny packets of smack wrapped up in silver foil and cling-film inside their cheeks. When a punter scores, he discreetly

11

tucks the money into the dealer's hand, the dealer drops the rock or the smack out of his mouth and into the punter's palm. The whole transaction takes only a few seconds. 'Why aren't the police doing anything?' moans my journalist friend. 'It's all so blatant.'

And it is. But what can the police do? Snarl up the whole of King's Cross in the middle of the rush hour while they try and nab a few street dealers? Supposing they do manage to collar them: the dealers will have swallowed their stash. Fear is a fantastic lubricant.

We've seen the street action, and my journalist friend wants to check out a crack den: do I know of one? Well, yes, as a matter of fact, I have some friends in the East End who are well-established crack and smack dealers, but they're not the sort of people who accept house calls, especially from journalists. What a shame I can't take my voyeuristic friend, but I can take you . . .

The day's action is just beginning up at Bob's place. It's about seven in the evening. Someone has been to see the Cypriot and they're washing up a quarter ounce of powdered cocaine in the kitchen of Bob's flat.

Bob's flat is situated at the very end of the outside walkway on the top floor of a thirties council block in Hackney. It's a good position for a drug dealer. The police have to come up four flights and get through a locked, bolted and chained door and a barred gate set in the flat's internal passageway before they can gain access. The windows are also barred.

Not that this deters them. To give the constabulary their due, they have turned Bob's place over several times recently, but they never find anything. Bob keeps his stash up his anus. The police know this but they can't be bothered to pull him in and fence with his brief while they wait for it to come out. Bob would have a good brief as well. Bob's family are well established in this area; this has been their manor for years. Three generations of the family have been hard men around here, respected men. Before they got into drugs they were into another kind of blag altogether: armed robbery.

Bob once told me how they made the switch: 'Chance, really. We were doing a number on this Nigerian bloke. We knew he had something but we didn't know what. It was six kilos of brown. I got the fucker down on the floor with my shooter in his ear and said: "You're fucking lucky we're not the old bill!"'

Bob is a talkative soul: bright, articulate and possessed of a gallows humour that counts for wit in this society. But Bob is mighty keen on that rock. Sometimes he'll be up for several days on end rocking it. Not that the crack is his core business – that's still smack.

As William Burroughs so pithily observed, smack is the only commodity that you don't have to sell to people; instead, you sell people to it. And the people who *it* buys come in all shapes and sizes. At Bob's, most of them get dealt with through the bars of the safety gate in the long, dark corridor that runs the length of the flat. The clientele are a really mixed bunch; all the way from shot-to-pieces street junkies, indistinguishable from alcoholics apart from the abscesses on their hands, to the smart end of the carriage trade: a young man, incongruously dressed in a velvet-collared crombie, is buying a rock and a bag of brown when we arrive. He has an accent that would sit more comfortably in St James's than in a Hackney council estate.

Bob doesn't have a pit bull or a Rottweiler; he doesn't need one. The other dealers around here all know who his family are and they respect them. But what about the Yardies? They don't respect man or beast. The word on the scene is that they carry automatic weapons and aren't afraid to use them. They have no respect for the conventions of the London criminal world. I asked Bob about it. 'Yardies?' he snorted. 'They're just another bunch of coons.'

In truth, there are always a lot of black people around at Bob's place. They're heavily involved in the crack scene. Most of them are second- and even third-generation English. They talk like Bob and his family, and a lot of them have done bird together. Bob's current dealing partner, Bruno, is black, and Bob himself has been scoring half ounces of smack through a Yardie.

I'll take you down the dark corridor to the kitchen where Bruno is washing up. Bob's place is always pretty cluttered, so mind the stuff lying around in the hall. Like a lot of professional dealers, Bob is eclectic in his activities. There are always consumer durables lying around the flat that have either been swapped for drugs, or are stolen goods waiting for a buyer. Bob loves gadgets, and he'll often detain an antsy punter and force him to watch while Bob takes the latest lap-top computing device through its paces.

Bruno is holding a whisky miniature over the steam that's spouting from an electric kettle. The little bottle has a solution of acetone, water and powdered cocaine in it. As we watch, Bruno takes a long metal rod and dips it down the neck of the bottle. A large crystal forms around the rod almost immediately. This is crack cocaine. The fresh rocks have to dry out on a bit of kitchen towel for a while, but then they're ready to smoke.

There are no Coke cans with holes in them round at Bob's. This is a piping household. The pipes are small glass things that look like they belong in the laboratory. The bowl is formed by pressing a piece of gauze down the barrel of a thin Pyrex stem; fragments of crack are sprinkled on top of a bed of ash; the outside of the stem is heated with a blowtorch until the crack begins to deliquesce and melt, then the thick white smoke is drawn off, through the glass body of the pipe and out through a long, flat stem. Smoking a crack pipe properly is an art form.

If you came at the right time, Bob might ask you to join him – if he likes you, that is. And you could while away the evening doing pipe after pipe, with the odd chase of smack in between to stop yourself having a heart attack, or a stroke, or the screaming ad dabs. If you stay, you'll have some amicable conversations with people – one of the Yardies might drop by. The English blacks are also dismissive of them. Bruno says: 'Yardies? They're just down from the trees, man.' It is almost universally agreed that the Yardies overplayed their hand in London. They were easy to spot, too flamboyant for our pinched, *petit bourgeois* drug culture. The Met has managed to have the bulk of them deported, but their influence as a catalyst to the drug scene has gone on working.

But now Bob is expecting his dad, whose flat this is and who is due out on a spot of home leave. It's not that he doesn't want his dad to know that he's dealing out of the flat; far from it. In fact, Bob's dad will expect a commission. It's rather that he won't want to see a lot of low-life punters hanging around the place. So we say our goodbyes:

'Stay safe, man.'

'Yeah, mind yer backs.'

Security is always variable at Bob's; sometimes, when he's especially lucid, it's fantastic. He drills punters to carefully wrap crack and smack and stash the little waterproof bundles, either up their anuses or in their mouths. As Bob says: 'The filth pull a lot of punters as they're leaving here, and they sweat you, so make sure you stash that gear 'cos I don't want to do ten because some dozy prannet had it in his hand.' But at other times, you'll find six or seven addicts scratching outside the door of the flat, waiting for the Man. And there are young black kids running up and down the walkways of the flats, taunting the addicts, especially the white ones.

Even out in the street, Bob's influence is still felt. A tall, young black dude in a BMW CSi notices us coming out of Bob's block and calls us over. 'Have we come from Bob's? And do we want to go somewhere else where we can go on rocking?' Well, of course we do! We have our public to satisfy.

Basie drives us back up towards the Cross. It's dark now. He keeps up a running monologue for our benefit; it's sheer braggadocio: 'Yeah, I've bin back to Africa, man. I hung so much paper in Morocco they probably thought I was decorating the place.' He isn't altogether bullshitting. I know from Bob that Basie is both successful at 'hanging paper' (passing false cheques) and at Bob's traditional blag: sprinting into financial institutions with the old sawn-off. I've seen Basie round at Bob's before. Sometimes he'll have a couple of quite classy tarts with him who look vaguely Mayfairy: all caramel tan streaky blonde hair and bright pink lips. If it wasn't for the hungry look and the strained eyes, one might almost take them for PR account handlers.

Up at the Cross, we turn into a backstreet and park the wedge. There's a crack house here that conforms a little more to our public's expectation. It's a squat with smashed windows and no electricity. Once Basie has got us inside, we are confronted with a throng of black faces. Everyone here is either buying, selling or smoking crack. Candles form islands of yellow light around which ivoried faces contort with drawing on the little glass pipes.

The atmosphere here is a lot heavier. Sure, Bob's place isn't exactly a picnic, but at least at his flat there is the sense that there actually *are* rules to be transgressed. Of course, it's bullshit to say there is honour among thieves, but there is a hierarchy of modified trust: 'I think you're a pukkah bloke, and I'll trust you and look out for you until it's slightly more in my favour to do otherwise.' It's an ethic of enlightened self-interest that isn't that dissimilar to any other rapacious free market where young men vie with one another to possess and trade in commodities. And, after all, isn't that what Mrs T wanted us to do? Tool around London in our Peugeot 205s and Golf GTis, cellular phones at the ready, hanging out to cut the competitive mustard.

But, at the crack house in King's Cross, we have no cachet, and we have the feeling here of being very isolated: a wrong move, a word out of place, and these people might get very nasty. The people here are much more 'streety' and they have very little to lose.

We've seen what we wanted to see, we've come full circle: you don't want to stay in the crack zone, do you? No, I didn't think so. Turn the page, get on with the next article, go home.

Evening Standard, September 1991

Mushrooms Galore

Aldous Huxley, that veteran psychedelic experimenter, once said of his younger and more turbulent acolyte, Timothy Leary, 'If only Tim weren't such a silly ass.' This could usefully serve as blanket condemnation for most of the philosophically inclined figures who owe their mind-set (these people must possess such an elusive attribute, as they themselves ascribe it so ubiquitously) to the cultural revolutions of the 1960s.

Certainly Terence McKenna is a silly ass. But his heart is so clearly in the right place, and so much of what he says is a fresh synthesis of a collection of 1960s ideas that are rumbling on into the '90s and acquiring further irrational adherents, that *Food of the Gods* deserves careful attention. It follows on from *Flesh of the Gods*, the seminal collection of papers on the ritual use of hallucinogens, edited by Peter Furst and published in 1972. The theory that McKenna puts forward is an honest and heartfelt attempt to move the issue of drug-induced intoxication from the wings to the centre-stage of our collective will-to-relate.

McKenna is a believer in an unusual form of dialectical materialism, for the material in question is any psychoactive substance, whether crack cocaine or cane sugar. He holds that cultural form can be 'read off' from the drugs ingested by any given population group. Thus 'Dominator' cultures, which McKenna thinks are a Bad Thing, are exemplified by their use of tobacco and alcohol; whereas 'Partnership' cultures – an emphatically Good Thing – are hip to the ingestion of psilocybin mushrooms, marijuana, and especially dimethyltryptamine, an extremely powerful, short-acting psychedelic drug, found in the ayahuasca and the yoppo or ebene of the Amazonian rainforest shamans.

DMT is McKenna's favourite drug – he's not afraid of telling us so. He writes of 'the most profound of the indole hallucinogen-induced ecstasies, the rarely encountered but incomparable experience of smoking dimethyltryptamine'. And in this lies one of the admirable aspects of McKenna's work: he is not afraid to join in the debate on drugs at the right level, namely one which implies giving a positive account of the social and spiritual value of intoxication. Most contemporary writers on drugs fall foul of this, precisely because of their fear of being tarred with the Leary brush. The taboos against the use of illegal drugs are currently as rigid as they ever were, and any commentator who admits to having 'turned on' is certain to be dismissed as an addled mind.

It is a common feature of psychedelic drug experience that the character of the eidetic visions is often influenced by the drug itself. Thus, those who ingest peyote buttons see human figures with peyote button heads, bus-shelters with wheeled peyote buttons pulling up at them, and tax returns with a suspiciously cactusy aspect. So it is that McKenna sees the world in the blue-grey flesh of the psilocybin mushroom. He is a meta-Kantian, holding that the very phenomenon of sentience itself is a function of a symbiotic relationship between *Homo sapiens* and the plant species that contain psychoactive alkaloids.

Just as phenomenologists with a Darwinian bent identify Lockean secondary qualities, such as colour, as being extended phenotypes (i.e. interspecies forms of informational coding that are impacted on by natural selection), so McKenna goes several steps further. For him the 'wetware' of our minds is profoundly bound up with our own ecosystem. This he characterizes, after Lovelock, as the 'Gaian biosphere'. By this McKenna means a self-regulating planetary organism, a 'Transcendent Other', a 'Vegetable Mind' – although why vegetables should necessarily have the upper designatory hand is beyond me. After all, the biosphere is just as much a function of purely chemical reactions; so this must be another unfortunate example of McKenna's proclivity for seeing the world in the gills of a mushroom.

McKenna has brought together Richard Dawkins's Neo-Darwinianism and Daniel Dennett's synthesized idea of 'memes' (concepts themselves as self-replicating organisms, subject to natural selection) to paint a picture of human consciousness as an evolutionary gestalt. This is a challenging and germane theory – the trouble is that McKenna develops it with a series of arguments that can be described as 'T-shirt syllogisms'. One such is: 'Agriculture brings with it the potential for overproduction, which leads to excessive wealth, hoarding, and trade. Trade leads to cities; cities isolate their inhabitants from the natural world.' This sounds uncomfortably like: 'If I drink, I get drunk. If I get drunk, I fall over. If I fall over . . .' etc. McKenna doesn't seem to see that his refusal to acknowledge the wholly reciprocal relation between human consciousness and drug 'effect' (Leary's concept of 'set' and 'setting', which he quotes with approval) leads to a biological reductionism that smacks suspiciously of the kind of scientism he is keenest to refute.

On a more prosaic level, it is by no means certain that the plant alkaloids that McKenna so reveres 'play an active part in the plant organisms they occur within'. This would, of course, be a crucial precondition if these substances are to play the role of extended phenotypes (or in his own formulation: 'extrapherenomes') that McKenna has assigned for them. A more traditional view is that the adaptive advantage of alkaloids (many of which are highly toxic) for the plant species that contain them is as poisons. This would make sense. After all, what could be a better way of ensuring – if you are a mushroom – that you will only be eaten by a small group of McKenna-minded hominids than synthesizing psilocybin?

McKenna trawls for the usual, suspect evidences and arguments in social anthropology and archaeology to put forward the now largely discredited theory that at some point in the human past there existed a pacific, pastoral ur-culture, an Eden from which we have all been expelled. McKenna is confused about self-consciousness, because, on the one hand, it is our bit of the Gaian mind, the 'Transcendent Other', and, on the other, it is so clearly the substratum of the nasty, meat-eating, tooth-rotting ego-obsession which he blames for the 'moral decadence' we now face.

But *Food of the Gods* is worth reading for McKenna's incisive way with the hypocrisy of our current attitudes towards psychoactive drugs. He argues persuasively for a freeing of the market in drugs, remarking pithily at one point that 'any society that can tolerate the use of a drug such as alcohol, can cope with just about anything'. But it's a pity that his monomania didn't allow him to recall that Bwitiists, the Fang adherents to the only extant psychedelic religious ritual in the Old World, hold that the 'ecstasies' they achieve through chanting and drumming are superior to those induced by ibogaine, one of McKenna's precious harmaline alkaloids.

McKenna also wishes to turn his back on all drugs he characterizes as exemplifying 'Dominator' cultures, and this leads him into tendentious reasoning concerning the use of *Nicotiana rustica* in Central American shamanic ritual: obviously the idea of human consciousness breaking through the meniscus of conditioned ontology under the influence of twenty Silk Cut is too much for him to bear. He echoes approvingly the words of Richard Evans Schultes, the 'founding father of ethnopsychopharmacology', who spoke of the shamanism of the Sibundoy Valley of southern Colombia as representing 'the most highly evolved narcotic consciousness on earth'. Naturally these people partake of dimethyltryptamine. McKenna also digs into the controversies concerning the identity of 'soma', the ancient ecstatic drug of the Rig Vedas, and Wasson's attempt to prove that it was fly agaric. Unsurprisingly, after numerous deliberations, McKenna plumps for another mushroom which contains his beloved psilocybin, *Stropharia cubensis* – while it seems just as probable that soma may have been derived from the opium poppy – not a plant of which McKenna approves. McKenna writes of Schultes, 'the reticent Brahmin', and muses disingenuously as to whether he and Leary, Harvard contemporaries, 'saw much to like in the other'. What is certain is that neither Schultes nor Wasson (who was horrified by the hordes of hippy experimenters who descended on Oxaca to 'do mushrooms', after his seminal *Life* article of the early 1960s) would find much to like in McKenna, who is subject to giving interviews in youth/style magazines, wearing Jackson Pollock sweatshirts, and pushing DMT at the kids, his only caveat being that you may 'die of astonishment'.

McKenna is an active guru. His ideas chime in with the lifestyles of the growing numbers of New Agers, or

MUSHROOMS GALORE

'Archaic Revivalists' as he would term them. And for that reason it is depressing to have to conclude that if – as one of McKenna's source thinkers, Marshall McLuhan, opined – the medium is indeed the message, then we may look forward to a steadily lengthening, ever-billowing, cosmic clothes-line of McKenna's T-shirt syllogisms.

Times Literary Supplement, January 1993

Reeling and Writhing

Avital Ronell is the professor of comparative literature at Berkeley, and, according to Sandar Gilman, 'perhaps the most interesting scholar in America'. In so far as the subject of comparative literature implies the most eclectic possible ranges of comparison, Ronell does not disappoint. In *Crack Wars* she subjects Flaubert's *Madame Bovary* to a meta-analysis predicated on the conceit that literature was the first form of narcosis and Emma Bovary a main-lining junkie, scoring intially from subscription libraries, but latterly hitting up whole volumes of Walter Scott in order to get a decent rush.

In *Crack Wars* Heidegger, Freud, Nietzsche, Baudelaire, Gautier, Arendt, Burroughs, Benjamin, Derrida and Lacan are brought together by Ronell the choreographer to weave a delicate pavane of pretension. And that's only the pre-credits. If you can make it to the end of this wilfully prolix work you will have been treated to an entire cast and crew list that meets the problematic of deconstruction by naming the clapperboard boy as the clapperboard is clapped.

This work is like crack itself in one very important respect: even a dosage of as little as twenty lines (an approximate equivalent of, say, 100 milligrams of cocaine hydrochloride – or a quarter of a commercial rock to those of you poor sods who are out hustling on the street) may be sufficient to induce cardiac Arrhythmia, incipient aneurysm and subsequent fatality in almost any British literary academic. For Ronell's prose fizzes and deliquesces like crack; it is at one and the same time ultimately compelling and ridiculously febrile.

Of course the real lie to the validity of *Crack Wars* could be the availability and cost of crack itself. In the United States, where, according to my informants, the precincts of most institutions of higher education are spread, not with gravel, but with discarded crack vials, as little as $5 can secure a rush to carry you through the most tedious of lectures. Here on the sceptr'd isle you would have to part with ten times that amount. And even then you would probably find yourself coming down just as the poor Fellow was clearing his throat.

Ronell takes the Heideggerian philosophical schema, whereby the presupposition of an ontological ground to identity is self-evidently impossible – a sort of epistemo-logical version of Gödel's incompleteness theorem – as the starting-point of all literary criticism. She is right in this: the whole of the twentieth-century eruption in French literary criticism was, after all, nothing but a sophisticated ligging of German metaphysics. It is no accident that one can hardly think of a major French cultural figure who hasn't been accused of collaboration. But thereafter Ronell departs hard and fast for the wilder shores of speculation. The quotation from Heidegger's *Sein und Zeit* – 'Addiction and urge are possibilities rooted in the thrownness of Dasein' – with which she prefaces *Crack Wars* cuts the ground from under her feet. For, as Professor Ronell cannot help but be aware, Heidegger himself explicitly denied the validity of any interpretation of his work not conducted in German itself. But try telling this to a bunch of Berkeleyans cruising on crack.

Her other principal conceit is the conflation of *Abhängigkeit* with *süchtig*, allowing her to foist an awareness of the metabolic stringencies of addiction on a man who probably had none whatsoever. But once she's got going, there's little that will stop her. The first half of the book is a farrago of existentialist and deconstructionist terminology that for sheer involuted obtuseness would take some beating. I would recommend that Professor Ronell herself be beaten about the head with a copy of Adorno's *Jargon of Authenticity* and returned to the campus for further teaching duties.

It's a shame really, because the kind of cultural reading she is urging on us does have some validity. The parallels between the 'intoxification' of literature, both reeling and writhing, and those of drugs are manifold. Ronell observes correctly that the experience of drugs cannot be adduced to any one schema; rather philosophy, chemistry, therapeutics and aesthetics are all equally implicated. Indeed it is worth noting that in the last ten years an entirely new subset of anthropology has grown up, christened with succinct charm, 'Drink Studies'. But Ronell's feeble puns – 'Thomas De Quincey cited Wordsworth. These texts are on each other. A textual communication based on tropium'; 'the history of our culture as a problem in narcossism'; 'literature . . . the breeding ground of hallucinogenres' – can provoke only the hollowest laughter.

Crack Wars is a four-in-the-morning book. It's the sort of book one finds while scrabbling at breadcrumbs that have become lodged in the twist pile. One's cracked-up sensibility is convinced that this crumb is a fragment of crack. One inserts it into the glass maw of the crack pipe and applies the wavering tongue of the blowtorch. But instead of the longed-for cohobation – the liquid twist of the viscous white smoke of ecstasy – there is only the particular smell of singed Wonderloaf.

As befits Ronell's ideology, she delights in the elision of genres. She has some sections that are playlets: dialogues between Heidegger, Freud, Nietzsche and Gautier; others that are mock-technical, like the pseudo-pathologist's report on 'Ms Bovary'. This, together with the way that the University of Nebraska Press has lavished an assortment of typefaces on her text, ranging from Garamond to Helvetica Ultra for marginal notations, brings *Crack Wars* closer in spirit to the works of, arguably, America's Greatest Living Philosopher. I refer, of course, to Woody Allen.

Allen, it may be recalled, wrote a skit for the *New Yorker* on the idea of a professor of literature at Columbia being magically interpolated into *Madame Bovary*, where he becomes lover number two, in between Rodolphe and Léon. This causes students all over *mittel*-America to look up from their copies agog, and cry out, 'Who's the Jew in the leisure suit on page 212?!'

Another Allen gag relevant to *Crack Wars* was his prefatory remarks to the essay 'Notes from the Overfed', which, Allen said, was written after nightmares occasioned by reading *The Weightwatcher's Guide* and *Fear and Trembling* during one insomniac night.

I would venture that much of *Crack Wars* may conceivably have been written during the aftermath of a heavy crack-and-Heidegger binge. I like to picture Professor Ronell gobbling down the occasional handful of Dalmaine, with a swig of Chivas Regal, while her mental gorge struggles with the nauseating effort of regurgitating half-digested gobbets of the *Lectures on Metaphysics*.

How long can it possibly be before she loses her tenure altogether?

Modern Review, Summer 1992

Let Us Intoxicate

So, the Liberal Democrats have voted to legalize marijuana and their 'leaders' are refusing to go along with it. So much for liberalism, so much for democracy. I heard one of these wallahs on the radio news the other night: 'Do you want to see a hash-sponsored Grand Prix? Do you want marijuana cigarettes on sale in tobacconists?' As if this were the very height of folly. Well, in some senses, no. While I, like many many other people, would like to see marijuana decriminalized, I don't want the intoxication it engenders to become conflated with the dreadful rituals already surrounding our society's drug of choice. I refer, of course, to our old friend ethyl alcohol.

What is wrong with intoxication in our society is that it is becoming increasingly decoupled from any meaningful ritual. In so-called 'primitive' cultures intoxication is almost always incorporated into ceremonies, whether they be rites of passage, shamanistic feats of auspication, or the visible expressions of social bonds.

You need look no further than the rituals surrounding kava in Tahiti to see just how elaborate these can be. In traditional Tahitian society, where you sit during the mastication of this distinctly unexciting drug (Westerners who have taken it say the effect is pretty much like a whole-body shot of Novocaine) defines your social status more exactly than your social status itself. Indeed you can read off from the kava ceremonial an entire structural analysis of Tahitian power-relations, much in the manner that Lévi-Strauss defined the complex tattooing of the Amazonian Bororo in *Tristes Tropiques*.

What the kava ceremonial serves to show is that the use of a drug is just as much a function of set and setting as it is of any irreducible neuropharmacological property of the substance. This theory of 'set' and 'setting' was initially propagated by Dr Timothy Leary and Andrew Weil (most notably in the latter's seminal work *The Natural Mind*). It states what is obvious to anyone who has ever experienced any form of intoxication. Namely, that your anticipation of a drug experience, and the setting in which you take that drug, influence its effects just as much as – if not more than – the drug itself.

How else to explain the radically different effects that the same drugs have on the same people at different times? Put bluntly: if you drop acid with a sense of trepidation and then head off for a late-night showing of *The Texas Chainsaw Massacre*, you can more or less guarantee yourself a bad trip. But at a less extreme level, sometimes you can find ethyl alcohol making you gregarious, sometimes you can find it turning you into Mr Blubby. Same drug – different set and setting.

Anthropologists who study the use of intoxicants in different cultures have a radically different view of the phenomena we call 'drug addiction' and 'alcoholism' than do the medical and legal establishments who make it their business to police what we do with our consciousnesses. In her foreword to a collection of essays embodying this anthropological approach to intoxication, entitled *Constructive Drinking* (one of my favourite book titles), Mary Douglas writes: 'The concept of "alcoholism" is not understood outside developed cultures.' For a vivid account of constructive drinking, look no further than Norman Lewis's *A Dragon Apparent*, in which he describes the rice spirit rituals of the Vietnamese M'nong. Although by our standards the entire people are chronic alcoholics, by theirs they are just living in the way they always have.

By the same token, while I was resident in Orkney over last winter I was amused to see that in the local doctor's surgery there were no less than fifteen pamphlets warning patients of the dangers of illegal drugs – which are pretty scarce in Orkney – and just the one advertising the services of Drinkwise Scotland. This in a place where it is not unknown for people in their twenties to have chronic stomach ulcers from imbibing 'the odd dram'.

The point is that drinking or drug-taking is only 'pathological' in so far as it departs from meaningful ritual. 'Alcoholics' and 'drug addicts' are merely that statistically definable component of our collectivity who are paying with their lives for our inability to take a more constructive view of intoxication. Of course, I'm not the first person to have hit upon this view. I remember being absolutely gripped some ten years ago by Thomas Szasz's *Ceremonial Chemistry: The Ritual Persecution of Drugs, Addicts and Pushers*. In this book the veteran Viennese anti-psychiatrist argued that the illegal status of drugs in our culture was a function of what he termed 'professional closure' on the part of the medical and pharmacological professions.

To a doctor, who wishes to maintain his exclusive right to prescribe drugs, the spectacle of people self-medicating is an intolerable infringement, a challenge to his income source and expertise. Szasz argued that the rituals that have developed around the use of illegal drugs are a kind of intoxicated black mass, a counter-religion to the established orthodoxies of popping benzodiazepines, drinking ethyl alcohol and smoking cigarettes. Certainly that's the way that many drug-takers view them themselves: the more illegal the drug, the more ritualized the behaviour. The lineaments of the 'hard' drug culture I have found to translate across almost all other cultural barriers. People shoot smack in the same way in Sydney, London and Los Angeles.

Doctors, politicians and jurists talk about drugs as if they were some scourge attacking our society. They personify 'drugs' as if they were sentient beings, deciding to wreck our children's lives. The same old shibboleths are tirelessly repeated in the press day after day, about how unscrupulous pushers are targeting our kids. Although, as William Burroughs so justly remarked: who would want a child as a customer – they're unreliable and don't have much money. But on the other side of the argument, the people who wish to legalize, or at any rate decriminalize, drugs don't propose any meaningful way of using them, which brings us back to Alan Beith, the aforementioned Liberal Democrat spokesman.

No one would want to see drugs freely available so that they could be used in the way that alcohol currently is. I don't want to see Needle Park any more than I want to see the grass arena of Camden Town. I don't want to see the Crack County Championship any more than I want to see cricket sponsored by tobacco companies.

But attitudes and practices of this kind cannot be determined from above, by governmental fiat. That's the mistake of all of those currently engaged in the so-called 'debate on drugs' (a debate which Thomas Szasz has quite rightly defined as boring). This loose coalition of doctors who believe they have the right to force us to be healthy, and politicians who kowtow to them, imagining that the law exists to encourage our best impulses, not disbar our worst, are engaged in a futile pursuit.

Of course, not all of our current drug rituals are antisocial and antispiritual. You can still experience the odd evening in which the collective imbibing of ethyl alcohol appears not simply enjoyable, but in some way instinctively right: a proper expression of the conviviality that should bind us together. But all too often this doesn't hold up. Young people aren't taught how to drink 'constructively' any more, instead they are brought up to view all intoxication as 'naughty but nice'.

Young people should be educated to use drugs in a meaningful way. Our culture should have its own defined initiation ceremonies involving the use of drugs, just as other cultures do, and these rituals should be socially approved and perhaps even enjoined. I'm not talking about some awful, contrived cobblers made up in equal parts of spliff, Khalil Gibran and Bob Dylan, but something that is generated by the people themselves. For that reason, I believe there is more genuine 'spirituality' in most acid-house raves than you'll find in a pub.

The great thing about the language of intoxication is that it is a more compliant idiom, it helps people to bridge the gap between less mutable aspects of themselves: looks, confidence, social and economic status. Being high is a great leveller. What I think confuses people about the whole drive to intoxication (which some theorists, notably Ronald Siegel, have proposed as an instinctive drive like any other) is that the positive and negative urges to get stoned can exist side by side in the same individual, let alone the same society.

And it is at this collective level that the problems associated with drug-taking need to be addressed. The move to pathologize habitual drug-takers and drinkers is now so well established that we hardly give it a second thought. 'Put them in clinics,' we cry. 'Give them treatment.' But as the redoubtable Szasz has observed, putting alcoholics and drug addicts together to discuss their problems is as asinine as confining tuberculosis sufferers in one place and getting them to cough on one another.

No, our relationship to intoxication is something that we all need to think about. We cannot delegate the job to some rarefied group of 'experts'. To do so is to hand over management of a key aspect of our spiritual lives to a gang of bureaucrats. In the meantime I'm off to have a beer, but not before making the requisite ninety-seven obeisances to the Great God Bacchus, a deity I happen to believe in fervently.

Observer, October 1994

Strike and Crack

Richard Price's fine novel *Clockers* is set in a milieu that most of us would go to great lengths to avoid, the drug- and crime-ravaged streets of the American city. It is to Price's lasting credit that he not only penetrated this lethal environment, but also took the four years necessary to research the material for a literary portrait which goes as far towards fulfilling the Stendhalian definition of 'art as the mirror of life' as anything I have read in a long time.

The 'Clockers' of the title are young, black street kids who deal in crack (a smokable form of cocaine). Their field of operations is the projects, grim ghettoized housing estates on the fringes of New York City; and their bizarre nickname refers to the fact that they live by a 'two-minute clock'. On these mean streets life is cheap and Price's two main protagonists exemplify in different ways the struggle to find some spiritual meaning in a darkened world.

Strike, a nineteen-year-old drug dealer, feels himself already on the verge of retirement. Rocco Klein is a homicide detective who is due for retirement, burnt out at forty. The body of Price's novel is concerned with the redemption of these two characters, as a series of events traps Strike between the police and the teenage gunmen of his drug-dealing confrères.

Strike runs a 'crew', or team of still younger dealers, who actually exchange the drugs for money. Strike is a puritanical model of devotion to drug-dealing. He never touches his stock, or even carries it on him.

By adopting his protagonists' perspective, Price is able to show more graphically than other writers just how intractable the problems of drug-related crime are in modern society. By his own lights Strike is working hard. He feels that there is no other way to escape from the ghetto. This truth is given a tragic counterpoint by the example of his brother Victor. Victor works sixteen hours a day at two jobs and is churchgoing and law-abiding; and yet he is the one who eventually snaps under the pressure.

Rocco Klein, who feels the senselessness of his detective work as a kind of endless recycling of violence and death, struggles to find himself by understanding the world he inhabits, rather than opting for the easy transcendence of affluence.

Price shows us a world in which the line between right and wrong has become hideously warped. Policemen can be honest or utterly corrupt, drug dealers can be regarded as 'good' because their drive for profit at least imposes a modicum of order on these lawless streets.

To read this novel is to be plunged into a strange and incomprehensible world, which then begins to swim into clarity as Price's superb ear for the crisp rhythms of street argot imposes itself. This is a book that needs to make no reference to a world outside itself because its own internal consistency is a mark of its veracity. Price does not allow himself any easy options in judging the behaviour of his characters, rather he asks his readers to re-examine their own assumptions about society at the most fundamental level. I urge you to read it.

Oldie, July 1992

Drugs and the Law's Pursuit of Virtue

Despite Douglas N. Husack's resolute disclaimer that he has anything directly to add to the 'debate on drugs', *Drugs and Rights* represents a valuable contribution to that debate. As he contends, arguments about the permissibility of recreational drug use which focus on utilitarian considerations and cost-benefit analyses of public health policy fail entirely to address the issue of whether or not adults have any moral right to use drugs recreationally. In a reasoned philosophical argument about drug use, public utility and consequentialism must be secondary to deontological considerations. Husack is also careful throughout consistently to compare the underlying assumptions of the current laws against drugs with the logic of our regulation of alcohol and tobacco consumption; and he labours tirelessly to expose the moral hypocrisy inherent in those laws.

Husack argues that the so-called 'War on Drugs' is predicated on the assumption of an 'Augustinian philosophy of the self', whereby the goal of virtue subsumes concepts of individual autonomy. He attacks the legalism and legal moralism implicit in the current laws against drugs in the United States, and although public policy-makers in Britain might imagine that the 'British System', whereby addicts are 'treated' by state-licensed physicians, somehow represents a more ethically sensitive response, Husack is quick to point out that it is no longer a guarantor of people's basic moral rights.

Husack presents a wealth of empirical evidence to support his contention that most political and philosophical thinking on drugs is 'determined by unwarranted generalizations from worst case scenarios'. Proposing a substantive rather than a formal concept of individual autonomy, he concludes that despite rhetorical flourishes there is no reason to suppose either that recreational drug use is non-autonomous, or that the pleasure people gain from it is in any way 'pathological'. Husack avoids the traditional pitfalls of philosophers discussing this subject by correctly observing that the concept of addiction itself is 'in a preparadigmatic period'. He points out that the empirical evidence about so-called 'addictive' or compulsive drug use is insufficient to warrant the strong paternalism of current laws against drugs.

Thus far his arguments rest clearly within a Rawlsian conception of the way in which individual rights and public utility should be played off one against the other. He rejects libertarian arguments for full legalization on the grounds that, while existing drugs do not exhibit characteristics to justify the denial of adults' right to use them, it is possible to conceive of drugs that no one would have the right to use.

It is at this point that Husack's argument to some extent displays its specifically American provenance. Whereas in the United States natural opiates such as heroin and morphine are held to have 'no legitimate medical use', in Britain the situation is somewhat different. By the same token, Husack's exclusive concentration on what he terms 'recreational drugs' means that he neglects the evidence concerning benzodiazepines: drugs that individuals may initially have been legitimately prescribed, but which they subsequently use recreationally; and from which rapid withdrawal may result in serious medical problems. It is undoubtedly the difficulty of making a comprehensive distinction between recreational and medical drugs that has led libertarian philosophers such as Thomas Szasz to push the logic of legalization far further, to propose a free market in all drugs, and an end to the state monopoly of medical licensing.

Husack, however, doesn't want to do away with medical regulation, and his arguments have a tendency to collapse into the agenda of liberal pluralism. But this is not to discount the sensitive and reasoned contribution he has made to an area of debate far too often clouded by prejudice and collective hysteria.

Times Literary Supplement, March 1994

Inside Her Majesty's Powder Keg

I drove through the clotted traffic of South London, feeling as claustrophobic as if I were already behind bars. I was going to visit a prison – never exactly a pleasure trip at the best of times. But this occasion promised to be more than averagely fraught, because I was going to see the first treatment centre for alcoholism and drug addiction ever to be established in a British prison: HM Prison Downview, just outside Sutton in Surrey.

We all know that British prisons are more powder keg than *Porridge*-like. Over the past decade there has been riot after disturbance after riot. But while the ending of the iniquitous 'slopping-out' may have happened, another hot situation is developing on the inside. The prisons are acting as a form of incubator for a problem child of potentially horrific dimensions: the HIV virus.

My guide was Jonathan Wallace, a vigorous man in his fifties, compact and grey-bearded, who is himself a recovering addict and alcoholic. As we drove he filled me in on the situation and the work of the Addictive Diseases Trust, the body that has set up the treatment centre, of which he is the chief executive. He spouted statistics, opinions and observations with manic abandon. 'Of course the real impetus for letting us get the project going has been the HIV virus,' said Wallace. 'The Home Office are prepared to publicly admit to a few dozen cases of

HIV throughout the entire prison system, while we know for a fact that there are over thirty HIV-positive prisoners in Downview alone.'

There are two unpalatable factors that lie behind this. First the sharing of needles, and second unprotected anal sex. Wallace told me: 'I heard about a landing in Wandsworth where thirty-eight men shared the same needle for three months.' Once we got to Downview, I heard different versions of this: one needle to ten men for a month; two needles to five injectors for a year, and so on. Prisoners use makeshift needles made out of Biros. The thought of these blunt instruments tearing flesh, carrying septicaemia, hepatitis B and Aids, was revolting. A sort of DIY death-wish.

And lest anyone be sceptical about this, or imagine that it's simply the prison culture itself that engenders such horror stories, they are also reported by many, many former inmates. One who was in Pentonville in the mid-eighties told me: 'Everyone knew when a bit of tackle [heroin] came on to the landing, and everyone knew who had the fit [injecting equipment]. There was never any question of not banging up, even if there was still some claret [blood] left in the barrel.' It's this ubiquitous practice – the 'flushing' of the barrel of a syringe with blood in the process of injecting – that makes intravenous drug use such a sure-fire way of transmitting disease.

But it's the drugs in the needle that are at the root of the problem. Even the *Report of Her Majesty's Chief Inspector of Prisons* – hardly an example of crass sensationalizing on this topic – makes perfectly clear the direction we are currently headed in. It acknowledges that 'the rate of increase in drug offenders was 20 per cent per year from 1986 to 1990'. And that while it is – for obvious reasons – impossible to do a direct survey of drug use in prisons, if we extrapolate from information about the drug use on the outside of those sent down, a chilling picture emerges.

In a survey of 1,751 men sentenced for all manner of offences between April 1988 and August 1989, 43 per cent admitted to regular use of drugs on the outside; 11 per cent met all the criteria of dependency – including injecting. But statistics alone are a very flimsy way of gaining a true picture of the problem. The report goes on to acknowledge: 'In nearly all closed establishments we hear accounts of pressure being applied to prisoners to smuggle in drugs through their visits or on return from temporary release.' And further: 'Drug smuggling is a significant area in which staff can be tempted to indulge in corrupt behaviour.'

If these statements weren't shocking enough in themselves, the real corker is: 'We found many staff who openly acknowledged the benefit of moderate amounts of alcohol and cannabis being available to prisoners.'

Of course, officialese and statistics – whatever their source – always create a sense of impersonality about any such problem. It is only when one goes to talk to the people on the ground, hear their first-hand accounts and sense the atmosphere of the modern drug-infested prisons, that a proper picture emerges.

There is no substitute for the depression created by entering a prison. You may think that a prison is like any other large, mundane institution, a hospital or a school for example, but it isn't. It's not just all the bunches of keys slung from uniformed hips, or the walls, topped either with grey Swiss rolls of anti-climb metal, or anti-festive decorations of razor wire. No, it's something more than that.

Dave (all names and identifying details of the prisoners in this piece have been changed for their protection), a man with a great deal of experience of prisons, summed it up in this way: 'In prison people are always waiting for something to happen, some incident. And whatever that incident is – you know it's not going to be good.'

Dave is a lifer, a softly spoken Tynesider who went down for murder in 1974. A slim man in worn denims, Dave has the lazy manner of someone who has seen so much violence that he knows the value of maintaining moment-to-moment calm. 'Oh, sure,' he says, 'I've seen so many men stabbed in prison I've lost count.'

The murder conviction arose out of a fracas relating to Dave's main blag, which was armed robbery. 'I wouldn't actually go on a job high,' he said as we chatted in his cell, 'I'd cool out for a couple of days. Then as soon as it was over I'd go on a colossal bender.'

Dave is the first 'peer counsellor' to be trained at the ADT unit. Having achieved a drug- and alcohol-free lifestyle himself, he will go on to spread the message among other prisoners, particularly lifers or those serving long sentences.

Dave, who has done time in no less than forty-four different prisons over the past nineteen years, was walking proof of the respect that being on the programme carries with it. Downview is a category 'C' prison – not the hardest, but by no means the softest. Downview is not an open prison, like Ford, but towards the end of their sentences thirty to forty of the prisoners are allowed out to work on weekdays. Yet everyone I spoke to there – staff and prisoners – admitted that drugs were rife. And one of the first things that happened to us when we went out on to the yard was that we were approached by one of the prison's principal drug barons.

He was a wild-looking individual, heavily tattooed: 'Dave, Dave . . .' he spluttered, 'you've got to talk to them about my lost property, man. You've gotta sort it for me!' His pupils were dilated and his movements spasmodic. The man radiated aggression like the high-pitched whine of a television.

As we walked away Dave explained: 'Well, you see, I'm still respected even though I've cleaned up from drugs. If anything I'm even more respected now than I was before!

'This is really a very good nick as far as staff attitude is concerned,' he went on. 'We have the most AA and NA meetings of any prison in the country. There isn't the kind of siege mentality you get in other prisons. It's become common knowledge very quickly that nothing that is said by prisoners who come on the programme will have any impact on their parole. There is 100 per cent confidentiality.

'There wasn't really a day inside that I didn't use a drug before I got on this programme,' he added. 'My drugs of choice were coke, speed and alcohol. I never had any difficulty whatsoever getting hold of it. It would be brought in for me as regular as clockwork every two weeks.'

Dave is up for his licence in November. (Lifers are not paroled in the ordinary way – they are only ever released from prison on a special licence from the Home Secretary involving stringent conditions.) When I put it to him that a cynic might suggest that his cleaning up from drugs was in some way determined by this, he was more than forthright: 'If you said that to me, I'd tell you to fuck off!'

The 'programme' in question is the Minnesota Method of treatment for drug addiction and alcoholism. It is based on the 'twelve steps' of Alcoholics Anonymous and Narcotics Anonymous. The first principle of the programme is total abstinence from all mood-changing chemicals, including alcohol. The addict or alcoholic (they are regarded as essentially one and the same) is encouraged to view his problem as a 'disease' – 'progressive, incurable and fatal'. The only way to arrest it is to admit 'powerlessness' at a deep and fundamental level. Treatment centres on the outside that use the programme employ confrontational group-therapy sessions to foster self-honesty, both in addicts and among them. It is felt that only by breaking down 'denial' ('I am not an addict because of factors X, Y and Z') can the process of recovery begin.

You might have thought that this kind of honesty would present insuperable problems in prison, where keeping quiet is the order of the day. 'Many people in the Prison Service thought it would be impossible to get inmates to come on the programme,' said Jonathan Wallace. 'They said the drug barons would prevent them, out of fear of both losing clients and being grassed up. Actually our relationship with the drug barons at Downview is pretty good. We've even had one prisoner who applied to get on the programme because of pressure from his drug dealer! Apparently the dealer told him that he was becoming a liability and had better sort himself out.'

Jonathan Wallace set up the Addictive Diseases Trust as a charity in 1991, with the express intention of working to bring recovery from addiction to drug addicts and alcoholics serving time in prison. In December 1992 the trust, working in close co-operation with Derek Aram, the governor, set up the treatment unit at Downview.

Wallace was outspoken about the real motivations behind allowing the ADT to set up its unit at Downview. 'The Government need to be seen to be doing something about drug abuse in prisons,' he said. 'For a long while they haven't been prepared to admit it, but the link between drug use and recidivism is astonishing. As many as 80 per cent of all cases heard by London magistrates involve drink or drugs.'

As we talked it emerged that there was an added fervour to Wallace's rap that day for a very good reason. He had just heard that he would have to cut his staff to only two full-time paid counsellors. The trust managed to raise £130,000 to set up last year and this paid for the programme director, four full-time counsellors and the training of peer counsellors. But without statistical proof of the efficacy of the programme, the Home Office is unwilling to provide statutory funding. This statistical evidence will take at least three years to gather. In the meantime, such is Wallace's dedication that he is prepared to go on administering the project while living on income support.

Although I'd only been in Downview for a couple of hours, I too felt a certain amount of relief when Dave and I reached the ADT's Serenity Shack, where the treatment programme is actually run. It was the only part of the prison decorated with flowers. In treatment centres I've visited on the outside, signs reading 'Hugs not drugs' seemed faintly risible, but here in the big house they looked downright seditious. If you went to hug a fellow prisoner, wouldn't he suspect you of attempting a 'gob-grabbing' (lunging for concealed illegal drugs)?

At any one time there are fourteen prisoners on the programme. Those who are accepted have to sign an undertaking not to use any drugs or alcohol during the twelve weeks of the course. The course is full-time, and, while attending, a prisoner is released from all work commitments. At Downview – considered one of the better prisons as far as facilities for working are concerned – there is an extensive carpentry shop, where we were shown a number of bird tables being made. Downview is a popular prison and ordinarily it takes a couple of years to be transferred there if a prisoner requests it. But applicants for the programme can expect to get in in a few weeks. 'We haven't actually publicized the programme too much,' Wallace told me, 'because, after all, what's the point? We only have fourteen places and there are forty thousand people in prison, of whom anywhere between a third and two-thirds may require help with drink and drug problems.'

Once prisoners have come on the course they are subjected to regular urine tests during the twelve weeks and 'bounced out' if they fail. In any such programme peer-group pressure is a crucial factor in success. In a prison-based programme this pressure would, presumably, be even tougher.

Six of the current programme 'members' (so called because the term used outside, 'client', is the favoured euphemism of the probation service) are serving time for murder. One of them is a parricide. But as I talked to the men, who were trickling in for their afternoon group-therapy session, I found neither a gang of clones – all spouting the same homilies – nor a colloquium of cynics.

'The thing about this programme,' said Gary, a stocky lad in shell-suit bottoms, who's been attending the Serenity Shack for a month, 'is that people really listen to you. It makes it possible to take the good and the bad as it comes. I'm beginning to feel that I'm coming back down to normal.'

Henry, a young black guy who joked that he had been labelled a 'plastic Rasta' after going on the ADT programme, reinforced this view: 'This is the safest place to be in a nick if you want to come off drugs.'

Others chimed in. Bill, who had actually been on the run from another jail when he'd heard about the ADT programme on television, turned himself in in order to get on it. 'Since being on this programme I've even been out for a weekend's home leave and didn't even have a drink. It's something I've never done before in my life. When I was last inside my wife divorced me – after twenty-five years of marriage. Before I'd gone in I'd been back up to three bottles a day. Now she's seen the change in me, she's allowed me to go back home on my leaves, she's come to visit me, she's been 100 per cent behind me.'

John McKeown, the senior counsellor at Downview, and, like all the other ADT staff, himself a recovering addict, put some of the methods they use in further perspective: 'It's true that we don't tend to push the members here perhaps as hard as they might do in treatment programmes on the outside. Some of the stuff these guys are looking at – some of the things they have done in the grip of their addiction – is very heavy indeed. We tend to try and give them an hour or so of winding-down time before they go back to their cells.'

But while the men currently on the programme were sounding highly optimistic – as well they might – Jonathan Wallace was more sanguine about their prospects. 'We reckon that of the ten men who have been through the programme seven are still clean. About 50 per cent of the men who come on the programme get bounced out for some reason. But really men's prisons are by no means the worst. Everybody in the Prison Service knows that the situation in the women's jails – particularly Holloway – is desperate. Perhaps as many as 80 per cent of the inmates there are regularly using, and they just can't get a handle on it . . . because the programme that they set up didn't depend on complete abstinence.'

Jonathan Wallace would like to see HM Prison Downview turned into one big treatment centre, with 240 places, catering for the whole British Prison Service. 'It makes sense. It's far cheaper to treat people while they're inside anyway – you don't have to pay for room and board!'

But enthusiasm alone may not be enough to bring this about. For the moment the ADT is struggling for its life. It desperately needs cash, cash and more cash, if it's to continue its work of defusing the powder keg in British prisons.

Evening Standard, September 1993

The Naked Tea

There's a bullshit element to all of this, says Dr Phil Robson. He's standing in his office at the Chilton Clinic, Oxfordshire's regional unit for alcohol and drug dependency, looking out at an empty football field. We're discussing – of all things – William Burroughs's philosophy of drug use as it relates to creative endeavour. Phil goes on: 'Everyone wants to believe that they can write "Kubla Khan" when they're on drugs, even when they're gouching out on a sofa with a burning fag in their lap.'

I'm at the Chilton Clinic to conduct a critical experiment. Phil Robson and I are going to screen David Cronenberg's soon-to-be-released film of William Burroughs's cult book *Naked Lunch*, to a group of his drug-addicted patients. It's an exercise very much in the spirit of Burroughs himself. In his preface to the novel (published in 1959), Burroughs had written that the naked lunch was 'a frozen moment when everyone sees what is on the end of every fork'. By screening the film to opiate users we would be giving the forkful an opportunity, at last, to comment on its own depiction.

After all, the vast majority of the audience who go to see Cronenberg's film will have had no experience of drug addiction, nor will they have read Burroughs's novel. They will not know whether the film has achieved that 'frozen moment', or if it has merely added to the vast number of films, books, records and TV programmes that make up the 'drug-porn' canon.

This will be a strange kind of busman's holiday. Phil Robson has invited six of his out-patient addicts to attend the screening; this means that we will have, collectively, eighty-six years of heroin experience in the room.

They came into the room one at a time. First was Paul, plump and benign, in his early thirties, looking too gentle for his role as public health enemy number one. Two older men followed, Robin and Laird, both on long-term methadone scripts, both in their late thirties with seventeen years on junk apiece. Robin was feisty and talkative, his grey hair tied back in a pony-tail, his eyes dug in behind deep black wrinkles – the desert stare of the addict. Robin brought a William Burroughs book with him and began to discourse volubly on drugs and creativity. Laird, on the other hand, was quiet and contained; his voice marked him out as a professional person, even if his scuffed hands and broken nails spoke of the manual labour of intravenous drug use.

Alistair was the baby of the bunch, twenty-three with only six years of opiates behind him. He had read Burroughs as well, and travelled to Tangier, where much of *Naked Lunch* was written and the film is largely set. He lounged in his chair with the casual insouciance of a young hoodlum – a ringer for one of Burroughs's own fantasy creations, the eponymous 'Wild Boys'.

Steve and Karen came in together. Steve in tracksuit and trainers, Karen in leather car coat. These two seemed different from the rest, less self-conscious, more like people who had ended up on smack for no better reason than that it was available. And this turned out to be the case: Karen told us later that she had got her first habit without even knowing what it was she was taking.

THE NAKED TEA

A chubby-faced young drug worker punched the lights, temporary night fell on the institutional room with its caramel easy chairs and blue and beige carpet-tile chequerboard. The video whirred and my addict-critics hunkered down to the wail of Ornette Coleman's saxophone. They slurped on their plastic beakers – the naked tea had begun.

Of course it would be foolish to suggest that every book of a film should be true to its original. Cronenberg himself has said, 'It's impossible to make a movie out of *Naked Lunch*. A literal translation just wouldn't work. It would cost $400 million to make and would be banned in every country in the world.' So what he was offering us instead was a fusion of his own writing with that of Burroughs to produce something 'in the spirit of the book'.

But as time passed it became clear, to me at least, that Cronenberg's movie bears hardly any relation to Burroughs's book, either in form or content and certainly not in spirit. What we have instead is 'late Burroughs', the Burroughs who wrote in the 1985 preface to his novel *Queer* that he had been forced to the conclusion that he would never have become a writer were it not for his accidental killing of his wife, Joan. This admission, combined with the text of *Queer* itself, an inordinately powerful homosexual love-story, led critics at the time, such as the self-confessed Burroughsian Martin Amis, to say that the book 'retroactively . . . humanizes his work'.

His work and, of course, his life. For there is one thing that brooks no opposition, there was never a writer like Bill Burroughs for self-mythologizing, for wilfully mixing 'the life' and 'the work'. Throughout Burroughs's books his fictional alter ego William Lee cavorts, a secret agent of the junk underworld. Cold-eyed and existential, he leaps from one dreamscape to the next, reporting with deadpan detachment on the atrocities of the unconscious

51

he has witnessed. But in Cronenberg's film this alter ego has transmuted into the William Lee of *Queer*, the withdrawing addict 'subject to the emotional excesses of a child or an adolescent, regardless of his actual age'.

Cronenberg's *Naked Lunch* is thus Burroughs's equivalent of J. G. Ballard's *Kindness of Women*; a volte-face by the literary outlaw, a belated attempt to say: 'Look, I felt awful about taking all those drugs, and shooting my wife and my son dying – all of that stuff.' Cronenberg uses Burroughs's accidental shooting of his wife, Joan, as the key motif of the film. The camera lingers lovingly as the glass she places on her head while Bill does his 'William Tell act' rolls to a standstill, intact. In real life it was this macabre detail that gave the lie to the 'act' for one eyewitness: 'We were temporarily deafened by the sound. The next thing I knew the glass was on the floor, and I noticed the glass was intact . . . And then I looked at her and her head had fallen on one side. Well, I thought, she's kidding . . . and then I saw the hole in her temple.'

The driving force of Cronenberg's narrative is Burroughs's theory that he was 'possessed', much in the medieval sense of the word, by an 'ugly spirit' at the time of the shooting. In the film, having shot his wife on the instructions of a giant cockroach, William Lee flees to Interzone (Burroughs's fictional recreation of post-war Tangier). Here the ugly spirit metamorphoses into a coackroach-cum-typewriter. This prosaic entity commands Lee to type a series of reports on Interzone. It is these, we are led to believe, that eventually make up the book *Naked Lunch*.

Cronenberg's film is, then, a film about the writing of the book, rather than a conventional film-of-the-book. Given Burroughs's own status as a literary experimenter, an *éminence grise* of the post-modern and the inventor of the cut-up method, whereby texts are created 'randomly', this approach might seem to have some artistic credibility. In Ted Morgan's biography of Burroughs, the story is told of how *Naked Lunch* itself was a 'cut-up' text: 'the sections were sent to the printer in random order, but when the galleys came back the order seemed to work'.

But whereas it may be possible to cut up and recombine texts, I'm not sure you can do the same thing with the spirit of a book. There seems to have been a ghastly synergy involved in producing this film. Burroughs's own quest for redemption has allowed for the injection of sentimentality into a text that never had any. Burroughs's book is a vicious Swiftian satire that uses the shock of the pornographic to jolt the reader out of his complacency.

It is a further irony that Burroughs himself, in a way, set the agenda for the kind of icky special effects that directors such as Cronenberg have made their stock-in-trade. Burroughs's visceral images of unspeakable creatures like the Mugwump, an insect-like entity who stores in his body 'a substance to prolong life of which he is periodically milked by his masters', were too much for the British and American censors of the early sixties. But now they have been translated back from the page into drug-dream visual imagery, they seem to have lost their bite.

But what about our panel? What did they make of Cronenberg's attempt to deal with the theme of addiction itself? The lights came back up, more tea was called for, we scraped our chairs into an informal circle.

Initial comments took in the formlessness and abstract quality of the film. 'It's a mishmash,' said Robin. 'I liked Burroughs's *Junky* because it was a good narrative, but this thing doesn't have any direction.'

Alistair, on the other hand, reckoned that this was the film's strength: 'That's what the cut-up method is all about.'

Robin was pissed off by what he saw as Burroughs's self-rehabilitation: 'Let's face it, he's trying to make himself look like bleedin' RoboCop – that's why Burroughs got what's-his-name [Peter Weller] to play his character. But he's not like Burroughs really is. Burroughs was a cold calculating bastard, not a victim, and he always had money to fall back on.'

The amiable Paul was more forgiving: 'It's very personal – you can't dispute his view of drugs an' that. I liked all sorts of little touches, like when he's groping on the wrong side of his mouth for his fag – that's what it's like when you're gouching.'

While the junkies thought the film did have some merits, giving either an evocative or a realistic picture of drug experience was not among them. 'Everyone's going to get the wrong view,' said Robin, 'especially of what it's like on smack.'

No one present had ever hallucinated cockroach type-writers. Alistair spoke for the whole group when he said, 'They may be good symbols, but if that's what they're meant to be, it takes too long to interpret them.'

This brought us fairly logically on to the issue of drugs and creativity. If Cronenberg's film leans on any conceit it is the idea that drugged experience somehow puts you in touch with your muse. Alistair felt that drugs did 'unlock' his creativity; the others were more sceptical. Both Laird and Karen admitted to doing very intricate drawings while they were stoned on smack. But Robin was more cynical and emphatic: 'It doesn't give you anything that you haven't got already. I like to write and do stuff like that, but it's not worth nothing if you're stoned, is it?'

The consensus was that the first part of the film – when the Lee character is working as a cockroach exterminator and his wife is becoming addicted to the 'bug powder' (pyrethrum) that he uses – was the most true to drug culture. 'But even so,' said Paul, referring to one of the film's starkest images, 'I've never seen a woman find a vein in 'er tit.'

We went on to discuss another aspect of Burroughs's philosophy of drugs – his obsession with the medical establishment as alternative drug-pushers, control freaks with qualifications. Since Phil Robson was out of the room, it seemed like a good opportunity to ask them whether they shared his view. Robin was emphatic as ever: 'There's no difference whatsoever, if the doctor's private. I had this doctor in London and I loved her, I really did. Going to get a script from her was like going to see a lover.' This neatly echoed the words of Burroughs's 'wife' in the film, who, getting hooked on her husband's bug powder, says: 'I felt drawn to it . . . you know . . . like you feel drawn to an old lover.' But everyone present agreed that when the treatment was on the National Health there was a profound difference. 'Take Phil,' said Robin, 'I never thought it would be possible but he's got me down to a fourth of what I was on a year ago.'

So what of Phil Robson, a consultant psychiatrist, a former lecturer in clinical psychology at Oxford? To what extent did Dr Robson conform to Burroughs's portrayal of the drug-dealing psychiatrist, the sinister Dr Benway?

In Burroughs's *Naked Lunch*, Benway is one of the central characters, 'a manipulator and co-ordinator of symbol systems, an expert in all phases of control'. He is in charge of a dystopian clinic where he inflicts various kinds of ghastly experimentation on his junkie patients. In Cronenberg's film the Benway character is reduced to a cameo part for Roy Scheider, but he still occupies a pivotal position in the 'pyramid of control' that is addictive drugs.

It's difficult to imagine anyone less like Benway than

Phil Robson, a rather cuddly-looking man with a beard and an enthusiastically maniacal chuckle. But if he wasn't a bit weird why had he allowed me to show this disturbing film to his patients? 'I thought it would be interesting to see whether or not someone who has experienced the drug life can communicate real meaning to people of another generation.' But like his patients, Phil has doubts about the Cronenberg *Naked Lunch*: 'I thought bits of it were enigmatic and interesting. Weller acts being stoned extremely well, but all the bug and cockroach hallucinations – they're disappointing. You know it isn't a good depiction of addiction.'

I leave Phil Robson's office. Outside, a patient is nodding out in the strip-lighted corridor. His hands, swollen from being fixed into, are resting on his knees, as if they've been detached.

I feel confused about the naked tea. It's as if, having enacted a Burroughsian conceit, I have become subject to one of his own fictional methods. Bits of his books come before my eyes intercut with medical and psychiatric accounts of addiction. The film criticisms of Phil Robson's patients start to mix 'n' match with my own.

Not that I begrudge Burroughs his retroactive humanization, nor his wide distribution courtesy of David Cronenberg. It's just this lurking suspicion I have that, in allowing the film to drift away from the true spirit of Burroughs's *Naked Lunch*, its creators will put people off reading the book. But then, there's nothing more likely to put people off reading the book than the book itself.

Guardian, April 1992

Junking the Image

There were two cultural revolutions in the sixties. Both appeared to involve the overthrow of established orthodoxies, both were spearheaded by almost mythic figures, and both of them had undertaken long marches. But whereas the Orient had a Great Helmsman, we in the Occident merely had a Great Junksman.

The Great Helmsman has been in his grave for over a decade, but defying the exigencies of the toxified body, the Great Junksman is still with us, and celebrates his eightieth birthday today.

During *his* long march William Burroughs went south from New York City, fleeing a federal rap for forging morphine prescriptions. In New Orleans in the late forties he marshalled his revolutionary cadres – Jack Kerouac, Neal Cassady and Allen Ginsberg – before fleeing still further south to Mexico City, this time on the run from a marijuana possession rap. In Mexico City Burroughs accidentally shot dead his common-law wife, Joan Vollmer Burroughs, and while on bail once more skipped the country, this time headed for South America.

From South America to Tangier, from Tangier to Paris, from Paris to London, and then eventually back to New York in the early eighties. In his absence Burroughs's *magnum opus*, *Naked Lunch*, the arcane text which became the little red book of our spurious cultural revolution, had been published. Initially it was only available in a samizdat form, courtesy of a Chicago-based alternative magazine, *Big Table*, which, appropriately enough, self-destructed after the issues that carried *Naked Lunch*. But subsequently the Olympia Press in Paris brought this explosive text out in book form. The rest, of course, is history.

These are the bare bones of Burroughs's long march. Put down in this fashion they already take on the lineaments of some biblical tale. Burroughs's mark of Cain was homosexuality and drug addiction. And his 'sin' was both destructive and creative. He himself has written (in the foreword to his autobiographical novel *Queer*) that were it not for the accidental shooting of his wife, he doesn't believe he would have become a writer.

Why did the Great Junksman survive, while so many of his confrères fell by the wayside? What specific qualities have allowed him to become that rarest of things: a legend in his own lifetime? But perhaps more pertinently, what does the Burroughs myth have to tell us about our attitudes towards the creative writer in the late twentieth century?

I think it tells us this: that ours is an era in which the idea and practice of decadence – in the Nietzschean sense – has never been more clearly realized. And that far from representing a dissolution of nineteenth-century romanticism, the high modernism of the mid-twentieth century, of which Burroughs is one of the last surviving avatars, has both compounded and enhanced the public image of the creative artist as deeply self-destructive, highly egotistic, plangently amoral and, of course, the nadir of anomie.

This is why the cultural revolution of the sixties has been shown up to be so spurious. This is why the avant-garde has never been deader than now. This is why there is no meaningful input from youth into the cultural mainstream.

JUNKING THE IMAGE

A friend of mine once said: 'When I was fifteen I read *Junky*, when I was sixteen I was a junkie.' I could say the same of myself. My form prize in the lower sixth at Christ's College, Finchley, was *Naked Lunch*. As far as I was concerned, Burroughs demonstrated that you could have it all: live outside the law, get stoned the whole time, and still be hailed by Norman Mailer as 'the only living American writer conceivably possessed of genius'. When I awoke from this delusion, aged twenty, diagnosed by a psychiatrist as a 'borderline personality', and with a heroin habit, I was appalled to discover that I wasn't a famous underground writer. Indeed, far from being a writer at all, I was simply underground.

Of course, it would be simplistic to regard this as a causal relationship. No responsibility for my delusion can be laid at the feet of Burroughs. He is blameless. He never claimed any suzerainty over the burgeoning cultural revolution of the sixties. In fact, he was appalled by the sloppiness and lack of tone displayed by the counter-culture as early as 1952, when he was resident in Mexico City and saw the first wave of Beats follow in his wake.

The idea of the pernicious druggy writer spawning a generation of emulators far antedates Burroughs. De Quincey was accused of having just such a dangerous influence after the publication of *The Confessions of an English Opium-Eater* in 1822. In the years that followed there were a number of deaths of young men from opium overdoses that were laid at his feet.

The truth is that books like *Junky* and De Quincey's *Confessions* no more create drug addicts than video nasties engender prepubescent murderers. Rather, culture, in this wider sense, is a hall of mirrors in which cause and effect endlessly reciprocate one another in a diminuendo that tends ineluctably towards the trivial.

Thus it is that in the heroin subculture – a crepuscular zone which I feel some authority to talk about – the Great Junksman is known of, and talismanically invoked, as a guarantor of the validity of the addict lifestyle, even by those who have never read a single line of Burroughs's works. By the same token, the image of the artist that the Great Junksman represents has now pullulated into the realm of popular culture. His true heirs are not junkie writers at all, but pop musicians who fry their brains with LSD and cocaine, ecstatic teenagers who gibber at acid-house raves, and urban crack-heads who dance to a different drum machine.

The status of 'drugs' as panapathanogenic – inherently evil or nasty – is something that artists such as Burroughs, and the law enforcement agencies he would affect to despise, have conspired to create. One man's creative meat is another's social poison, but both parties in some strange way wish to keep it that way. It was Burroughs himself who in the preface to *Naked Lunch* drew his readers' attention to the fact that there was something inherently 'profane' about opiates, in contrast to other kinds of drugs.

But this is false. The fact of the matter is that the self-destructive image of the artist, and the failure of occidental culture to develop meaningful and valid drug rituals, are two sides of the same coin. It always puzzled me that I was unable to sort cause and effect out in this fashion. The reason was that, while I understood the above intuitively, I was still in a very important way an *apparatchik* of the Great Junksman. I, like him, came to believe – as many addicts do – in the reality of a magical world of hidden forces. I, like him, came to writing as a function of a dialectic of illness and recovery. The heightened sensitivity of heroin withdrawal produces a ghastly reactive sensitivity, which in turn calls forth a stream of grossly sentimental imagery, an imaginative correlative to the spontaneous and joyless orgasms experienced by the kicking addict. This is the origin of De Quincey's *Suspira de Profundis* and Coleridge's 'The Pains of Sleep', just as much as it is of Burroughs's *Nova Express* and Cocteau's *Opium*. It follows that the nineteenth and twentieth centuries form a dyad. And in both, some of the finest creative minds have traded the coin of their own self-realization for the noxious draught of notoriety. The Great Junksman's perverse and – given his own femicide – macabre obsession with the 'right to bear arms', his affected, militant homosexuality and consequent misogynism, his – and our – confabulation of an image that owes as much to the facts of his fiction as it does to the fictions of his fact – all of these reach a peculiar apogee in this one perverse fact: he is eighty and alive whereas by all rights he should be long gone.

By saying this I mean no disrespect. I merely wish to point up the paradox of this anti-establishment establishmentarian; this sometime junkie with a ribbon in his buttonhole that shows he is a member of the American Academy of Arts and Letters; this bohemian exile who lives in Andy Hardy, small-town America; this 'Hombre Invisible' who has become so terribly visible.

If the Burroughs story tells us anything, it is that we are in a pretty pass. We desperately need a new image of the creative artist with which to replace this tired old *pas de deux*. At the moment we circle round creative genius like hicks visiting a freak show. And this is, of course, the attitude that has spawned an industry of literary biography which threatens to overtopple the production of fiction itself.

So, let us use this anniversary, not to celebrate and further garnish the legend of the Great Junksman, but instead to re-examine the continuing relevance of his alter ego's great fictions; his satirical visions of cancerous capitalism and addictive consumerism; his elegiac and poetic invocations of sadness and dislocation; his enormous fertility of ideas and imagery. And let us say: rest in peace, Bill Burroughs; may you live to celebrate many more birthdays, but a pox on the Great Junksman, let's topple his monumental statues and move forward on our own long march towards some more spiritually valid conception of the writer's role.

Guardian, February 1994

Street Legal

It's five-thirty in the morning and I'm walking up the Gelderse Kade canal towards Amsterdam's Central Station, skirting the red-light district, which at this hour is quiescent: the ebb of last night's trade washing against the flow of this morning's. Hobbling on the leaf-plastered cobbles is a Surinamese woman, obviously a drug addict. She's wearing a bilious velour tracksuit and begging in a desultory fashion, proffering her upturned claw of a hand to each indifferent face as she passes. For once, the expressions of the Chinese gamblers, wending their way home, live up to their racial stereotype: they are inscrutable.

For me this woman is a point of strange orientation. The previous evening I had seen her further up the same canal, again panhandling, this time outside a traditional Amsterdam bar. The kind that sells mostly shots of jenever, the Dutch gin, and wittebeer, the light lemony beer favoured by Dutch drinkers. She had chosen the wrong place to beg. A couple of the drinkers, Dutch indigenes sporting long fair beards and the tattered colours of the Amsterdam chapter of the Hell's Angels, had grabbed her and were administering punches and kicks to her arms and legs.

This wasn't the kind of work-out her tracksuit had been intended for. It was a beautiful evening, and the canal looked unbelievably picturesque, with its tip-tilted houses, their high gables like fretwork against the sunset. And in the middle of it all, the Hell's Angels were laughing, their girlfriends were laughing, while the Surinamese woman yowled, and the tourists and Amsterdammers went about their business, scrupulously turning a blind eye.

Amsterdam. I remembered the city from my first visit some ten years before. Coming out of the Central Station and heading towards the Zeedjik, the snaking lane which leads to the heart of the red-light district, I had been mobbed by a crowd of some twenty South Moluccan heroin dealers. As they pushed their wares into my face I caught sight of a large sign that had been put up on a bridge: 'Absolute power,' it declared in English, 'corrupts absolutely.' Quite.

But then this was where it was at. This was the city where elected officials smoked dope in the council chamber; the city where the junkies had their own union; this was where the permissive society had come home to roost.

Amsterdam, a city synonymous with the 'Dutch Experiment', a combination of enlightened policing and harm-minimization health care that has, its proponents claim, effectively divided off the nasty hard-drug market from its benign cannabis cousin.

The Dutch Experiment has become a kind of shibboleth for people concerned with drug policy in Britain. For pro-legalization liberals it is an example of an enlightened approach that has paid dividends. They visit Amsterdam to sop up the atmosphere of its cannabis cafés; to revel in the naughty liberty of being able to puff a joint in the street unmolested. But for prohibitionists it is the exact reverse: a sexual Sodom and a narcotic Gomorrah rolled into one horrific sin bin.

What is the reality? This time round the junkies weren't just clustered along the Zeedjik, they were all over the town centre. They were crouched on the benches thoughtfully provided by the municipality, manipulating bits of tin foil. Chasing the dragon, while children kicked footballs around them. Down in Neumarkt station, the platform was lined with junkies. They were dealing, smoking, scratching and altercating. Ordinary Dutch commuters went about their business, seemingly ignoring what was going on.

An Anglo-Dutch friend who lent me her centrally located flat had told me: 'Before the Olympic bid a few years ago, you knew where the junkies were, so you could avoid them. But when the police cleaned up the Zeedjik it was like lancing a boil: the pus has spread all over the centre of town.' How right she was. The morning after I arrived, there crouching on the basement steps was my own personal addict. He looked up and smiled. He was smoking his morning hit of heroin, as casually as an alcoholic on the streets of London, supping a Special Brew.

Later that day, a Dutch journalist related an anecdote which summed up the native attitude. An Amsterdammer was coming out of his apartment one morning when he saw a shabby figure crouched on the basement steps. Without looking too closely, he assumed that it was a junkie fixing up. 'Make sure you clean up afterwards,' he quipped. The 'junkie' looked up and flashed a warrant card. It was an undercover cop. 'Make sure you clean up afterwards,' the Amsterdammer reiterated, and went about his business, whistling.

The Amsterdammers are a bizarre inversion of the English concept of Nimbys. They don't mind it being in their backyard – as long as it's cleaned up afterwards. Or that's what they would like you to believe. But as I got deeper into the drug world of Amsterdam I began to realize that there were two quite separate versions of the events going on around me.

One version was for the consumption of foreign professionals: policemen, health-care workers, journalists and lawyers, who had come to see the Dutch Experiment in action. The other version was more truthful. A truth that was as unpalatable for the Dutch as it would be for the foreigners; a truth that hides behind the apparent accessibility of Dutch society; a truth that is politically and morally complex, and therefore not readily packaged for public consumption.

If you contact the Ministry of Health before undertaking an investigative trip to Amsterdam, a helpful secretary will arrange an itinerary for you. There will be visits to Drs Dirk Korf and Peter Cohen, academic specialists in criminology, who have conducted numerous studies on the prevalence of drug-taking in Amsterdam and the Netherlands. There will also be a visit to the Jellinek Clinic, which provides detoxification treatment for addicts and alcoholics.

And, finally, you will be treated to an interview with Dr Theo van Iwaarden, head of the Alcohol, Drugs and Tobacco Policy Department, part of the Ministry of Health. Dr van Iwaarden is a relative newcomer to the job, replacing the more flamboyant Eddy Engelsman, whose writings and publications over the last fifteen years have represented the crystallization of a policy towards drugs that the Dutch themselves invariably describe as 'pragmatism'. You get a selection of Mr Engelsman's articles by mail before you set off, together with statistical bulletins on the drug abuse situation in the Netherlands, and a copy of an instructive book called *Cannabis in Amsterdam: A Geography of Hashish and Marijuana*.

This tome, by A. C. M. Jansen, is a dope smoker's ramble masquerading as a sociological text. Impressionistic and facile, it concludes with a specious micro-economic study of the price elasticity of 'hemp products' in relation to the competition between coffee shops that sell them. And this is what the government puts out! It's as if a journalist investigating alcohol use in Britain were sent a selection of Jeffrey Bernard's columns by the NHS.

Dr Dirk Korf is relentlessly pragmatic. 'I suppose it's true to say that my research has retrospectively alibied [sic] government policy.' Dr Korf's research shows that the prevalence of cannabis consumption in Holland has actually fallen in the wake of effective decriminalization. 'Heroin,' he tells me on the other hand, 'is perceived by Dutch adolescents as a "junkie drug". The visibility of heroin use helps to make it appear unattractive, just as much as it helps the authorities to practise harm-minimization policies.'

He agrees that as police statistics are unreliable, it's impossible to prove that the availability of methadone to addicts has actually meant a decline in drug-related theft. But he said that 'the older the addicts, and the more they've been in contact with the methadone programme, the less criminality they exhibit'.

When I charge him with the visibility of heroin use in Amsterdam he retorts: 'Amsterdam is atypical. You wouldn't see anything like it in the rest of Holland. The policy is: make things visible and you can control them. The point is only that the tip of the iceberg you can see is bigger here than it is in countries with a more repressive policy.'

But Ien Jensen, who runs the Jellinek Clinic, is more fatalistic. 'The point is,' she says, 'that all the addicts who are on methadone supplement it with black-market heroin.' And there are a lot of them, an estimated five to six thousand for a city with a population of 1,079,702 (January 1992 figures).

Indeed, the registered addict population of the Netherlands as a whole is quite high: 21,000, exactly the same as that of the UK, a country with over five times the population. Of course, the Dutch would argue that this is simply because their figure represents a true picture of the problem, whereas, as British epidemiologists would admit, the British figure captures only a fraction of the true population. When the Dutch call their policy 'pragmatism', they are voicing a historical truth. During the 1960s, Amsterdam became one of the first European cities to be badly affected by urban blight. Traffic in the centre was appalling, rates were high. Businesses moved out, leaving behind a vacuum into which junkies, prostitutes and criminals moved.

Amsterdam was the northern entrepôt for the 14K Tong, who at that time controlled the trafficking and distribution for South-east Asian heroin. The drugs scene was large and vicious, attracting addicts and users from all over Europe. The only way to deal with it was 'pragmatism'; it simply couldn't be eliminated. Having accepted that, the Dutch have moved to make the best of a bad thing, retrospectively labelling this 'pragmatism' as an enlightened policy.

'Really the Dutch are very, very conservative people,' my friend told me. 'Try suggesting that Queen Beatrix should abdicate. Even in a hash coffee shop you'd get some very angry replies. The thing is,' she continued, 'that the "liberals" are really just the descendants of the Calvinist conservatives they allegedly oppose.' One such liberal is thirty-three-year-old Inspector Rob van Velsen, head of the Amsterdam Narcotics Bureau. Inspector van Velsen, as well as being one of the most liberal policemen I had ever met, was also the handsomest.

The two of us were chatting in a rather empty squad room, decorated with the pennants and insignia of other drug squads from around the world. The Inspector started off by giving me a lecture about the British involvement in the opium trade, and went on to say: 'There is no drugs problem here in Amsterdam. We regard it either as a health problem, or as a public order problem. We are interested in drugs only in so far as they contribute to the proceeds of organized crime. We are not interested in drug use itself.'

Back in Britain I had spoken to Customs and Excise sources about Holland. 'We regard the Netherlands as a country of origin for drugs. Not so much heroin, but certainly synthetics. We think that Dutch criminal gangs, possibly those ones traditionally involved with cannabis, have seen the Ecstasy market in Britain, and have acted to fill the demand.'

Inspector van Velsen denied that the Dutch authorities regard Ecstasy in the same semi-legitimate light as cannabis, but the way he did so was significant: 'We don't see a problem with using Ecstasy here. There is no public order problem, and we haven't seen any deaths from it. We are aware that some of the criminal groups have been exporting to the UK, and we've started to take an interest in it.'

Inspector van Velsen was also sceptical about the existence of organized crime in Holland. He talked to me about 'groups that know people, that have connections, but no "mob" in the style of the USA'. This is at best a half-truth. While it is undoubtedly the case that there is little high-level corruption in the public service, the Amsterdam police itself has been rocked by corruption cases at middle level. Furthermore, the Dutch not only refer to organized native criminals as 'the mafia', they also point to a particular area of Amsterdam, the Leidseplein, near the Rijksmuseum, as the mafia part of town.

'We are a little bit successful at what we do,' says

Inspector van Velsen, 'that's why people from around the world come and see us.' But while he and my other Dutch interviewees struggled to convince me that it was simply a case of 'more of the iceberg' being exposed to view, all my research, and casual encounters, led me to believe that the iceberg was, quite simply, bigger overall.

Monica, an eighteen-year-old prostitute who offers 'suck and fuck' at 100 guilders (about £30) a throw, operates out of one of the infamous shopfront windows in the red-light district. I caught up with her in The Rocket, a hash café near the Neumarkt which is frequented by young 'drug tourists', English and German kids who have come for hash and Ecstasy. A working-class Amsterdammer who's been on the game for a year, she was happy to talk about prostitutes taking drugs.

'Sure, it happens all the time. A girl goes on the pipe or the brown. She gets very skinny, she loses all her clients. She goes away for three months and comes back better.' But what are the people who run the brothels like? 'They're very reasonable. A doctor comes in twice a week to give us a check-up. We get a flat fee, with bonuses.' Do you think these people are involved in any other illegitimate business, like drugs? Monica didn't even answer, she refused to talk to me further.

The police, the criminologists and the Head of Policy at the Ministry of Health may deny it, but there have been a number of newspaper stories recently implicating Amsterdam as the centre of a European network of child prostitution and white slaving. Certainly Amsterdam is a pornography production centre, and some of the most vicious child pornography is known to be produced there. It strains credulity to imagine that it isn't the same 'groups' of criminals who are mixed up in these different trades.

Inspector van Velsen did, inadvertently, give the lie to

the political agenda that underpins all this. Apropos of nothing, when discussing the famed 'Balkan route' for heroin coming into Europe, he said, 'Ask yourself why the Americans are so keen to support the Kurds.' I came up with some fatuous explanation, and the handsome narcotics chief smiled enigmatically.

Another Dutch contact filled in the blanks for me. 'Oh, it's easy,' he said, 'they think the Americans are allowing the Kurds to deal in heroin for arms. They sell to the Moroccans, who then bring it into Holland.'

Stuart Wesley, director of the Drugs Division at the National Criminal Intelligence Service, was sceptical. 'I haven't heard anything,' he told me, 'but then there's always a lot of rumours kicking around about the DEA [the American Drug Enforcement Agency].'

We were sitting in the Service's offices off the Albert Embankment in London. 'We don't know about what we don't know,' a detective inspector in charge of a regional drug squad had once said when I was working on another story; and really that's about the most truthful statement I have ever heard about the drugs trade from a police officer. Stuart Wesley and I sat calculating the street value of a kilo of Ecstasy; it was something he hadn't figured out before: 'Err . . . that's three 920 hits per gram, about 960,000 a kilo . . .'

That makes the street value of the British 1991 Ecstasy seizures roughly equivalent to the NCIS's entire budget. And that's just the seizures. Ever since the mid-1980s when the Thatcher government cut the Customs and Excise budget by a third, policemen and customs officers have discovered a new realism about the drugs traffic. 'You calculate that you get about 10 per cent of the drugs that come in, don't you?' I said tactfully to Stuart Wesley.

'We don't know,' he sighed, 'we just don't know. It could be much less.'

'Don't your policemen get cynical?' I had asked Inspector van Velsen back in Amsterdam.

'Oh no,' he replied.

Later that day at the Neumarkt station, the junkies were all gone. Two burly Dutch metro police were patrolling the concourse. 'You've cleared out all the junkies,' I said.

'Oh yeah,' they replied, 'but they'll be back as soon as we've left.'

'Don't you get cynical?'

'How do you say it in England?' he replied. 'It pays for my roast beef. It's a living.'

'We will never accept a harmonization of drugs policy throughout the EU if it involves a step backwards from our current situation,' Theo van Iwaarden had told me. 'Formally we are not proposing a full legalization of cannabis, but informally we are investigating a number of options . . . I personally think it would be very difficult under our current State Secretary for Health, and under our current Minister of Justice. If we take another step there will also be a lot of international political pressure, which wouldn't please the Ministry of Foreign Affairs.'

So the Dutch go on; their 'pragmatism' means that their tax inspectors submit estimated bills to the hash cafés and the brothels, both of which are technically illegal. 'They've come to believe in their own rhetoric,' an older Dutch friend told me, 'but really the city is ungovernable.'

The Netherlands has an enlightened social policy, and an enlightened drugs policy, and yet nothing seems to help. Like the hero of their best-known folk tale, their fingers are stuck in the dyke, while a tidal wave of drugs pours over the top of it. But really they are taking the buck for the rest of Europe, and their only real crime consists of trying to put a brave face on it. Perhaps if they admitted that, without a supranational dimension, their policy is just as ineffective as evveryone else's, then perhaps everyone could sit down and plan a sensible, enforceable drug policy. One that, for a start, fully legalized cannabis. But then, not even a burgomaster likes to admit that his new clothes are really transparent.

Guardian, February 1994

Fixing Up a Vinyl Solution

The Disposable Heroes of Hiphoprisy are asking for trouble in the press release that accompanies their little foray into mixed-media, *Spare Ass Annie & Other Tales*. They are – their publicists assure us – 'heavy ironists'. Well, that's lucky, because they are definitely the disposable element in this package. Burroughs's laconic delivery and assumed carney man's banter have for a long time represented one of the best-packaged writers-as-readers that we've had to latch on to. Indeed, the resuscitation of Burroughs's career achieved by James Grauerholz in the early eighties was as much a function of getting the old man on the road and gigging as it was down to any inspired late flowering of his creative powers, wasn't it?

Quite the reverse. The material Burroughs retailed during his showcase, rock-band-style tours during these years was none other than the key routines from things such as *Naked Lunch, Soft Machine, Nova Express*, and the fragmentary early jottings, now collected and published under the title *Interzone*. Once again, this is the kind of stuff the Great Junksman has decided to push at us with his Disposable Heroes (DHs).

While it's true that for all I know the DHs – a 'Bay-based' combo – may have fulfilled their stated aim of 'bridging the divide between hardcore gangsta rap, industrial dance and live jazz . . .' on their last outing on their own account (the album *Hypocrisy Is the Greatest Luxury*), on *Spare Ass Annie & Other Tales* they are confined to bridging the gap between their own credibility and our suspension of disbelief.

The only ostensibly Burroughsian aspect of the DHs is the description retailed in said release of Michael Franti, the band's guiding spirit, as 'the first rapper of his generation with an up-to-the-minute grasp of international events . . .' You can almost hear Uncle Bill snarl, 'Whaddyamean ferchrissakes? Has the goddamn punk done a cut-down on his cerebellum and had it wired directly into CNN. What is he? Some kind of a mutant already . . .'

To put it straight, this is an album where the words and the music reached a parting of the ways very early on. The words took the high road and the music the low. If you sit down and listen in any moderately lucid state of mind the impression you have is of an old man muttering and ranting on in the aural foreground, while some young lads, engaged on some completely unrelated project, footle around with the controls on a mixing desk in the next room. Hal Wilmer's role in all this, as impresario, link-man between the stria of the counter-cultural sediment, is defined solely by little seams of Wurlitzer chords or Movietone News-style soundtrack that are dropped in for 'added effect'. This can pull you up short; for a moment the layers stack up and a trowelful of wobble-boarding riddim bass cements it all together. But soon we're back in *Interzone*, in some velour-encrusted dive. The Great Junksman attaches his lips to your inner ear, and, fellating you with his Midwestern whine, makes a pitch for your orgones.

Why does Burroughs feel he has to do these things? The answer is surely that he's a nice enough old codger, and when some spirited bucks make a play for his attention, he's happy enough to oblige. A more portentous explanation is axiomatically less flattering. For, like Marx, Burroughs is a thinker who has been subject to a major epistemological break. This occurred sometime between his re-encounter with Brion Gysin, in Paris in 1958, and the publication of *Naked Lunch*. Until this winter of sublime 'wigging out' (Burroughs and Gysin would sit for hours scrying mirrors, their eyelids propped up with half matches), Burroughs had succeeded ably in the decadent tradition of confabulating the art and the life. As the recent publication of the Burroughs–Ginsberg correspondence from these years makes clear, it was the compulsive need to entertain and capture an audience for emotional purposes that made the classic routines what they were: full of bite and desperation.

Pre-'59 there is the deadpan realism of *Junky*; the nostalgic *roman-à-clef Queer*; the epistolary belle-lettriste take on Rimbaud, *Yage Letters*; the high camp of *Naked Lunch*; and the reheated left-overs in *Interzone*. But everything that has come afterwards has been garnish or embellishment. Worse still, the very 'revolutionary' methodologies that Burroughs coined in this fertile period of insemination by Gysin are not brave new media that anticipate the innovations of the sixties (installation and performance art, multimedia experiences, sub-lim etc.), but rather a literal cut-up and rearrangement of his previous larder of ideas.

The subsequent trilogies of 'novels', the numerous pamphlets, the tapes, the films; what does this corpus of work really amount to? An analogy would be with an artist who I once saw on show at the ICA in London. This character would assemble on a table a number of her personal artefacts. She would then draw, photograph and model them, placing the representations in front of that which was represented. Next she would draw, photograph and model the representations themselves, creating a second order of nostalgic self-referentiality. This is essentially what Burroughs has been up to since 1959.

He is an artist enacting the same ritual as his own character Bill Gains, the decrepit addict-overcoat thief in *Junky*. At one point in the story Gains pulls out a package of old papers from the broken-down bureau in his tatty flophouse room. His Knights of Columbus certificate, his army discharge (dishonourable) and so on. These he fondles and pitifully rearranges 'as if trying to supply himself with an identity'. All the while he mutters 'just a victim of circumstance'.

That's Burroughs in a nutshell – a victim of circumstance. He is fated to end up on rap albums, guilty of the hubristic inclination to take his status as avant-garde avatar to its anachronistic limit. This is why the arch inflamer, the most-high censored one, is reduced to being backed up by people who, when supporting those spiritual barkers U2, 'instead of letting the size of the venues dictate [their] message . . . made an effort to communicate with local community groups, inviting them into stadiums to set up stalls and distribute leaflets'. Naturally. This has to be the way to dissolve the negative conditioning inculcated by such mass and unreflective entertainment: invite in local community groups.

But really we're all victims of this particular circumstance. Just as the pabulum of liberal guilt was to incant 'we are all to blame', so that occasioned by the capitulation of the avant-garde is 'we are all victims'. We are all victims of the cut-up, of a thousand talentless leotard-wearers, of the hideous synaesthetic miscegenation provoked by the reckless intercouse between high drugs and low culture. It can be argued that the very quotient of torque measurable in any given cultural moment is a function of just how highly geared it is, how much of a declivity exists between the status quo and those individuals who determine with clarity to be contrary. In the progress (or otherwise) of Burroughs's work we can see this writ small. The Beats were a genuine movement in that collaboration was central to success. It took a decade and a half of the posse burnishing one another by association to have an impact on the mainstream. But now every single new departure, every instance of a crystallization of a new 'style', is leapt on by the marketing men without its having a chance to ferment or foment.

Of course, *Spare Ass Annie* isn't a rap album *per se*. I think on perhaps one of the tracks there is a little attempt, a moue towards syncopation on the part of Uncle Bill, but otherwise he does carry on as if blissfully unaware of what the kids are getting up to. It was John Clellon Holmes who in a *New Yorker* piece summoned up his 'trinity' at the theological core of the Beat Generation: the hipster, the spade and the junkie. But while Jack Kerouac covered these bases, writing extensively on bebop jazz and even penning a narrative written entirely from the point of view of a nineteen-year-old black single mother, Burroughs's own 'beat trinity' was considerably different.

He may have lived in North Africa for upwards of ten years, but he didn't go there on pilgrimage to the Master Musicians of the Riff. Nor has Burroughs ever been much of a negrophile. The serried ranks of cock-sucking boys that populate his texts are reduced – once you blur the focus of remembrance – into a pointilliste splatter of writhing copper-coloured skin. Burroughs never really left the South America of his imagination, the pullulating city of the red night. Furthermore, in his earliest published work there are the disparaging references to the 'new breed' of hipsters that is emerging in the USA; Burroughs finds them disturbingly apathetic and asexual. Already there is disdain for the mass adoption of the aesthetic he has been helping to spawn.

I suppose someone might argue that the focus of gangsta rap on firearms gives some credence to its co-option as a form of the Literary Outlaw, but it's a flimsy contention. The truth is that contemporary youth culture is as far from Burroughs's work as is imaginable. Moreover, rap itself is already an ersatz medium. If you are talking about the work of artists such as Gil Scott Heron and the Last Poets as being seminal, then you are speaking of the creation of an 'authentic' medium only to the same extent as you speak of Hugh McDiarmid's 'Scots-language' poetry as being authentic. In both cases the impetus has come from the intellectual and seeded a popular substratum. But Burroughs's trinity would never have been hipster, spade and junkie. It would have been junkie, intellectual and junkie, or even just three intellectual junkies – why not fire the supernumeraries?

On this particular album Burroughs's reading of his own work is as good as ever. The agile mind is in and of itself continually circling around the possibilities of rhythm, assonance and sibilance present within the words. The dramatic cadence of his inflection retains that rusty flatness, giving the impression that a tuning fork coated with verdigris is stuck in the old man's craw. The opening track features the album's eponymous heroine, who has 'an auxiliary asshole in the middle of her forehead'. She is first among a group of repellent equals, all of whom have been offered asylum by Uncle Bill in his Freedonian dystopia. As he plaints, a walk-on-the-wild-side-type chorus comes in, yodelling 'Spare Ass Annie' and the Hiphopcrytes do their best to sound like the Art Ensemble of Chicago after a heavy largactil session. It's all so predictable, and when the Great Junksman pronounces weightily, to the accompaniment of farting horns, 'This is an object lesson in how far human kicks can go', it's an effort not to mutter: before they become no kick at all.

The sad thing is that the routines themselves are as brilliant as ever, but trivialized by their context rather than ennobled. Individual lines still leap out and grab. In 'Talking Asshole' there is a certain atmospheric to the plaintive skirling of a synthesized clarinet in the background. In 'Mildred Pierce Reports' Burroughs imparts the line 'Well, aren't you going to do something . . .' with a fine catty emphasis as the drums hit the backbeat. But how many times can we hear 'Dr Benway Operates' before the idea of washing the toilet plunger in the commode before using it to massage the patient's heart becomes a tad stale? Burroughs can still create more of a sound picture than anyone else, simply by saying the line 'I saw women thrown down in Fifth Avenue and raped in their mink coats.' He doesn't need the cab noises and traffic susurrations added in to prove realism. In such surroundings the creeping formlessness of the Burroughs routine is enhanced rather than contained.

The only real gem on the album, the only place I found myself remotely carried away, was the rendition of 'Junkies' Xmas' that dominates the second half. This early short story displays Burroughs at his best, conjuring up an entire parallel world out of a supply of sepia backdrops of wartime New York in the grip of winter. The junkie of the title, Danny, is released from jail on Christmas Eve and wanders the city looking for money and a score: 'enough for an eighth, and something to put down on a room'. The elision between warmth, security and heroin is entire. This is a kind of mutant O'Henry story that might have been penned for the *Saturday Evening Post* in a post-war America with no illusions whatsoever. The only thing Danny can manage to steal is a suitcase that's been used as a prop by a torso murderer. As he dumps the two bloodless legs it contains, the junkie mutters: 'The routines some people will put down nowadays . . .' He manages to sell the suitcase to a fence for two dollars, but then can't score. Eventually he manages to hit an alcoholic doctor for a quarter-grain tablet of morphine. He repairs to a cheap hotel – and here Burroughs's voice acquires a truly loving tone, caressing the listener as he meticulously describes the ritual of cooking up a fix. But just as he's about to have his hit – 'the shot in front of him, his defences gave way and junk sickness flooded his body' – he hears an unearthly groaning from the next room. Against his worst nature he goes next door to investigate and finds a young man suffering torments from kidney stones. This makes Danny laugh bleakly because it's exactly the fake routine he would put down to get junk out of a doctor. Danny takes pity on the kid and gives him the morphine. But Danny is rewarded for his Christian act: 'Suddenly a warm flood pulsed through his veins and broke in his head like a thousand golden speedballs.' 'Hark the Herald Angels Sing' swells in the background; it is a beatific moment: 'Ferchrissakes, Danny thought, I must have scored for the immaculate fix.'

It's a great gag and delivered with consummate panache, but it has absolutely nothing to do with the *Zeitgeist*, it says nothing to the racist rappers in the ghetto, or the dweebs in the 'burbs. It's a pure satirical conceit, a comic reversal.

J. G. Ballard, reviewing the Burroughs–Ginsberg correspondence in the *Guardian*, trotted out once again his opinion that great writing can only be produced by individuals who are prepared to take up Burroughs's posture of determined non-conformism. I would have thought that on the contrary, the past few decades have demonstrated perfectly what happens when the great mass of people begin to believe that an admixture of narcosis and attitudinizing can stimulate artistic production.

The consequence of such an aesthetic is this muddy sonic swamp, this plurality of feeble little genres, struggling with each other to achieve some pre-eminence, some hold on posterity. And the greatest irony of all is that these high modernists, these self-immolating creators, should have turned out to be both so durable and so romantic. My guess would be that *Spare Ass Annie* and the rest of the memorabilia, the shotgun paintings and the Dutch Shultz ramblings, will be confined to the stalls at U2 concerts. The great books will remain.

Modern Review, October 1993

Drug Dealer by Appointment to Her Majesty's Government

An acquaintance of mine, a columnist on a national newspaper with a penchant for cocaine, has often said that, if he ever found it difficult to get hold of supplies in London, he would only need to shoot up the M6 to Widnes on Merseyside, and there Dr John Marks, the druggies' friend, would prescribe for him all the coke he needed.

It is to Dr Marks's credit that when I relayed this to him, he disclaimed any knowledge of the person concerned. But, be that as it may, Dr Marks's policy of prescribing pure heroin, cocaine and amphetamines to addicts registered at his Widnes clinic has aroused a good deal of attention in the media, earned him a lot of enemies among the drug treatment establishment, and made him a cult figure in the drug addicts' underworld.

The media attention Dr Marks can live with, judging from the smooth way he deals with inquirers. A visit to see him is preceded by an information pack arriving at the interviewer's house a few days in advance. This sets out the Marks philosophy on drug treatment in exhaustive detail, and includes photocopies of the editorials and articles he has published in numerous professional journals such as the *Lancet*. In these he puts forward his persuasive arguments that the war on drugs has failed, and that a more humane and realistic approach to the problems associated with drug use needs to be taken in our society.

On arriving in Widnes, I found that I had been double-booked to see Dr Marks. A tall man with the old-young face of a politician was ensconced in his office with him. This turned out to be the New South Wales Shadow Minister for Health, come to survey the Marks method. Dr Marks has also been the subject of a *Panorama* documentary, and while I was working on this article, another journalist said that he, too, was profiling Dr Marks.

That was the upside. The downside was that sources from within the Merseyside drug treatment services were loud in their condemnation. One spokesman says, 'Marks gets journalists up here and claims that he single-handedly introduced the policy of harm minimization to Merseyside. It makes us very angry. He says his prescribing policy is responsible for the low level of HIV here, but that's rubbish. Liverpool is a backwater with high unemployment and few transients. The needle exchange programme wasn't Marks's brainchild anyway.'

Those were the milder criticisms. There were harsher accusations flying around. The world of drug treatment and drug politics is perforce a murky one, and on Merseyside it all becomes even murkier.

It is easy to see that any individual putting forward a radical approach to drug treatment which involves attacking some of the principal shibboleths of our society can fall victim to professional rivalries and entrenched interests.

Dr Marks makes strong claims for the success of his approach, and it is these claims as much as anything that have generated interest. But to what extent are they justified? And what is it that will make a man risk public opprobrium in order to help drug addicts?

'It's anger,' Dr Marks says. 'It makes me furious that a group of young, able people – they have to be able to survive the harsh drug underworld – should suffer from the same death rate as people with smallpox, between 10 and 20 per cent, simply because of inhumane laws. I'm not a bleeding heart, and I don't think there's anything glamorous about drugs; I try to make my clients realize that what they are doing is boring, bloody boring.'

According to Dr Marks, his prescription policy, together with the provision of sterile injecting equipment to addicts, has resulted in a 0 per cent rate of HIV among intravenous drug users on Merseyside. He also claims a 'fifteenfold' decrease in drug-related acquisitive crime in the area covered by his clinic. In his opinion, there is 'no black market' in hard drugs in Widnes.

Asked to defend his prescription policy, Dr Marks refers to his flip charts and unleashes a string of statistics. He is at pains to point out that the prescription of 'drugs of choice' to addicts is merely the traditional British system as laid out by the Rolleston Committee in 1926. The committee advocated that addicts could be maintained on heroin or cocaine, by their GPs, where it was felt that there was little chance of withdrawing them successfully, or where the drugs were deemed necessary for them to lead a productive existence.

Dr Marks acknowledges that it was the coming of cheap air travel in the 1960s, together with the over-prescribing of a number of British doctors, that led to a partial abandonment of this system, and to today's network of drug dependency clinics, mostly offering only methadone reduction to addicts.

But he angrily dismisses the observation that we cannot turn back the clock. 'It's millenarianistic [sic] to claim that there's anything special about the age we live in. After all, the Romans thought that their adolescents were the worst that the world had ever seen.'

Dr Marks has 400 patients (or 'clients' as he refers to them) spread between two clinics. The procedure for getting registered is complex, and he has evolved a complicated method of assessment combined with random testing to ensure that his prescribing isn't being abused. Only addicts registered with local GPs can be maintained, and they must attend a group therapy session every week, or forfeit their prescription. Once registered, addicts may receive heroin in injectable ampoules, or in the form of heroin 'reefers'. Some are on the traditional heroin substitute, methadone, and, in addition, some receive cocaine or amphetamine ampoules or 'reefers'.

But 'treatment' isn't the right word, because Dr Marks doesn't really believe that drug addiction is a medically treatable condition. 'But try telling anyone that 99 per cent of drug users don't need treatment, it goes down like a lead balloon with the people who are giving out the £16 million in cash.'

When asked why he insists on a therapy session for his clients, Dr Marks is equally forthright: 'It's political,' he says. 'When I hand out drugs I'm not acting as a physician, I'm acting as an agent of the state monopoly on drugs.' As far as Dr Marks is concerned – and he produces yet more statistics to back this up – there is a more or less determinable period of drug using for any given addict. 'The job of the physician is to keep the addict healthy until he sees the light, or his EEG normalizes, whichever way you want to put it. People stop taking drugs despite the interventions of doctors and police, not because of them.'

But Dr Marks doesn't go so far as to advocate complete legalization of drugs. Rather he points to what he calls the 'quadratic relation' between supply and demand. 'Up until the sixties there were far tighter controls on the sale of alcohol. Since they've been relaxed we've had an epidemic of alcoholism. But, by the same token, if you entirely prohibit a drug like heroin you encourage epidemic black-market trading, because people have to deal in order to sustain their habit.'

This quadratic relation implies, says Dr Marks, that there should be a controlled supply to 'users', both of opiates and of alcohol, and he points to the Norwegian state monopoly on alcohol as an example of the way forward.

It's a shame that the claims that Dr Marks makes for his methods are so exaggerated, because it tends to lay him open to charges of charlatanism. His radical stance is a fascinating example of the way that breaking any long-held social taboo is bound to result in vilification.

There are lots of rumours surrounding Dr Marks personally, he is the first to admit it. 'They say that the probation officer sleeps with me and I give her a script. They often say that I give drugs in return for sexual favours.' There is no evidence for this, any more than there is that drugs prescribed by Dr Marks are leaking on to the black market in substantial amounts.

Dr Marks is happy for me to talk to the police in order to verify his claims. Detective Inspector Phil Williams and Detective Constable Mike Lofts of the Cheshire Drug Squad soon modify Dr Marks's claims of having 'eliminated the hard drug market' in Widnes. 'Oh, you'd find heroin in Widnes, if you looked for long enough,' says Mr Williams.

In fact I didn't have to look far at all. I simply had to cross the road from Dr Marks's Chapel Street clinic to the pub opposite. In the public bar I found Norman and Ian, scrap merchants and committed boozers. 'See that,' says Norman, twitching aside a beer mat to reveal a notch cut in the Melamine bar top. 'A mate of mine did that with an axe, he was on the needle. He died three years ago.'

Ian had a friend who was one of Dr Marks's patients: 'He gets speed in a bottle, has a drink of that and he's off!' They scoffed at the alleged non-availability of heroin in Widnes. 'I could take you up to Ditton [a suburb of Widnes] where I live and we could find five smack dealers in as many minutes, not that they'd thank me for taking you.'

Mr Lofts and Mr Williams also corrected the impression of falling drug crime statistics as a function of Dr Marks's prescribing policy: 'The Merseyside police,' says Mr Williams, 'are now operating a policy of cautioning all first-time offenders for drug possession, that's why there's been a reduction in crime.'

The Cheshire police are also now operating a cautioning policy, but they're resigned about the real motivation. 'The aim of the formal caution is to get people out of going to court,' says Mr Williams. 'It's down to the backlog at the courts, and that's a political thing.'

Both officers agreed that the addicts Dr Marks maintains show less marked criminality, better health and better socialization, but they were more sceptical about the actual impact on the drug-dealing infrastructure. 'There has been a reduction over the past eighteen months as far as street dealing in Widnes is concerned, but the dealer structure is still intact,' says Mr Williams.

'We're only playing at this policy because of lack of funds from central government,' says Mr Williams. 'I'd like to give Marks's methods a proper trial, say lasting five years, if the money was available. Then we'd see whether this approach was really effective.'

Mr Lofts adds: 'The point is that John Marks is our only chance for a new initiative. I've spoken to other consultant psychiatrists at drug dependency clinics, and all they have to offer as a solution is more methadone.'

One such consultant psychiatrist is Dr Tim Garvey, who runs the Bootle drug dependency clinic in Liverpool. It is through comparisons with Bootle that Dr Marks seeks to point up the success of his methods. Dr Marks claims higher mortality rates for Bootle as against Widnes addicts; higher crime rates and more new registrations of addicts.

'I don't disagree with all the substance of John Marks's ideas, but I do object to his style,' says Garvey. 'Almost the only time we ever get any media attention here is in connection with Marks and his views. None of them points out that we treat twice as many addicts here in Bootle as he does in Widnes, and we have a waiting list. If what he says about addicts not wanting methadone is really true, why do we have a waiting list?

'The point is,' Garvey adds, 'that prescribing policy on Merseyside is in general more liberal than in, say, London. I maintain lots of addicts long-term on methadone, but I don't feel the need to shout about it, I actually think it's counter-productive to the kind of work we are trying to do here. And as for HIV, the truth is that the rates of infection are just as low here as they are in Widnes, so once again it can't be the heroin prescribing that's making the difference.'

Dr Marks admits that the role of 'drug doctor' is a thankless one. 'They used to say that failed doctors become psychiatrists, and failed psychiatrists go into the drugs field. We're the lowest of the low.' And although he was scathing about Dr John Strang, one of the government's favourite drug doctors ('We know that he has two addicts that he has maintained long-term on 1.8 grams of heroin a day. Pure, unadulterated heroin, so if he's prepared to do this for some patients for years, why isn't he prepared to do it for new ones?'), he also admits that it couldn't simply be professional or self-interest that motivated him.

'I don't agree with Dr Strang or Professor Griffith Edwards,' he says of more establishment figures in the drug treatment world, 'but I do assume that they know something about what they're talking about, they have a modicum of intelligence. I know they have a vested interest in staying on top, but that isn't sufficient to explain their ideas.'

Perhaps the truth about Dr Marks is that by his own lights he shouldn't really exist. He is enthusiastic about the work of Thomas Szasz, the maverick American anti-psychiatrist who believes in a completely free market in all drugs. While Dr Marks wouldn't go that far, his views do imply that there can be no particularly meaningful role for doctors in defining a society's drug policy; he has written himself out of the debate as regards his professional expertise.

At the same time, Dr Marks does defend his arguments with statistics that are questionable, as he himself admits. 'I keep expecting someone to come along and say I've added it up wrong, that I've put two and two together and made five.' But the point is, rather, that in the Stygian gloom of the drugs black market, statistics are bound to take on a creative rather than a descriptive role.

No one knows how many addicts there are in the country, and no one knows the quantities of drugs that are in circulation, all we have are guesstimates. By the same token, academic studies that aim to demonstrate statistically the efficacy of this or that policy fall foul of the inability of any social science to be value-free. Did the drug addicts get well or die because of the therapy, or because of the social context? And how can these factors be disentangled?

The paradox of Dr Marks is: is he quack or idealist? Is it really a function of our failure as a society to confront the issue of our drug use responsibly and collectively? Dr Marks's ideas imply that rates of alcoholism and addiction can be altered by command policies, and in that belief he ironically mirrors the very convictions of those he implacably opposes.

Observer, September 1992

PLEASE DON'T FEEL I'M REJECTING YOU
SIMPLY BECAUSE I'VE THROWN YOUR GIFT AWAY......

THE MOLECULAR STRUCTURE OF BANK MANAGERS

INVESTIGATIVE REPORTER OF THE YEAR

ALTHOUGH HARRY HAD BECOME A TABLE, HE STILL FELT AT PERFECT EASE IN SOCIAL SITUATIONS

'IT SAYS "PLEASE INTRODUCE THIS BEAR TO A LIFE OF PROSTITUTION AND DRUG ADDICTION"...'

'OF COURSE I'M GOING TO MAKE YOU BIG KEVIN, BUT FIRST I'M GOING TO MAKE YOU 'ACTUAL SIZE'...'

'I HAVE A WET DREAM'

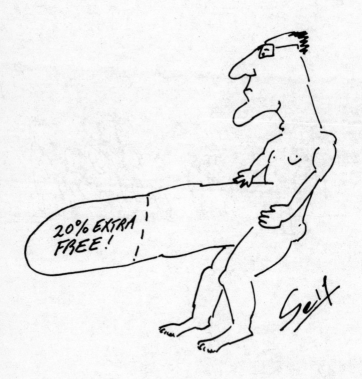

PART TWO

ON OTHER THINGS

HUMOUR

Off the Box

Something strange has happened to me; I've lost the ability to watch television. I can't hack it any more. Ten or twenty years ago this might have been a source of *bien pensant* snobbish pride, along the lines of those hot-housing parents who would say: 'Oh, we don't let Saul or Laetitia watch television for more than half an hour a week, and anyway there's no time for it what with the sitar lessons, the gestalt therapy and boules fixtures at the Lycée.' Not any more. Now you cannot admit to anybody that you don't watch television without them withering at you. Even writers cock an eyebrow as if to say: 'Come off it, what are you trying to pull?' No, especially writers are prone to this. They accept the medium's unrivalled status as the story-cycle of our epoch, a great braiding together of fact, fiction and confabulation. They've also seen the writing on the cheques.

I have no doubt that V. S. Naipaul likes *EastEnders*, Margaret Atwood can't bear missing *Roseanne*, and Kenzaburo Oe, the Nobel laureate, looks deep into the ur-semiology of the *Mighty Morphin Power Rangers* for inspiration. To suppose otherwise would be folly. No one argues with the fact of television any more. Sure, there are still minor disagreements about what programmes should be shown on it, but this is mere banter. Television has triumphed.

ON OTHER THINGS

It's not my fault, this quintessentially modern, dare I say it, even post-modern, malaise. I didn't set out to quit television, it just sort of left me. I admit I may not have exercised those vital television muscles enough, for the thing about television is that it actually requires a vast amount of energy, at least two of your senses going at more or less full stretch. Nowadays I'm lucky if I can keep one of them in play for more than a few minutes; a blind Camembert tasting looks like hard work from where I'm reclining.

And the suspension of disbelief required, my dear! *Such* hard work. The theatre was always bad enough, trying to convince yourself that a gang of epicene twerps fresh out of RADA were in fact languid Russian aristocrats, incestuous Ancient Greek monarchs, or neurotic Danish courtiers. But television teases you constantly with the certain knowledge that just off-screen hover a lot of men called Trevor, carrying clipboards and wearing sleeveless anoraks with too many pockets.

I blame all those programmes where they think it's clever to show you the nuts and bolts of the operation, the sound stage, the cameramen and technicians. Fools! They opened a Pandora's box of twisted supposition. Now I can't see a presenter sitting behind a beige, modular console (where do they get that furniture? You never see it on sale anywhere) without entertaining the idea that they are naked from the waist down and being vigorously fellated by a man called Trevor, carrying a clipboard . . .

This parlous condition has begun to marginalize me, but not as much as you might expect. The fact is that television and life are now so intimately entwined that you don't actually have to watch that much of either to know what is going on in both. I now have a sufficient memory of plot lines, characters and scenarios to cruise into conversations about the box with benign insouciance, scattering 'Has Michelle had her baby?' here and 'How's Keith Chegwin now he's off the bottle?' there, safe in the knowledge that I won't be called out on it.

And why should I be? In this culture of high reflexivity, deep virtuality and media interpenetration, the hardware of television has become increasingly superfluous. It doesn't take much vision to imagine a world in which broadcasting itself has died out, leaving behind a kind of folk memory of what it was like.

In this post-TV society, people will go round to the houses of wise elders. These greybeards will transfix with their yarns of amazing devices, pulsing with life, that when activated would beam the teeming world into your consciousness. They will recount the plots of ancient soap operas and antediluvian television plays with the rhythmic cadences of the Norse sagas, leaving appropriate pauses for their listeners to interject: 'And then she said . . .' or 'And then he went . . .' until the whole company is rocking and swaying in a trance of communal myth-making.

Perhaps on high holidays or solstices the ark of the covenant will be processed, so that the masses will be able to catch sight of the beaming visage of Isla St Clair, the Mother Goddess, on the cover of a copy of the *Radio Times* dating from 1974.

I fear this future. I'm not so sure that it's a fantasy. Television quite clearly can't do without me. Why else would the licensing authority keep importuning me with notices stating that I have to inform them, in writing, that I don't have a television in my house or they will take me to court for non-payment of their fee? Whatever next? Will we soon have to inform the requisite authorities if we don't have a microwave on the premises? 'No deep-fat fryer, sir? Complete form E2459 and hand it in at that window.'

And I miss television, I really do. I miss it for its marvellous quiddity, its status as the psychic carpet underlay of our world. I used to look forward to seeing all those people, the Peter Snows, Tracey MacLeods and Bill Gileses. I used to look upon them as – sob! – my friends.

But there is help at hand. Recently a friend told me about a bold and courageous psychotherapist who has begun to work with the televisually bereft. His methods are a combination of traditional behaviourism (the patient is punished for watching animated shorts from eastern Europe and rewarded fulsomely for sitting through an episode of *Buccaneers*) and the distinctly whacky. I have been attending his clinic as an out-patient for the past four weeks. To begin with I was only required to watch epic films such as *Ben Hur* on tiny televisions, the ones with one-and-a-half-inch LCD screens, on the grounds that suspension of disbelief is so impossible under these watching conditions that it needn't even be attempted.

It's worked, and I'm now up to watching at least fifteen minutes of television a day on a healthy four-inch screen. And this morning there was some truly heartening news. A bed has become vacant at the clinic and I can now be admitted as an in-patient. I can feel it in my bones – I'll soon be watching television all day long.

Observer, April 1995

Island Life

I've always liked the title of W. H. Hudson's great autobiographical work *Idle Days in Patagonia*. And, of course,
I've read the book itself a number of times. However, the
content has rather slid through the gaps in my recollection,
much as water – stained by vegetables – flows through the
holes in a colander. Nowadays I confine myself to reading
the title alone.

I thought of this the other night, sitting in my local pub,
the Taversoe Hotel, in Orkney. There used to be a joke
when I was at school, the substance of which was that
instead of actually telling a joke you simply told a number,
which referred to a list of jokes, whereupon everyone fell
about cackling in a knowing fashion.

Well, at the Taversoe we have taken this one step further.
Tired of one another's insistent prattle during the long
winter evenings, we have put social intercourse on a more
efficient basis.

There is now a list of possible conversations tacked next
to the list of fine malt whiskies the pub serves (my favourite
is an Islay malt with a fine, peaty nose and clean, slightly
salty finish, called 'Old Apathetic'). If you want to talk to
anyone, you simply select one of the conversations listed,
turn to the person you wish to have it with, and utter the
relevant number.

These range from:

ON OTHER THINGS

1. 'Getting to know you'. A brief exchange of essentially inane pleasantries is followed by more circumstantial questioning. Employment, sexual orientation, marital status, political opinions, spiritual yearnings; all are touched upon but not belaboured.

Certain stresses within the dialogue and lengthy pauses give rise on both sides to an intimation of a potentially closer relationship, but without the conversation becoming in any way oppressive.

Rounds: three. A short and either two pints or two glasses of wine.

All the way to:

37. 'Gurdjieff Special'. A brief exchange of essentially inane pleasantries is followed by a whirlwind descent into deep, mutual, spiritual questioning. After identifying a shared yearning that seems to transcend both space and time, the conversationalists employ such techniques as the Rorschach ink-blot test, free association, meditational yoga and co-counselling to free themselves from the hidebound constraints of a socio-culturally constructed 'identity'.

Towards dawn the conversationalists quit the pub and, much in the manner of the final sequence of Bergman's *Seventh Seal*, join hands and, forming a chain, dance across the heather.

Rounds: fifteen. May comprise any combination of drinks as long as they add up to the unrecommended twenty-two units per person.

This, I'm sure you'll agree, is a brilliant solution to the problem of pub conversation.

I'm always trying esoteric conversations like 14 and even 32 on the locals, but invariably they stick to the tried and tested, like 9 (planning application refused), 11 (new borehole sunk) and 25 (man coming over from the mainland to scan the ewes).

One of the problems with being an idler living on a small, isolated island is what I term the 'Groundhog Day Effect'. This occurs because there simply isn't enough happening to go around. Undoubtedly there are people on the island who are leading incident-packed lives, but fortunately I'm not one of them. Nor is my friend Eric who works in the local salmon fishery.

About two months ago Eric bought a second-hand Ford Granada 2.3 litre. A day or so after this life event, I met him in the Taversoe. 'What's happening then, Eric?' I asked.

'Not a lot,' he replied coyly, 'except I bought a new car the day before yesterday.'

After the shock waves of this conversational bombshell had died down a little, we went out to examine Eric's new motor. I was enthusiastic – perhaps too enthusiastic. In some parts of Britain it's still considered bad form to fellate a car aerial – even if it is second-hand.

A month later I met Eric in the Taversoe again. We swapped yarns for a while (or Orkneyaga sagas as they are known in this part of the world). After a while I said: 'What's happening then, Eric?'

'Not a lot,' he replied coyly, 'except I bought a new car.'

After the shock waves of this conversational bombshell had died down a little, we went out to examine Eric's new motor. I was enthusiastic – perhaps too enthusiastic. In some parts of Britain it's still considered bad form to fellate a car aerial – even if it is second-hand.

Someone once said that those who do not understand their history are doomed to repeat it. Well, I can't understand what I'm doing wrong, but now I've had the 2.3 Granada conversation with Eric half a dozen times. It's even acquired its own number, '2.3'; and I've heard other people in the pub having it as well.

Of course, another function of the slow pace of events is that people here have long and accurate memories. Events that happened many years ago are recalled by almost everyone with startling clarity.

This island, like most of the Orkneys, is rich in prehistoric remains. The largest extant chamber tomb in Britain, Midhowe, is about two miles from my house.

It's a formidable structure, some fifty metres long and ten wide. It was built by neolithic people in about 3500 BC. When it was excavated in the 1930s, the bones of twenty-two adults were found, symmetrically arranged in the stalls the tomb is divided into.

According to the archaeologists, Midhowe was in use for as long as a thousand years. I find this incredible. To think of a small, tribal society, in which the average life expectancy was nineteen, using the same tomb for that many generations. To my mind it implied that these people must have been considerably different to ourselves, perhaps having some kind of bizarre group mind, or collective unconscious. But when I taxed Simon, the local builder, with this theory, he merely gave me a sanguine look and replied: 'Nine.'

Living by myself, in an isolated house with few means of contact with the outside world apart from a fax-machine, a telex, a networked computer (linked via modem and satellite to all major ethernets) and a videophone, I am often thrown back on my own inner mental resources for days at a time.

Initially I found this incredibly lonely and dispiriting. I seized upon any excuse I could find to make conversation with people I ran into. I would go down to the local shop and say things to the girl who works there like: 'It says here that this margarine contains 30 per cent unsaturated fats, 40 per cent polyunsaturated fats, 28 per cent rancid ghee, and

2 per cent reconstituted rennet. But I can't believe it's not butter.'

I even tried more risqué conversational sallies, such as: 'Why do you think they've discontinued Camp Coffee?' But eventually I decided I would have to learn to cope with isolation. I began working on developing an appreciation of that mental state the Buddhists call 'sartori', or 'doing fuck all'.

To begin with I could only do fuck all for a few moments at a time. I would concentrate too hard on the doing of fuck all. As everyone familiar with this technique is no doubt aware, such an attitude can be a major blow to progress. One Ch'an master wrote: 'It is not in the doing of fuck all that the fuck alledness of fuck all exists.'

I took this to heart and began to make real progress. I soon became able to enter a state of sartori without any conscious effort. Now I can be doing something – making a cup of tea, or tidying a room – when I cease to be conscious of my actions at all.

When I snap out of these reveries I'm unable to tell how much time has elapsed. It can be minutes, or hours. The only way I can discover it is by trying to assess exactly how little I've done. On a good day this can be refreshingly little, just a paper-clip moved to one side, or a cigarette paper lightly crumpled; but on bad days I may find that during my fugue I've scanned the odd ewe, or even submitted a planning application.

Idler, April 1994

Eight Miles High

Make no mistake about it, first-class flying is the heroin of travel. A few flights might not give you a bad yen, but push it too far and you'll never, ever escape the consequences: your metabolism will alter at a cellular level; you'll have to become rich – or a whore. Fuck it, I've only had one hit of this shit and I'm still swaddled in its velvet paw ten days later.

But – ah, how did you start? I mean, did someone give it to you, or what . . .?

It's like this: I've been up all night at the fag end of a rolled-up 72 hours of missed obligations, street corner burns and tiffs with desk clerks. My face is a kind of *impasto* of willed disintegration, and I'm checking in for the Saturday p.m. Virgin flight to New York. I've spent the last twenty hours spreading myself around town like some kind of new, err . . . spread. Pulling the carriage of my body into bar-after-bar-after-bar on those most exiguous of rails, the ones just thick enough to get you to . . . the bar. I'm feeling my gusset – it's feeling me. I'm also sensing the airport as a gusset – soiled of course. See those baggage conveyors, how they yaw and grab at the air's damp perineum . . . I'm all fucked up. It's not funny.

There's a gusset in front of me for the mid-class check in. Except I don't think it's called mid-class anymore, it's called something like 'priority class'. They've euphemised the shit out of it. How like Major's Britain. Perhaps Virgin Atlantic is a microcosm of Major's Britain. The gusset in front of me is wearing brown Terylene trousers and the body of a largish Asian man. Ahead of him some old gusset is buying a ticket. It's taking several millennia, Ancient Sumer has risen once more, Gilgamesh appears on the cover of *Radio Times*. Inside my trousers a rain forest is being established, an entire ecosystem. Miniature Colobus monkeys swing from the hairs on my testicles.

I start to study the staff behind the desk. They are wearing beautifully neat uniforms in bright, bright primary colours. They are young and shapely. Their faces are not willed impastos of disintegration. The last rail they rode on was Network South East. Their pants are uniformly gussetless. They look like heavenly extras in a remake of *A Matter of Life and Death*. I approach the white-clad senior angel and cough up some sort of gurgle of discontent. She beckons me round to the Upper Class check in. And then it starts, the plunger is pressed home: the slippery descent into bliss.

The desk clerk slaps and tickles the keyboard, his lovely brow furrows, he can't hack it. He looks up and says: 'I'm sorry, Mr Self, we have no mid-class seats left, we'll have to bump you up to Upper Class . . .' He's *sorry!* I do nothing but splutter, and stand there while he goes on slapping and caressing the moulded plastic for about twenty seconds real time (the Queen Mother goes on mega-H.R.T. and is artificially inseminated, the donor is Phil Collins, the intention: to beget a master race . . .). It's too much for me to bear; deranged at the prospect I attempt to run off in the direction of the aircraft, until called back to get a boarding card.

He's thanking me. I'm thanking him. This is a little darling slice of luck. I don't know what's in store yet, but even now I'd give the most fulsome encomiums to

VA. Best Airline 1995? Fuck it: Best Airline of the Whole Fucking Decade. And If I knew then what I know now? No encomium would suffice. If necessary I'd go round to Richard Branson's house, or barge, or whatever it is, and rim him to get another seat in Upper Class.

Then I'm clunking through something called 'fast track'. Not, as I had hoped, a kind of super-rail, running incandescently ahead of my stooped membranes, but really a taped-off extra lane along which the rich limp, burdened by their responsibilities. It has its own metal detectors and security staff, and apparently its own immigration officials. Truly, wealth is another country.

Then, ahead of me stretch more wavering, vibrating gussets. Giant, black gussets along which passenger-gussets yomp. My gate is so far away that I may have to take on bearers. I'm flagging, when another Virgin seraphim appears driving one of those little rubber-wheeled trolleys. 'Virgin Atlantic, sir?' I assent. 'Hop on.' And we're off. I've prematurely aged to this extent: being carted around Heathrow like some thyroid case on a fork-lift. The faces of the healthy, as we pass them, register amusement and contempt. But I don't care, I've lanced into an Arcadia of the idle. We approach the gate, the seraphim says, 'Have your boarding card ready, please,' and then we almost drive *on to* the plane. I totter off the trolley, the cherubim at the door examines my boarding card and directs me all of eight feet to my seat.

I say seat, but really this is a terrible misnomer. It isn't a seat – it's a *bed*. Another heavenly chore-whore appears and sort of tucks me into this thing. 'Champagne, orange-juice, or buck's fizz?' she asks. I opt – unsurprisingly – for champagne, and she brings me an *entire bottle* of Tattinger brut. This I cradle protectively, a child safe with its teddy bear in its cot, as we lumber along the runway and take off.

EIGHT MILES HIGH

Take-off is always a big disappointment for me. Of course, there is always the sensation of being wrenched from the earth as if the plane were God's friction toy, and He a child determined to break it. This is never entirely vitiated by the fact that modern 747s are bigger than Chartres, with whole transepts and choirs full of gussets playing *Donkey Kong* and reading novels by Jeffrey Archer. We still know the sublime is somewhere out there.

During take-off I often console myself with imagining how John Martin, the great 19th-century apocalyptic painter (check out his *Plains of Heaven* and *The Fall of Babylon* in the Tate) would deal with the depiction of the interior of a Virgin 747, as its nose rammed into some reservoir in Staines at 32 ft per second/per second. The buckling of entire phalanxes of mortgage brokers and PE teachers could only really be satisfactorily achieved using oils. Thick, thick oils.

I'm mature enough to understand that air travel has to be rendered thus: from check- in, through terminal, to aircraft itself, a kind of illimitable boredom of corporate design. The point being that flying – even in 747s – is intrinsically *so* exciting, that everything must be done to make it dull. That's why there aren't full-length windows, or transparent floors. That's why the steward(esse)s don't wear Buck Rogers-style uniforms and shout 'Wheeeee!' during take-off. That's why the pilot doesn't come on the PA as you're taxiing and say something like the following:

'Hi! I'm Dave, your pilot this afternoon for our flight to New York. We're taxiing down to Runway Four, and personally I'm as wired-up as a baboon on methedrine. Shit, I'm going to hit that throttle and we're going to have over two million pounds of thrust jamming up our arses before you can say "Richard Gere". If you really want to wrap your head around the event-horizon of take-off, keep your eyes on the video screens, we're going to be relaying a set of deeply strange trance-enhancement graphics that will make the *Beyond the Parhelion* section of *2001* look like a broken lava lamp. Clamp on those earphones and clock the Mad Professor's remix of *Interstellar Overdrive*; and when those oxygen masks fall into your lap be sure to take a good long blast – it's specially formulated Virgin DMT. I think you'll agree with me: it's the food of the gods. Remember, every flight with Virgin is a profound, collective drug ritual. Here weee goooooo!'

No. None of the above.

Then we're airborne. We level off (I say that advisedly – I've been levelled off for some years), and the 'no smoking' sign winks out. I spark up. I'm at 22,000 feet, and I'm smoking and drinking *in bed*. A senior sort of *putti* appears. In a New York accent, she asks me if I would like a cocktail. Asks me by name. Asks me as if my welfare really concerns her.

And not just my current welfare, I feel she knows my whole poignant history intimately, just from the tone of her voice. I feel she was with me in the playground when that 13-year-old thug took the piss out of my zip-up, suede ankleboots; and then when I called him out on it, beat me to a reasonable pulp. I whimper, choking back the appellation 'Mummy', that I would like a Bloody Mary. 'Is that with Tabasco and celery salt, Mr Self, or would you prefer a more Worcester sauce-oriented version?' I like it here.

I'm going to crash soon. I can do that here. I've got a window 'seat', but there's enough space between my bed and the aisle bed that I can walk around the end of it without even getting near to the feet of its occupant. Damn it, the guy in the next-door bed is so far away that I could have one of my full-scale *Jacob's Ladder*-type nightmares, complete with arm-thrashing and convulsions, without him even noticing.

There's that, and there's the blissful absence of the video screens as well. They've been stowed somewhere in the interstices of the beds for take-off, and need never be pulled out again. That's fine by me. I've never been able to cope with those miniature LCD video screens since the time I got on a Virgin flight to New York – admittedly well over the herbaceous border – and became convinced that they were accurately portraying the thoughts of the person sitting in the seat in front of me.

Needless to say, it didn't surprise me in the least to learn that at the core of the very being of the woman sitting in front of me, Mick Jagger pranced, wearing a leather jacket that had last seen service in an episode of *BMX Bandits*.

When I awake, we're beginning our descent. Mummy appears next to my bed and says: 'Diddums haveums a nice sleepums?' Touchdown is as slight as a repressed homosexual vice cop putting the cuffs on a rent boy. I swing my feet out of bed and stroll off the aircraft, waving goodbye to my close, close Virgin friends. I'm through immigration and customs with indecent haste. Why? Because I'm the first fucker off the entire plane.

I'm in a cab, jolting along the Van Eyck Expressway, watching lissom black kids shoot hoops outside frame houses before you can say Martin Scorsese. It's all been such a painless progress that I cannot believe I'm actually in New York, until the cabbie (who's a Haitian or some such), on discovering that I write fiction for a living, enquires with great seriousness: 'Say, this thing called "Writer's Block". Does it really exist or what?'

The Idler, July–August 1995

Slack Attack

Some people are born to slack – others have slacking thrust upon them. Perhaps it's a measure of how seriously I take my own status as a slacker that I've long since forgotten which it is that applies to me.

Take this article for example. It was commissioned some weeks ago by a young man with a bright, eager voice: 'Will you do fifteen hundred words on slacking?' he asked.

I adjusted one of the servo-mechanisms on my fully powered Parker-Knoll recliner, bringing my flabby mouth into closer contact with the padded mouthpiece: 'Of course,' I fluted. 'Consider it done already.'

Since that day the poor commissioner has phoned me a number of times, on each occasion the note of anxiety in his voice moving up the scale: 'Err . . . that piece on slacking,' he begins hesitantly.

'My dear boy!' I snap back. 'Can you not hear the facsimile machine already whirring in the next room?'

But it's a lie. The truth of the matter is that my piece on slacking has become like the arrow fired at St Anthony in the philosophical paradox. It crosses half my mental terrain on its way to being written, and then half the remaining half, and then half of that half, and so on. For the slacker both time and distance are necessarily linear and incremental – there is no finer and more dedicated clock watcher than the true

118

slacker – and at this rate the article will clearly never be written.

However, in the meantime I can at least entertain you with some digressive remarks on the business of slacking. Slackers are very fond of digressions, glosses, marginalia, indeed anything that falls short of producing a genuine piece of work. Coleridge and Nietzsche, who between them formed the great Anglo-German axis of nineteenth-century slacking, were both addicted to the practice of drawing up elaborate plans of works supposedly on the verge of being written.

Indeed, when Nietzsche was found nodding out and glazed-eyed over the manuscript of *Ecce Homo*, his bizarre autobiography, it was clear from the title-page that he had got around the problem of failing to write the projected five volumes of his great *Revaluation of All Values* by simply assuming that they had already been written!

Poor Nietzsche has been maligned in many ways, but in my view the worst omission has been the neglect of the last eleven years of his life during which he did little but drool. I hope to remedy this in my soon-to-be-published work, *Nietzsche: The Slack Years*.

Like a lot of slackers, I started out as an academic slacker. I remember the terrifying figure of Mr Marsden, my Latin teacher, wrapped up in his academic gown and poking an adamant digit at me from the front of the class: 'You, Self,' he bellowed, 'are a slacker!' What occasioned this judgement was my placement – for the second year running – at twenty-fifth out of twenty-six in the Latin exam.

But I soon realized that academic slacking was small beer. No one ever really pays that much attention to it, because after all you might simply be stupid, rather than indulging in a complex response to a world crazed by needless activity.

ON OTHER THINGS

I'm going to come back to this question of slacking in academia later on – or at least I think that I might. Alternatively, I could eat an entire packet of Bourbon Cream biscuits and reread *The Raj Quartet*. But in the meantime what I most want to convey to you is that slacking is really quite different from other forms of inactivity. Your true and authentic slacker is not like a dosser, or a shirker, or a truant of any description. Indeed slackers are often surprisingly productive people. The reason for this is that the 'slack' itself, the actual head of inertia that the slacker builds up whilst doing nothing, is to the slack psyche as the stretched rubber of a bungee is to the bungee jumper.

When the slacker reaches the very bottom of this descent into inactivity, he finds himself with an unconscionable amount of energy which has to be dispersed as quickly as possible. This is the only explanation I can come up with of how I have managed to do anything at all in my life.

Slacking is in the air at the moment (do I mean this? Perhaps it's simply that the air itself is slack at the moment – temporarily unperturbed, leaving us in a kind of Slackagossa Sea), but it means different things to different people. Not only that, but there are also many distinctive kinds of slacker – what we might for convenience call 'slackotypes'.

In the United States, where the film *Slacker* has gained some notoriety, the designation implies a kind of happy-go-lucky life on the margins of society, cruising around, doing drugs and hanging out. Well, while this is a perfectly honourable kind of slacking it hardly captures the whole majesty of the slacking *Weltanschauung*. American slackers are like Australian dole bludgers: people who refuse to work. This makes them part of a class.

SLACK ATTACK

Now, your true slacker can belong to any class. Perhaps the greatest literary slacker of all, Oblomov, the eponymous hero of Goncharov's great slack novel (which, incidentally, is one of those classics that almost no one has ever managed to finish), is an aristocrat. Whereas the most important slacker in our culture – Andy Capp – is defiantly working class.

The reasons for this lie in differences of national character. For Americans, to slack is necessarily to be beyond the social pale, but in Britain, where many slackers enjoy both prestige and power, we have never had any difficulty in appreciating the slacker wherever we may find him.

One has only to look at the status of *The Graduate* as a cult film. What do we have there but – horror of horrors – a young man in between university and his first job? Hardly a great picture of rebellion, but in 1960s America the fact that he didn't go straight into plastics was seen as positively revolutionary.

Had Benjamin been British he wouldn't have had to shirk in this fashion. In British industry slackers are given the recognition they deserve, and often promoted over the heads of their more tediously active colleagues. I think it was G. K. Chesterton ('think' because I can't summon up the energy to look up the reference) who said that the British love a talented mediocrity; by this he obviously meant someone who can slack with a certain panache.

Like most of us, I really came into my own as a slacker at university. The atmosphere of Britain's universities – particularly Oxford and Cambridge – is one of immemorial slacking. On arriving, the freshman feels a deep sense of pride at being inculcated into a culture where very intelligent people have done very little for many centuries. Together with like-minded friends I founded the Minimalist Society. This was a club devoted to doing as little as possible both physically and mentally. Our patron was Anna Sewell, the paraplegic author of *Black Beauty*. We were like the Apostles and the Souls before us, and many former Minimalists now occupy prominent positions in the political and cultural establishments.

It was also at university that I discovered that invaluable aid to slacking, drugs. I soon realized that there are certain drugs that make for better slacking than others. William Burroughs said of heroin that when he was on it: 'I could stare at my shoe, with great interest, for hours.' It's difficult to imagine someone wired on cocaine extracting the same intellectual sustenance even from a Gucci loafer. The current prevalence of Ecstasy use amongst teenagers is something we should all be worried about.

All that gyrating around dance floors is distressingly active. But when parents share their anxieties with me I tell them not to worry, Ecstasy is just a phase and most of these young people will soon become indoctrinated into the socially acceptable drug ritual: putting large portions of the forebrain to sleep with ethyl alcohol.

But it was the early 1980s that saw slacking really come into its own. It's a misconception of modern popular culture that the counter-culture of the 1960s and 1970s provided great opportunities for slacking. Not only is tie-dying an exhausting and time-consuming business, but right up until 1976 it was difficult for the most committed shirker to walk down the street without someone offering lucrative employment.

Baroness Thatcher changed all that. When I signed on in 1982 I received a letter from the DHSS telling me that due to administrative overload it wasn't even necessary for me to come into the dole office on a fortnightly basis. I took to my bed and entered a golden age of slacking. During this period, when people asked me what I did – that most hateful and insulting of enquiries – I would reply, 'Lie in bed and read philanthropic novels', which was the honest truth.

In economics it is the Phillips curve that expresses the assumed relation between unemployment and inflation. It was this coefficient that along with a few other simplistic pabulums provided the bedrock of monetarist – and therefore Thatcherite – economic policy. But the Phillips curve attracted me for wholly different reasons: it was so evocative of the gentle swoop of a hammock, or the languorous arch of a sloth's back depending from some branch. Like many others I lay down in the Phillips curve for several years.

But the saddest thing about mass unemployment is that it forces people to slack who really don't want to. I would like to propose a national register, whereby those who really truly want to do nothing can swap with those who have been compelled to be idle against their wishes.

I suppose that it's tempting to view the current return to favour of slacking after the temporary insanity of the late 1980s as the delayed dividend of some of the youth cults of the past two decades coming lolloping on behind. Are we now seeing the flowering of a slack culture headed by political leaders who didn't even have the energy to inhale? After all, what was punk but the crudest essence of the slack?

It's a nice idea – but I'm afraid it's not true. In fact punk was an awfully energetic business, all that leaping about and rending of clothing. Furthermore the creators of punk, like Malcolm McLaren, were actually entrepreneurs teeming with energy. No, the truth is that we are witnessing the coming of age of a new generation of slackers. These tyros of ennui have no time for the decorous languor of their elders. They want to do nothing at all, and they want to do it now.

ON OTHER THINGS

They have even begun to develop immensely sophisticated equipment in order to facilitate this advanced slacking. I believe they call it virtual reality – I call it sitting in the corner and fidgeting.

Observer, January 1994

Man Enough to Have People Operate on Your Penis

Unlike other men, I have never been horrified by the idea of an operation on my penis. Recently I have put myself into deep hypnotic trances in order to discover the key to this will-to-mutilation, and I now think I have the answer. You see, I am that rarest of things – an uncircumcised Jew. I think this is why I feel so drawn to people who wish to stick scalpels into my todge. Without actually being able to face up to the fact that I want to be circumcised, I suppose I like to put myself in situations where a little extra whittling might be engaged in.

After all, on the face of it circumcision isn't that great an operation. When my brother's second son was born, his girlfriend – in a lurch of Semitic atavism – decided that little Jack needed the snip. As the closest male relative other than the baby's father, I was called upon to hold him in my lap while the mohel (the rabbi who is authorized to perform circumcisions) did the job.

The mohel clucked around the flat, saying racially unstereotypical things like: 'Let me guess, what did this place cost you? One hundred and eighty? Two hundred thou?' and getting fearsome-looking scalpels out of a Gladstone bag. Then, with the baby spread-eagled on top of me, his penis directly in line with my own, the mohel pulled up the foreskin, fastened it with what looked like a paper-clip, and lopped it off with his scalpel. Blood? The beaches ran red.

But for some reason I was fascinated rather than repelled. I talked for some time to the mohel about his work. He told me that he operated out of a storefront in Hendon with a display of clocks in it. 'Why clocks?' I asked.

'What would you put in the window?' he replied with a grin.

My next brush with penile surgery happened a year or so later. It started with a familiar dawn inspection of the old todge. I noticed, idly at first but then with mounting trepidation, that it had acquired a second glans. Either that or it was a growth of some kind. Despite the somewhat chaotic life I was leading at that time, I still hied me to my local croaker. She wasn't overly impressed. 'It's a penile cyst,' she said. 'I'll refer you to the genito-urinary surgeon at University College Hospital.'

In the manner of these things, it must have been a full nine months later before the appointment came through and I 'slipped down my things' in the cubicle on the sixth floor at Gower Street.

The surgeon came muscling in and cursorily examined me. 'Oh, it's a penile cyst,' he said sadly. What was he expecting? A member with the fully formed, animate, miniaturized head of Marilyn Monroe growing out of it? He gave me a vulpine grin. 'I suppose it might be benign,' he said. 'But just to be on the safe side I think we'd better operate, though on the whole we don't like to operate on the penis. It's full of blood vessels, as you no doubt know, and the risk of infection is very high.' Good of him to put me at ease like that.

It took another four months before a suffering child was thrown out of its hospital bed to make way for me 'n' my penis. As I sat on the bed waiting for the registrar, ghastly visions plagued me. It was obvious, I mused, that given the extreme divisions of labour in the world of medicine more than one surgeon would be required for a delicate operation of this kind.

The actual 'cyst man' was probably in somewhere like Colchester. My man just did penises. So he would remove my penis and send it up to East Anglia on the back of a Honda 500 with a 'LIVE ORGAN IN TRANSIT' sticker on the back of it. In Colchester the cyst man would perform brilliantly, while I lay anaesthetized and unmanned in the heart of London. But I felt certain that, while the trip back down the A12 would be fine, just as the operating assistant was hurrying towards the theatre with my John Thomas nestling in a kidney dish packed with ice, he would trip . . . and the mouth of the lift shaft would beckon. By the time they retrieved it, my penis would be covered in fluff and oil from the winding mechanism.

In the event none of this transpired. A nurse came up to me with my notes. She was nervous. 'It says here,' she said, 'that you are registered as an intravenous drug user.' Fate had stepped in in the form of a compulsory HIV test.

They sent me home while they did the test. I drank Wild Turkey and played Brahms's *Requiem* and the 'Siegfried Idyll' all night, imagining myself in a horned helmet pushing off for Valhalla in my death ship.

Needless to say, the result was negative. I was so relieved that I bunked off the penis operation, figuring I wouldn't need it in my new state of immune bliss. The cyst went away on its own.

It's some years now since my last close encounter of this kind, and I'm beginning to regret the lack of opportunities to test my mettle. However, the other week I read about an obscure tribe in Borneo who require every male to have a wooden peg hammered vertically through their penis as a rite of passage. Once this excruciating and unanaesthetized operation is performed, a wooden ball is attached at either end of the peg. The aim is, you see, to provide the tribeswomen with greater clitoral stimulation during intercourse.

Apparently at least half the men die as a result of this practice, but I don't know, it sounds like it may be worth the risk. At any rate, I've booked two tickets. One for me and one for the mohel. I figure I may as well have both operations at once, it'll cut down on the overheads.

GQ, August 1995

Mad About Motorways

It is difficult to say when my motorway obsession really began. As a child I was subjected to eternal-seeming car drives. My father's parents lived in Brighton and each weekend we set out to drive to the south coast. My father is a man who has the rare gift of being able to block out not simply – as many others do – those emotional truths that we all find unpalatable, but also those aspects of the communications infrastructure that he finds unpleasant. So it was that it would regularly take us anything up to three and a half hours to get there. Dad wouldn't even use the newly constructed bypasses around Horsham and Leatherhead. It was as if anything with more than one carriageway was anathema to him.

I remember staring at the loamy-brown surface of the newly built A23 (later the A23(M), and eventually the M23), as it humped away through the North Downs on a more or less direct route to the sea, wondering why it was that we were forbidden the motorway. I know now, for the truth is that motorways are highly addictive. Once you've acquired the habit of motorway driving, it's damned hard to kick it. You may set out on completely innocuous excursions, fully intending to take the scenic route, but yet again the slip-road will suck you in, a lobster-pot ingress to the virtual reality of motorway driving.

The truth is that my father had good reason for his

attitude towards motorways. During my childhood he was a professor at the London School of Economics, but also prominent in pressure groups concerned with the impact of urban and regional planning. Dad had friends who had written books with titles such as *Wittgenstein and the Arterial Road System in South-East England*. He took me to visit the new towns that were beginning to necklace London.

So it was no surprise to me when he ended up emigrating to Australia, to Canberra, of course. For 'Canberra', as we all know, is an ancient Aboriginal word meaning 'Milton Keynes'. When I stayed with him in the early 1980s, he would take me for walks down by the ornamental lakes that are the centrepiece of this garden city, and sweeping his arm in a wide arc, exclaim: 'Incredible, isn't it? Here we are in the middle of a conurbation of 250,000 people, and you wouldn't know it for a second. You can drive from the outskirts of Canberra to the centre in ten minutes without ever realizing you're in a city at all.'

Arguably, this is precisely why Canberra has the highest suicide rate in Australia. It is not an 'edge city' like those growing up in America, but a 'verge conurbation'. It all looks as if it is merely the result of a giant landscaping exercise intended to camouflage the motorways that pulse through it.

But if my father's somewhat ambivalent attitude towards motorways is responsible for germinating my interest in these great works of twentieth-century monumentalism, my own wilfulness has cultured interest into obsession.

Joseph Heller, in his great satirical novel *Catch-22*, invented the 'Lepage gun'. This bizarre weapon could 'glue an entire formation of planes together in mid-air'. This, for me, is a condition most devoutly to be desired. In terms of motorways, the 'Lepage-gun effect' is observed when, toddling along at around sixty-five in the middle lane, you suddenly become aware that all the other vehicles around you are static in relation to one another. At that moment you cannot be certain whether you are hurtling forward, or if, on the contrary, the great grass and concrete trough of the motorway is being reeled back behind you, like an enormous piece of scenery.

When I first experienced this, it was a profound epiphany. I was inside a synecdoche of society itself – a perfect figure of modern alienation. After that I was hooked. I got a job that provided me with an utterly inconspicuous dark blue Ford Sierra and a remit that allowed for plenty of motorway driving. Fifteen thousand miles the first year, 20,000 the next. Up and up it went until in 1989 – my peak year – I managed more than 35,000 miles.

I became a connoisseur of service stations, a seeker after complex gyratory systems. I observed that the A41(M) was the shortest motorway in Britain (barely longer than it was wide), while the M4 provides the longest continuous straight stretches.

The time I got stuck at the back of a vast jam heading out of London on the M4 on a Friday evening was a peak experience. We've all known this: the traffic comes to a halt and we sit mired in frustration, thinking to ourselves ghoulishly that the only possible compensation for this awfulness – the pregnant unnaturalness of this situation – will be to see the wrecked cars ringed by emergency vehicles when this tailback finally clears. But horror of horrors, when the great steel testudo finally gets under way again, we see no evidence of the cause of the jam.

On this particular occasion, while I was actually stuck in the jam, an academic whose subject was 'traffic studies' was explaining this phenomenon on the radio. Apparently, what the flying eyes call 'sheer weight of traffic' comes about when the motorway is particularly densely packed.

If one car brakes even millimetrically, the one behind brakes harder and this sets off a chain reaction of increasing scale that passes back down the motorway, until the cars in the rear come to a grinding halt.

The academic's explanation segued perfectly with my experience of the phenomenon itself. Ever since, I have been unable to use the expression 'sheer weight of traffic'; instead, I call it 'mere weight of traffic'.

For a long time, I felt ashamed about my motorway obsession because Britain seemed so notably deficient in motorway culture compared with other countries, particularly the United States. The idea of a proper British road movie was laughable – there just wasn't enough track. We didn't even have the sort of stylish attitude towards road transport that gave Fellini the pretext for *La Strada*.

Not only that, but British cars until the mid-1970s had a tendency to look more like Silver Cross prams than Cadillacs. Ironically, aerodynamics only really impinged on British car design at the same time as congestion began to make our roads impassable, crowded dance floors upon which we are condemned to perform the endless heel-toe quickstep of grinding synchromesh.

New motorways are vital – I feel – not, of course, because they will ease congestion, since it is axiomatic that road availability must always lag behind demand. No, they are vital because to my mind they represent the enhancement of social control and an augmentation of the greatest monuments that our culture will leave to posterity.

Enhanced social control, because, as the government's tax breaks for business motorists imply, our rulers actually wish a significant proportion of the workforce – particularly middle management – to be stuck in tailbacks a lot of the time. For if they weren't, they might well become still more bolshie about our national relegation to the status of Airstrip One.

And posterity, because it is my contention that the motorways of today are our pyramids, our ziggurats, our great collective earthworks. Perhaps 10,000 years from now, when they are grassed over, the archaeologists of this distant era will be puzzled by the harmony between the motorways, with their sweeping curves, banks and revetments, and neolithic monuments such as Silbury Hill and the Avebury stone circle. Possibly they will advance the theory of the existence of a continuous motorway culture lasting some 7,000 years.

Whatever the case, we would do well to remember that mere weight of traffic may in fact be our passport to immortality.

The Times, September 1993

BOOK REVIEWS

Where Did I Go Wrong?

A Father's Story, Lionel Dahmer's analysis of his hopelessly flawed relationship with his son Jeffrey, is particularly unpleasant for a parent to read. It might be possible to dismiss the book as just another example of the breast beating occasioned when someone lights on a new-found jargon to explain his life mistakes ('denial' is made much of in this book), were it not for the palpable pain and despair that gusts from the text.

Of course, nothing is easier than to impose a retrospective interpretation of events. What makes Lionel Dahmer's narrative so compelling is that he is trying in this ascription to peer not just into the soul of his son but into his own.

A Father's Story is fairly straightforward, running chronologically from the son's birth and childhood in the Middle West through to his arrest in July 1991 at the age of thirty-one, conviction seven months later (for killing and dismembering fifteen boys and young men to gratify his sexual desires with their bodies) and his incarceration for life.

Throughout, the sense of someone constitutionally ill-equipped for introspection of any kind groping toward a realization is gripping. Lionel Dahmer comes across as he presumably intends to – as an emotionally and spiritually absent parent. A chemist who describes his emotional make-up as 'a broad, flat plain', he buried himself in the laboratory where 'the ironclad laws of science governed', rather than face up to the 'chaotic' world of human relationships and to the impact that his disintegrating marriage to a seriously depressed woman was having on his younger son.

The details of Jeffrey L. Dahmer's life – from his increasing lack of affect to his growing obsession with bones, his teenage alcoholism and his arrest for child molestation – are brought into grotesque salience. And as Lionel Dahmer writes of his chronically moody, asocial son, one wants to grab hold of the author and shake him out of his withdrawn state.

Clearly Lionel Dahmer is not a professional writer, and the text bears the evidences of strong editing. Whether or not this makes its execution and publication a wholly meretricious act is quite difficult to judge. Undoubtedly Lionel Dahmer believes he is acting in good faith, but then according to him, he has always done that.

The tone of *A Father's Story* stands in interesting contrast to that of Brian Masters's fine *Killing for Company*, which I first read in 1985, when it was published in Britain (it came out in the United States a year later and was minimally distributed). Mr Masters's unconventional biography of the British mass murderer Dennis Nilsen is long and graphic, yet in reading it one doesn't feel macabre or like a voyeur. Lionel Dahmer's memoir of his homicidal son, Jeffrey, is a lot shorter and a lot less graphic, yet the sense of spying on the mechanics of evil can be almost overpowering.

I was fascinated by Dennis Nilsen, for he lived and killed in the same area of North London where I grew up and still live. He was an interviewer for a state employment bureau in Kentish Town – his task was to assess people's suitability for employment – and one of the people he interviewed was me.

WHERE DID I GO WRONG?

It is now almost aphoristic to say of evil that it is banal, chillingly ordinary. But the fact remains that the Dennis Nilsen I met seemed to me, as he did to his colleagues and acquaintances, to have had no charge, no resonance, no aura about him whatsoever. His chain of fifteen murders between 1978 and 1983, when he was arrested at age thirty-seven, their attendant necrophilia and dismemberments, and his hoarding of the body parts, had yet to be discovered.

Like Jeffrey Dahmer, Dennis Nilsen had a largely loveless and isolated childhood (he came from a poor background in the Buchan, a culturally distinct enclave of Aberdeenshire in Scotland). In attempting to scour this upbringing for evidence, Brian Masters seizes on one episode that in the time-honoured tradition of psychoanalytic biography he sees as key to what Nilsen became: as a five-year-old, he was without preamble thrust into the parlour to pay his respects to the bloated corpse of his grandfather, a fisherman who had drowned. Masters identifies this as the point at which eros, agape and thanatos became hopelessly commingled in Nilsen's mind.

Whether or not this is a good explanation, it suits the dramatic cadences of this perceptive book, which Random House brought out in the United States late last year with a preface linking Nilsen's and Dahmer's pathologies. Masters, the author of books on less unsettling figures like the British novelists Marie Corelli and E. F. Benson, has a style remarkable for its clarity, and that is a good thing, because he had unusual access to the killer's own writings after his arrest; Nilsen is now serving a life sentence. Not since Dr Karl Berg wrote *The Sadist*, his book on the German serial killer Peter Kurten, in the 1920s has such a garrulous and intelligent embodiment of evil come forward to tell us of his inner life.

For if listening to the Celtic mystic pop music of Clannad while drinking Bacardi and Coke, preparatory to sawing up the corpse of a young drifter you have garrotted, performed various sex acts with and then kept sitting in an armchair for several days isn't evil, then I don't know what is.

Masters himself isn't sure about this question. At some points he seems to suggest that the moral-religious perspective on evil and the forensic-psychological definition of mental disorder converge. At others he implies that Nilsen worried him enough to bring him to question his acceptance of the Freudian view of the need to acknowledge rather than repress violent impulses.

Masters is among those who make the point that serial murderers like Nilsen and Dahmer are becoming more common. Some would argue – indeed, Lionel Dahmer comes close to doing so – that this is a function of the violence and anomie of modern mass society. This may be true, but I would be inclined to see both the killers and the society that obsessively contemplates them as involved in a colossal fabrication of collective memory and moral perception.

Lionel Dahmer writes about a recurrent dream in which he is aware of having committed a violent murder but with no knowledge of why, and then identifies it as a wellspring of homicidal intent that he shares with his son. I have such a recurrent dream, and I would wager that many reading this do as well. 'I see and hear my son,' he writes at another point, 'and I think, "Am I like that?"' I can think of no better place to begin the much-needed examination of the dark side of our natures than with a careful reading of these two remarkable books.

New York Times Book Review, April 1994

Three Dots to Heaven

Louis-Ferdinand Céline's great work *Death on the Instalment Plan* comes with some powerful disincentives for the reader: it is French, it is difficult to read, it is long and the author was (with some justification) accused of anti-Semitism. Céline's first novel, *Journey to the End of the Night*, was a critical and popular success when it was published in 1931, but he himself felt his prose style had reached its apogee with this second novel. Apart from short descriptive passages in which orthodox punctuation is employed, the great bulk of the book is written in single clauses interspersed with three dots. Critics took this device to be evidence of chronic legerdemain, but really the three dots are crucial to Céline's aim of breaking down the moribund formality of written French.

The action of the story forms a prequel to the better-known *Journey*, and isn't so much a *roman-fleuve* as a *roman-torrent*. Céline triumphantly fulfils his objective, which is not so much to describe reality but, as André Gide observed, to describe the hallucinations provoked by reality.

Once the reader has absorbed the unusual style, she is carried away into a world of visceral description, fantastical riffs and raw emotion. The sense of incompleteness and the sudden changes in direction mirror the nature both of speech and of thought more exactly than do the experiments of better-known modernists. There are many passages which for sheer verve and attack are unsurpassed, but particularly strong is Céline's evocation of anger. He elevates the police's commonest call-out, the 'domestic', to it's true tragic status: 'I come part of the way down to look . . . He's dragging her along the banister. She hangs on. She clutches his neck. She bounces down the stairs . . . I can hear the dull thuds. She struggles to her feet . . . She goes back up to the kitchen. She has blood in her hair. She washes at the sink. She's sobbing . . . She gags . . . She sweeps up the breakage . . . He comes home very late on these occasions . . . Everything is very quiet again.'

At a more philosophical level Céline deals with the whole impact of technological progress on the modern psyche, especially, in this novel, in the extended interlude of the narrator's apprenticeship to Courtial, the universalist inventor.

Until 1989, when John Calder published a hardback edition of this book, the only English-language edition in print came from an American house, New Directions. Both editions use the Ralph Manheim translation, which, while admirable for its fidelity to Céline's love of Parisian argot, now suffers from the transposition of that dialect into anachronistic figures of speech. To say that the time is ripe for a new English translation of this great novel is a gross understatement.

Independent, March 1993

B and I

Nicholson Baker, in his wry and touching essay on the nature of literary hero worship, *U and I*, sets out to write on the impact John Updike's *oeuvre* has had on . m, without referring to the works the.nselves. Instead, he wishes to create a new genre of criticism founded only on what the critic can proximately recall. To this end he honestly – and not especially shamefacedly – calculates that he has read at best some 40 per cent of what Updike has published in book form.

I can go better than this. I have now read everything that Nicholson Baker has published in book form. Five titles in all: *The Mezzanine*, *Room Temperature*, *U and I*, *Vox* and now the new one, *The Fermata*. If Baker can justify a book off the back of a 40 per cent reading, then I, with my cool 100, can probably make a realistic push for the Bakeronian Chair of Micro-Observation, whenever and wherever someone sees fit to endow such a thing.

If the chair is founded, I would make a strong case for it having a functional Melamine finish, with counter-sunk transverse bolts along both arms. I look forward to many, many hours spent in this chair, observing the infinitely subtle gradations of wear on the graphically patterned nap of the chair's covering. I shall stare seer-like into space, on the lookout for the Brownian swirls of dust motes as they fall to earth. *De temps en temps* I will produce a paper, which, through its teasing refraction of the Bakeronian aesthetic, will leave the rest of academe gasping. These will have titles such as 'Tying Up Marcus Aurelius in a Shoelace: Images of Bondage in *The Mezzanine*' and 'Showing the Shower: The Equivalence of Sexual and Literary Exhibitionism in the Work of Nicholson Baker'.

Actually, to be honest (and have you noticed, by the way, that this expression has achieved total ubiquity over the past ten years as a kind of verbal tic? Obviously, as human intercourse becomes more and more circumscribed by half-truths and even downright lies, so people feel driven to guarantee the veracity of even the most uncontentious statements), I haven't read every last word of Baker's in book form, I gave up on *Vox* about ten pages before the end.

I wish I could say that I did this in much the same spirit that I left off reading Proust at the last volume, so that I could preserve *Time Regained* for my old age, but it isn't the same at all. Rather, having waded through about 150 pages of not particularly inspiring winky-wanky-woo, I felt I could do without a climax – both literary and masturbatory – that was bound to be a let-down.

Put baldly, Baker has written two good books – *The Mezzanine* and *U and I* – two bad books – *Vox* and *Room Temperature* – and one book that falls so excruciatingly on the middle of the vaulting horse that reading it sent a ball-crushing twinge from the base to the nape of my critical sensibility.

The basic conceit of *The Fermata* (the Italian for 'pause', used in musical notation) is that an undistinguished Bostonian office temp called Arno, while in the fourth grade at school, developed the ability to halt the universe, that is, except for himself. Arno can move about in the paralysed world doing as he pleases, and when he wills it everything returns to normal.

This is too good a conceit to let alone, and indeed Baker is not alone in having investigated it. In the text itself, his protagonist is forthright enough to admit to having read Bierce's and Borges's attempts at the 'frozen time' story. I might also make some small claims on the genre myself, for there is a parallel between Arno's time-freezing abilities and the 'enhanced eidetic capability' of Ian Wharton, the protagonist of my novel *My Idea of Fun*.

Again, like Ian Wharton, Arno gains access to this bizarre noumenal realm through the ramshackle marriage of magical thought to personal ritual. But in Arno's case these ritual calculi are far more clearly linked to Baker's own obsession with the penetration of the manufactured into the quotidian. Thus it is that Arno's first fermata is engineered by him chancing upon the transformer of an electric car set, and his second is sparked with the help of a spin-drier and a length of thread sewn through the calluses of his hand.

As Arno gets older so the time-freezing rituals become more complex. In one episode – which recalls the sublime obfuscation of Borges's 'Tlön, Uqbar, Orbis Tertius' – he commissions an engineering student to build him a time-freezing machine out of a gallimaufry of oscillators, capacitors and rubber bands. He justifies this to the engineer on the basis of a bizarre story about a fictional nineteenth-century philosopher, who thought that the machine would be able to – you guessed it – freeze time.

But far more important to the development of *The Fermata* as a novel is the use that Arno makes of his extraordinary ability. Baker has played upon an almost universal childhood fantasy in summoning up the idea of the fermata. His elision of magical thought and personal ritual is another universal, but Arno's excursions through the petrified forest of bodies that is Massachusetts in suspended animation will, I imagine, leave the majority of his readers abandoned by the wayside. For if the male protagonist of *Vox* is an admirer of manual relief, a connoisseur of hand jiving, a devotee of pocket billiards, then Arno is a kind of Supreme Wanker, what with his ability to commandeer the entire universe for his masturbatory playlets.

Like Baker, in *My Idea of Fun* I identified sexual interest as the spur towards this kind of ideation of the experiential, but whereas in the character of Ian Wharton I wanted to explore the nature of the semi-permeable membrane between 'neurosis' and 'psychosis', in the character of Arno, Baker seems to be exploring only that link between the public face of acceptable sexual interest and the private world of nerdy wank-obsession.

Arno doesn't freeze time so he can acquire money, power or influence – all of this strikes him as immoral. Nor does he use it to facilitate the getting of wisdom, through spending long hours in the fermata studying (although he does claim that he will get around to this sometime). No, Arno's chief occupation, once he has stopped the world, is to get off on the spectacle of naked women: he goes around stripping these insensible creatures, fondling them, and very often masturbating over them.

And this is where Baker lost me; instead of matching a third universal apprehension to the first two, he comes up with something that it's debatable whether most people want to do at all. If I could freeze the universe at will I might want to look at the occasional pair of tits, or maybe the odd cock, but I doubt I would retain the compulsion to go on doing it day in day out, for year after year.

And Arno is not only a richly innovative wanker – like the telephonic sexers in *Vox* – he is also a pornographer (or 'rotter' as he terms it), and he uses his extraordinary ability to insinuate his pornography into the lives of women. In one staggeringly complex set-piece Arno freezes time whilst overtaking a woman on the freeway, spends seven hours writing a pornographic story, tape-records it and then places the tape in the woman's car cassette player. He is acutely disappointed when the woman pitches the tape out of the car's window after having only listened to half of it.

But on another occasion he has more success: the pornographic story is buried beneath the scrabbling fingers of a woman sunbathing on a beach, and Arno is able to surreptitiously follow her home and witness a scene of delightfully graphic dildo-driven masturbation that provides him with imaginative fodder for ages to come.

I can conceive that many critics will recoil from some of these episodes, because at a gut level there is something obscene – for them – about the pollution of an allegedly 'literary' text by such 'filth'. This was the same kind of reaction that I received for *My Idea of Fun*. Somehow the description of the raw actuality of sex or violence in unashamedly high literary style strikes some people as the equivalent of attending Lady So-and-So's little soirée and taking a monumental dump in her teacup.

Such a perspective is as ridiculous as it is hidebound. Literature has always been powered forward by these kinds of irruptions of sex and violence, and it can be argued (notably most recently by J. G. Ballard in his marginalia for the new edition of *Atrocity Exhibition*) that it is during periods when pornography infiltrates high art that there is the greatest level of creative innovation.

But it is not the spunking-off on women's temporarily arrested eyelids that turned me off *The Fermata*. Rather it is the intrinsic nerdiness of Arno as a character. It's not that I demand that a character be 'sympathetic' in any commonly understood way – indeed, the wish to show the impossibility of achieving this in the contemporary novel is what lay behind my creation of Ian Wharton – but I do want his lack of sympathetic qualities to point to some wider issue, whether social, psychological or metaphysical.

I do believe a case can be made for Baker's *The Fermata* as a satire on contemporary mores. The very laboriousness with which Arno conjures up for the reader the peculiar qualities of the fermata state (how it affects people who were in motion at the time he froze them; sound, light, electricity and so on) points to a fine appreciation of the way the arcane vocabularies of technology have infiltrated our view of the world. Likewise, Baker's consummate grasp of the lexicon and schema of pornographic writing introduces a note of genuine uneasiness into the book which lays the table, if not for a naked lunch, then at least for a partially clothed breakfast.

But in the final analysis, while *The Fermata* contains some great gags and some fine writerly observation, it fails to convince. Just as Baker's rather shadowy narrator, Arno, collapses into the identity of all of Baker's shadowy narrators, so *The Fermata* collapses into the schema of Baker's earlier books: from micro-observation to intellectual conceit to sensual feeling and back to micro-observation. When his technique is at its best it reveals a world in a grain of sand, but when it isn't working it makes the world out to be nothing *but* a grain of sand.

Modern Review, 1994

The Book of the Film

One of the more asinine arguments advanced during the recent 'death of fiction' debate was that of Gilbert Adair, who opined that in the production of 'artemes' – key artistic ideas which graft themselves, as motifs, on to the lives of the mass – literary fiction has become notably defunct. In the twentieth century, Adair asks us to believe, the torn shower curtain in *Psycho* has trumped any potential literary artemes from the off. Walter Abish is a writer who hatches artemes the way a frog spawns – with apparent ease and in great quantities. He is also a writer who takes from film and renders unto it. In three slimmish works of fiction, some poetry and now the relatively chunky novel *Eclipse Fever*, he peers into the lens of the projector as it spews out imagery. Thematically, he has circled around the core of the United States, though at a careful distance – like Kafka, who wrote *Amerika* without visiting the country.

In Abish's earlier *Minds Meet* the central character, Marcel, opts for extraliterary retirement in Albuquerque. With *Eclipse Fever*, Abish goes further south still, to Mexico itself, using a traditional narrative lens to focus his thematic beam to a scintillating point. Alejandro, the hero, is at the tip of a pyramid of deracination. He is doubly compromised, having betrayed the American financier Preston Hollier in one of the shuffles of the corrupt tarot that constitute the auspicatory game of Mexican politics, and also lost both his critical and sexual integrity to Jurud, the American novelist who has been screwing Alejandro's wife, Mercedes. Mercedes also happens to be Jurud's Spanish translator.

Alejandro may faintly despise the work of Jurud, a New York Jewish intellectual, but this doesn't stop him agreeing to fête Jurud on his forthcoming trip to Mexico. By the same token Francisco, Alejandro's best friend, cannot resist a commission to 'write something favourable' about Preston Hollier's plan to put a lift in the Pyramid of the Sun. Meanwhile, Jurud's daughter Bonny, a sixteen-year-old runaway, experiences both the United States and Mexico at a more visceral level. Her tangent takes her from a fundamentalist motel-owner, via a Hasidic Felasha to Yucatán. Here, sick in her hotel room, she witnesses the eclipse of the novel's title on CNN.

Alejandro is like a quicksilver bead of self-consciousness moving through the historical self-forgetting of the twentieth century. He has never visited the United States, but has built up a picture of its magnificent ordinariness entirely from film. Nevertheless, when he summons up an image of his own cuckolded self, it is the cretinous husband in Chabrol's *La Femme infidèle* that Alejandro seizes on: 'Idiot, idiot, he kept repeating. The epithet an expression of his chagrin, aimed at what he had not explored.'

There is nothing arch about the way Abish intrudes such allusions into his work. When Buñuel's use of two actresses to play the same character in *That Obscure Object of Desire* makes its appearance here as the substance of an argument between Alejandro and his best friend, Francisco, it is greeted by the reader as an old acquaintance. In *Eclipse Fever* film is eaten up by life and then expelled in little farts of recollection.

Throughout the novel Alejandro's identity folds in on

itself. So does his memory, and so do the very subclauses that Abish rivets together with his functionalist punctuation. Speech here is always reported in the historical present. Parentheses are abandoned – this is the realm of the interjection – where dashes intersperse the banal, the ridiculous – and the profound.

For Abish, language is still freighted with the technical taint of the *Tractatus*. Words are so many little pictures, each corresponding to another reality. Emotion cannot be fixed by them – it can only well up between them. It is a mark of a great cinematographer that when you leave the cinema you find yourself cutting, panning, tracking and composing in the same manner. How much more heady is the impact of a novelist who can do this at the level of ideas?

But Abish, unlike a populist film-maker, doesn't simply produce snapshots to be passed among the mass. He tears treasured portraits from our culture's family album and thrusts them into his cunning slide carousel. Clicking from one page to the next, we reflect not on the death of literary fiction but on its vitality.

Independent on Sunday, July 1993

The Burnt-out Shells of Men

Stopping to buy petrol outside Oxford on a winter's evening, I noticed a skinny lad dressed in the casual uniform of puffa jacket and Reeboks, lingering beside the pumps. He was eyeing a green Toyota Celica 3.0i, the owner of which was paying for his petrol. Suddenly the lad darted forward, wrenched the door of the car open and began fiddling with the ignition.

The car owner – a ringer for Mr Yuppie, in his suit trousers, stripy shirt and tie – came running full tilt out on to the forecourt. He was too late. He flung himself on to the boot of his car, but was thrown off as the lad screeched away in an S-bending tailspin that took him out on to the bypass.

Beatrix Campbell's *Goliath: Britain's Dangerous Places* is a book for everyone in modern Britain who has ever witnessed an incident like that and wondered why it is that neither of the traditional party-political analyses of contemporary criminality seems to explain what has occurred. It is a book that deals with what has happened to the social anatomy of Britain under fourteen years of authoritarian, market-driven government and delivers a thesis which, while open to obvious criticisms, does at least provide a way of seeing the issues in question divested of their protective ideological clothing.

Campbell takes the late summer riots of 1991 as her

starting-point and offers a painstaking analysis of the events on the Ely estate in Cardiff, the Blackbird Leys estate outside Oxford and the Meadow Well estate and West End district on Tyneside. Her account is most notable for its introduction of different voices. This is a text through which ordinary men and women, whether public servants, politicians and conscientious community activists, or joy-riders and ram-raiders, speak about the way their collective space is defined and then shared out.

'Space' lies at the core of Campbell's thesis, which is that the distinctive face of contemporary criminality and riotous assembly in our society is a male one. On the marginalized estates of modern Britain, devastated by unemployment and economic deprivation, the traditional gender-based social distinctions have been fractured. With young unem-ployed men thrown back into the physical spaces normally occupied by women, they exorcize their impotence in the form of internecine warfare. The burnt-out cars that litter these suburban landscapes are poignant symbols of male destruction, as a function of male impotence.

Campbell is a meticulous researcher, at her best when looking in depth at a given locale. Anyone who still wishes to believe that the worst-off in our society are somehow inexorably becoming better off would be well advised to read her cataloguing of the collapse of the Meadow Well estate on Tyneside throughout the 1980s and early 1990s. This is an estate where not only are the vast majority of young men unemployed, but even the activities of state, local government, and citizens' agencies have been attenuated and eradicated by persistent, violent criminality.

Campbell argues that our will to respond to such social ills is a function of the way we regard them. She attacks those on both the right and the left who seek an explanation for what has happened in the designation of an 'underclass'. By delving into the way that the police, as a social institution, have responded to the new criminality, Campbell is able to draw out the mutually supportive antagonisms that perpetuate the macho theatres of 'hotting' and joy-riding. She is also unafraid to examine the way that the Alison Halford sex-discrimination case illuminated the male authoritarian culture of the Merseyside constabulary, at a time when it was manifestly failing to provide effective community policing. And indeed, the whole phenomenon of 'community policing' and 'neighbourhood watch', with its rubric of 'us' and 'them', comes under Campbell's analysis.

This is a book dense in allusion and argument. The great sadness that it locates and exposes is that, on all sides of the divides of race, gender and class, there are voices of great compassion and reasonableness. Britain is a country where communication channels still exist, even if they are partially blocked.

Despite the alarm bells that a 'feminist' analysis may raise in some readers' minds, it is worth noting that Campbell never descends to doctrinaire tub-thumping in marshalling her views. *Goliath* presents a panorama of modern Britain that we have to acknowledge. And for those of us who are unwilling to do so, the spectacle of North America, with its lawless urban hinterlands, lies in wait.

Sunday Times, July 1993

Not a Great Decade to Be Jewish

Like a Member of Parliament about to enter a debate, I feel that at the outset I should declare an interest – the influence of Woody Allen's comic style on my own. Two out of the three collections of humorous pieces included in Allen's *Complete Prose* were my primers, my textbooks, the canonical forms to which I have returned time and again when considering what it is to be funny in print.

I must have been given the American edition of *Getting Even* in about 1974, when I was thirteen. A year or so later, I actually staged a version of the short play *Death Knocks*, in which Nat Ackerman, a balding Jewish schmutter manufacturer, plays gin rummy with Death. At that age I was, of course, unaware that the playlet is an exquisite parody of Bergman's *Seventh Seal*. I may have been a pretentious and culturally omnivorous adolescent, but it was exclusively the strength of Allen's one-liners, and the precision of his comic timing, that fuelled my admiration. There can have been nothing more absurd to the audience of North London middle-class parents and schoolboys than my production.

My mother was a Jewish New Yorker, and one was as likely to come across Mort Sahl, S. J. Perelman and James Thurber dotted around the family home as H. B. Morton or Wodehouse. Despite this, Allen's Yiddish vocabulary (his kvetching and kaddish, his schlep, kasha and noodge) was as alien to me as to any other English boy; and so was his fictional topography, which effectively mirrors that classic cartoon 'A New Yorker's View of the World'. And yet I read, and reread and even memorized, whole passages of *Getting Even* and *Without Feathers*. Almost twenty years later I still find myself cribbing and restructuring some of Allen's gags in conversation. It wasn't until I came to reread these pieces that I recognized the origin of the joke: 'K. would not think to pass from room to room in a conventional dwelling without first stripping completely and then buttering himself' – which I had freely adapted over the years to become: 'he/she has to strip naked and grease themselves to get through a door'. Ditto for exploded metaphors such as: 'She had a set of parabolas that could have caused cardiac arrest in a yak.' Or: 'the zenith of mongoloid reasoning'.

Any canonical work is more than a point of origin, an inchoate text from which others derive: it also acts as a refracting lens. As I grew older I began to appreciate the way Allen's humour both anticipates the evolution of late twentieth-century comedy – the crystallization of the absurdity of urban alienation – and simultaneously reaches back to incorporate the styles and modes of Dorothy Parker, James Thurber, Perelman and Groucho Marx.

For my young self, the crucial juncture occurred when, thanks to *Annie Hall*, Allen became famous in England. Up until 1976 he was an oddity, a little-known Jewish funny man, a minority-interest comedian. With *Annie Hall* all this changed, and, at least for the art-house-inclined, his film became a primary point of cultural reference. I was appalled in the way that only someone can be who feels he has discovered something in advance of the masses. Allen was *my* comic inspiration, and what's more, although I was profoundly deracinated, he had also become the touchstone of whatever Semitism I accorded myself. The idea that the goyim should even be allowed to laugh at this self-lacerating, mordantly Jewish comedy was more than I could stand.

In retrospect I find it difficult to believe that Allen's humour became widely appreciated in England at that time simply because of the Oscar award. Rather, the English were becoming more self-consciously urbanized and decadent in the mid-seventies. Traditional Little England anti-intellectualism was on a partial wane. In a word, the English were becoming more Jewish. So it was that they began to find Allen funny.

Interestingly this acceptance of Allen in England coincided with what critics have identified as the 'epistemological break' in his work. John Lahr, in his 1984 essay on Allen, wasn't the first to take the view that the comic's early films, thin narrative skeletons on to which Allen could graft his anarchic one-liners, were somehow more honest. After the break, according to Lahr and many others, Allen committed the comic's worst crime – wanting to be taken seriously. He made the stilted, boring Bergmanesque *Interiors*, and his execrably self-obsessed version of Fellini's *8½*, *Stardust Memories*, in which he tried to deflect such criticisms, by placing them in the mouth of a grotesque, importuning fan: 'I prefer the early funny films.' But Lahr's essay, in which he accuses Allen of 'teasing and flattering a middle-class audience with its hard-won sophistication', and defines his humour as deriving from 'emotional paralysis', was written before *Hannah and Her Sisters* and *Crimes and Misdemeanours*, films which arguably united Allen's 'cosmic kvetching' and his nice appreciation of the tragic ironies of ordinary lives.

There has now been an even more profound 'epistemological break', the kind that only an unusual artistry could survive: Allen's life has begun to overshadow his work. Hardly anyone on the planet has been able to watch *Husbands and Wives* without picking apart the seeming artifice to peer at the emotional realities which we now know lie beneath it. At some screenings – although not the one I attended – sophisticated audiences have tittered knowingly as the Allen character, a creative-writing professor called Gabe Roth (shadows of Portnoy?), discourses to the camera on his attraction to younger women, his belief in fidelity (tee-hee) and so forth.

Husbands and Wives was a depressing experience for me. No one likes to see his idols brought so low. When the news first broke about Allen's alleged child abuse I was appalled. Surely, I mused, this cannot in any way be true? The whole point about Allen's metaphysical schmuck persona was that it represented a fundamental honesty; a willingness to admit to sexual inadequacy, lust, emotional missed connections. How could such a man turn out to be a comprehensive suborner of trust? To compound the unease there was the film's cinematography. Allen's increasing artistic pretension has been mirrored by his use of sophisticated camerawork. But in *Husbands and Wives*, it looks as if Allen forced Carlo Di Palma to undergo a two-week speed-and-brandy binge before shooting the picture on the comedown. Obviously the hand–held judder and frenzied jump-cut were intended as visual counterpoints to the narrative's muddled emotional compromise and painful honesty. But what came across was a kind of dodginess, an evasiveness which of course one knew was there, as Allen denied the reality of his off-screen misdemeanours face-on to the wavering lens.

On returning to the fifty short pieces contained in the *Complete Prose*, a different order of criticism occurred to me. Naturally, post-Soon-Yi, every reference to nubility leaps off the page. In 'The Lunatic's Tale', Allen's enduring obsession with Jehovah's failure to put the mind of a 'charming and witty culture vulture' into the body of an 'erotic archetype' is given full rein, as he enacts a dry run of the fantasy scene in *Stardust Memories*, by performing the Frankensteinian psycho-sexual transplant surgery himself. It is now very difficult to view his plainting on this theme (no less than five of the fifty pieces are concerned specifically with the impossibility of finding a sexy woman who is his intellectual equal) as anything other than retrogressive and callous. If it is true that Allen cannot locate a woman whom he finds both intelligent and sexy, it is surely – we now feel – a function of his own shortcomings, rather than the cosmic joke he would have us believe.

It is in his use of pastiche and parody that these pieces represent the seedbed of Allen's humorous vision. And, as such, all too often I found myself agreeing with Lahr: in Allen's work – unlike that of, say, Groucho Marx or Thurber – parody represents 'an imagination submerged more in art than life', although I would be inclined to say more in culture than in art. 'Look,' Allen seems to be saying, 'I may have been expelled from university' (an event which provided him with the memorable gag: 'I cheated on the metaphysics paper by looking into the soul of the student seated next to me'), 'but I'm still just as clever, well-read and philosophically literate as the people I would like to be.'

The author's note for *Getting Even* was one of the Allen lines that I found funniest as a child. He stared out from the jacket, a misshapen little man with glasses, holding a stick or a twig, with a mien of utter hopelessness. Underneath he declared: 'My only regret in life is that I'm not someone else.' But, contrary to the impression which his films give, Allen doesn't want to be Bergman,

Renoir, Fellini or Lang. In the *Complete Prose*, it is clear that he wants to be Sontag, Benjamin, Adorno or Arendt. His comic one-liners are a painful involution of the existential aphorism, which traces its lineage back through the Frankfurt School to Nietzsche: 'Death is an acquired trait.' His parodic cultural disquisitions – a critique of a Nietzschean character's laundry lists; an elision of Dostoevsky and eating disorders; a pseudo-memoir of a contemporary of Freud's – are in effect his attempts at the exegetical essay form, which has come to represent the summit of contemporary intellectual achievement. When Allen quips, 'Epistemology: Is knowing knowable? If not, how do we know this?' he is not simply flattering his audience, he is flattering himself as well, showing us that he, too, has a vast matching set of Samsonite intellectual baggage. Possibly my discomfort on rereading these pieces was as much a function of recognizing this pretension within myself as of seeing it in Allen.

The influence which Allen exercises on my own comedy, and on that of many others, is based less on the subject-matter of his pieces than on the particular form of the Allen gag. It is important to remember that Allen cut his teeth writing jokes for Johnny Carson, churning out, it is claimed, as many as five hundred a week. The Allen one-liner has three basic forms: the 'bathetic let-down' the 'surreal elision' and the 'silly word'. Here, in the same order, are examples: 'So little time left, he thought, and so much to accomplish. For one thing, he wanted to learn to drive a car.' 'I did not know that Hitler was a Nazi, for years I thought he worked for the phone company.' 'Once, on holiday in Jena, he could not say anything but the word "eggplant" for four straight days.'

Most of the pieces in this collection were first published in the *New Yorker*, and it is to the classic comic vignettes of the 1930s that they so clearly owe their primary inspiration. The *Complete Prose* is an ideal bedside companion, to be dipped into for quick hits of enjoyment. Treated in this way, and severed from the Allen persona and its tendency to topple over into his own work, the pieces remain examples of unalloyed comic genius. In 'If Impressionists Had Been Dentists', Allen produces a hilarious pastiche of the American bio-pics of Van Gogh, Toulouse-Lautrec and Gauguin. Seurat is a hygienist who cleans his patients' teeth one at a time, in order to build up 'a full fresh mouth'. Toulouse-Lautrec is too proud to work on a stool and so, fumbling away, manages to 'cap Mrs Needleman's chin'. Eventually Vincent, unrecognized, reduced to 'working almost exclusively with dental floss', and unhappy in love, confesses to Theo that 'the ear on sale at Fleishman Brothers Novelty Shop is mine'.

In 'The Kuglemass Episode', Allen conceives of a magician, 'the Great Persky', who is able to project his clients into any work of fiction. So it is that Kuglemass, a Jewish academic at Columbia, trapped in a loveless marriage, is able to enjoy an affair with Emma Bovary: '"My God, I'm doing it with Madame Bovary!" Kuglemass whispered to himself. "Me, who failed freshman English."' More surreal still is the fact that Kuglemass actually crops up in the text as it is being read: 'At this very moment students in various classrooms across the country were saying to their teachers: "Who is this character on page 100? A bald Jew is kissing Madame Bovary?"' This kind of conceit goes far further than the simple schemas of Allen one-liners, creating a *reductio ad absurdum* of fantasy/reality, reality/fantasy, that is the hallmark of true satire.

In 'The Discovery and Use of the Fake Ink Blot', he seems to be cutting the ground from under himself, with a mock-serious commentary on the very unfunny nature of the pratfall. However, Allen has never been shy of slapstick, either in print or on film, and these pieces abound with casual instances of the cruellest and most pointless violence, visited on those who expect and deserve it least: 'The old man had slipped on a chicken-salad sandwich and fallen off the Chrysler Building.' The Mafia 'are actually groups of rather serious men, whose main joy in life comes from seeing how long certain people can stay under the East River before they start gurgling'. In 'Viva Vargas!' the first-person protagonist cascades off the front patio, 'luckily breaking the fall with my teeth, which skidded around the ground like loose Chiclets'.

Allen's sado-masochism is another slant on his self-hatred. This in turn is inescapably linked to his Jewishness, and the idea of Jewish humour as a pre-emptive strike: we'll run ourselves down so far that the gentiles won't be able to say anything worse. The quintessence of the Jewish joke is not simply its self-deprecatory character – the Jew as mensch gaining strength through oppression – but also the fact that it must be told by a Jew. If a gentile tells a Jewish joke he is an anti-Semite, if Woody Allen tells an anti-Semitic joke he is being funny. And here is the crux of my anxiety. The revelation of the nebbisch-as-possible-child-molester may be enough to destabilize the careful balance of pressures that have made Allen's comedy such a good vehicle for promoting tolerance and understanding between Jew and gentile. With Allen paraded as the caricature Jewish child molester, defiler of Christian (oh, all right, Korean–American) virtue, the other elements of his comic persona fall into alignment with the traditional slurs on Jewishness, and specifically on Jewish men: androgyny, thanatos, sexual obsession, febrile genius. With neo-Nazis burning down refugee hostels in Germany, the nineties may not be such a great decade to be Jewish in. With Woody Allen committing crimes of pretentiousness and breach of trust, it may not be such a great decade for Jewish humorists either.

London Review of Books, February 1993

Couch Surfing

It is a common enough experience in life to read a book that, while possessing some elements of style and lucidity, nonetheless contains at its core an absence of real bite, substantial meaning. How much more unusual to read a book that is freighted with annoying jargon, seemingly wilful obscurantism, and yet which has at its heart some profound and original truths.

Such a book is this collection, *On Kissing, Tickling and Being Bored: Psychoanalytic Essays on the Unexamined Life* by Adam Phillips. Phillips quotes J. L. Austin's remark in his preface, that 'it is not enough to show how clever we are by showing how obscure everything is' and then goes on to demonstrate quite the reverse. I cannot perceive it as anything but disingenuous for a member of the psychoanalytic profession to imagine that the general reader won't be put off by a text that employs phrases such as, 'The body . . . is by definition both a subjective object and an object objectively perceived.' But then perhaps Phillips's idea of the general reader and my own differ radically.

Phillips begins his collection with an introduction that sets out his belief that – contrary to Freud's own, essentialist view – psychoanalysis is a 'transitional language, one possible bridge to a more personal, less compliant idiom'.

This is a view that both echoes Wittgenstein's anti-metaphysic, and reflects a fashionable desire on the part

of analysts and therapists to perceive their work as more
in the manner of an artistic exercise, in which they join
with the analysand in creating a more satisfactory 'story'
about the analysand's inner life than the one she is currently
telling herself.

But what Phillips does share with Freud is an insidiously
pessimistic view of human nature. In the opening essay
'First Hates: Phobias in Theory', he agrees with Freud
that 'what has to be explained is not why someone is
phobic, but how anyone ever stops being anything other
than phobic'. On this assumption, phobias can play a vital
role for a person by focusing and localising what would
otherwise be a terrifying omnipresent paranoia.

This may be true enough, but to conclude with Phillips
that as phobias confront the psychoanalyst 'very starkly,
with the dilemma of a cure . . . the aim of psychoanalysis
is not to cure people but to show them that there is nothing
wrong with them' is to beg the question so often asked by
the layman: in that case why pay them?

However, as Phillips moves on to discuss more nebulous
and less obviously analysable psychological states, in the
essays 'On Risk and Solitude' and 'On Composure',
another current emerges in his thought. Phillips contrasts
the ideas of Winnicott, the British psychoanalyst and
founder of the Object-Relations school of thought, with
those of Freud. He reaches the conclusion that for Freud
solitude could only be described as an absence, whereas
for Winnicott it is first and foremost a presence. While
for the atheistic Freud this is a readily explicable view, is
Phillips right in extending the absence of God to include
Winnicott and the rest of us? Surely it is still possible to
imagine a deistic neurotic?

In the essay 'Worrying and its Discontents', Phillips
comes up with the memorable line 'All of us may be

surrealists in our dreams, but in our worries we are incorrigibly bourgeois.' He advances the theory that worrying is an attempt both at simplification of the human predicament, and a kind of 'overprotection of the self'.

Yet it is in this essay that a problem that can best be described as ontological reductiveness starts to emerge for Phillips. Given his espousal of the impossibility of a 'true self', only a schema of multifarious personal narratives, it becomes unclear who exactly it is who is doing the dreaming, the worrying, the kissing or the being bored?

As Phillips's Procrustean labours bend and stretch jargon in new and more elegantly tortuous ways, one is reminded insistently of the cartoon where the man asleep is depicted dreaming himself asleep, and when the man in the dream awakes the 'real' dreamer disappears.

Phillips continues to throw out good one-liners, pithy examples of near-wisdom. He characterises Winnicott's developments in the field of childcare as a post-imperial restitution: 'a theory of good-enough mothering as the antithesis, the guilty critique, of what was always a bad-enough imperialism'. He is also acute on boredom.

In the essay 'On Being Bored' he draws a vital and interesting distinction between the boredom of children and that of adults. The boredom of adults, Phillips seems to suggest, can border on the pathology of despair, whereas for children it is 'integral to the process of taking one's time'. And in a throwaway line that echoes Tennyson's 'In Memoriam', he remarks plangently, 'So perhaps boredom is merely the mourning of everyday life?'

In 'Looking at Obstacles' Phillips undertakes more ortho-dox psychoanalytic explorations, and here as elsewhere in the collection, he laces his bewildering text with the occasional lucid case history. Particularly notable is his sleight-of-mind whereby he leads a repressed homosexual to a truer understanding of the nature of his desire.

But Phillips also seems to share Freud's bleak view of romantic love as 'everyman's psychosis'; he opines that our first relationship is 'not with objects (i.e. other people) but with obstacles'. He goes on to say that, 'People fall in love at the moments in their lives when they are most terrorized by possibilities. In order to fall in love with someone they must be perceived to be an obstacle, a necessary obstacle.'

The essay ends with a coda that both implies Phillips's view of love, desire, what you will, and also retroactively informs much of what has gone before. He says that although he has tried to demonstrate that the word 'obstacle' is full of meaning, he is left with 'the feeling that comes when one endlessly repeats a word only to be left with an enigmatic obstacle as to its sense'.

There is a nice echo here of the Thurber story 'More Alarums at Night', wherein all kinds of mayhem is released into the Thurber household because the author has been lying in bed unable to remember the name of the town 'Perth Amboy'. Gradually as he struggles to grapple with finding the name in his own mind, the sense of words themselves begins to drain away, until in terror Thurber goes next door to wake his father. Shaking him into consciousness Thurber cries, 'Name some towns in New Jersey!' Needless to say his father thinks he has gone mad.

It seems to me that the Phillips methodology, which is a kind of hydra of relatavism, leads inexorably to just this kind of madness. As each epigrammatic head of the id-creature is lopped off, so another two – or more – take its place.

This all comes to one big head in the concluding essay 'Psychoanalysis and Idolatry'. What commences as a *divertissement* on Freud's collection of antiquities turns into a disquisition in which Phillips all too painfully reveals the bogus syncretism that lies behind much psychoanalytic thinking. Phillips correctly nails down Freud's view of religion as analogous to that of Marx: 'The effect (of religious consolations) can be likened to that of a narcotic.' He also bravely observes that the notion of psychoanalytic transference itself can be termed 'a form of secular idolatry'.

But where does all this take us? Only to another paradox, the one with which Phillips concludes the entire volume. That psychoanalysis is a cure of idolatry through idolatry, and furthermore, 'The one thing psychoanalysis cannot cure, when it works, is belief in psychoanalysis. And that is a problem.'

Phillips is right to acknowledge it, and it goes a long way to explaining why people continue, apparently fruitlessly, in analysis for many years.

Phillips has written a provocative and interesting collection of pieces here, one that benefits from more than one reading. And although the occasional piece of sloppiness (such as toying with calling Winnicott a 'proto-Nietzschean', when of course Nietzsche had been dead for several decades before Winnicott was born) gives the impression of a young intellectual surfer showing off on some of the bigger waves of twentieth-century thought, Phillips is to be admired for his courage in so gaily committing theoretical suicide.

European, July 1993

Catch-23

The book was thick and red. It was almost thicker than it was wide, a thickness that somehow enhanced its bookishness. There was that, and there was also the fact that its very title was already a figure of speech: which had come first? It was – to me aged twelve – quite clearly more of a book than most, if not all, of the other paperbacks untidily stacked on the shelves in my father's study.

Furthermore, it was a book of absolute superlatives. Instead of a mere littering of one-liners on the covers, there were about eight pages of paragraph-long citations, all vying with one another to encapsulate the brilliance of the book. Bold headlines proclaimed: 'Over three million copies sold in this edition alone!' and 'The most successful novel of all time!' Even aged twelve I was in no doubt that this *Catch-22* was a very superior book indeed.

I read it and didn't understand it. The whole tone of the book was unknowable to a child. I wouldn't have been able to fathom a straight depiction of the events covered by Heller's novel, let alone a satiric one. Yet everything about the book niggled at me. I had the sense of the prose delineating a topography, a fictional landscape, that swam into and out of view. And I also had an intimation that the act of deciphering this strange terrain would coincide with apprehending perplexing aspects of the adult world that had heretofore eluded me.

Over the next four or five years I read and reread *Catch-22* some twelve times. It became a sort of bible for me, or at any rate a universalist and encyclopaedic tome that contained the answers to just about everything. The scenes that had initially revolted me with their strangeness – like the one where Havermeyer persecutes mice by snapping on the light in his tent, smiling while they hunt round with tiny, frightened eyes for their tormentor, and then blows their little, furry bodies to pieces with a .45 round from his service revolver – revolted me instead with their tense analogue of humans' cruelty to humans.

So, while it wasn't love at first sight, it was sustained and firm affection for what is indisputably a great book. And when I came to reread it for the first time in many years I was shocked to discover just how influential Heller's masterpiece had been on the development of my own satiric style and project. *Catch-22* is a veritable manual of satire. It has it all: superb comic one-liners and apophthegms: 'Death to all moderators', 'What's good for M&M Enterprises is good for the country'; high-speed dialogues to rival the Marx Brothers: '"But what if everybody else felt the same way as you?" "Then I'd certainly be a damn fool to think any other way"'; and a pithiness and terseness of description that is highly evocative. For me, ripe plum tomatoes have, in Colonel Cathcart's memorable formulation, always been 'the firm breasts of young girls'.

The Soldier in White – the ultimately redundant middle-man; Dunbar, who cultivates boredom so as to increase his lifespan; Captain Flume, who dreams so convincingly that he is awake, that in the morning he is exhausted; Major Major Major Major, who's only available when he's out; Chief White Halfoat, whose family can't help finding oil; Milo Minderbinder, who can buy eggs for seven cents and sell them for five whilst still making a profit; the maid in lime-green panties, who puts out for everyone with cheerful abandon – the list of characters, snapshotted and frozen for atemporal relevance, if not exactly endless, is longer than that of most other writers' entire *oeuvre*.

And there was also the elegant complexity of the book's narrative and temporal structure. It must have been about the fourth time I read *Catch-22* that I fully appreciated the way this allowed the action of the novel to emerge like some free-floating DNA spiral of satirical inheritance: consecutive chapters drawing chronologically closer to one another, then pulling apart, until narrative time and 'real' time eventually converged.

But most of all, *Catch-22* was notable for its tone: a welding together of deep cynicism and deep humanism. A tone that was profoundly unsentimental and for that very reason fully engaged with the miserable fate of individuals tossed about by gargantuan and aggressive forces. The book was all of a piece: whole for part and part for whole. The conceit of the 'catch' itself, endlessly repeating itself, permutating throughout the consciousnesses of characters, writer, readers. And the tone, the style grouted it all together. Here was a book, one felt, written by a man who sat down at the blank sheet fully juiced, got going and kept going in exactly the same vein until he was finished. Hence the book's beautiful subtlety of comic timing.

Given all of the above, it's hardly surprising that *Closing Time*, a sequel thirty-three years in the coming, is a terrible disappointment. No. No, that's wrong. It isn't a disappointment, because no one would imagine, given Heller's fictional track record in the intervening three decades, that it could be anything else but the mismatched collision of sentiment and lapsed comic timing that it is.

The action of the novel begins once again with Yossarian lying in a hospital, but in the nineties, and the once enigmatic Assyrian bombadier has become a white-haired 'consultant' to the now global M&M Enterprises (his remit is simply to object to Milo's exponentially awful capitalistic scheme). He still gooses the nurses – as of old – and is tormented by mysteriously heraldic figures, such as a Belgian diplomat incarcerated beside him, and a series of disparate spooks who seem to be following him.

The plot of the novel, such as it is, involves Yossarian's attempt to get to the bottom of why it is that Chaplain Tappman (yes, the Anabaptist of old) is internally manufacturing heavy water. The action rambles through the ageing minds of Yossarian and two Heller-alikes, Samuel Singer (who, like Heller himself, worked as a Time-Life executive) and Lew Rabinovitz, a scrap-metal dealer and all-round *mucher* from Coney Island who is slowly dying of Hodgkin's disease.

The first thing that alerts the reader to the monumental failure that is *Closing Time* is the imprecision of Heller's tone. This oscillates between an attempt to recapture *Catch-22*'s sublime burlesque, and the sub-Proustian effluvia of a cashiered Brodkey. The tone of the passages written in the third person about Yossarian, and those written in the first person as Samuel Singer or Lew Rabinovitz, is jarring in its inconsistency – not that either of the styles taken in isolation is any better.

Next there is the portentousness of the book, attempting as it does to ram together all the great 'universal' concerns – sex, death, public versus private morality, technological progress – into an almost unreadable goulash. Thirdly there is the apparent childishness of the surreal and fantastical underpinnings of the book: a secret government facility that involves the recreation of nine-hole golf courses and amusement parks for the crazed President's post-nuclear holocaust delectation. This concern with nuclear armageddon (perhaps wrongly) appears hopelessly recherché given the political developments of the past few years.

And then there is the attempt to join the plot dots, to give clever little link-ups between the various characters and *mises-en-scène*. In *Catch-22* this was always managed with a great lightness of touch; *vide* the way Yossarian appears naked in a tree at the funeral of Snowden. In *Closing Time* such devices are invariably heavy-handed and contrived, culminating in the appalling solecism of Heller referring to himself *en passant* as 'poor Joey Heller from Coney Island'.

But there's worse still. Possibly crazed by having lived a great part of his working life as a writer, with the sure knowledge that his first book will achieve posterior recognition as a great work of satire, Heller has seen fit to incorporate the scenarios – and even the characters – of his peers into the action of *Closing Time*. Thus we are given a whole riff on the fire-bombing of Dresden, complete with a 'character' called Vonnegut, who subsequently becomes a writer. And throughout there is the bathetic intervention of a character called Schweik, who we are continually reminded is 'a good soldier'.

Heller doesn't spare us the reappearance of some of the best gags from the original, but in this context they come on stage knock-kneed, like the failed vaudevillians of *Broadway Danny Rose*. Even the re-entry of Milo Minderbinder's chocolate-coated Egyptian cotton failed to give me the ghost of the smiles and belly laughs of yesteryear.

And the novel's set-piece denouement, a phantasmagoric society wedding held in the PABT bus terminal in midtown Manhattan that is an obvious homage to the galleon sequence in Céline's *Voyage au bout de la nuit*, falls flat, overloaded by great skeins of repetitive descriptions of food, clothing and decoration.

But, to return to my initial observation, this is hardly a disappointment. And further, while criticize I must – that being the very name of the game – I still feel nothing but admiration and respect for the author of this book. It is interesting to speculate how it is that a writer of Heller's stature could have his own internal critic depart so comprehensively. Interesting and not unknowable. For just as it is a truism to observe that the best critical minds are often utterly incapable of producing original creative work, so it is to point out that while a writer may be able to continue writing creatively, his ability to judge his own work's quality may well desert him: the two faculties are disparate, but require unity.

It is also notable that satire is an art form that thrives best on a certain instability and tension in its creator. The satirist is always holding him or herself between two poles of great attraction. On the one side there is the flight into outright cynicism, anomie and amorality; and on the other there is the equal and countervailing pressure towards objective truth, religion and morality. Is it any wonder that most satirists collapse towards one extremity or the other? And can you blame them? The world of *Catch-22* was undoubtedly a painful vision to summon up and the material consequences of its creation a great enemy of promise for its creator; how much worse it must have been to live with its aftermath for the next thirty-three years.

Modern Review, October 1994

'SIDNEY....!?'

ACCOUNTANTS

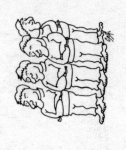

CHARTERED ACCOUNTANTS

CERTIFIED ACCOUNTANTS

SECTIONED ACCOUNTANTS

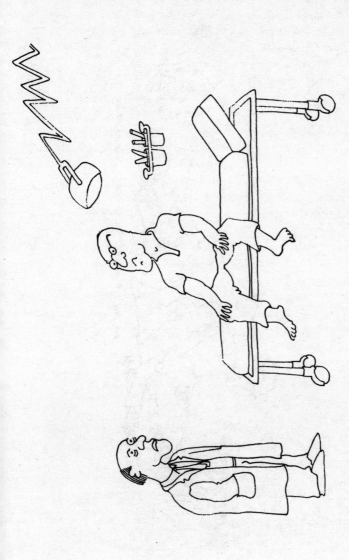

' IT'S TOO LATE MR HODGE – WE'VE DECIDED TO REMOVE YOU AND REHABILITATE THE TUMOUR '

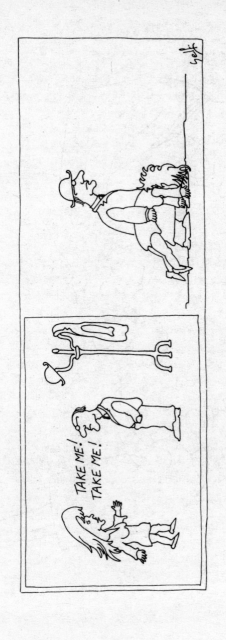

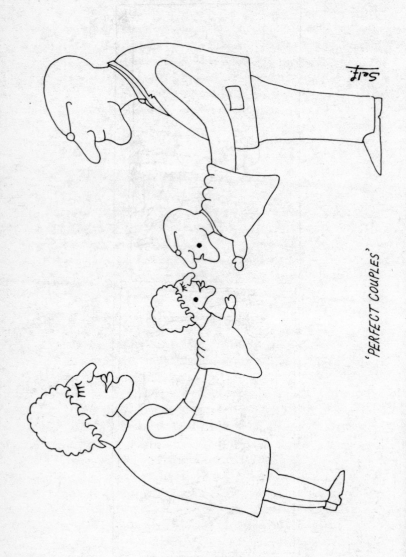

'PERFECT COUPLES'

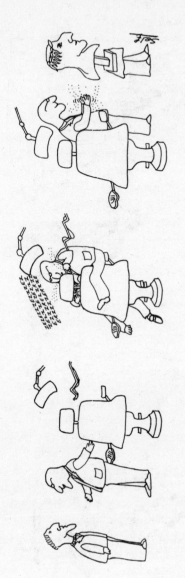

MANY DENTISTS ARE THWARTED SCULPTORS

"AHH! AT LAST, THE ALTERNATIVE JESTER ......!"

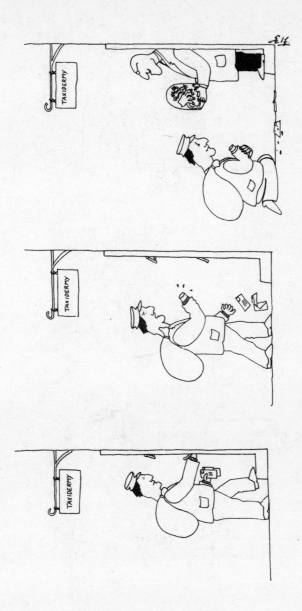

FEATURES

A Little Cottage Industry

'You're loss adjusters for the Northern Ireland Office?'

'That's right.'

'So you come in fairly quickly?'

'Yeah, we come in very fast, as soon as we can get here.'

'I'm here doing a feature for the *Observer*, so I'm interested in the whole process.'

'Well, we got the call at around 2.00 p.m. and came straight down here, but we have to wait until the army and police have cleared the area before we can actually get in.'

'So the Northern Ireland Office pays out compensation to private individuals . . .?'

'. . . Even commercial property as well they pay out on.'

'And do you think the reason you come in so fast is a psychological one, to show that the NIO cares in that way?'

'Yeah, it's a little bit of both. It's psychological to show, number one, that they care, but it's also that they want to see the damage as quickly as possible, so they have an idea first-hand exactly what it is; they want to create reserves for this incident, to see how much money they need to put aside for it. Plus, there's also the factor that they want to make sure that nothing happens over the weekend that is added to the damage in any way sort of thing, you know, they don't want ornaments getting knocked over or anything else. So, the idea is they want us here fast to see it straightaway.'

'So you'll hang in now until they let you in?'

'We'll hang in until they let us in.'

'And where are you based?'

'In Belfast.'

'You've driven all the way down? This only happened at ten past one . . .'

'Yeah, well we were instructed at about half past two, and we literally left the office about ten minutes after that.'

'And what you're involved in is basically a kind of negative quantity surveying?'

'Err . . . I suppose it is really. I started off as a quantity surveyor and we do come from either an insurance or a quantity surveying discipline. Most people have their own loss assessors acting for them, who will present a claim to us, ahh . . . and then we will agree the amount of damage with them. Most people on . . . on domestic property have their own insurance cover, so they'll involve the insurance company as well. But the company will then get their recovery from the Northern Ireland Office . . .'

'. . . I see . . .'

'. . . We will ultimately put forward a figure and if the insurance company pays out they will be covered by the NIO.'

'But people must have to pay out a pretty brutal premium to be fully covered in this area?'

'Well, yeah, that's right, it would be hefty from that point of view. Although some people – to be honest with you – don't claim, especially more than one claim. They don't want to have their insurers sit back and think . . . one company here has actually said to some of the people:

one more claim and you're off cover for everything. Forget about it, we won't give storm cover, fire cover . . . So the people have just literally stopped claiming from the insurance company, and just rely upon the NIO, just work it that way.'

'There's a lot of stuff written in the press about how that's bad politically, because it's building up a sort of negative economy, where there's a lot of money slushing around.'

'Oh yeah, oh yeah, that's very true. It does become a little cottage industry at times.'

'Oh well . . .'

'We don't even know what extent of damage there is, they say there's some properties down there pretty extensively damaged, but . . .'

'The impression I got was that the house had been pretty much blown out.'

'I've dealt with claims down there not that long ago.'

'In this patch here?'

'Yeah, actually there was a bomb in the square here not that long ago. Very minor damage down here, as you can imagine, just some plaster cracks or whatever but . . .'

'But the RUC station here was taken out . . .?'

'Yeah, that was the 25th of April . . . it was Saturday the 19th of March, the whatever . . . 10th of January. I think this is our eighteenth incident down here in the last, sort of, three or four years. They're getting fairly regular. But from our point of view it's quarter past four now on a Friday, and we normally finish at five . . .'

'Thanks for talking.'

'OK. All the best.'

He left me and walked off down to where the security forces had stretched white lengths of tape across the road. A big, gingerish man wearing a sharp, dark double-breasted suit, an aggressively op-art tie – all bold geometric patterns

– and accompanied by a colleague attired so similarly that the two of them looked like some strange paramilitary insurance unit.

The NIO loss adjusters were the most concrete thing I had managed to latch on to in Crossmaglen, South Armagh. How suitable, I thought to myself, that an English ironist should light on these figures of consummately jokey normalcy, whilst Lynx helicopters buzz the rooftops. In its own peculiar way this summed up the sensation I had had of entering a hall of mirrors ever since I arrived in Northern Ireland. It was the business of the place to supply the stuff of narrative, of anecdote, of story; and it was the business of the English voyeur to provide the necessary irony, the distancing, that could render the situation simultaneously comprehensible and yet redundant.

I went to Northern Ireland with no firm convictions about anything other than my own inability to make a reasonable comment. In Belfast three nights before the Crossmaglen incident, the novelist Robert McLiam Wilson had bellowed at me across a dinner table: 'But don't you see, we need people to come from outside and comment on what's going on here. It's no good you saying you're not qualified. You have to have the courage to be sincerely insincere – if that's what you feel.'

But I didn't even feel sincerely insincere – I felt worse than that, I felt ashamed. Robert Wilson, like the two other novelists I spent time with in Northern Ireland, Glenn Patterson and Carlo Gébler, extolled the virtues of the long piece on the Province that Rian Malan wrote for the *Guardian* last year. But, of course, Malan could bring a valid outsider's view to the Troubles. He's a South African and when he says that the Troubles are as nothing compared to the suffering of his own country, it carries clout.

In Britain we've become accustomed to only accepting

such validity: the high moral ground of someone else's suffering. But if there's to be any movement at all in the intractable nastiness of politics in Northern Ireland, then we must cease adopting such perspectives, confront our insincerity and our shame. I feel ashamed about the Troubles because for many years I supported the Republican cause, if not the 'armed struggle', for reasons that were so simple-minded that they now make me blush.

The events that 'politicized' me in relation to Northern Ireland were the hunger strikes of the early 1980s. I became a signatory of a human rights declaration that was meant to do for Northern Ireland what Charter 77 had done for the Czechs, but which in reality was probably little more than a front for the Republicans. I remember marching on a wet day in 1981, from Trafalgar Square to Quex Avenue in Kilburn, together with the oddest mixture of trendy lefties and working-class Irish people. Constantly harassed by the police, the demonstration was eventually broken up altogether, while H-Block Committee activists shouted through megaphones.

The reasoning was thus: if Thatcher is bad, then, QED, it follows that the hunger strikers must have some good in them. Furthermore, any minority group that forces the British state apparatus into such galvanisms of military activity must be acting as a proxy, drawing down on to them the repressive measures that the British government might well like to deploy against the left wing on the mainland.

But more than that, there was the fact that an espousal of the Republican cause was absolutely guaranteed to reduce all sorts of people to apoplexy. It was the acid test of British patriotism. If you wanted to *épater* them to the hilt, you merely had to challenge the right to exist of the United Kingdom. I've never had a Damascene conversion from this point of view. Rather it has ebbed away, just as the political certainties of most youth seem to ebb away, to be replaced by the fuzzy, 'I'm not fit to comment' lack-of-attitudinizing so redolent of incipient middle age. But contributing to this falling away of my 'convictions' was the growing acknowledgement that, not only did I not know much about Northern Ireland, for much of the time Northern Ireland hasn't existed for me.

The Australian writer Peter Carey wrote a story called 'The Cartographers'. In it, the portions of a vast country that are not regularly mapped start to disappear. Gradually this attrition of the very landform begins to effect things closer to home. Buildings in the centre of the capital city that people have taken for granted for too long and never properly regarded begin to disappear as well. Eventually, people who are not loved begin to evaporate too. The story ends with the narrator's father screaming at him, as through the old man's back we begin to ascertain the pattern of the wallpaper.

Northern Ireland is, for me, the country described in Carey's 'The Cartographers'. A country where 'politics' has ceased to function as the arena within which to manage the concerns of the people. When that happens the very physical geography of a place begins to deteriorate. The disappearing parts of Northern Ireland are the no-go areas on either side of the sectarian divide. The most extreme examples of disappearance are the gaps in cityscapes where buildings have been bombed, and the gaps in people's lives when those they loved have been killed.

In Northern Ireland people were keen on telling me what politics were, I think because the word 'politics' no longer serves to describe what is happening. 'Politics isn't politics here,' Robert Wilson told me, 'it's geography.' 'Elections aren't fought on political issues here,' pronounced Richard

McAuley, the Sinn Fein press officer, 'they're fought on constitutional ones.' There was another shibboleth that I heard time and again, until it was polished smooth by repetition: 'There aren't any current affairs in Northern Ireland, only history.'

'I'm doing some research for my new novel,' a snort of laughter from Robert Wilson – he's about to coin an epithet. 'I'm studying Irish history seriously for the first time. Studying it so that I can lie more effectively!' He was pinpointing another get-out for those of us on the other side of the Irish Sea. We sit here, and bewildered by the 'complexities', relapse into the idea that both sides of the divide are guarding historical arcana, privileged knowledge we cannot hope to understand. It salves our conscience, renders the conflict in some way tribal, puts it beyond the purlieus of reason.

My time in Belfast was a busman's holiday. I surveyed the conflict not through the eyes of a reporter, or a journalist, but through those of fiction writers. How did they respond to the challenge to their imaginations that their country represented? How was it possible to write true fictions in a place where fictional truths were being produced with such frantic abandon?

I felt embarrassed about pushing Robert Wilson, Glenn Patterson and Carlo Gébler to mull over these issues for hour upon hour, but needn't have. It gradually dawned on me, as we talked and talked and talked, that this was another of the little cottage industries that has been created by the Troubles. Whether it was the loss adjusters in Crossmaglen or the prize-winning novelists in Belfast, all had become narrative artisans. People had to fabricate their stories with a will, because the story the society was telling itself was so warped.

In Crossmaglen I stood and watched as cliché after cliché framed itself, hackneyed images from a million news reports. Squaddies talking to children leaning on a fence, an elderly woman ambling up the road while a prone rifleman draws a bead on her shopping, another squaddie in a sniping position under one of the ubiquitous 'Sniper at Work' mock road signs. The images were worn thin – I talked to the news reporters instead: 'Well, you see, that was one of the things, whenever you were working on the *Irish News*, or the *Newsletter*, whenever there was an incident you sometimes had to phone up and find out if they were Protestant or Catholic victims before you decided to go. If you were working for the *Newsletter* and it was a Catholic victim you might not bother going. And when I was working on the *Irish News* I remember the shootings up in Castlerock, those four workmen, you remember? We spent a good half-hour, wasting time, finding out if they were Catholic or Protestant before we went. Eventually I was sent only to find out they were Catholic. Crazy really.'

But the young radio reporter had another anecdote as well, concerning himself. His story, so to speak, and that was that he was from a mixed family, but had been brought up a Protestant in a highly Protestant area. But while he felt under no threat, his sister lived in the Shankill Road in Belfast, and she was under threat: 'Because someone might finger her as a Mick.' The situation made him angry – angry at people 'at home' who didn't realize the danger she was facing.

And so every anecdote in Northern Ireland has to come accompanied by its refutation. One person will tell a story pointing up the ubiety of the sectarian divide, and how both groups can instantly identify one another – and then someone else will chime up and say: but what about so-and-so. I had no idea he was a Catholic. Glenn Patterson told this anecdote: 'If you walk around certain areas of Belfast you're bound to be stopped and asked what you are. So one night Robert and I were coming back from somewhere and this drunk asked us. And we looked at each other, trying to guess what the right response was, but then we just shrugged and told him the truth. Then the drunk said: "Are youse two actors?"'

Neither Patterson nor Wilson was comfortable with an ascription of nationality at all. I asked Glenn if he thought of himself as Irish. 'I don't really have any understanding of that . . . people are always trying to get you to define yourself in their terms.'

Then Wilson chimed in, lighting what seemed like his eighty-seventh Silk Cut of the evening: 'Last year I went to a conference in Dublin with the exciting title "Imagining Ireland". I got there and I looked around at all these bloody writers and I thought, you fools, you aren't the people who are imagining Ireland, it's guys wearing balaclavas with names like "Stompy" and "Squinty".'

It was an emphatic comment, well up to standard, and yet earlier that same evening Robert had contradicted himself: 'For years,' he had said, 'I couldn't see this whole business of violence the right way round. I couldn't understand that the basic fact is murder, all the persiflage that comes with it, is entirely logical. Look, you have to understand, you remember those three soldiers who were lured up on to the mountain by those girls, right when the Troubles began? Well, they were all shot with the same gun, they were shot by somebody who had seen what a bullet does to the head. You see, the act of political murder isn't a moral act – it's an act that's possible because of a fatal lack of imagination.'

There was the paradox: Ireland was being imagined by people with no imagination. Both Wilson and Patterson were attempting to deny the absolute relevance of the political violence that surrounds them to their work: 'It's the increasing urbanization of Ireland that dominates my thoughts as a writer at the moment,' said Wilson, 'not the questions of nationality.' Yet his own first novel, *Ripley Bogle*, is steeped in 'questions of nationality', just as Glenn Patterson's *Burning Your Own is*.

Carlo Gébler had persuaded me long and hard about the marginal character of the men of violence; their lack of constituency; their status as political dinosaurs, intransigently reacting to the nexus of pressures defined twenty-five years ago and now cast in concrete. Yet his own writerly preoccupations in recent years seem to have been more and more with the narrative of political violence where he lives. When I arrived in Belfast he was just finishing the last of a trilogy of films about Belfast, two of which were concerned directly with the impact of the Troubles. His new novel (as yet unpublished), while ostensibly concerned with the last recorded witch burning in Southern Ireland, is nonetheless couched within a story about what it means to be a writer, what it means to be Irish, and how violence queers the pitch.

'Go up the Falls Road,' Robert Wilson instructed me, 'tell them exactly what you see . . . tell them it looks OK . . . that it's full of ordinary middle-class houses.' So I went up the Falls Road and I saw some middle-class houses, but I also saw plenty of RIR Scorpions driving around (the Royal Irish Regiment can be distinguished from mainland British Regiments, both by cap badges and by the 'Confidential Hotline' numbers stencilled in yellow on the sides of their vehicles), and outside Sinn Fein's 'Advice Centre' some Stompies and Squinties were being searched at gunpoint by a patrol.

The problem for the novelists was that they just couldn't

get enough product out to do the 'imagining' that was within their remit. 'We've over three hundred works of fiction concerned with the Troubles here,' Yvonne Murphy, assistant librarian at the Linen Hall Library told me, 'of course the vast majority of them are exploitative thrillers, using the Troubles as a violent backdrop.' Yvonne Murphy was helping to preside over an effluvium of fatal lack of imagination, a comprehensive archive of the Troubles' ephemera. At the Linen Hall Library they had it all, from plastic bullets to bibs inscribed with the Red Hand of Ulster and the slogan 'Baby Prod'. There were bumper stickers reading: 'Keep Ulster Tidy – Throw Your Litter in the Republic'; paperweights inscribed 'You Are Now Entering Free Derry'; a message of support for Bobby Sands from the Ayatollah Khomeini.

'It's a problem for us to keep all of this stuff,' said Yvonne, 'I mean what do you do with a "Kick the Pope" lollipop when it starts to melt?' It would have been flip to point out that that was probably what the 'Baby Prod' bib was for, but on the other hand there is a niceness of fit between signified and signifier in Northern Ireland that recurs over and over again.

At about ten past one, when the IRA active service unit (ASU) hit the security forces checkpoint on the Cullyhanna road out of Crossmaglen, I'd been eating fat, white ketchuppy chips. Eating them from a cone of paper poised between my thighs, and toddling along the lanes from Newry. I had no particular plan of action. I was acting like the worst ironic voyeur, listening to pop music on the hire car radio, goggling up at the stark army listening posts that sat atop every hill bristling with aerials; and every so often stopping to take a photograph of another piece of IRA iconography.

As well as the by now familiar triangular 'men at work'-style road signs that proclaim 'Sniper at Work' and show a hooded silhouette brandishing an Armalite in one hand and a clenched fist, there were other usurpations of the Highways Department that seemed to me even more telling.

Outside Camlough, on the A25, there was a crudely lettered sign with letters and numerals done in green, white and orange. It proclaimed: '30 mph', and underneath: 'IRA'. 'We control everything here,' the sign seemed to be saying, 'even the speed limit.'

And then on a minor road heading into Crossmaglen there was the sign I'd been waiting for. High up on a telegraph pole a piece of blackboard had been tacked. The lettering was white on black, and around the slogan a few quavers and semiquavers had been inscribed to underscore the reference. 'Mull of Kintyre,' it read, 'Bodies Rolling into the Sea . . .'

This was on Friday 10 June, eight days after the RAF Chinook carrying twenty-nine people, most of them members of the Northern Irish security establishment, had crashed on a Scottish hillside. Say what you will about the IRA – they aren't slow when it comes to translating events into postures, attitudes and ultimately narratives.

Around the time I was taking this in, the ASU had already detonated its mortar and was presumably making its way across fields, back into the Republic, or somewhere else where it could go to ground. The mortar was of the local manufacture that has become known as the 'Mark 10'. A group of three or four oxyacetylene cylinders sawn off, packed with the explosive charges and then levelled at an angle of forty-five degrees. This assemblage was then attached to the back of a truck and driven to within range of its target.

A LITTLE COTTAGE INDUSTRY

The charges travelled about 150 yards, hit a house and the side of the checkpoint. One civilian, two RUC personnel and a soldier were injured and flown out by helicopter to hospital in Newry.

I reached Crossmaglen at about 2.20 p.m. I'd been there the day before and had my car searched by a young squaddie from the Scottish Regiment. But today the queue of cars stretched back for a couple of hundred yards from the checkpoint. The area surrounding the two camouflage- and khaki-netting-draped bafflers was buzzing with RUC men and soldiers, all with firearms levelled rather than ported. I didn't think much of this, for all I knew the extra activity could have been part of a routine sweep of some sort. It wasn't until I pulled up in the main square and the Radio 1 news came on that I realized something had gone down: '. . . Two mortar bombs have hit and partly damaged a checkpoint near Crossmaglen in South Armagh, a civilian and three army personnel were slightly injured . . . A new crime of racial harassment is to go on the Statute Book . . .'

But where had the bombs hit? I'm no hard newsman, and the idea of asking a passer-by didn't exactly appeal, so I drove out of the village on the road that leads most directly to the Republic. Through a hamlet with a sign at its crossroads proclaiming: 'Second Battalion IRA', and then down a tree-lined lane. By a bridge two blue-uniformed Gardai leant against the bonnet of their van: 'Where've you come from, son?'

'Crossmaglen.'

'Is it true there's been an incident up there?'

'I just heard it on the news . . . a mortar attack on a checkpoint. I'm press. I was sort of looking for it.'

'I think you'll find it's back up in the village there.'

'Oh really, well then you'll see me coming back again in a few minutes.'

And as I recrossed the invisible border and drove back into the whirring noise-zone of army helicopters, and the fear-zone of hyped-up young soldiers staring at me through the sights of their rifles, I reflected on this nice irony: that it should take foreign policemen and a news report from London to inform me of an event that had occurred some 300 yards from where I'd been sitting.

Truly this had to be a metaphor for the Troubles themselves: a real incident is rendered progressively more unreal by overlay upon overlay of narrative obfuscation. What is physically close becomes instantly distant; and what is temporally remote is yanked into the present moment. By the time I was driving back to Newry, three hours later, the mortar attack at Crossmaglen had fallen down the Radio 1 hit parade of human tragedy; and by the time I reached Belfast that evening, it had been dropped altogether.

I went to see the people who were imagining Ireland, the people who proclaim 'Tiocfaidh Ar Lá' (pronounced 'Chucky Ar La') or 'Our Time Will Come'. I found myself waiting on a vinyl bench behind the barred door of the Sinn Fein Advice Centre. Party activists were coming in and getting assignments – it was the day of the European elections. On the wall there was the 'Roll of Honour', volunteers who had died in action against the British forces were listed. It was the tangible expression of one of the most successful of contemporary Irish fictions – that there is a real disjunction between the political wing of the IRA and those who wage the armed struggle.

Eventually Richard McAuley, the press officer, arrived, and we went upstairs. We settled ourselves in a room with flaking plaster, a scratched kneehole desk and worn carpet tiling on the floor. There followed one of the most soporific interviews I have ever conducted in my life. If McAuley felt the same way, he wasn't showing it.

He talked on and on, his response to every one of my questions unvarying in its espousal of the party line. 'We have no objection to Albert Reynolds talking to Loyalist groups, both the Irish and the British governments have to become persuaders for change. If you don't have a dialogue the alternative is aiming for military victories. And I think it's generally accepted – although possibly not by the Unionists – that that is not going to provide a solution . . .' Other writers have remarked on this sense of the implacable that surrounds Sinn Fein rhetoric. Whatever tactics I tried to draw McAuley out, to get him to admit some of the known facts that seemed to contradict his line, he side-stepped and came up with another reply remarkable only for its vapidity, its failure to add anything substantive.

It was ridiculous. I was sitting in the hub of the Republican movement, a building that had been attacked three times by rocket grenades in as many months, and I felt myself falling asleep. McAuley was imagining an Ireland in which, as he put it, 'It is possible to square the circle. People said it couldn't be done in South Africa and it has been. They said the same thing about Palestine . . .' This was an imagination run rampant. The facts were that he gave absolutely no hint that Sinn Fein would be climbing down on its position regarding the Unionist veto over future constitutional change in Northern Ireland. I don't believe that the party's response to the clarifications of the Downing Street Declaration will contain any movement on this issue. The unstoppable force will continue to butt its head against the immovable object.

After an hour or so I resorted to tactics. I shamelessly employed my own shame, spoke of my own Republican sympathies, implied that I was still more than sympathetic. Nothing doing. Only in the dying minutes did he start to show a little true colour: 'If we can advance the peace process it may no longer be necessary for British Intelligence to control Loyalist death squads, for them to supply information on how to kill me, or my family, or my colleagues . . .' And then, with the tape recorder off, on our way back down the stairs, we stopped to survey the wreckage caused by the last rocket attack.

I probably can't do justice to the change in his manner when McAuley described these events, but my hunch was that as he traced the path the projectile had taken, through plasterboard, brick and paper, he sensed that I knew – and I knew that he knew – imagination had, in a quite ghastly way, given in to intuition.

It isn't the novelists' fault, their inconsistencies and self-contradictions are the only reasonable response of good men to a bad situation. All three of them, Wilson, Patterson and Gébler, are so implacably opposed to the men of violence that they cannot help but try to deny some of these realities. They were no more willing to countenance the idea of a 'split' in the IRA than Richard McAuley. They have to retain a view of the paramilitaries as monolithic, an incarnation of this evil, because to do otherwise is to start negotiating with that fatal lack of imagination.

Wilson had spoken of his concern, as a writer, with the growing urbanization of Ireland. That urbanization has of course a subtext: the urbanization of the conflict, the links between the paramilitaries and the more blatant face of organized crime is ineluctable in any context where there are firearms and social deprivation. But in South Armagh, where the sniper is at work with his Barrett Light Fifty rifle, five feet of gun weighing thirty pounds that can deliver an armour-piercing round over a mile, it is a different story.

It may only be small wedges of territory, but these zones – the so-called 'Bandit Country' of South Armagh and South Fermanagh – are occupied by the British army. The road signs tell you that more than anything else. And I would have liked to have got one of the leaflets that had been distributed in Crossmaglen a week or so before the mortar attack on the checkpoint. Leaflets that cordially suggested that residents of the houses near military installations might like to spend as much time out of the house as possible. In Crossmaglen the IRA parades petty offenders, and even, it is said, adulterers, around the main square after mass on a Sunday, placards around their necks proclaiming their transgressions. I wonder if the British army patrols that saturate the village draw a bead on these tormented people, just as they draw a bead on everyone else.

We're all bound up in imagining Ireland, but I wonder if for the English this activity has become increasingly lackadaisical. I grew up with the armed struggle in my ears, just as my contemporaries in Ireland did. When I was twelve, the London ASU of the IRA bombed the Angus Steak House in Hampstead village, 100 yards from my prep school. I cannot remember a time when the dull rumble of the Troubles hasn't been going on in the background, erupting time after time into purposeless squeals of public agony and collective rending of hair and garments.

Last year I was on holiday in the Republic, staying in the house that belonged to those great imaginers of Ireland, Somerville and Ross. The house is in Castletownsend, an enclave of the Protestant Ascendancy in West Cork, which was the most implacable area of IRA support, both in the Tan war and the civil war that followed.

At dinner one night the conversation drifted on to the subject of the relationship between the Ascendancy landowners and the native Irish. An Irish woman – the kind who might be described as a 'Castle Catholic' – chimed up saying: 'But you don't understand. The relationship people had with their servants was very different to that in England. Here the servants were – and are – far more familiar. They felt it was their perfect right to involve themselves in every aspect of their employers' lives. There was a refreshing lack of any formality. But, of course, at the same time they would never dream of thinking themselves like "the quality".'

I was gobsmacked. I sat there staring into the mahogany pool of the table. Immediately before dinner I had been reading the memoirs of Earnán O'Maillie, *On Another Man's Wound*. O'Maillie had at one time during the Tan war been the IRA commander in Cork. In it he had written almost exactly the same thing: '[The English officer] had been used to Ireland as a good hunting country in the same way as he had looked upon northern Scotland as a fine place for grouse, deer, fish, and the wearing of kilts. As long as the country provided a Somerville and Martin Ross atmosphere of hounds giving cry, strong brogues, roguish wit, discreet familiarity of servants, and a sure eye for picking out "the quality" and letting them know it; then Ireland could be understood.' Here was another niceness of fit, revealing a terrible gulf of incomprehension.

'Anniversaries are important here,' McAuley had said, ever the man for stating the obvious. He didn't see anything meretricious or objectionable about the BBC's forthcoming twenty-fifth anniversary bonanza on the Troubles. And why should he? It's another contribution to the little cottage industry, another stab at imagining Ireland.

I'll leave the last anecdote to Robert McLiam Wilson, for it unites all concerns: the media, the conflict, the imagination. 'Last July 12th I went down to watch the bands come by at the end of the road. I got down there and this RUC man turned to me and said: "Have you seen the *Newsletter*?" I told him no, and he said: "Well, you better get inside, son." You see, they'd carried a story that morning reporting the publication of my second novel. There was a photograph of me and under it the caption: "Robert McLiam Wilson, prominent West Belfast novelist".'

Observer, July 1994

The Valley of the Corn Dollies

We were standing on the beach at Sizewell in Suffolk – my dad and I. To our right the Kubla Khan dome of the fast-breeder reactor hall gleamed in the wan sunlight. Daddy was expounding. Foolishly I had provided him with an opportunity – I'd admitted that I was writing an article on the state of English culture.

'Mmm . . . English culture. Well . . .' he paused, rocking on his heels, a great dolmen of a man. 'In about 1981 I had to give a lecture at the embassy in Tokyo on the subject of English culture.'

'Oh, really.' I was underwhelmed. 'And what did you have to say about it?'

'Funny thing is I can't remember . . . Shall we go and get a pint?'

Not exactly an epiphanic moment in most cultural contexts, but the truth is that the mention of the words 'English culture' prompts more bathetic lines, from more disparate individuals, than anything else I have ever hit on. At times I began to feel that the term 'English culture' might conceivably be an oxymoron, or worse, as flimsy a journalistic pretext as Hunter S. Thompson's search for 'the American Dream' in *Fear and Loathing in Las Vegas*.

Given this, I could imagine the denouement of my quest well enough: Self floundering across a field of rape in pursuit of a toothless, old smock-wearer.

SELF: What is that in your hand, old man?

SMOCK-WEARER: Thaat? It be a corn dolly.

SELF (capering): At last! At last! I've found English culture! Fol-de-rol! Hi-diddley-hey!

Self and smock-wearer execute a passable Mexican wavelet and then quit the rape field in a severely truncated conga line.

As a fellow novelist (Irish, of course) put it to me when hearing about my improbable remit: 'The English have such a reliable appetite for hearing what shite they are.' Yes, we may not have a culture we can call our own any more, but never let it be said that we're slow off the mark when putting the boot into our own. Indeed, this tendency is now so well advanced that it could reasonably be argued that English culture is entirely constituted by self-loathing.

I'm no stranger to this tendency. I always make it clear, when talking about the cultural exhaustion of my country, that I do not mean those other thriving, exciting cultures, tacked on to the edges of the land mass. I dissociate the parlous condition of the 'English novel' from the rude health of the 'English-language novel'. I make damn certain that, when I'm in Scotland, Wales, Northern or Southern Ireland, I don't make the absurd solecism of referring to 'British culture'. It would be like a Nazi asking for a cream cheese bagel in Grodzinski's – would it not?

Well, no, not exactly. The truth of the matter is that while English culture may be moribund when considered in isolation, suspended like some bisected bovine in the formaldehyde of cultural criticism, the reality is that it positively pullulates with invention and polymorphous perversity.

Not all of this is to be desired. Culture cannot be read off from social circumstances in a form of straight equivalence:

good society = good culture. The opposite is rather more often the case. Freud, Kraus, Schnitzler, Klimt, Kafka . . . All were working to the full extent of their powers, cradled by the dying limbs of the Austro-Hungarian Empire.

It's a bit like this in England. It's all very well for my co-essayists of the last three weeks to trumpet the triumphs – and the weaknesses – of their respective cultures. They may quote this theatre director, synopsize a writer or two and comment on the odd festival, but let's call a spade a spade: their cultures exist like satellites, within the gravitational pull of something far bigger, a kind of cultural dark star, capable of sucking all the available Welsh, Scots and Irish deep into the hinterlands of Portland Place Television Centre, Fleet Street and Soho.

Yes, send us your poor, your huddled masses and we'll dress them in Paul Smith, Agnes B, Vivienne Westwood and Jasper Conran. Then we'll employ them in writing multi-supplement newspapers, filming television retrospectives, Merchant-Ivory films and Carling Black Label commercials.

It would be facile to condemn this as 'cultural imperialism'. No, contemporary English culture is both colonizer and colonized – and all the stronger for it. It is a culture of profound and productive oppositions. And I believe, personally, the best possible country for someone with a satirical bent to live in. I'd go further: England has the world's top satirical culture.

The English have, in the two and a half centuries since Swift (a man who really knew what a reliable appetite we have for hearing what shite we are) ascended a parabola of facetiousness to achieve the very zenith of irony. We have managed this by fostering a culture of conflict and opposition. Is English culture bigoted or liberal? It is both. Is it hermetic and introverted or expansive and cosmopolitan? It is all of these.

One of the recent English cultural events that garnered much attention in the print media was the deathbed interview of Dennis Potter by Melvyn Bragg. Like many other closet Englishmen I felt my capacity for dismissive irony being cauterized and my heart beginning to stir as Potter spoke, saying: 'We British in general, English in particular – I find the word "British" harder and harder to use as time passes – we English tend to deride ourselves far too easily . . . because we've lost so much confidence, because we lost so much of our identity, which had been subsumed in this forced Imperial identity which I obviously hate.'

I too find the word 'British' harder and harder to say. It sounds as implausible a description of where I live as Airstrip One. But Potter's televised leavetaking from us was freighted – predictably enough – with irony. For, while setting up a Utopian socialist, essentially working-class culture in opposition to the Heritage Industry, chocolate-boxy pomp and circumstance that the current regime still wishes to hide behind, he was nonetheless acting in a way that is possible only in a post-Imperial culture.

His use of television to broadcast the absolute spiritual importance of a 'good death' was not far short of being Ciceronian. Only – I would argue – in England could this have taken place. His dryness, his self-possession, his honesty, his caustic wit in the face of extinction. Damn it all – his sang-froid (as with most quintessential English characteristics, only a French tag will do it justice) made me, for a wrenching, choking second or two, proud to be English.

We're big on dignified death at the moment – as suits a culture of rich decline. We were treated to Derek Jarman's expiry in the past year as well. Once again our newspapers, image-hungry and commentful, treated us to photographs of Jarman wasting away with Aids. When he was on the brink of death even the *Daily Telegraph* carried it as a news item. And this the man reviled for his gayness, his cruising, promiscuous lifestyle and last – but by no means least – his achingly pretentious 'arty-farty' films.

I've been as quick off the mark as the rest of us to dissociate myself from Jarman's creative excesses. As a gay friend of mine once remarked lovingly: 'He just has to put Tilda Swinton in a corner and get her to emote!' There's a tendency among the chattering classes – another of our great coinages – to trash our own before anyone else can. In this sense we're like a collective personification of Anthony Blanche in *Brideshead Revisited*. We loiter by the statue of Mercury in Christ Church's Peck Quad, desperately frightened lest some gang of vicious hearties come and debag us for our aestheticism.

But the truth of the matter is that Jarman was a great English film-maker. And in *The Last of England* he offered us a set of discursive and yet plangent images of our own divided nature: its beauty and its brutality, its sensuality and its darkness. Each frame that Jarman contrived in this film appeared to me to be at one and the same time wholly arbitrary and yet exactly right. The sense of frenzied enervation that it produced in me was unmistakably English in character. After all, as I've often had occasion to remark, London is a great city, which has genuine edge, and which is still in some ineffable way terribly dull.

So the contradictions pile up. We may bemoan the English for their obsession with class – on some dark days it seems to me that English culture is defined entirely by class preoccupation – yet without this preoccupation it is inconceivable to imagine there being the films of Mike Leigh, Terence Davies or Ken Loach.

THE VALLEY OF THE CORN DOLLIES

While there is a conformist tradition of exploiting class division for 'light comedy' or bogus satire that runs in an unbroken line from P. G. Wodehouse through the Waughs (Evelyn and Auberon) to Stephen Fry and Hugh Laurie, there is another class-influenced tradition that is surreal, irreverent and genuinely subversive. In the post-war period this begins with Spike Milligan, snags in elements of Alan Bennett and Peter Cook, hooks up the Monty Python team and comes to rest with the alternative comedians of the early eighties, in particular Alexei Sayle.

That much-derided Monty Python team. Oh, my God! They ended up in Hollywood, they make corporate videos, they sold out big time! But they were also – let's not forget – good. How good is open to dispute, but they were an Oxbridge gang of bourgeois boys who took on their own class and its preoccupations with a vengeance. They took the piss out of the English ruling class and its mores in a way that hadn't been done on television before, and I don't believe has been substantially improved on since. Let us not forget 'Upper-Class Twit of the Year'. And let us not forget either possibly the most incisive film satire on England in the early eighties, Terry Gilliam's *Brazil*. Made by a Canadian, I grant you, but infused with all the awfulness of the Thatcher regime, its bizarre mixture of antimacassars and atomic weaponry, of aspidistras and the absolutely fabulous.

Thatcher is, of course, the real bogey woman of this essay. There was never anything more English than Baroness Thatcher née Margaret Roberts. She proved once again that anyone in this country who had elocution lessons could aspire to a hereditary title. Thatcher made explicit the peculiar cultural bond that has always existed between the English lower middle class and the English upper middle class, the two groups dancing a gavotte around one another, aping each other's attitudes.

It would have been nice to imagine – what with the monarchy so convincingly working itself via the Method into the mind-set of a tampon – that this quavering chord of snobbery was at any rate being stretched in the present if not snapped altogether. But, of course, nothing could be further from the truth. The English obsession with class is in great shape and over the past fifteen years has received a booster course of anabolic steroids in the form of government-inspired promotion of gross economic inequality.

The fact remains that, in the past decade and a half in England, the poor have got resolutely poorer while the rich have got resolutely richer. Statistics came out a month ago (rating minimal column inches in newspapers that had more important things to comment upon, such as new trends in advertising) that, while the middle classes in England have doubled their wealth in real terms, the least well-off have got progressively poorer.

This leaves the bulk of cultural commentators in an uneasy – not to say tendentious – position of having to nip and nibble at the hand that so conspicuously feeds them. Going back to that Potter interview, I think he voiced a sentiment that many of us feel when he said that there was a real demand for radicalism in England in the eighties – it happened to come from the right wing, but the demand for change was insistent.

We got the change – but it wasn't exactly what we were looking for. But to reprise what I said above, a great culture is not necessarily derived from an egalitarian or socially responsible political and economic culture. In the eighties we saw rickets and tuberculosis reappear in our cities; along with new kids on the block: firearms and crack cocaine, and

I would argue that as a direct result England came of age as a particular kind of culture.

A year or so ago I did an interview with Martin Amis for an American college review. It was at the end of our conversation that Amis inadvertently identified the nub of the cultural exhaustion suffered by the English middle class – and what underlies it, adumbrates it, gives it substance.

We were discussing the notion of 'cool'. The Americans definitely had it, opined Amis. All Americans? I countered, or perhaps only Afro-Americans? They did, after all, coin the term in the first place. Well, Amis didn't know about that, but whatever 'cool' was, it was a quality that the English were incapable of possessing.

I would like to dissent from this view. Not only do I think that English culture is cool – I also think we have been getting cooler. But this 'cool' is a tricky thing. Decidedly double-edged. Cool feeds off poverty and injustice, that's why the Americans have always had so much of it. Cool produces great dance music, great drug culture, the insistent iconization of violence and sensuality.

It's fashionable enough to deride America, and to single out its influence on English culture as being wholly negative. A couple of months ago the literary editor of the *Guardian*, Richard Gott, wrote: 'There is now no English fiction to speak of, no English theatre, no English art, no English music, no English films, and no English newspapers. What survives is provincial, anecdotal, without reach or significance . . . For years now we have learnt to live with American politics and culture as though they were our own. They are our own for we have no other. We are permanently in a mood to read American writers, see American art, listen to American music . . . etc.'

If Gott's rant (another fine English cultural tradition – we even named a political tendency after it in the seventeenth century) displays anything, it's the bogusness and attitudinizing of those on the left just as much as those on the right. The willingness to search for culture in terms of some specious purity. Gott is just as guilty as John Major of longing residually for some English arcadia. His may not be defined by the sound of leather on willow, but it's no more or less asinine.

If Gott wishes to deride English culture in this way because of American influence, then he presumably would also wish to deride the influence of the Afro-Caribbean, South Asian and Central European immigrants to this country, let alone all the myriad other peoples who have made their homes here. (He also presumably has a great deal of sympathy for the way in which New York has been 'invaded' by legions of English journalists, writers and publishers over the past ten years.) Let us not forget that it was England that found a place for Marx to park his carbuncled bum while he wrote *Das Kapital*, and for Freud to push his couch when Vienna became a tad too intolerant.

And contemporary English culture gifts us the delights of this in the form of the writings of Ben Okri, Hanif Kureishi, David Dabydeen, Kazuo Ishiguro, Anita Desai, Ruth Prawer-Jhabvala, Caryl Phillips and Salman Rushdie; the thoughts of Ernest Gellner, Adam Phillips and Germaine Greer; the music of Yehudi Menuhin, Joan Armatrading and UB40.

If you chuck out the bathwater of 'pernicious' cultural influences, the baby of exciting and productive ones goes along with it. If you see culture as a one-way street you neglect the fact of just how influential English culture has been on the rest of the world – and America in particular. Forget *Four Weddings and a Funeral* and remember the Stone Roses, the Orb, Primal Scream and the whole Manchester

Rave scene, which has washed up in America in just the way that so many other delirious waves of English dance music culture have before.

Yes, you would have to say that, when it comes right down to it, what the English are best at at the moment – and have been for some little while – is the synergy of dance, drugs and street fashion. The youth of just about any English provincial city look infinitely cooler – to my mind – than their contemporaries in either Seattle or Turin.

We're also good at something rather numinously termed 'retail services', by which is meant marketing, advertising and merchandising, as well as franchising. Indeed 'retail services' constitute the largest part of our invisible earnings. You can go to any city in the world and see the influence of English retail services. How pitiful it is to moan about American consumerism and commercialism when we have so enthusiastically pursued it ourselves for many years.

When I was last in the States, number six on the MTV video chart was Morrissey, as camply English as they go, warbling irresolutely: 'The more you ignore me, the closer I get.' And in truth this is what has been happening with the cool side of English culture, the more the self-appointed élite of cultural critics has ignored it, the closer it has got.

Part of the reason for this is the way that the English middle class excels at cultural appropriation. No sooner has something been generated than it can be twisted into a suitable shape for intelligent 'comment'. Football has been one of the recent victims of this superior yobbism. A lot of rather etiolated, epicene, middle-class, male intellectuals have discovered a new authenticity when they come to identify themselves as football fans.

What are they playing at? After all, it's one thing to enjoy a bit of a kick-around, or standing on the terraces with a plastic beaker of Bovril, but it's quite another to churn out newspaper articles and even books – damn it all, that's culture! And it is a culture of appropriation. Flagrantly uncool, the English bourgeoisie has gone hunting for new, farouche culture. But it hasn't ventured very far – just down the social ladder a few rungs to raid the working-class larder. And that's what this football thing is about: cultural appropriation. It's really no surprise – because that's what the English pop culture has been about (in part) for many years: i.e. sons of Dartford PE teachers wailing that they're 'street-fighting men'.

There are two nations in England therefore, the cool nation and the undeniably uncool one. It follows that there is a cool culture and an uncool culture. It's the sort of exercise that a great many English journalists take to with great enthusiasm, separating cultural artefacts and creators into these two categories, or others similar. It won't be too long before there are magazines in England consisting entirely of lists of what is deemed to be 'in' or 'out'. Of course the irony here (and please note the frequency with which the word 'irony' is recurring in this essay) is that those who undertake such activities are about as far from the notion of cultural cool as it is possible to be, without relocating to EuroDisney.

Yes, you've guessed it, the arbiters of cool are the least qualified people for the job; and further, the vast majority of the people who are responsible for defining the parameters of contemporary English culture are also woefully inadequate for the task. This is not simply a function of the old adage: if you have to ask what rhythm is then you ain't got it. It's more to do with the dread influence of the media and in particular the namesake of Dennis Potter's pancreatic cancer, dear old newly American Rupert Murdoch.

I'm not going to go into yet another rant about the

deadening influence of television, or the parlous state of the English novel, or the lack of quality in the quality newspapers, but certain facts about the relationship between the English cultural scape and the media do seem to me to be indisputable.

In Raymond Chandler's novel *The Long Goodbye*, the multimillionaire Harlan Potter remarks: 'A newspaper is an advertising vehicle predicated upon its circulation, nothing more and nothing less.' In the United States this was evident as long ago as the fifties. Here, we have continued to cling to the cherished delusion that the bulk of good newspapers and periodicals are driven by some 'line' or other. But other media – notably television – have now made the same kind of inroads as they have across the Atlantic. English newspapers, magazines and even books now find themselves fighting for a smaller and smaller share of the attention span available. With declining circulations, the only way to bolster profits is by more advertising and cutting editorial costs.

You can now have the delicious experience of opening a quality newspaper and finding many, many column inches not only filled with extemporized comment, but also lists of the 'in' and 'out' and, most pernicious of all, a vast amount of highly self-reflexive material: journalists writing about journalists, about television programmes, about the way in which certain cultural phenomena have impacted (but not about the phenomena themselves), and about items of such persiflage that you wonder fervently how the subs could bring themselves to key the stuff in. I myself have considered asking all my journalist friends to contribute to a collection of the most facile and meretricious examples of this genre. It would be entitled 'The New Glib'.

J. G. Ballard has said that the shocking thing about English television is that it treats serious subjects glibly, the Americans only treat glib subjects glibly, which is a far less serious crime against the culture. What is true about television is also true, *mutatis mutandis*, about other media as well.

Another contemporary English cultural shibboleth concerns that word 'irony' which I asked you to note earlier. A decade or so ago there was a film scripted by David Hare called *The Ploughman's Lunch*. This was a state-of-the-nation type film, a timely comment on how the Thatcher era was beginning to shape up. The eponymous, central irony of the film was that the idea of the ploughman's lunch, far from being some immemorial component of the English agricultural worker's diet, was in fact the coinage of a sixties marketing man trying to vitalize pub snacking.

Nowadays such a device would be given the ubiquitous – and invariably incorrect – ascription 'post-modern'. This has come to refer to almost any example of cultural self-reflexivity. It wouldn't surprise me in the least to hear some self-appointed 'cultural critic' refer to the Carling Black Label advertisements as tremendous examples of English post-modernist irony. They're not, of course, they're merely another way that advertising people have hit upon of selling us indifferent lager.

What kind of claim is it anyway to say that, while our culture may on the face of it be hopelessly decadent, we are at least capable of having a good snigger at ourselves? Such a claim opens the door to a peculiarly un-English state of mind: despair. And another concomitant to the specious post-modernist contention is that the old divisions between 'high' and 'low' culture are somehow being eradicated. The people who advance this view – best summed up by the masthead slogan of the *Modern Review*: 'Low Culture for Highbrows' – are in fact our old friends the middle-class football fans under a different guise.

You note that they aren't remotely interested in presenting high culture for lowbrows, by which I mean that they have no intention of regarding their hold on the print media as an opportunity to provide education or enlightenment for anyone. Rather they seem engaged – and I don't just mean the *Modern Review* people by this, I think the tendency is far more widespread – in a kind of lower-sixth-form common-room approach to our culture: it's all much of a muchness really and a bit of a laugh, so let's not take it too seriously. What lies behind this is not the professed aim of elevating popular culture, but the urge to drag high culture down to a level where it can be discussed in the same way that Carling Black Label advertisements are.

I think that popular culture can be good on its own terms and so can high culture. I don't see any particular need to mate them with one another in order to produce some exciting new chimera. It merely seems to me to be the result of the despair that afflicts people when they realize that their culture has simply become too amorphous and too large for them to get any kind of grasp on it at all.

It was said of Coleridge that he was the last man in England to have read everything. Well, he was none too happy with this feat in the early nineteenth century – imagine what a horror it would be today. It strikes me that, while the business of marginal cultures that have had their cultures denigrated and deracinated is to preserve and renovate them, the business of cultures like England's, which has been and continues to be remarkably influential, is to somehow distress the cultural fabric, so that the people aren't faced with the Coleridgean dilemma. Coming back to newspapers, how many times in the last ten years have you heard people moan that there is simply too much stuff around for them to read/listen to/watch? Imagine how dreadful this predicament would be if it were really the case that the majority of this material were worth reading/listening to/watching?

But of course no nation – not even the English – has a monopoly on the business of cultural self-loathing. Why, even those triumphalists the Americans are no mean practitioners. During a recent book tour of the States, if I had been given a dime for every time someone chimed in during the Q & A session at the end of the reading, saying how much better contemporary English writing seemed to be to them than American, I would have become a comparatively wealthy man. When people would say this, there was nothing else to do but point out that most of last year's reading in the English literary press was about just how dismal our literary outpourings were, particularly when compared to those of contemporary America.

But then America is a newcomer to that field of declining cultural self-loathing, and while Americans can attitudinize self-revulsion with the best of us, they still haven't acquired that distinctly English kind of self-abuse, that thoroughly reliable appetite for hearing what shite they are. But I'm confident they'll catch up. They'll catch up because their culture is being changed and compromised in many of the same ways that ours is.

Let me tease this out a bit further for you, and in doing so start to resolve the strange conundrum I presented earlier when I claimed that, despite all of this negativity, superfluity and redundancy, English culture was cool and getting cooler.

All of what I have said above applies to culture when considered as a passively received phenomenon, it does not apply to culture in the making. It most definitely applies to the self-reflexive nullities of much 'cultural criticism' but it certainly does not apply to what these myriad critics are attempting to examine. Let me make it simpler still; it applies to the superstructure of our culture, but not to our base. The superstructure of English culture is still overwhelmingly white, middle class and metropolitan. The people we are forced to listen to on matters cultural have by and large seldom actually immersed themselves in the culture they purport to be explaining. They are the cultural PEVists, the Psycho-Empathetic Voyeurs. They no longer need to immerse themselves in culture, they simply need to know that it's going on somewhere. 'Here be culture,' reads the map that is attached to almost every publication nowadays in the form of some 'what's on' or events guide.

Although these arbiters would seek to distance them-selves from the reactionary postures implicit in so much English culture-mongering from the national curriculum on up, the fact remains that they have joined in a silent compact with those people who believe a culture's strength depends somehow on its purity. They have entered the Valley of the Corn Dollies, and are to be seen there eating ploughman's lunches voraciously. They come under many guises: anti-American, anti-European, anti-Caribbean, anti-Semitic, homophobic, misogynistic, anti-just about anything.

They want to preserve a vision of England that is equally compounded of Lowry and Wodehouse, of dappled afternoons on the croquet lawn at Blandings Castle and beclogged figures clunking their way across the cobbles of northern industrial cities. Theirs is a world in which the despair and resentment of Philip Larkin is still the best show in town: It fucks you up, your culture, / It doesn't mean to but it does . . .

A pox on all their houses. Last year, along with nineteen

other unfortunates, I was named as being one of 'the best novelists' (under forty) in contemporary Britain. This ushered forth a storm of cultural self-abuse in the press. Pundit after pundit declaimed on the 'death' of the English novel. Together with my fellow novelists I was somewhat bemused by this. What exactly was it that we were doing if we weren't writing English novels?

As you can imagine, there was much discussion late into the night. And while we agreed that a particular kind of English novel, a Trollopian (Joanna or otherwise) recrudescence of the national persona, was indubitably extinct (and perhaps never really existed except in the minds of members of the Trollope Society), the English-language novel was doing just fine, thank you very much.

Surely the same is true of English culture? While the old idea of a monocultural scape is impossible to sustain, England as the centre of that great roiling, post-colonial ocean of cultural ferment is alive and kicking. So I say: English culture is dead – long live English culture! But then I would say that, wouldn't I, being defiantly English, Jewish and half-American to boot.

Guardian, August 1994

Dealing with the Devil

Last night, I finally penetrated the veils of false memory that have shrouded my mind. It was a chilling and exhilarating moment, the culmination of a personal odyssey which has taken me to some of the darkest regions of my psyche. Over a period of about fifteen minutes – as I became increasingly dizzy and dissociated – I came to understand that for my entire conscious life I have been subjected to a sophisticated form of mind control.

As this impinged upon 'me', I felt my astral body detach itself from my material body and float up towards the ceiling of the room. There it hovered, gazing back down at the figure of the man who lay on the bed. The assumption of my true identity was like a surge of electricity. I was wholly vivified; if you like, enlightened.

This 'Will Self', the lanky form prone on the duvet, was manifestly little more than a puppet, constructed by a cabal of powerful magicians – Satanic cultists. For many years their agents, licentiates, acolytes and creatures have shadowed Will Self, providing him with the sly cues and psychic cover stories that have made it possible for him to believe himself an autonomous, self-aware individual.

Freed finally from this awesome delusion, I realized my true nature, which I will now reveal to you: I am an Illuminatus, a member of a conspiratorial cult that has existed for many thousands of years, in fact as long as human history itself. My thirty-two years spent as Will Self were a kind of initiation rite. All Illuminati must discover their true nature in their own way. Once you have crossed this assault-course abyss you can assume your rightful capabilities and powers.

What was written in 1486 in the *Malleus maleficarum*, or *Hammer of the Witches*, was the truth. I am one of those creatures who 'infect with witchcraft the venereal act and the conception of the womb. First, by inclining the minds of men to inordinate passion; second, by obstructing their generative force; third, by removing the members accommodated to that act; fourth, by changing men into beasts by their magical art; fifth, by destroying the generative force in women; sixth, by procuring abortion; seventh, by offering children to devils . . .'

The two Dominican friars who wrote the *Malleus* were our sworn enemies and their horribly accurate portrait of the Illuminati has pursued us down the ages. Originally intended as a handbook for Inquisitors working in southern Germany and endorsed by Pope Innocent VIII, this Observer Book of the realm of darkness is – as you can see – spot on. It could be offered as corroborative testimony to that of the British children who have given evidence of being involved in the practice of ritual abuse; and that of the 'survivors' of ritual abuse – both here and in the USA – who over the past few years have begun to recover their own buried memories of cult membership.

These are accounts of inter-generational Satanic cults, in which young children are persistently sexually abused and forced, if female, to become 'brood mares' as soon as they are able to conceive. Their function is to provide more sacrificial victims for the cults' hideous rituals: the dismemberment and consumption of foetuses and babies.

But whereas the 'survivors', as they and their therapists

style themselves, have woken up to the hideous revelation that they have been victims of a cult to such an extent that they have fashioned multiple sub-personalities, thus blocking out whole swathes of experience, I have found myself to be one of the perpetrators and my authentic being to be one of pure evil.

If the above strikes you as a sick joke of some kind, a piece of malicious fabrication that impugns the very real distress of a great number of people, then you are entirely wrong. My capacity as a writer of fictions means that I must call in such material, allow my imagination free range over the territory of the collective psyche. This has placed me in an interesting position vis-à-vis Satanic abuse.

My novel *My Idea of Fun* is an attempt to examine what is happening to the belief systems of individuals in an age when our relentless practice of applied psychology has kicked the legs out from under our social ethic; in an age when the light of reason, far from burning brightly, is guttering terribly.

It is my contention that the current extraordinary delusion concerning child abuse, Satanic abuse, so-called ritual abuse (this latter is very hard to define), is significant in ways that people are extremely unwilling to accept. My own experience and thought on the matter leads me to believe that there are a number of highly unpalatable truths about our own culture bound up in this phenomenon.

In the process of researching this article I found myself becoming profoundly psychically disturbed. The fantasy sequence with which I began this article is a piece of emotional confabulation that – as I wrote it – had real force for me. The human mind – as I hope I can demonstrate – is indeed a malleable thing. The really secret cult in our cult-ure is the one we all belong to. And it is precisely because membership is so universal that it is proving so hard to get us to break ranks and confess.

'There are,' said Jim Harding, director of children's services at the NSPCC, 'some children who are abused, with some ritual activity or behaviour as an aspect of that abuse, but there is no evidence to suggest the existence of families or extended families where there is an embedded culture of Satanic abuse.

'But look,' he sighed, 'we only speak from experience here – or not at all – and we have only looked into a small number of cases.' Harding spoke with gravitas. When he suggested that the media preoccupation with Satanic abuse had the effect of 'trivializing' the reality of adults' sexual abuse of children, I believed him. When he suggested that the number of children on the NSPCC's 'at risk' registers might be a poor indication of the number actually abused, just as – in the past – the number of women reporting sexual assaults was a poor indication of the number who had actually been assaulted, I believed him as well.

'Look,' he sighed again – a decent man freighted with producing sound bites on the culture's indecent preoccupations – 'it could be true to say that there are some unhelpful depressions heading across the Atlantic as far as child protection is concerned. But I think things are different here. We don't have the sheer scale of witnesses coming forward for a start . . .' He tailed off, eyes sliding away to the window. We are trebly compromised – his reticence seemed to say – by our functions, our status, our very preoccupation. What happens to trust in the realm of abuse? 'I think,' he resumed, 'the truth may lie somewhere in the middle.'

Harding told me about studies that were under way to try to fix the extent of the problem. His absence of rhetoric, his determination that the NSPCC was unapologetically committed to children's welfare – and nothing else – had begun to turn the issue around in my mind.

'We have come across a case,' Harding had told me, 'where children were terribly abused and no doubt ritual was involved. But the point is that the significance – in the context of that abuse – of an upside-down cross is from the children's point of view totally unimportant. What's far more significant is understanding a form of coercion such as this – if you're going to help the victims overcome it.'

Heading north towards Birmingham, on the service centreless M40, I read the fact file from the NSPCC on 'Child Abuse Trends in England and Wales 1988–1990'. Lying open on the passenger seat, black type set against blue vinyl, the quotidian was never more ugly. The summary presented was precise, shading 'abuse' with the solidity of 'neglect'.

The facts amassed about those whose children come to the notice of the social services could have been guessed at in a lounge bar, by anyone with the nous to state the obviousness of suffering at the bottom end of society: 'The findings showed that marital problems, financial difficulties and unemployment were the main factors affecting registered families . . . The sexually abused children were the oldest, followed by the physically injured, emotionally abused and neglected children, with the non-organic failure to thrive cases [where infants are not growing healthily and there's no medical explanation] the youngest . . .'

Sure: they will fuck you, your mum and dad, but only once you're old enough. Before that they beat up on you, scream at you and if you're small enough starve you, or dash your brains out against the wall. But there was one statement in the summary that marked the line between what has been happening in the USA and what has occurred in Britain: 'The number of physically injured children registered increased between '88 and '89, while the number of sexually abused children decreased. Possible reasons for the decline in registrations of sexual abuse could be increased caution on the part of child protection professionals following the events in Cleveland and subsequent inquiries, or the end of a reporting peak.

'The numbers for children in the emotionally abused, neglected and other categories remained constant during the study period, while those for grave concern [cases where they suspect sexual or physical abuse but cannot prove it] almost doubled.'

The NSPCC were talking about 18 per cent of 9,628 children who had been registered between 1988 and 1990. They were talking about fewer than 2,000 instances where actual sexual abuse was proven. In the USA, last year alone, over 30,000 adults came forward with 'recovered memory' evidence of having been subjected to Satanic ritual abuse as children. Even allowing for discrepancies in population base, the NSPCC were clearly not identifying a pool capable of generating such a future upsurge.

The cases in Britain in which evidence of Satanic abuse led to children being taken into care were, most notably, those of Orkney and Rochdale. The 'truth' in both cases – as in that of Cleveland – became engorged by evidence and then ruptured into 'the subsequent inquiries' the NSPCC summary gnomically referred to.

The Butler-Sloss inquiry into the Cleveland case led to new 'guidelines' being issued for the relevant agencies and to a discrediting of the RAD (Reflex-Anal Dilation test) that had set Drs Higgs and Wyatt on the path to placing 123 children in care. But even at the time (1988) of the inquiry's report being published, journalists were asking why it didn't tell the public what the ratio of correct to false diagnoses had actually been.

A highly placed source in the relevant child protection agencies told me while I was researching this piece: 'We think that up to 60 per cent of the children taken into care at Cleveland probably had been abused. But there's nothing we can do about it now.' Likewise, in the Orkney case no one ever disputed that actual abuse had taken place. The father of the 'W' family on South Ronaldsay (who were at the heart of allegations) had actually served time in jail for abusing his children. What the Clyde Report on the Orkney case reiterated was what the Butler–Sloss Report had already implied: that the extent to which social services had believed children's testimony, to that extent were they confabulating, a confabulation being the creation of truth through the admixture of fact and fantasy.

In the USA the accusations of confabulation have been far more widespread and far more damaging. The 'con-fabulation' school trace the surge of 'recovered memories' of Satanic abuse to the publication in the early eighties of a book entitled *Michelle Remembers*, written by a Canadian called Michelle Smith and her psychiatrist, Richard Padzer. Smith's accounts of Satanic ritual abuse (SRA), as it rapidly became known, were in line with the *Malleus maleficarum* check list: the abuse, torture and mutilation of people and animals; being forced to participate in the sacrifice of human adults and babies; being ceremonially married to Satan.

In 1988 two young psychiatrists, Walter C. Young and Bennett G. Braun, and the psychologist Roberta G. Sachs published a paper which became immensely influential. It was entitled 'A New Clinical Syndrome: Patients Reporting Ritual Abuse in Childhood by Satanic Cults'. Sachs was a specialist in dissociative disorders, states of mind character-ized by a confused or diminished sense of identity. The most flamboyant and recognizable of these disorders is termed MPD, or Multiple Personality Disorder. The three authors of the paper interviewed thirty-seven patients diagnosed with MPD and found that over 25 per cent produced congruent accounts of Satanic ritual abuse.

What seems to have happened next is that the cart of effect got put before the causal horse. With only internal and corroborative evidence for the veracity of these accounts of Satanic ritual abuse, the three authors hypothesized that these accounts implied Multiple Personality Disorder. They had unleashed a bush fire of diagnostic supposition. Multiple Personality Disorder, which until then had been a comparatively rare diagnosis for psychiatrists and psychotherapists to make, began to become commonplace.

In the USA three principal responses to this phenomenon have been adopted. First, there are those who, in line with the testimony of *Michelle Remembers* and another self-help guide, *The Courage to Heal*, have taken the evidence of 'recovered memories' of SRA at face value. Second, there have been those who, along with Dr George K. Ganaway (the programme director for the Ridgeview Center for Dissociative Disorders in Smyrna), have accepted the significance of 'recovered memories' of SRA, but seen them as 'screen memories' masking the more prosaic forms of abuse that are inflicted on children – the kind of things the NSPCC 'at risk' register records. Last, there have been influential professionals, such as Professor Richard Ofshe (professor of sociology at Berkeley), who have put forward the thesis that the MPD diagnosis and the SRA memories themselves are a complete confabulation between distressed patients and inept therapists.

Ofshe's publications on the subject question the validity of Freudian psychoanalytic psychiatry in general. Ofshe (along with such critics of Freudianism as Jeffrey Masson) points to the dithering that surrounded Freud's original reclassification of his analysands' accounts of childhood sexual abuse as fantasies or 'projections'. Masson has accused Freud of hypocritically turning his back on what he knew to be the truth: namely that these patients actually had been sexually abused. Ofshe makes the reverse point that Freud was utilizing the same techniques that 'recovered memory' therapists use today, namely hypnosis, interpersonal pressure, leading and suggestion. And that furthermore he never considered the possibility that the 'memories' of abuse were pure confabulations. Rather, he chose to see them as true fantasies, the result of repressed instinctual sexual drives.

None of this would be remotely important or worth running over again were it not for the tremendous impact that Freudian ideas have had on our culture. None of it would be germane were it not that, at the time of writing, fifteen American states have altered their constitutions to admit testimony derived from 'memories' recovered in therapy. There are men and women either already in jail or awaiting trial in the USA on the basis of such evidence.

It is possible to argue that the particular way in which the SRA phenomenon has spread in the USA is unique to that society. The USA is a country where there is still a strong Christian fundamentalist minority. Forty per cent of Americans are regular churchgoers, as against 5 per cent in the UK. The USA is also the culture where Freudian ideas caught on and were institutionalized most rapidly. And lastly there is the relative impact of the various 'strong' schools of feminist psychotherapy. It is ironic indeed that, in seeking to discredit the Freudian attribution of memories of sexual abuse to 'pure fantasy', many feminist psychotherapists may have fallen into the same trap as the

Great Paternalist: namely, refusing to accept the role of the therapist herself in leading an unstable or neurotic patient towards a delusory 'answer' to her or his problems.

If I wanted a graphic illustration of the difference between British and American cultural response as regards this issue, I couldn't have chosen a better person to visit than Dr James Phillips. It would be fair to say that with friends like Dr Phillips, the believers in the validity of recovered memories of Satanic ritual abuse don't need any enemies. Entering his surgery in Northfield, Birmingham, was like coming into the fateful snicker-snack atmosphere of a closed psychiatric ward.

Dr Phillips has been carving a media presence for himself as a result of his allegations of Satanism both high and low in British society. He is an enthusiastic propagator of the Multiple Personality Disorder diagnosis. He has been suspended by the General Medical Council (the result, he claims, of a 'Satanist conspiracy'), and is being forced to wind down his practice as a GP.

Dr Phillips and his associate in the 'Jupiter Trust' he has founded, Gordon Lochead, present the 'strong' thesis that up to one in ten Britons are members of a Satanic cult that permeates our entire society. They would both find the first-hand testimony with which I began this article highly credible. Indeed, as I talked to them in a cramped sepia room at the top of the gloomy, deserted surgery, the sunny Sunday outside receded, to be replaced by the fusty coldness of despair and grasping at psychic straws.

I presented myself to Phillips and Lochead as a potential patient, someone who had suffered throughout his life from problems with alcohol and drug addiction (I was misdiagnosed as a chronic alcoholic and drug addict in 1986), someone who felt the presence of an amorphous leviathan of disturbing – but repressed – memory nipping at the heels of his consciousness.

It didn't surprise me at all that they went for this like hounds after a scent: 'If only we could have you with us for a couple of weeks,' said Phillips, 'then we could really do some work together.' The more I showed myself to be compliant, the more flamboyant their revelations of Satanism became. They named government ministers as Satanists, pointed to the suicide of Jocelyn Cadbury as a cult 'hit', and spoke of 'thousands of corpses' buried at the 'ceremonial site' of the Rollright Stones.

It was spooky being with them. They both spoke of their own multiple personalities as if they were in the room with us, floating overhead like dreamers in a Chagall painting: 'Oh, yes,' said Phillips, speaking of his 'John Barleycorn' drinking persona, 'he's a real bugger to get along with, a real drag to have around, isn't he, Gordon?'

Gordon, a pale, intense Scot with a ginger beard, voiced vigorous assent to this. At one point during our conversation, first Gordon and then 'the Doctor' himself had to absent themselves to help a woman alcoholic they were treating in the surgery. 'She has the DTs,' Gordon explained, 'the Doctor is just giving her something to help her out.'

I couldn't wait to get out of the place. But I wasn't being entirely disingenuous. What experience I have of the attribution or diagnosis of childhood sexual abuse as a causal factor lying behind other more obvious psychological disorders comes from my own past on-off membership of twelve-step programmes such as Alcoholics Anonymous and Narcotics Anonymous, and my residence at a Minnesota Method treatment centre for four months in the mid-eighties. It was here that I first ran up against the idea that repressed memories of childhood sexual abuse could be the actual cause of subsequent alcoholism and drug addiction.

Interestingly, of course, the nexus of religion and psychotherapy that you find around the twelve-step programmes resembles the cultural ambience of the USA. Furthermore, the Minnesota Method of treatment for addiction and alcoholism is itself an American import. Among the psychotherapeutic disciplines that have clustered around the twelve-step programmes are such 'eclectic' schools as Psychosynthesis. This is a therepeutic method wherein clients are encouraged both to enact various 'sub-personalities' and to look for some fundamental, buried, repressed trauma, which can explain their subsequent flight from reality into the neurosis of drinking and drugging behaviour.

It had long occurred to me that both the diagnosis of alcoholism and drug addiction as a 'disease' and indeed the very structure of the twelve-step movement itself represented a microcosm of a wider cultural malaise. I myself underwent therapy with a psychosynthesist for some time at the beginning of this year. The therapist – who I would regard as highly responsible within all reasonable bounds – was nonetheless firmly convinced of the significance of memory repression within my malaise. I broke off the treatment when I began to feel that the search for this elusive trauma was beginning to eclipse more immediate concerns.

But now, as I gratefully powered my way out of Birmingham and on to the southbound M5, more of the rows of ratiocination in this strange Rubik's cube of socio-psychological speculation appeared to be clicking into place.

My last port of call was to visit a man called Roger Scotford, who has been attracting a fair share of media interest in the last few months. Scotford has set up an organization called Adult Children Accusing Parents (ACAP). This is the British equivalent of the False Memory Society, the support group for parents in the USA who say they have been wrongly accused of inflicting (usually Satanic) sexual abuse on their children.

Scotford's daughter claims to have 'recovered' memories of his sexual abuse of her during homeopathic treatment. These recovered memories are brutal and graphic although not specifically of SRA. Scotford, an attractive, greying man in his fifties, slightly fey but with an engaging manner, was a positive torrent of information on 'False Memory Syndrome' and all related matters. Everything in his manner said: 'You can't possibly believe that these accusations are real, can you?' His charming house and flower garden were a picture of Kate Greenaway-style homeliness. He was scrupulous in his need to differentiate between the 'robust' hypothesis of 'recovered' or 'false' memories of childhood sexual abuse, and those memories that had elements of continuity, which therefore should be regarded as being probably true.

Since Scotford set up ACAP he told me he had been 'approached by some people who quite possibly were paedophiles. We don't accept people into our organization unreservedly, we ask them to complete a questionnaire which provides a contextualization for the accusations.' Scotford himself is clearly agonized – but by what? the doubters ask. One journalist friend who had already interviewed him voiced reservations about his testimony. His response to the accusations was after all congruent with either guilt or innocence.

His first wife (the mother of the adult daughter who has accused Scotford) has been reported to have said, 'There is no smoke without fire.' Scotford showed me a letter from a former neighbour. The neighbour wrote to a journalist at the *Daily Mail* who had written a piece sympathetic to Scotford: 'I have observed and admired the courage of those two young women [Scotford's daughters] in their attempt to cope and deal with their horrific memories. If Roger Scotford cared about his daughters why would he wish to publicize his views in this way with thinly disguised photographs and his home number?'

But then isn't this the true definition of a modern witch-hunt? A situation in which the accused's very protestations of innocence can be taken as evidence of guilt? I have no wish to come down on one side or the other in any particular case. Which is why, despite Scotford's urgings, I didn't take up the trail that led to his elder daughter (the one who has made the most graphic accusations). Rather, while I was talking to Scotford, I began to arrive at a vivid picture of a culture that has lost its way.

To reiterate: I would agree with Jim Harding at the NSPCC that the widespread existence of sexual abuse of children is an unpalatable truth that has only recently and coaxingly begun to be acknowledged. However, the climate within which it has come to light is not one lit up by 'common sense' or reason. Rather we are a society in which the way we govern our sexuality has become uncoupled from collective ethics. What can we make of a culture in which the rituals associated with menstruation are those of advertising rather than religion? 'Look, no blood!' exclaim the ubiquitous advertisements on the television. In semiotic terms they represent a simultaneous celebration and suppression of a biological reality. In the USA the declivity between feminists and the alleged 'backlash' against feminism has come to encompass the debate about Satanic ritual abuse as well. Feminists here, such as Suzy Orbach, are appalled by the idea that accepting the fictitiousness of 'recovered' memories may lead to some kind of climate in which it becomes difficult, once again, for adults who have been abused as children to come forward and talk about what has happened to them. This is certainly something we should all be worried about.

But when I lay down on my bed after a hard day's driving and talking I found it only too easy to confabulate my way into the hideous scenario I set out at the beginning of this piece. The furniture of the delusion comes from the vestiges of Christianity that lie within my mental prop department. Satanism is after all a construct which owes its existence to its opposite. The mechanics of the delusion I adapted from psychoanalysis with its concentration on the 'false bottom' of self-conscious memory. I can admit to my own suggestibility; what I cannot admit to is being the Devil's disciple.

But however implacable and empirical the testimony of people like Jim Harding, there really is no commonsensical view of these matters. He told me that the NSPCC saw many cases 'where sexual interference with children took place within a context whereby it was judged less damaging to leave the children in their homes than remove them'. Judged by whom? And according to what standard? Which brings us full circle to the proposition I first set out: that we live in a culture elements of which are under threat from forms of cultism. And one thing is for certain: it's not going away.

It is egregious to quote one's own work, but in my novella *Bull* I made an observation which seems to sum up the current introjection of our culture's moral queasiness: 'In this world where all are mad, and none are bad, we all know that the finger that points, also points backwards.'

Harpers & Queen, November 1993

Head-Hunting for Eternity

On a hot day in May I took Highway 99 and drove as fast as I could inland from Los Angeles. Trundling along the broad swathe of concrete, I felt as if I were trying to escape the inundation of this limitless city, which like some urban tidal wave kept on coursing in from the Pacific. But even in the outermost 'burbs, where Mainstreet USA laps against the bleached bones of the Californian hills, there was still an orange tinge of smog in the air. It made everything look underexposed, like a photograph which had been rejected by quality control.

After three hours in Riverside at the headquarters of the Alcor Life Extension Foundation, it was no longer the smog that imparted a sense of unreality, but the fact that I'd been in earnest convocation with a group of people who are deeply committed to sawing each other's heads off after death and then plunging them in liquid nitrogen. Their objective? Nothing short of immortality. They call themselves cryonicists. Lots of other people, including the vast majority of the scientific establishment, call them Dagenham – two stops beyond Barking.

The place where the 'suspensions' take place is far from being some citadel of *Blade Runner*-style hardware. It's just another breeze-block building on another industrial estate, right down to the textured louvres in the diminutive vestibule.

234

I had seen the smiling likenesses of the already suspended Alcor members. I'd admired the rather dated ambulance the cryonicists had kitted out as a rapid-response vehicle. And I had stood and goggled at the operating table where the 'patients' are prepared for possible immortality.

Now it was show-and-tell time. I was ushered into the aluminium-sided, concrete-floored warehousing unit which contains those members of the Alcor Life Extension Foundation who are already in suspension. The cumbersome lid of the 'neuro-suspension chamber' was being unbolted by Hugh, a huffy cryonicist in his fifties, dressed scoutmasterishly in a tan shirt with epaulettes and pressed chinos.

Coddled inside the chamber were seventeen individual heads. The heads of people who had died of cancer, cardiac arrest and even Aids. Not that these heads could actually be seen, of course – that would have been macabre. No, no, they were all tidily packed away in individual canisters, in cold store until at least the next millennium. It was like some low-budget version of *Alien* with set design by Texas Homecare instead of H. R. Giger.

The liquid nitrogen gave off a froth of condensation. Hugh and I stared down into the chamber. Among the submerged head-boxes (or 'neurocans', as they are properly called) I could see something else, something that looked decidedly prosaic, something made out of blue linen. 'What's that?' I asked, pointing.

Hugh huffed. 'Oh, it's a pillowcase.'

'I see, and what's it got in it?'

He grunted again. 'Miscellaneous objects.'

'What sort of miscellaneous objects?' My mind reeled. I knew that these people believed in the possibility of whole body cloning; that's why they were prepared to lose their heads after death. Could it be that they also imagined a future science capable of recreating them from still more slender leftovers? Was the blue pillowcase full of ears? Fingers? Perhaps even toenail clippings? Ralph Whelon, a thin, young cryonicist, spoke up.

'They're pets,' he snapped, 'the pets of people who've been suspended.'

Those pets stayed with me throughout my sojourn among the cryonicists, and long afterwards – the pets and the severed head of Saul Kent's mother, Dora, of which more later. Naturally the blue pillowcase was full of pets, for were you to be brought back from death far in the future, with human society incalculably altered, having your very own doggie to hand would do more for your mental adjustment than a spaceship full of psychologists.

That is cryonics in a nutshell: a bizarre marriage between scientism run amok and dewy-eyed sentimentality. As I journeyed around California from one freeze-dried fanatic to the next, a picture of the cryonics community emerged that was at one and the same time reassuring – all too clearly these people were Dagenham – and yet unsettling, because the very form that their delusion takes mirrors the profound spiritual difficulties our culture has in coming to terms with death.

I first became aware of cryonics in the seventies when, as a sci-fi-obsessed teenager, I read an article in the *Observer* magazine, eerily illustrated with pictures of cadavers lain out like presentation salmon on back-lit beds of crinkle-cut ice. It seemed fairly logical to me as a thirteen-year-old materialist. If the mind and the brain are one and the same, I reasoned, and could somehow be preserved at the moment of death, it would be possible for the highly advanced scientists of the future to reboot it, to switch it on again.

But there was another sci-fi story that also gripped me. It portrayed a future in which wealthy people who were terminally ill had their diseased bodies amputated and then went on living as disembodied heads mounted on life-support racks. The first line of the story went something like this: 'For breakfast this morning I had twelve dozen Dover number one oysters and a jeroboam of Dom Perignon – then they removed the bucket.' This seemed an ideal life to me.

Of course, I know now that if I'd joined the Alcor group, or some other gaggle of cryonicists, I'd be spending my summer holidays at life extension conferences at Lake Tahoe. For I had all the psychological factors in place: a genuine willingness to entrust my head to science – whether real or fictional – and an exaggerated fear of death. All the committed cryonicists I met in California had that make-up.

Arguably, the cryogenic dewars (storage canisters) I saw at the Riverside Alcor facility are the lineal descendants of the chamber tombs of the Orkneys, the Sutton Hoo burial ship and the pyramids themselves. But the idea that preserved bodies might be animated by some scientific process dates back to the eighteenth century and Benjamin Franklin, who wanted to be pickled in Madeira: 'I wish it were possible . . . to invent a method of embalming drowned persons, in such a manner that they may be recalled to life at any period, however distant.'

Freezing as a method of preservation came to the fore in this century, predictably from science fiction, which has a lot to answer for in spawning cults. L. Ron Hubbard, the founder of Scientology, was a sci-fi writer, and there's a congruence between Scientology and cryonics. True, cryonicists have no similarly charismatic cult leader. No, the more they spoke, the more

237

I understood what they worshipped. It was their own heads.

The cryonicists' bible is actually a 'factual' book, *The Prospect of Immortality*, published in 1964 by one Robert Ettinger, a junior college physics instructor in Michigan. He argued that cryogenic (or 'tissue freezing') technology and medicine were already well enough advanced for the 'front end', the practical bit, of the cryonics procedure to be worth undertaking. He now runs the Cryonics Institute in Oak Park, Michigan. However, the honour of the first suspension belongs to the Alcor group and Dr James Bedford, who died in California in August 1967, and who now resides, along with the pillowcase full of pets, at the Alcor facility in Riverside.

It was Steve Bridge, a rather doggily earnest cryonicist, who welcomed me to Alcor and took me through cryonics history. He explained that the Alcor people deny the sovereignty of death – in the literature I had received, the word death wasn't even mentioned; it's referred to as 'deanimation'.

I steeled myself: would Bridge make a play for my head from the off? In the event, he was happy to laugh at some of his odder beliefs. We talked about the early suspensions. 'Oh, they were extremely crude!' he giggled. 'They knew very little about chemistry or biology, and even used mortuary pumps to do the perfusion!'

'Perfusion', a much-used word in Alcor literature, is the pumping out of the blood and its replacement with a cryoprotective fluid, a glycerol and sucrose-based compound which retains its liquidity once the 'patient' is chilled to −196°C. Really, the efficacy or otherwise of perfusion is at the very core of whether or not cryonics has any validity whatsoever.

Contemporary science maintains that cells can be irreparably damaged during freezing: any remaining water in the cells forms ice which expands and ruptures them. But, say cryonicists, those clever third-millennium boffins will know what to do. They will send in vast armies of 'nanomachines': tiny, molecular-sized devices, each carrying an on-board computer and capable of physically repairing cellular damage. The nanomachines will communicate with each other, and with vast computers outside the body, in such a way as to reanimate us – not as we were, decrepit and worn out, but restored to the full flower of our youth. And where a 'neuro' (severing the head) rather than a whole body suspension has been done, our missing bodies will be cloned from DNA in surviving cells.

The cryonics literature takes gruesome delight in the makeshift surgery of the suspension procedure. But, as I read case histories of individuals who have fought to be suspended, I found myself becoming emotionally involved. These people spent the last harrowing days of their lives fighting battles with doctors and coroners to ensure that they were pronounced 'dead' as quickly as possible, so that the Alcor team standing by could get perfusing. I felt myself working alongside, champing at the bit, waiting to assist with the insertion of a catheter or a femoral artery cut-down.

Here is the description of the pivotal moment in the cryonic suspension of Eugene Donovan: 'Gene died at 8.19 a.m. on the morning of 21 March 1989. All of us were with him. The hospice nurse pronounced death and from somewhere in the room someone said, "Let's go!" We all quickly wiped our tears and the transport began.

'Jim did manual CPR [cardiopulmonary resuscitation] while Mike and Steve hooked up the HLR [heart-lung resuscitation]. Jerry placed an endotracheal tube. I tried to place an intravenous catheter, and Diane, Gene III and Ray assisted all of us . . .'

Hardly what you'd call a graceful departure from this world. But it drew me – another wannabe surgeon – inexorably towards the question of what it would feel like to start hacking away at the body of someone I'd personally known. Ralph Whelon, the Alcor vice-president, was gung ho on this: 'Even on the first suspension I assisted with, no doubts crossed my mind. It isn't something that's done lightly or nonchalantly. Sure, it takes a strong stomach, but that in itself strengthens commitment.'

But what would Steve Bridge feel, holding my head as it was 'carefully separated surgically at the sixth cervical vertebra'? 'Well, I have to admit,' he said somewhat ruefully, 'once your head has been removed, that becomes the patient. The rest of your body is just a cadaver and we treat it accordingly. But put it this way, I wouldn't have made a good doctor. I can't stand to find myself in a situation where I can't do something for someone.'

Bridge, in fact, used to be a children's librarian, and it transpired that not one of these cryonic pioneers had what amounted to a formal medical training. Had I sought suspension over the past two decades, my front-end man-ager would have most likely been either a jet-propulsion engineer, a dialysis technician, a surgical assistant, or a vet. But Bridge was unashamed about this apparent lack of formal qualifications. 'In the early days, we thought that once they saw what we were doing, establishment scientists would quickly get involved and improve the technique. But that wasn't the way it worked out. We found we had to do it all ourselves.'

The Alcor Life Extension Foundation is the largest cryonics

group, with twenty-seven patients suspended so far, ten of them 'whole body' and seventeen 'neuro': there are three hundred or so cryonicists worldwide, but only forty-eight are suspended. They still offer competitive rates: £80,000 for whole body suspension and £25,000 for neuro. Storage and maintenance costs are only £44 a year for your head and £570 for the whole body. This covers topping you up regularly with liquid nitrogen so that you don't get too clammy and, presumably, changing your pillowcase as well. If money is a problem, insurance policies can be amortized. A modest sum invested will provide the income for storage, maintenance and, who knows, maybe a little nest egg with which to buy your first space station.

Reading these costings was like being droned at by a financial adviser: 'Right, Mr Self. We've sorted out your accident insurance and your PEPs for the kids' education. Now there's just your suspension payments left to arrange.'

Alcor, nonetheless, make no profit, and every board member is fully committed and signed up for suspension. Perhaps mutual aid has ensured their survival. Other cryonics societies have come and gone. When I went to visit Thomas Donaldson, an Alcor member in northern California, he told me of one failed cryonics group where they had all simply 'walked away from the situation, which caused a big stink . . . literally!'

But, notwithstanding Alcor's high ideals, something made me feel slightly uneasy about signing my head over to them. As I talked to Whelon and Bridge, a picture emerged of embattled cryonicists fighting legal battles with the Riverside Coroner and the California Department of Health Services over their right to do suspensions. In 1987, this legal battle had focused on one person – Saul Kent's mother, Dora, and in particular her head.

ON OTHER THINGS

It was the cryonic suspension of Dora Kent which brought the Riverside Coroner's Department down on Alcor. According to the Riverside Press Enterprise for 3 October 1990: 'The coroner's office determined that Kent died of a lethal dose of barbiturates and sought homicide charges. Alcor officials said the drugs were administered after Kent's death to prepare her body for freezing.'

Alcor won its legal battle with the coroner and the California Department of Health Services, and now has the right to continue doing suspensions and storing bodies. But to this day no one will reveal where Dora Kent's head is. The boys at Alcor will only say that it's not in the neuro-suspension chamber with the other patients.

My head – Dora Kent's head. That night, as I lay tossing and turning on my bed at the Shangri La Hotel in Santa Monica, I dreamed of immortality. I was awakening from a deep sleep, swimming up through the grasping tendrils of Morpheus towards the light. I could feel within my body a strange sensation. It felt as if myriad little pulsing things were moving about in there. Then it came to me. I was being reanimated! The suspension had worked.

I'm a little unsteady as the attendants help me out of the reanimation chamber. I look down groggily at my legs. They definitely are my legs, but they look better than they did during my previous animation: smoother, more muscular, more youthful. One of the reanimation technicians comes over. She's shy but a bit puffed up. Like a child about to bestow a gift. She holds up a mirror. 'Would you like to see what a good job we've done for you?' she says. I look at my reflection and then wake up screaming and screaming. They muddled me up! For in the mirror, crudely attached to my own lanky neck, was the wizened bonce of an elderly woman. I was half Self, half Kent.

The following morning, vowing never again to stay in

a hotel with any connection to Lost Horizon, I headed off back up Route 99. I was going to confront Son of Head.

Saul Kent was one of the first ten people to become seriously involved with cryonics in the sixties. It was he who persuaded Ettinger that he needed to do something practical in support of his theories. Kent helped to found the Cryonics Society of New York and then came west in search of more converts. Although still a member, he is no longer directly involved with Alcor.

I found him deep in the suburban hinterland of Riverside, holed up in a typical faux adobe Californian house with a large Alsatian called Franklin. 'Franklin is a wonder dog,' he explained, kneading the dog's scruff with a large hand. 'He's been technically dead for over six hours. All the blood was drained out of his brain and he was taken down to around 4°C. No EEG activity at all. Then he was brought back – and look at him!' Franklin wagged his tail reanimatedly. He was in frisky contrast to his master, who looked distinctly liverish.

Kent is the ideologue of cryonics. He has written three books and numerous magazine articles. These are a strange gallimaufry of concepts drawn from the wilder shores of artificial intelligence, futurology and cognitive theory, all of which when added together depict a future in which science will be omnipotent, immortality assured and mankind will be living in self-created worlds gently orbiting the sun.

He fixed me with sag-bag eyes and expounded at length on how as a child of four or five he had decided it would be 'a bad thing' to die. This kindergarten epiphany had led him to a life of cryonics. 'Mind you,' he continued, 'I really view being suspended as the second worst thing that can happen to me after death itself. What I really want is to live healthily for as long as possible.' Now he hardly thought about death at all.

As Saul banged on, I started casting furtive glances around the room. Was there, perhaps, a neurocan tucked behind one of the canework bookcases? After all, Oedipus schmoedipus, what greater love can a son have for a mother than to chop off her head and stash it about the house?

But if Dora Kent's head had gone AWOL, what chance for my own? The boys at Alcor had given me alarming news. They were confident about their ability to keep their patients cool, but at the same time they gaily informed me that Riverside was the Californian city with the highest risk of an earthquake. They were now seeking a new site for the facility, possibly in northern California or Arizona. I began to suspect that, once I had entrusted my head to these people, it might end up doing more travelling when deanimated than it had with me still attached.

So I left LA and took the shuttle north to San Francisco. I was going to meet Thomas Donaldson and encounter the cryonics credo in full flight. For here was a man who had become obsessed by cryonics in the early seventies, and had then discovered in 1985 that he had a brain tumour.

His house was an hour's drive through the rain, down the coast from San Francisco towards Big Sur, and a very modest house it was, too – a little house made of ticky-tacky. The uninformed might imagine that plenty of millionaires would sign up for suspension, just for the hell of it. But, in fact, most cryonicists are fairly typically middle-class. Donaldson was no exception. A former maths teacher and computer software designer, he confirmed my impression of cryonicists as the ultimate computer nerds, with his trollishly sparse hair (for natural and therapeutic reasons) and his vocal delivery, horribly reminiscent of the comedian Emo Phillips.

I found him hunched up in his cardy. 'Aaaaah . . . OK! If they know enough to bring you back, they're going to know enough to grow you a new body . . . aaaah . . . OK?' That's why he was signed up for the head job alone. 'As soon as I knew I had the tumour, I thought: this is it, this is the battle I've been waiting for.' But his fight to have himself suspended immediately, before his legal 'death', proved unsuccessful. Some might think him lucky. His tumour hasn't spread and he is now in his fifth year of remission.

Perhaps it was his distance from the cryonic cockpit in LA that allowed him to talk more casually about his fellow cryonicists. 'When the coroners came for Dora Kent's head,' he confided, 'it wasn't there!' He giggled rather loonily. 'It had been removed.'

But then he went on and on, trotting out exactly the same tedious arguments. Sitting in his dun little room, with the rain coursing down the windows, my head began to deanimate with boredom. I sensed that it was time to leave the cryonicists.

However, back in England, I kept thinking: what if I had a deathbed conversion and decided, after all, that I wanted immortality on the instalment plan? Ralph Whelon had told me there was a front-end facility in England. I called the number he had given me and got one Garret Smyth. Was it true? 'Well, yes,' said a young, educated voice. 'We can perfuse you and lower your body temperature to dry-ice levels, around −79°C. Then we have a cool box to transport you to California. We don't handle storage here.'

'Where's here?' I asked guilelessly.

'Eastbourne,' replied the immortalist.

I could see his point about storage: there are already far too many deanimated people on the south coast of England.

But I didn't feel comfortable about gifting my head to the British cryonicists. There are only sixteen of them and none have actually done a suspension yet. It sounded like entrusting your head to them would be a recipe for guerrilla theatre at the Wintergardens.

That night, Dora Kent's head came to me again, grinning cheesily like a low-rent version of Hamlet Senior's ghost. At 3 a.m. I called Ralph Whelon in California. 'Come on, Ralph,' I said. 'Open up on the question of Saul's mum's head. For Christ's sake, where is it?'

'It's not a question we answer,' he purred. 'I told you that. We won't tell anyone until we're absolutely sure she's safe.'

And when will that be? Orthodox science is still a long way from complying with cryonicists. Saul Kent had told me he had a renegade cryobiologist working at his new laboratory, but that he preferred to remain incognito. The Society for Cryobiology, an official medical organization, states that its board of governors may either suspend or deny membership to anyone who engages in or promotes 'any practice or application of freezing deceased persons in the anticipation of their reanimation'.

Dr David Pegg of the East Anglian Regional Blood Transfusion Service sighed when I cited this. 'What the cryobiological community objects to is the impression these people give that the science has reached a point where some basis for this procedure exists. The suspension process just isn't meaningful when a patient is well and truly dead. They've died of something and there is no known remedy for it. That puts what these people are doing well into the realm of fantasy. What we object to as cryobiologists is the way they use the trappings of science to create a mystical atmosphere. They're just like priests dressing up for some ritual.'

But, in fairness to the cryonicists, isn't their response to the tyranny of death in a godless world at least understandable? They point out that in modern Western societies the vast majority of health expenditure tends to be in the last few months of a person's life. We seem to have created a culture of medical expertise dedicated to squeezing the last pips of consciousness out of near cadavers.

The modern way of death is already tied up in the tubing of an ostensibly life-saving technology. We die in hospitals, laid out on scientific altars. Perhaps the cryonicists are only taking this manifest faith in science to its logical and startling conclusion? The strange truth is that, since cryonicists started perfusing corpses with mortuary pumps in the late sixties, scientific research has been advancing towards the cryonicists' somewhat expanded view of the possible. Parallel computing; nanotechnology (or molecular machines); concepts of cyberspace and, of course, genetic engineering – these are no longer just the dreams of cranks, they are fields of legitimate research eating up many millions of dollars.

And what a delicious irony it would be if cryonics were to work, after all. Saul Kent had told me he had no doubts about his own reanimation: 'If you're being suspended now, you're not going to be one of the first ones back. The people being suspended fifty or a hundred years from now are going to be far easier to work on. If you're being suspended now, you'll have a long time to wait, perhaps thousands of years.'

But there will come a time when even those subject to the guerrilla theatre of the early suspensions will be revived – brave survivalists of time itself. And it will be a shock for the immortals of the future to discover that the pioneers, daring non-conformists all, are just a small posse of rather strident bores. I'll have to sign up for suspension so I can at least have a natter with Dora Kent's head, a frolic with Franklin the wonder dog. We'll all have such a lot of catching up to do.

Esquire, September 1993

Do You Believe in the Westway?

I come over all emotional when I think about the Westway. Really, I do. I can remember its completion in 1970 and my first 'grown-up' ride on it a few years later. High, on the pillion of a moped, caroming across all four lanes in the heat of a summer night.

It was so shockingly futuristic, an embodiment of all the science fictions I had ever read. A road sweeping across the city's cubist scape; clean, shiny, slicing by block after block in elegantly plotted curve after curve. Then tantalizing with a final roller-coaster plunge over the Marylebone Flyover, before depositing you, dazed by the hubbub after the cool heights, in the bebop beat of Central London.

Perhaps such eulogizing seems excessive. I think not. The fundamental experience of driving the Westway remains the same. And drive it I do. In the last week alone some twenty-odd times. On each occasion it never fails to work its magic. Especially when I come on at the White City junction and am driving completely on automatic, registering nothing but the subconscious 'chnk-chnk-chnk' of tyres over the deck sections of the flyover, only to come to when the road narrows at Paddington Green, and appreciate yet again the perfect movie-poster image that the windscreen provides as I swoop by the Buck Rogers British Rail maintenance depot and commence my descent.

I'm not alone in finding this building, set as it is on the

most vertiginous yet satisfying of the Westway's curves, a monument to the best that architectural modernism has to offer. Chris Petit, the film critic turned director, used just this windscreen-framed image for the poster of *Radio On*, a brave attempt at a British road movie.

The maintenance depot was built at the same time as the bulk of the flyover itself and the same consulting engineers, Maunsell, worked with Paul Hamilton the architect. For some years now I have wondered why it was that the building looked so neglected. To my way of thinking this has to be one of the finest pieces of real estate in the capital. Although, I concede, it's not everybody's idea of fun to have 70,000 vehicles driving straight towards you every hour of the working day, only peeling away at the last second.

The answer is predictable: the maintenance depot is scheduled for demolition. Ironic, really, that what twenty years ago was regarded as a hideous piece of urban brutalism now looks elegant and elegiac, set against the bypass-bound corporate banality which is to replace it.

David Lee, now the chairman of Maunsell, is the man who, for want of a better designation, I would call the Father of the Westway. Would he object to this? 'Well, yes,' he told me, 'because really I was quite a young man when I worked on the road.' Young, maybe, but a visionary for all that.

I spent a couple of hours indulging my Westway obsession with Lee, in the prosaic surroundings of Room 401 at the Civil Engineering building of Imperial College, where he is a visiting professor. But as we talked and he started to describe the flowing curves of my favourite flyover with capable, constructive hands, I could see that within his breast there beat the heart of an artist.

At last I broached this very point. Naturally he demurred. 'It's true,' he said, 'that I was the project designer and had overall responsibility. But the line of the flyover itself, which is in many ways the most aesthetically pleasing aspect of it, was determined more by necessity than design. There were only certain places that we could situate the piers, so we had to create a line that conformed to this and at one and the same time produced a good driving surface.'

In this respect I think Lee and his team were triumphant. The Westway is foremost a drivers' road. It was no surprise to learn that he himself is the 'addictive' owner of a Maserati Spyder, and that at the time of the flyover's construction he was piloting a stylish Jaguar 2+2 around London's roads. 'We also wanted to create a kind of triumphal entry to the city,' he went on. 'My company was involved in designing the Hammersmith Flyover, which is in many ways revolutionary. But when we built the Westway it was entirely innovatory, both technically and as the longest elevated roadway in Europe at that time.'

A road linking Central London with the west had long been on the drawing-board at the old London County Council. Looking back over the clippings, I found references to the agitations of tenants' groups to prevent such a scheme as early as 1937. It wasn't until the 'white heat of technology' was climbing the thermometer in the 1960s that the possibility of putting the road in the air became feasible at anything like a realistic cost.

'The scheme was ground-breaking as far as legislation was concerned,' Lee said. 'Up until then there weren't really the mechanisms in place for buying the land needed for a project like this. The Westway changed that.' Nevertheless, he conceded that 'Nowadays we wouldn't dream of constructing a major thoroughfare quite so close to people's houses.'

Lee was as enthusiastic in describing the flyover's techno-logical specification as I am in talking about driving it. Now

I know that the first section, which lifts you in one clean swoop from White City to the main deck, is a single piece of pre-stressed concrete, as is the elevated roundabout below. Now I know that where the Harrow Road underpass dives down towards Royal Oak, and the road is on three separate levels for a brief period, the construction required that the actual deck itself be free-floating over static piers. Now I know that the Westway was originally designed to have only two carriageways throughout, and that the hard shoulder was added towards the end of its construction. Lee's team used some of the first big computers employed in such tasks to crunch the mighty numbers required to make such a quick change with pinpoint accuracy.

Most of the political agitation that surrounded the road's construction has died away. 'They said that it would destroy communities,' said the Father of the Westway mournfully, as if speaking of a hooligan son, 'but I made provision in the Ladbroke Grove area for business and community spaces to be actually built into the body of the structure, and I believe that today there are over seventy businesses operating out of the flyover.'

He's right, of course. Anyone who strolls down the Portobello Road on a Saturday afternoon cannot help but be aware of the area under the flyover as a particularly vibrant, ineluctably commercial little community. Yet it is also here that the worst of the Carnival riots have been centred in past years. Here, around Albany Place and Basing Street, where the big bass-driven sound systems are set up and the Sensurround dub music provides a concrete-jarring rhythmic counterpoint to the heavy engineering of the flyover itself.

The flyover tends to have had a bad cultural press for just this reason. Films of recent years, such as *Breaking Glass* and *Sammy and Rosie Get Laid*, have set scenes of riot and urban alienation under the grim lips of its jutting deck. One of the few entries the flyover makes into popular song is, predictably enough, in the Clash's 'London Calling'.

If you head west towards Latimer Road you enter an area where, despite the presence of workshops and a large children's daycare centre, the monumental presence of the flyover seems to have leeched the life out of the adjacent streets, leaving behind boarded-up buildings, burnt mattresses, zigzag graffiti, the detritus of urban decay.

Carrying on towards White City, the decks above divide to form the massive dilator of the elevated roundabout. It is here that, from below, the Westway is at its most visually spectacular. The sky is sliced into a series of curving wedges by the aerial carriageways. They form a basketry in the air that is at one and the same time free-floating and unbearably heavy.

In the centre of the roundabout at ground level there are a series of football pitches, a cricket net and even an area for exercising horses. A group of Queen's Park Rangers reserves were playing five-a-side when I strolled by. The ball came sailing over the netting towards me. As I booted it back, one called out to me: 'Thanks, mate, it normally goes up on the motorway.' Of course. I could imagine it only too well. Powering around the tight curve of the roundabout, thinking oneself far removed from the ground, when suddenly a football comes smashing through the windscreen!

This area is pivotal for the Westway in all sorts of ways. It is its cultural as well as its social nexus. To the left of the football pitches as you head west there is the official travellers' site for Hammersmith and Fulham. It never ceases to amaze me, and I'm sure many others, that anyone should be made to live here, where there isn't so much lead and carbon monoxide in the atmosphere as atmosphere in the lead and carbon monoxide.

Ten years ago, when the site was little more than a muddy piece of waste ground, I came for a job here as a children's playleader. At that time it looked like Calcutta, now it's more like Beirut. Nevertheless, as is ever the human way, some of the travellers have not just spruced their caravans up, but also created little gardens, window-boxes full of daffodils and geraniums, bright splashes of colour set against the ziggurat swathes of slurried stone above and behind.

The triangle of land the travellers' site occupies is important for another reason. For if Lee is the flyover's father, the Westway's poet and chronicler has to be the novelist J. G. Ballard. It is here, in the shadow of the westbound slip-road linking the main body of the flyover to the West Cross route, that the action of his masterpiece of urban alienation, *Concrete Island*, takes place.

The premise of the book is stark. An architect, driving from his Marylebone offices to his home in Richmond, comes on to the slip-road too fast and plunges off on to the waste ground below. Ballard wrote the book in the seventies, soon after the flyover was constructed and when this area was still waste ground. His hero, Maitland, then becomes trapped on this concrete island, a victim of the inhuman urban scape he himself is helping to create.

A long-time fan of Ballard's, I thought this article would be the very premise I needed to go and see him. I dashed off a letter to the great man and received a faintly despairing reply: 'I don't think I have anything very interesting to add to what I've already said about motorways and so on – all a great many years ago . . . those were the days when I was enraptured by the notion of organisms with radial tyres, etc. – how dull life seems today . . .'

Ballard's vision of the impact of the car on the city is, of course, highly ambivalent. His books *Crash*, *Concrete Island* and *Atrocity Exhibition* are at one and the same time condemnations of automotive alienation and celebrations of technological achievement, the sheer exhilaration of high speed.

Another artist who has been infected with the same ambivalence, and turned it to superb effect in considering the Westway as an artwork, is the painter Oliver Bevan. It was Lee who gave me Bevan's number. Maunsell sponsored Bevan's exhibition of Westway paintings at the Barbican in January 1993.

Bevan also came to the Westway via car trouble, although not as serious as that of Ballard's protagonist. His old Ford broke down and was towed to a garage under the elevated roundabout. The painter was entranced by the shapes the flyover's decks described and embarked on a series of large-scale canvases that elegantly capture the strange dichotomies the road represents: its beauty and its terror, its light and its darkness.

'I think the flyover conforms to old notions of the sublime,' he told me as we chatted at his Shepherd's Bush home, which also doubles as his studio. 'It has a kind of awful beauty. I can't paint anything that doesn't fill me with conflicting feelings. The Westway flyover is also a marvellous fulfilment, on a great scale, of the sort of lines and curves that we associate with the art deco period.

'It's my contention that, just as the rail termini of London, which were viewed in the nineteenth century as being merely civil-engineering works, are now held superior to much of Victorian architecture, so the Westway, the Hammersmith Flyover and other examples of twentieth-century monumentalism will be appreciated as being far more important than the modernist buildings.'

ON OTHER THINGS

Even David Lee, the bashful Father of the Westway, agreed with the substance of this. I had asked him whether or not he viewed its design as being in the spirit of Le Corbusier's brutalism? 'Oh, yes,' he replied, 'but far, far better! And I always knew that it wouldn't be until long after my death that the flyover would be properly viewed as a work of art.'

Evening Standard, May 1993

On the Edge of Blackness

In Nhulunboy even the four-wheel drives move slowly, as if tranquillized by the heat. The long stretches of asphalt are swished by sprinklers. Back off the road stand bland blocks of flats for the mining company employees. The company is Swiss and so are the blocks, which would look more comfortable in temperate Geneva.

Nhulunboy is a little enclave on the Gove Peninsula in East Arnhemland, Northern Australia. It's a warped enterprise zone where the white employees – some 3,000 of them – live, separated from the traditional black 'owners' of the area. The blacks are at Yirrakala, a fifteen-kilometre drive along roads smeared with the red dust of bauxite, between shimmering enfilades of gum trees. Everywhere you go in Gove there is this fine red dust. The bauxite forms a thickness, a layer over the entire area. The mining company is scraping this stuff off and carting it away.

Land rights for Australia's Aboriginal population is fast becoming the most pressing and controversial political issue on the country's agenda. And if you ever had any doubts about the cutting-edge nature of the Aboriginal land rights debate, Gove is the place to resolve them. For here, the land is literally being removed from beneath its owners' feet.

At the foot of the settlement, running behind the beach, all the way from the Surf and Life Saving Club to the precincts of the Gove Resort Hotel, runs a kilometre-long

257

chain-link fence, constructed in the past month. The aim of this little bit of repressive park furniture is to stop the Long Grass people from walking through the flats on their way to the beach.

It's a nasty bit of exclusion, and of course it doesn't stop the Long Grass people. They are still there, down on the beach, where the light is so sharp that their dark shadows waver and combine with the darker shadows under the trees. Here they sit, in the long grass that gives them their name, a sort of terminal moraine of discarded, silvery wine bags strewn all around. Synthetic bladders that have been torn from their cardboard exoskeletons and squeezed until they've gushed their last.

'Basically,' said Bill Moss, striding ahead of me, 'they come up here for a holiday for a month or two, do their drinking and then go back to their own communities.' For the rest of East Arnhemland – an area the size of France, with a population of around 8,000 – is dry. As you drive into Yirrakala, the sign by the road (complete with its own terminal moraine of discarded wine bags) reminds you that any vehicle that carries alcohol on to Aboriginal land will be confiscated – without compensation.

But that day there had been no question of confiscation. My old friend Bill, a white teacher who has worked for many years with the Aboriginal people, met me at the airstrip, off the Darwin plane. With him was Sam O'Brien, a 'consultant' on land and sea rights to the Yolngu people, the inhabitants of this steadily abraded paradise who've had claim on the land for many centuries past.

O'Brien, a thin, wire-wool-haired man in his mid-forties, of benign and earnest mien, was trying to gather together various of his Yolngu 'clients' for a meeting concerning the pursuit of sea rights, an area of native title not covered in any way by what is known as the 'Mabo decision'.

The Australian High Court Mabo decision, now embodied in the Native Title Act of the Australian Parliament, sets the agenda for the way in which the vexed question of Aboriginal land rights will be resolved by the Australian polity over the next decade. But while the act seems on the face of it to offer Aboriginals a means of claiming title to their traditional lands, in reality its provisions are hedged around on all sides.

Native title to land which has been alienated is extinguished; pastoral and mining leases are held to be valid forms of such alienation. There are instances where such leases have contained provisions for Aborigine rights, but their extent is disputed by both Aboriginals and white lessees seeking to retain title. Conversely, Aboriginals who wish to claim title, even to unalienated land, have to prove a 'continuous association'. This requirement hits not only at deracinated Aboriginal people – who may have difficulties proving such an association with any land – but also at more settled and traditional groups.

Pat Turner, the charismatic head of Atsic (the Aboriginal and Torres Strait Islander Commission, the chief quango through which Aboriginal affairs are handled by the Commonwealth), herself an Aranda woman from the centre of Australia, put it to me thus: 'We have to do this [become involved in Mabo test cases] for the whitefellas, so that they understand the rules . . . But the onus of proof is unbelievable. My people have to sell their souls to white judges to prove they own the country.'

While I was in Canberra the first round of fiscal brouhaha, concerning the size of the budget to be allocated for compensation (to all parties concerned), was getting under way in the House of Representatives. The Parliament House sits beneath a huge steel flagpole that looks uncannily like a monumental hypodermic syringe. Inside, desultory representatives intoned their way through preliminary minutes, while monocellular clutches of Japanese tourists were hustled through the public gallery.

Of such sights is Australia comprised: at times the white presence seems to strain to make itself felt in this oceanic continent. Like some smear of Vegemite on the edge of a giant piece of toast, the Big Five white cities turn their backs on the hinterland – still inhabited by an ancient and profoundly different race – and settle down to watch *Home and Away*.

There's a psychic as well as a physical fault line that runs between black and white in Australia, one that is being plotted by an army of academics. A Canadian anthropologist, based at the Australian National University, joked with me at a cocktail party in suburban Canberra (really a tautology, as all Canberra is a suburb): 'Oh, yes,' he smiled wryly, 'there is such an enormous exchange of academics studying various aspects of our respective indigenous peoples that I've considered setting up a special airline to transport them back and forth.'

But while much of the superstructure of Aboriginal Studies can seem bizarre viewed from the suburbs, the fact remains that many white Australian baby-boomers, instead of emigrating to Earl's Court and other points north, went into their own interior, discovered their black countrymen and women, and assisted them – ineptly and in efficiently – in their struggle.

In Canberra, a cantonment of legislators, academics and lawyers, the consensus was only that everyone could look forward to a 'shit-storm of litigation' as claim and counter-claim got under way, each and every one feeding into the network of cracks that runs beneath the supposedly secure edifice of the Australian nation. Yet there was also a more numinous aspect to all of this: perhaps the penetration of white-into-black was being accompanied in Australia by a reverse penetration, a colonization of the white sensibility by the Aboriginal world view.

The doyen of white Australian activists on Aboriginal affairs, Dr H. C. 'Nugget' Coombs, wrote in his recent book *Aboriginal Autonomy* that young Aboriginals might look forward to a time when white society would be analogous to the Continent for Young Englishmen of the nineteenth century: they might go on the Grand Tour, but they would return to the verities and shibboleths of their own culture, having happily sown their wild oats.

But wasn't the reverse also happening? And weren't the white Australians who went into the Outback to work with the Aboriginals embarking on a form of Grand Tour? Or was it perhaps a kind of internal exile, a way of parcelling off troublesome, radical elements, into the illimitable wastes, the hot Siberia?

To be in Australia is to be subtly aware of this vacuity at one's back, like a sixth sense of an open door. No wonder that the best of Australian art, film and literature alludes to this otherness, this strangeness. The landscapes of Sidney Nolan and Fred Williams; the early films of Peter Weir; the novels of Patrick White, Peter Carey and Xavier Herbert: all attempt to give definition to this penumbra, this dark shadow around the blinding southern sun.

In the past it was always said that white artists had gone too far in trying to mould their vision of the Australian landscape in terms of European conventions of representation, but what strikes the contemporary visitor to the continent is that now this process has been reversed:

in every suburban kitchen hangs a tea towel or a calendar with Aboriginal motifs on it; the Quantas 747 decorated by Pitjinjarra artists patrols the skies over Sydney. Is it that the European eye is stretching itself to embrace a different perception of the land? Or rather: is it being stretched despite itself?

Bill Moss was living in Gove, as far from Canberra as Istanbul is from London. I would go and see him and his fellow 'exiles'. Find out what the view was from those who straddled the frontier.

The morning of my arrival we tooled around the peninsula, stopping in Yirrakala so I could pick up a permit to be on Aboriginal land, then swimming in the pellucid Arafura Sea. We visited the museum where the 'bark petition', the declaration of Yolngu rights and title sent to Canberra in the 1960s, is kept behind climate-controlling glass.

Then sometime in the afternoon we settled down to drink by the deep green of the Gove Resort Hotel pool. After adjourning for supper we ended up back in the cavernous bar late that night, indisputably drunk and watching a collection of blacks and whites weave around the pool tables.

Sam had teamed up with Bungana, one of his Yolngu clients, a big, broad-shouldered man with a full moustache, wearing a blue singlet. Bungana had another mate in tow, a thinner, wiry man. The Yolngu are known as a fairly easy-going Aboriginal people not driven by the same asceticism, or the same rigour with regard to taboo, as some of the desert peoples. The first Aboriginal pop group to score any real chart success, Yothu Yindi, come from Arnhemland. Their promotional videos, which mix elements of traditional ritual with modern boogie, would be pretty much anathema to Aboriginals from the Centre.

Sam had been talking all day about his difficulties in getting his clients mustered, but Bungana wasn't one of the culprits. The consultant was the one being yanked around. As we staggered across the grass from the hotel to Bill's company-issue bungalow, Sam turned to Bungana and said: 'You people regard us as slaves, don't you?' Bungana muttered something in the negative. 'I don't mean that you think we have a slave mentality,' Sam continued, 'but you think of us as essentially your servants.' Bungana shrugged his shoulders. Later Sam explained to me what he meant. 'Someone once said to me that Aboriginal society is essentially feudal without serfs, and that white people like me fulfil that role. There are a lot of people in my position who do it because they think they are doing right, and they are recompensing for their bourgeois backgrounds. They do it for a short time and they get burnt out, because there is an enormous propensity for driving slaves around. Every Aboriginal person out there [he gestured towards the tropical darkness] can recognize a potential slave, yoke them and drive them along.'

Sam elaborated, developing a picture of Aboriginal political culture that differed quite radically from Bruce Chatwin's *The Songlines*-inspired romanticism that has coloured much contemporary perception. Aboriginal politics were, he said, 'incredibly Byzantine; Aboriginal people are politically active in a day-to-day way. Politics is an extension of familial relations . . . they live in a world of intrigue. They are Machiavellians. This is one of the best ways to understand them: often it is pursuit of power for its own sake.'

And within this vast, drawn-out labyrinth of political relations, jawlines rather than songlines, there were clearly defined, steeply vertical power relations: 'Power is measurable in their access to all sorts of rights, their ability to call in social credit. Status and rank is an obsession with most Aboriginals.'

Sam's introduction into this Machiavellian world had been stranger than most. A student at Sydney University, shortly after his finals he ran away with an 'unsuitable' girlfriend to stay with a relative, who was a missionary in Arnhemland. They hid out for three months in the bush, and Sam became acquainted with the Aboriginals: 'New South Wales was one of the blandest outposts in the Empire,' he says, 'I can remember going to the cricket when I was a kid and thinking that the members' stand was empty until someone hit a four and they all stood up. They were all dressed so identically. It was impossible to tell that they were actually alive.'

After such drear circumstances, he had found the Aboriginal people impossibly exotic. Like my archetypal Australian baby-boomer radical, Sam had spent time in Europe in the 1970s and come away just as appalled by its banality. He had ended up back in the Northern Territory. A job 'washing dishes' on the first land rights claim had led him to the Northern Land Council, where he had assisted in the building of the most significant organization for processing territorial claims in the country. But somewhere along the line his idealism – and possibly even guilt – had been shed. He now no longer viewed his role as a consultant to explain the Aboriginal peoples' views and society to the whites, rather the reverse was the case. 'My role as a bridge [between cultures] is a myth really. I'm not trying to explain what Aboriginals are to anyone else. My job is to explain to Aboriginals what the fuck we are on about. During this same work [on sea rights] I had to explain that the Queen of England claims the sea bed, the sea resources, the water column, the surface of the water and the air above it. My clients are absolutely outraged at this. They say: "No, it's ours. We own it." There is a major misunderstanding here.

'You would have thought that after two hundred years there would be enough insinuation for the penny to have dropped. The truth is that it hasn't. The notion of federalism and how representational democracies work is a total anathema to the way their political system works. Selection is the mechanism for power, not election. They find it hard to understand how our system works.

'But on the other hand most of the white people I know who work in this business know nothing about our culture. Their greatest problem is that they have nothing to offer. They sit down and listen to a piece of Aboriginal music and go: "Oh, wow!" They don't understand anything about their own culture and what they tend to do is characterize it as evil and shallow and not worth worrying about, yet somehow it can be substituted for the Aboriginal culture. This is a very dangerous idea. It makes it harder for the Aboriginals to realize who they are dealing with.'

Sam was adamant about his realism in the face of an alien and idealist culture. His own personal view of the resolution of the land rights issue, and the questions of sovereignty that lie behind it, was that Aboriginal people should be allowed to have self-governing provinces, linked to the Federation as are the other states. The introduction of Aboriginal senators into the upper house would be, he argued, a way of breaking the conservative stranglehold on the Senate.

But if the world of Aboriginal politics was Byzantine, and that of Canberra Byzantine in a different fashion, wasn't the interface between the two bound to be almost unknowably strange?

'Well, it's a combination of both,' Sam observed, before

launching into one of the most peculiar political anecdotes I've ever heard: 'The favourite method of political manipulation for Aboriginals is to take a prime minister out into the bush and do magic on him, throw stardust in his eyes. And then he will say whatever you want. This is their favourite political strategy: we want to see the chief, the boss, and we are going to get him on his own and we are going to do things to his brain.'

I was somewhat taken aback: do they ever succeed in this?

'Hell, yes. It works. They took Hawke out to a remote place in Barunga about five years ago and got him to sign a treaty. It's not a treaty in the strict sense of the word, but that's what it's called. It makes all sorts of pledges about what Australia is going to do for Aboriginals. His advisers were screaming. He did it because he was isolated and starstruck. They did it to Whitlam – he was completely won over in the same way.'

How about Keating? Have they taken him off too? 'Well, not exactly the same. In his case it was Parliament House rather than the bush, and slick Lutheran-trained black lawyers rather than witch doctors, but the essence of it was the same.'

It was not that this was preposterous – far from it. It was just that this talk of ju-ju, sympathetic magic, what you will, sat strangely between us in the neat, safe, suburban context. But then the other explanation I had heard for the relative success of the Aboriginal cause had been equally oblique.

When you thought about it, the fact that some 250,000 largely deracinated indigenous people had managed to claw back a substantial amount of land and benefits from 15 million rapacious whites did seem quite amazing. (Although, that being said, it needs to be stated unequivocally that,

ON THE EDGE OF BLACKNESS

so bad is the Aboriginal lot, even this constitutes at best a very partial restitution.) But what was this really down to? Credulousness on the white side interfacing with the Aboriginal propensity for Machiavellian tactics? Or something altogether more unknowable?

Down south, back in the Canaan from which Sam had taken a permanent leave of absence, Peter Craven, former editor of *Scripsis*, the literary journal, and now a dyspeptic columnist on the *Australian*, offered his take on why Paul Keating was supporting Native title and risking confrontation with the very elements of white corporatism that underpin his regime. Was this the prime minister's getting-of-Aboriginality?

'You've got to think in terms of Asean [the Association of South-East Asian Nations],' he replied. 'Keating wants to heave himself up to the same kind of status as he sees these South-East Asian countries having, but there's one central problem: no history. By hanging out with the blackfellas he can lay claim to their fantastic, 40,000-year history. That explains his enthusiasms for Aboriginal rights, pure and simple.'

At the time I had considered this observation as merely facetious: an Antipodean equivalent of a *Private Eye*-style piece of cynicism; but a week later, sitting under Sam O'Brien's mango tree as the flying foxes came winging in to chatter and feed above our heads, Craven's take was being rendered prosaic, mundane even.

Sam was emphatic about the way he dealt with sympathetic magic in his work: 'I use it,' he told me, and related an anecdote about sending out a traditional message stick to gather in a group of recalcitrant clients. But this was a practical use – the philosophical overtones were something he profoundly resisted. 'I know enough to be able to pass

267

as an acolyte – which is sufficient. I know enough to be able to say which totem I would nominally have – enough to be able to say I am a shark; if I go somewhere and say I am a shark all of a sudden this cabal of other people with symbols take me away and treat me as if I was the member of some sort of club. I don't really understand it.'

And you don't want to?

'No. It is not something I can be. I can't be an Aboriginal.'

And then I pushed Sam on this – because it chimed in with my own unease – pushed him until he admitted: 'I'm terrified. Absolutely and totally terrified about the whole business.'

In case it works?

'I know it works. I have absolutely no doubt about it. People say to me: "Come with me and I'll take you to a place where the trees drip with blood."'

But isn't there a real danger that someone in your position is going to make some sorcerer really angry? 'That's why I am very careful: I am terrified of these people. If they say "Jump", I say "How high?"'

I must stress that on Sam's part this is not wholesale abandonment to the idea of sympathetic magic as a political tool. What Sam, Bill and others like them are actively campaigning for is a reconciliation between 'animist inscrutability' and 'cultural cringe'.

In this context, encounters between black and white are crucial. They are the opportunities for each side to see one another as 'three-dimensional beings', to break down 'partitions'. The psychological, or cosmological, interpretations that are placed on these encounters are a different matter. One which, I would agree with Sam, is best left in partial obscurity.

*   *   *

ON THE EDGE OF BLACKNESS

I am not someone given to contemplation of the irrational, but suffice it to say that while I have relayed much of what I learnt while in Northern Australia, I have left out much else. Whether this is because of the sensibilities of those who imparted information verging on the taboo, or because of a genuine fear of sympathetic magic, I cannot say. But it seems to me that the very fact of such a quandary is instructive in itself. Australia is far more 'away' in this sense than 'home'; far more magical than dirty in its realism.

The identities of Bill Moss and Sam O'Brien have been disguised in this piece for just these reasons. This was at their request, but I agree they were right to do so. Whether their ability to function effectively in the political arena would be compromised more from one side of the racial divide than the other is unfathomable. That it would be is beyond doubt. The working out of the issue of Native title and Aboriginal land rights is surrounded by just this zone of the unknowable. However Keating acts in the next few years to provide his solution to the Aboriginal question, he would be well advised to listen to the counsel of those such as Nugget Coombs, Sam O'Brien and Bill Moss, who have traversed the chain-link fence and spent time with the Long Grass people. But then it may be a few years yet before we know what kind of stardust it is that is being sprinkled in Keating's eyes.

Observer, January 1995

"YOU REMIND ME OF AT LEAST FIFTEEN PEOPLE I KNOW..."

ADULTERY

" SIDNEY'S GOING WALKABOUT...."

" TAKE ME TO YOUR DEALER ...... "

THE POST-AARGUMENT-ABOUT-COITUS-CIGARETTE

'I DO HOPE I'M NOT DISTURBING YOU....'

' I WISH TO BE INSURED AGAINST BEING HARASSED BY INSURANCE SALESMEN....!'

CASUAL SEX

'I LIKE TO PUT EVERYTHING ON THE TABLE BEFORE I START NEGOTIATING...'

PROFILES

Thomas Szasz: Shrinking
from Psychiatry

Ross Perot was talking to CBS News. 'Raisin' taxes,' he drawled, 'is like givin' a cocaine addict maw co-caine.' I knew I was in the right place. Outside, the sirens wailed in the New York night, while on the flickering screen the presidential hopeful defined the collective American psyche in terms of obsession and compulsion.

When I walked out of my midtown Manhattan hotel the following morning, the discarded crack vials crunched like gravel under the soles of my shoes. I was on my way to interview Dr Thomas Szasz, the maverick 'anti-psychiatric' thinker who advocates the legalization of all drugs and puts forward the radical view that both drug addiction and mental illness are not diseases at all.

By noon I was sitting with Dr Szasz in his immaculately neat office at the New York University Medical Center in Syracuse. I started off by asking him what he felt about R. D. Laing, who had put forward theories similar to Dr Szasz's, and then, paradoxically, had himself suffered a mental breakdown.

'There are no second acts in academic notoriety,' said Dr Szasz. Paraphrasing Gore Vidal is very much Dr Szasz's style. 'Laing agreed with me that there is no mental illness but claimed to have a cure for schizophrenia. Perhaps that's something like the Greek idea of hubris. I think that in many ways what happened to Laing . . . obviously there is a problem with self-honesty.'

A small, neat man, who still has a pronounced Hungarian accent after fifty years living in the United States, Dr Szasz could never be accused of courting popularity for its own sake. On the contrary, his radical views on mental illness and drug addiction have been presented with great consistency and courage in the twenty-or-more books he has published since the 1950s. And Dr Szasz has stuck to his guns despite public vilification and professional skulduggery.

In his latest book, *Our Right to Drugs: The Case for a Free Market*, Dr Szasz returns to themes he first explored in his ground-breaking work *Ceremonial Chemistry*, published in 1974. Put succinctly, Dr Szasz holds that we have substituted scientism for morality and allowed a category error to permeate our thinking about mental illnesses and other 'diseases' such as drug addiction, alcoholism, anorexia and obesity. Szasz sees their current 'pathological' status as the inevitable result of a society that is unprepared to accept the hard work involved in personal responsibility. During our conversation he quoted Burke approvingly: 'Men are qualified for civil liberty in exact proportion to their disposition to put moral chains on their own appetites . . .'

'You can see when we allow doctors to take over the area of communal life that is concerned with how we communicate and how we morally judge, we open a Pandora's box. I'm not suggesting that there is a conscious conspiracy, it's rather a collective urge, a sort of Puritan desire to be smacked with one of Mummy State's hands, while being stroked with the other.'

But Dr Szasz is not just a conventional libertarian

philosopher, and his case for the complete legalization of all drugs rests as much on his sophisticated analysis of the language of medicine, and his careful reading of social mores, as it does on appeals to individual liberty.

'The whole area is full of absurdities,' he told me. 'On the one hand, if you can drink and drive, you can be jailed. But on the other hand, you can take a prescribed drug like Halcion, murder someone, and get acquitted. You can carry a loaded gun, but not a loaded syringe. It's almost as if we want to be punished in this way, deprived of our rights and turned into adult children. Or take the smoking debate. People forget the issue of private property. If I own a restaurant and wish to have people smoke in it – it's my own affair. No one has to come there.'

Dr Szasz's arguments rest, he says, 'on firmly held, rather traditional values. I am not conventionally religious, but I do think that personal responsibility is enormously important.' Had he ever taken drugs himself? 'Oh, no, never. Partly because they don't really interest me, but more importantly because of their legal status. I just couldn't afford to give any ammunition to my critics.'

In 1962 he published *The Myth of Mental Illness* in which he argued the symptoms of mental illness are not those of a disease but merely examples of behaviour that is generally disapproved of. Following this there were attempts by members of the American Psychiatric Association to have Dr Szasz removed from his post. 'They made mistakes,' he said, 'and I was lucky. They actually wrote a letter to the university saying that I was "unfit to hold the chair in psychiatry" because of the book. Imagine that! They tried to act as if the First Amendment didn't exist! Such foolishness. That's why censorship is a much better concept for the understanding of drug prohibition than any "disease model".'

Certainly, by arguing that state-run drug programmes are nothing but 'legalized drug peddling' and that the war on drugs is not only a waste of time, but also positively pernicious, Dr Szasz was bound to earn himself enemies. 'But it is ridiculous,' he says. 'Putting drug addicts in treatment centres is somewhat like confining people with tuberculosis together and then getting them to cough over one another.'

But what about the actual suffering involved in mental illness and drug addiction: surely Dr Szasz couldn't gainsay that? What would he have felt like if one of his two daughters had been a drug addict or a schizophrenic? Wouldn't it have made him alter his views?

'Well, you know a lot of people ask me that question. I have been fortunate. But, you know, what is the impulse to ask these questions? Surely it's an attempt to make me look bad . . . It's really compassion-mongering, trying to adopt the high moral ground of someone else's suffering. It's analogous to the way people raise money for charity: "Give us your money for people starving in the Third World," they say. But of course they live well using other people's money to indulge their own altruism.

'Of course I cannot imagine forcing my daughters to be hospitalized. To the extent that I style myself an "anti-psychiatrist" it is only the involuntary type of psychiatry that I mean.'

So what about psychotherapy, where the individual actively seeks help? 'Well, I don't call what I do "psychotherapy", I just call it talking to people. If I can help them, then that's good, but I hope I never fall into the mistake of believing that I can help people because of my professional status.'

According to Szaszian philosophy, self-help groups such as Alcoholics Anonymous would appear to be the most pernicious and misguided of 'therapies'. But at least they have the honesty to give their theories an overtly religious character.

Did he agree? 'I suppose so. If people think that they can be helped by these things, that's their own affair. Just as it's their own affair if they want to belong to a religion or take a certain drug. But as far as I am concerned they are all equally stupid. It's just a case of *chacun à son goût*.'

But there is an increasing amount of research that seems to show that drug addiction and alcoholism may be genetically inherited. Wouldn't this seem to fly in the face of his theories? 'No, not really. I mean I'm not competent to judge this evidence, but even if a person does have a disposition to react unfavourably to a drug, all his susceptibility does is to enlarge his responsibility to avoid it.

'Really all of this preoccupation with medical care of one kind and another, as a political and a social issue, is a displacement. Instead of giving the people bread and circuses, politicians give them wars against diseases and drugs, and all kinds of therapies. If you look at it carefully you will see that involuntary mental hospitalization at taxpayers' expense is really a kind of poor relief.'

Dr Szasz is no faddist or crank, nor a 1960s maverick who has had his day. Indeed he said that he had been hardly aware of the counter-cultural antics of the Learys and Hoffmans. Rather, the key to Dr Szasz comes from his cry early on in our discussion when I touched upon the tension in America between the collectivism of public health laws and the individualism of capitalism. 'But it's all in de Tocqueville,' exclaimed Dr Szasz. 'He understood this and wrote about it 150 years ago!'

And that is why I predict that Dr Szasz's work and

thought, prompted by the publication of his new book, will once again come to the fore: he takes the long view.

The Times, June 1992

Damien Hirst: A Steady Iron-Hard Jet

About twenty minutes before Damien Hirst arrives at the Serpentine Gallery to talk to me, the susurration begins. The leaved minds of those who wait – gallery workers, a photographer, an editor and me – are agitated by his preprence, the afflatus of what may – or may not – be his genius.

Calls are despatched to try and ascertain where the errant artist has got to. Pimpernel-like he has been sighted here, there and everywhere. I imagine some sort of incident-room map of Central London, with little coloured lights moving about it, showing the relative positions of Hirst, his critics, the buyers of his work. Possibly it could be entitled 'Moving Towards the Inevitable Impossibility of a Meaningful Encounter'. Or somesuch.

'He's definitely coming,' reports a head, poked round – and apparently partially severed by – the door jamb of the staff kitchen where we wait. A new agitation is generated among the waiters. There is discussion of Hirst's antics, the put-ons that have been tried on him by his critics:

'They asked him to draw a banana,' says someone referring to a television appearance by Hirst, 'and then he couldn't do it . . .'

'That's not true!' counters another. 'Damien is a brilliant draughtsman.'

I'm smoking moodily in a corner, reflecting that this

phenomenon is somewhat like J. G. Ballard's concept of the 'Blastosphere', as described in his experimental work of fiction *The Atrocity Exhibition*. The Blastosphere is the implicit shape of the way matter is perturbed by an explosion. It is atemporal: it may just as well precede the fact of the explosion as follow from it. We are all waiting in the Hirst Blastosphere, and as such it is inevitable that events, dialogue, thoughts even, should reflect the Hirst anti-aesthetic – a quotidian elision between the surreal and the banal.

A gallery worker shows a suit-wearing man carrying a clipboard into the staff kitchen. She says, 'Over there', pointing at a part of the room, and he replies, 'Mmm, mmm . . .' and notes something on his clipboard. They leave, without saying anything further, or even acknowledging the presence of the waiters. I wonder what the man with the clipboard would look like floating in a solution of formaldehyde.

And then he arrives. There's an almost audible thrumming that precedes the door being opened, an onanistic strumming, the essence of which is summed up by this question: Is it better to masturbate over the image of the Emperor if he has no clothes on, or is it preferable to stimulate yourself discreetly knowing that he is tightly sheathed?

In this sense Hirst's entrance to the kitchen is analogous to the way Ashley Bickerton's *Solomon Island Shark* – one of the exhibits in the current Serpentine Gallery show, 'Some Went Mad, Some Ran Away', which Hirst has guest-curated – impinges on the viewer's sensibility. Hirst is hammerhead down, tightly encased in PVC, rubber and leather, and already garnished with the fatuities of those who observe and comment upon him. Fatuities that are as ordinary and perverse as the coconuts and plastic bags of Scope mouthwash that dangle from Bickerton's shark.

What's immediately apparent is that Hirst has a genuine charisma. Like many spatial artists he is concerned with the interplay between individuals' senses of embodiment and their capacity for extroception. He manifests this as an aspect of his being: his being-in-the-room acts on the flustered gaggle of waiters like an ultrasonic whine on a school of fish; and so they quit it.

We wander out into the gallery to look at the work. Conversation is desultory. We examine details of the various works rather than commenting on their totality. Hirst is annoyed that some of the myriad plastic tags that stipple the surface of Angus Fairhurst's *Ultramine Attaching (Laura Loves Fish)* have been removed. I remark that it reminds me of my days as a shelf-stacker at Sam's Bargain Store in Burnt Oak.

Abigail Lane's *I Spy*, two glass eyes impaled on free-standing hanks of brass wire, calls forth from us both a warm recollection of the girder-impaling-eye sequence in Paul Verhoeven's film *The Fourth Man*, and we go on to bat back and forth anecdotes about other instances of bizarre discorporation, both real and filmic.

Another Lane – this time a full-size waxwork of a naked man crouching on the studio floor – calls forth a dialogue on the sense in which a sculpture can make the viewer aware of the distant provinces, the forgotten Datias and Hibernias of his own body. 'Actually, you know,' says Hirst, 'the genitals of the sculpture are modelled on the real genitals of the subject.' And we stand for a while, thinking about the sensation that the cold stone would make pressed against our own scrotal sacs.

Hirst talks about his interest in depicting 'points of light moving in space'. This, he tells me, was most of the inspiration behind creating the spot paintings, where the aim is to set up a kind of visual humming, a titivation of the air above the surface of the canvas. This calls forth from me a lengthy effusion on 'points of light in space' that runs all the way from the nature of the retinal after-image, through Zeus appearing in a shower of gold, to the experiences of Terence McKenna, the Californian drug guru, on dimethyltryptamine. Hirst grunts non-committally.

And indeed, as we tour the exhibition it becomes increasingly clear to me that not only does Hirst pay very little attention to the way that art critics are describing and categorizing his work, he doesn't even conceive of it in the same terms. For him the ascriptions of certain works as 'gestural', 'expressionistic' or 'conceptualist' are quite void.

What interests him are the details: the way that the butter curdles in Jane Simpson's terminal bird-bath *In Between*, a brackish fusion of brass, butter, halogen bulb and refrigeration unit; the implications of stress set up in Michael Joo's miscegenations of metal construction and Disney or scientific iconography; the way that Andreas Slominski's *Untitled* – a bicycle garlanded with bags of impedimenta – far from being difficult to assemble, in fact arrived at the gallery 'ready to be wheeled out of its crate'; the exact ratio of formaldehyde to water that he uses for his own animal works. He seems most engaged when I remark on the way that little golden bubbles are trapped in the fleece of the lamb he incorporated into *Away from the Flock*.

It's easy to see – talking to Hirst – why so many art critics should have seized upon him as grist to their word mills. They want his apparently gnomic comments on his work to be genuinely gnomic, evidence of a trickster mentality that teases the *cognoscenti*. The art critics who contemplate Hirst's work are like clever children playing with one of those stereoscopic postcards: they flick it this way and that, to show the Emperor alternately naked and adorned. Thus they get their kicks.

In fact Hirst quite clearly thinks about his work in just the straightforward way that he says he does. *Pace* this transcription of our dialogue, which shows Self attempting to schematize, and Hirst quite properly resisting:

W.S.: What I thought was interesting about the way people are writing about you at the moment is that the art critics have to describe your work in their own arcane language – one which prettifies what you are doing. And that does them for at least half an article.

D.H.: They do it all the fucking time . . . they've been doing it for years . . . There's nothing more boring. They say: You go in, you see a thing . . . blah, blah, blah, just fucking describe it.

W.S.: But it seems to me that what you're really interested in is this dark side, this anima, the ingressability and internality of the body, and the way that culture refracts that experience. Your art is very kinaesthetic, it's about the internal sensibility of the body.

D.H.: I remember once getting really terrified that I could only see out of my eyes. Two little fucking holes. I got really terrified by it. I'm kind of trapped inside with these two little things . . .

W.S.: Pin-hole camera?

D.H.: Yeah, exactly.

When I attempt to outline some kind of epistemological development in his work, towards a more 'visceral' approach, Hirst says: 'I think I'm basically getting more yobbish. Yobbish is visceral. There's an idea of reality that you get from working with real animals . . . and I like formaldehyde.'

And we go on to discuss the technicalities of suspending animal carcasses in formaldehyde: what the solution comprises, how he finds out about its properties, and so on.

Hirst tells me: 'It's ridiculous what I do. I can't believe in it – but I have to.' And this might reasonably stand as the motto of any serious contemporary artist. What the critic misunderstands is that the imaginative condition of an artist like Hirst is to be continually poised upon the fact of his own suspension of disbelief. The critic attempts to appropriate this queasiness as his own. This is because the critic, furthermore, wishes to appropriate the role of the artist for his own as well.

It's a mistake to be deceived by the ironic hall of mirrors that Hirst's work seems to present; to be distracted, like the waiters in the kitchen at the Serpentine Gallery, by the 'phenomenon' of Hirst. While it's true that Hirst – like Warhol – is an artist who is as much sculpting in social attitudes as he is in physical materials, his approach to those attitudes is Myshkin-like in its lack of guile.

D.H.: I'd love to be a painter. I love those stories about Bacon going into a gallery where one of his paintings was being sold for £50,000, and buying it and just trashing it. But you can't really do that with a shark, it would take a whole gang of men with sledgehammers.

W.S.: That's why I brought up that Mach thing [the man who immolated himself trying to burn a sculpture by David Mach]. Because what would you feel like if somebody came in and destroyed the work? Surely, it is part of a coherent vision and you would feel as if someone had hacked off your arm?

D.H.: I don't really mind, because I think the idea is more important that the object. The object can look after itself. It will probably last long after I'm dead. I'm more frightened of being stabbed myself. You can always get another shark.

In the course of our conversation Hirst describes many techniques that are explicitly Warholian: working with assistants who are inadvertently 'preprogrammed'; attempting to generate 'randomicity' in the spot paintings; the idea of a machine for producing 'great artworks'. But while it may be too much to assume that he has stumbled upon these concepts wholly independently – they are, after all, very much part of the air we breathe – there's no doubt that his formulation of them is arrived at with a certain freshness. Hirst is a naïve rather than a sentimental artist in Schiller's formulation.

The comments that Hirst makes that are most interesting disavow his refusal to articulate a coherent vision. Of fat people he remarks: 'They just want to fill up more space.' He opines that what really interests him about space is its purely formal properties: 'I think it's all like collage . . . d'you know what I mean . . . that's why doing my own work and the group thing is basically the same. It's collage, shapes in space. As an artist you have these constrictions, when you make a work you have to decide whether it goes on the wall or the floor . . . Well, I hate that. My idea of a perfect art piece would be a perfect sphere in the centre of a room. You would come in and walk around it and it would just be there . . . I love the refractions of light in the liquid pieces. With the shark I just love the reflections in the huge volume of liquid – you don't really need the shark at all.'

We went on to discuss Hirst's new work, entitled *Couple Fucking Dead Twice*. He described it thus: 'Just two tanks, with no formaldehyde in them, and there are four cows – two in one tank, two in the other – and they're just these peeled cows. One's just stood upright, and the other one goes on its back, giving it a really tragic, slow fuck. They're both cows, so it doesn't matter. And they'll just rot. By the end there'll just be a mess of putrid flesh and bones. I just want to find out about rotting.'

There's an eloquence in this description that underscores his comments about the importance of the inspiration for him. He agrees readily enough when I suggest to him that the impetus for the creation of such works is the fact of their having arisen in the imagination in the first place. But this is as far as he can be driven towards intellectualizing his own work or defining an aesthetic.

He is far more interested – both lying on the lawn outside the Serpentine Gallery, and much later drinking at the Groucho – in putting to me teasing choices: 'Which do you hate more, serial killers or flab?'; 'Are you an optimist or a pessimist?'; 'Are you someone who sees the glass half-empty or half-full?' I would hazard a guess that the need to throw up these niggling and trite queries is a dim reflection of the very real battle between appearance and reality that is always going on outside the cave of Hirst's mind, as the Platonic forms of his sharks, cows and lambs are carried by in the flickering firelight.

But I don't want to subside into the kind of waterbed of rhetoric that supports most art-critical speculation, any more than I want my prose to become a fancier description of a very ordinary accumulation of material objects. ('They do it all the fucking time . . . they've been doing it for years . . . There's nothing more boring. They say: You go in, you see a thing . . . blah, blah, blah, just fucking describe it.') William Empson described the introductory copy that prefaces exhibition catalogues as 'a steady iron-hard jet of absolutely total nonsense'.

DAMIEN HIRST: A STEADY IRON-HARD JET

The catalogue copy for 'Some Went Mad, Some Ran Away' is a perfect example of this. Richard Shone's essay kicks off with a statement of mind-bogglingly discursive universality: 'An urge to bring order to chaos – the search for meaning in the seemingly random flux of experience – has existed as a fundamental human motivation throughout history.' What are we to gather from this? That this is an art show that somehow manages to bracket and contextualize the fundamental conundrums of all human experience, for all space and all time?

I think not. Rather, this kind of bombast is an aspect of what I have alluded to above, just as Wittgenstein memorably remarked on the impossibility of a meaningful musical criticism, on the basis that it was otiose to describe one language in terms of another, completely alien language. So the excesses of contemporary art critics in attempting to define and fix the work of artists such as Hirst reflects a wrong-headed and truly pretentious attempt by manipulators of language to reduce formaldehyde, flesh and bone to some chintzy philosophical abstraction. In literary criticism we have seen the phenomenon of deconstruction – an attempt by critics to hijack the mantle of the metaphysician for their own scrawny shoulders; and this is what we are witnessing here as well.

Shone goes on to characterize Hirst as 'riding freely through the grasslands of art, finding nutrition in the company of his kind'. I hope only one thing, that that 'kind' continues to be artists as interested in the physicality of art as Hirst is himself, and not the pallid poetasters who see his enactments of tangible chutzpah as a springboard for their own aesthetic ambitions.

Empson's phrase is so correct in terms of Hirst's art because Hirst is creating 'steady iron-hard jets', not uttering them.

Modern Painters, Summer 1994

*The day after this interview was conducted, a disgruntled artist attempted to destroy Hirst's sculpture *Away From the Flock*. W. W. S.

Tim Willocks: Size Matters

Tim Willocks's second novel, *Green River Rising*, is a well-paced, well-written thriller about a 'lock-down' in a horrific penitentiary in east Texas. The book is insistently filmic: violent action prods the narrative forward somewhat viciously, as if it were a nightstick being jammed into the small of the reader's psyche.

There's plenty of gore: arms severed by band saws, skulls cracked by ball-peen hammers, men leucotomized by 'shivs'; and plenty of bodily fluids exchanged, mostly between the book's female protagonist, the rangy psychologist Juliette Devlin, and two supremely manly men. These are the book's hero, Ray Klein, a doctor sent down for a rape he never committed, and Reuben Wilson, a black, former contender for the world middleweight title, who has become leader of the Long Valley Runners, the black contingent at Green River.

It was no surprise to me to learn that Alan Pakula has optioned the book (for which Willocks has already completed the script), and that it looks a distinct possibility that Pakula will make the film as part of the three-picture deal he currently has with Warner Brothers. No surprise, because the book is above all a traditional buddy-buddy outing, much in the manner of *The Dirty Dozen*.

In *Green River Rising*, the highest accolade any man (or woman) can be accorded is to be deemed 'a bad muthafucka' by the bull-necked prison hospital orderly, Froghead Coley. Indeed, the awards of this auspicious 'bad muthafucka' title to Devlin and Klein, respectively, are the most poignant moments in the book; and conceivably the most poignant moments in literature since Cathy and Heathcliff hit the heather.

What then to expect of the author himself? I had already been disabused concerning the much-quoted slug-line Willocks's publishers Jonathan Cape have appended to their new prodigy: 'He looks like an angel, but writes like the Devil.' For the photograph of Willocks that seems to bear this out (showing him smiling seraphically, with red lips, dead pale face and cascading orange locks) was taken by Polly Borland.

Polly, whom I have worked with in the past, is by no means a realist portraitist and, indeed, for the last couple of years she has been engaged in a photographic project on my daughter Madeleine. In Polly's photographs of Madeleine, she looks like nothing so much as . . . well, as . . . Tim Willocks.

But, if he isn't angelic, will Willocks be like his hero Klein, a bad muthafucka, a Shokotan warrior, manly and capable of reducing insolent interviewers to a boneless pulp in a matter of seconds? I picture the two us, *Women in Love* style, wrestling nude in the bar of the Groucho, lathered in perspiration, smeared with fois gras, being egged on by a circle of epicene literati.

In the event, Willocks is slumped in a sofa at the aforementioned club, looking big and burly but by no means threatening. With him is his Spanish girlfriend. 'Is it all right if she sits in?' he asks. 'She doesn't speak any English.' Humph! I think to myself, so this is the ideal Willocks woman, beautiful and bilingually challenged.

We adjourn to eat. Both of us order the Cumberland

sausages – obviously. Two such manly men as us wouldn't dream of putting anything less phallic than a Cumberland sausage in our mouths. Conversation ranges over fields of obvious mutual interest. He: doctor specializing in drug addiction who writes novels; me: sometime drug addict and novelist.

The trouble is that we can't seem to get much of a disagreement going. Willocks ventures that 'the amount of social damage and unhappiness caused by the present social and legal structure of drug control could be enormously reduced by different policies'. And I assent. I challenge him with the idea that, by maintaining some addicts on opiates, he is acting as little more than a licensed drug dealer. He assents.

Obviously if I'm going to fire things up a bit, I'm going to have to press the conversation into more sensitive areas. In *Green River Rising* much play is made of penile size. Both Reuben Wilson and Ray Klein exchange fluids with Juliette Devlin. But although Devlin is Klein's woman, he is troubled less by jealousy than by the possibility that the black man is bigger. Size, in the Willocks *Weltanschauung*, clearly matters. So how big is the novelist's own appendage? I decide to inch round to this topic.

Has he come under attack yet for representing another aspect of the 'backlash' against feminism?

'No,' he tells me, 'not yet, although I suppose I am expecting it. I do think there are some fundamental differences between men and women, which in recent times people have tried to ignore.'

But by putting forward the view – which he does in the novel – that for a man to be a man he has to be able, in the right circumstances, to defend his womenfolk with bone-crunching violence, isn't he opening himself to the charge that he shows male sexuality being defined solely in terms of aggression?

'Intercourse,' says the softly spoken unangelic one, 'is a physically violent act in the same sense that a tree falling down or a storm is violent. Violence can have a neutral meaning just as a conjunction of extreme forces. It doesn't have to have a moral sense.'

I sit there, imagining the conjunction of extreme forces that will occur when I ask him, figuratively speaking, to drop his trousers. Was he, I then asked providentially, like his hero Klein, an adept of some martial art?

'Yes, I do karate and used to compete, but I'm too old for it now.' Phew! The determination to ask him about his penis goes all soft inside me and stickily retreats. While not averse to the odd rough house, this particular literary bad boy would prefer the odds a little more evenly stacked.

And that's pretty much that. Willocks, girlfriend and publicist depart for Manchester to celebrate publication. I adjourn downstairs to the bar, where I've spotted Jeffrey Bernard, a writer who's current notions of manliness are far closer to my own.

Evening Standard, June 1994

Martin Amis: The Misinformation

It's a dun, early afternoon in the basement of Julie's, a restaurant off Holland Park Avenue in West London. The décor is late Klingon, as are the waitresses, who sashay around in long, velour coat robes underneath big hair. The muzak plays, frog-tongues of receipt are being extruded from the cash register with an angry whirr. And I'm witnessing an oxymoron made flesh: Martin Amis lost for words. He's discussing the beast bumping under the bed of his life – a hideous chimera made up of teeth, women and a £500,000 advance for his new novel, *The Information*.

'It's just that it got out of hand is all I have to say about it . . . It just . . . It was a spiral . . . as these things are . . . I sort of . . . I am slightly thrown by it . . . I don't think I . . .' He breaks off to order an espresso from a Klingon who's wafting by and continues: 'The ironies inherent in it are very very striking, and every day something new about it strikes me. It feels like I really am caught up in some *post-modern* joke. You know it's very disturbing to feel *disliked* and that gravity exerted by that mass of dislike is not pleasant . . . um . . . But one of the things Salman lost for a while as a result of his situation was the right to sober literary consideration. And I feel a kind of danger that I might lose it for this book. I'm hoping the book will *bite* through that shit and stand on its own two feet.

299

But it's an awful thing to be treated phenomenally rather than in a literary way.'

Amis sighs. 'It's really a story about the English character and not about me. What *got into* people? Basically. It brought out a tabloid streak in people who shouldn't have a tabloid streak.

'It goes back to my unique situation, in that I do think I'm pretty thick-skinned because *I've seen it*, it's been around the house, I've *seen* my dad lampooned when he broke up with his wife, it goes with the territory. So, I think that's what qualified me to write the novel and it qualifies me to say that all this stuff, it ain't *my* trouble, it's England's trouble, it's A. S. Byatt's trouble.'

He pauses. There's a hollowness in the room – we're the only customers – the atmosphere is both nervous and enervated, if that's possible: 'It doesn't weigh on me . . .' His slight shoulders sag. 'Actually, sometimes it does put the wind up me a bit. It's just that it's all out of control and that I'm exposed . . . That's what happened early on in the deal and that's where everything went wrong. It *should* have been kept confidential. *Why* wasn't it kept confidential? The whole thing. How did it get out that I – supposedly I – was demanding this money? That's where it all went sour, right there, and then it was just a sort of *maelstrom*.'

Yeah, it goes with the territory. Or as one of the lowlife characters in *The Information* puts it: 'Terry-terry . . . That what it all come down to. Every man want to be cock of the walk. All the Indians want to be chief. That what it all come down to: terry-terry.' And today I'm lunching with the chief in the far corner of his particular terry-terry: Amiscountry.

If you cross beneath the Westway from Shepherd's Bush and then turn right, you enter a very particular region.

MARTIN AMIS: THE MISINFORMATION

From here to Westbourne Park in the east, to the Harrow Road in the north, and to Holland Park Avenue in the south, stretches Amiscountry.

One of Martin Amis's great literary heroes, Vladimir Nabokov, believed that in order to understand the fictional topography of a novel, you needed to have an exact appreciation of the physical spaces within which the action takes place. He would commence his lectures on literature at Cornell by rendering diagrams of the two crucial 'ways' at Combray, or the floor plan of Mansfield Park.

The implied comparisons with Proust and Austen are not as outlandish as you might think. Like Proust, Amis is a novelist of psychological interiority projected on to the world: skies, streets, cities are for him the tangible simulacra of states of mind. And like Austen, Amis is a miniaturist, dissecting the verbal tics and nuances of the middle class with a well-stropped razor. His characters may venture further afield – in *The Information* trips are undertaken to Soho, to Islington, the sticks, there is even a whirlwind tour of the USA – but their true nature remains defined within this ragged rectangle.

Amiscountry is a variegated place. It stretches all the way from 'Calchalk Street' in the north, home of Richard Tull, the failed-novelist, book-reviewing protagonist of *The Information*, to Holland Park Avenue in the south, where the egregiously glib Gwyn Barry, purveyor of literary 'trex' and Tull's enemy-cum-friend, lives in palatial splendour. Still further north the modernist silhouette of Trellet Tower, home to Keith Talent, the darts-playing yob of Amis's *London Fields*, looms up.

The elegant terraces and squares that flank Ladbroke Grove may have been built to form aristocratic estates, but they now comprise elements in one of England's most prized literary estates. There is little greenery in the area, just the occasional little patch of grass, usually shit-bedizened, where someone or other stands tethered to their dog. In *The Information* Richard Tull takes his children on regular sorties to 'Dogshit Park'.

I decided to walk over to see Martin Amis from Shepherd's Bush, in the hope of clearing my head. You want to have a clear head if you're going to lock antlers with Amis. To say he is not a man to suffer fools gladly is a gross understatement. He often pounces on misusages of English in conversation, and will demand the authentication of examples used in arguments – or even discussions.

Furthermore, Amis has achieved that most useful of occult abilities over the years: the ability to swap height. I don't know if he sojourned with sadhus at the headwaters of the Ganges in order to acquire this skill, but the fact remains that when I am with Amis (approximately 5′ 5″) I, Self (6′ 5″), feel small. I've known Amis as an acquaintance-cum-family friend for about six years and often wondered why it is that when we meet, instead of him, as you might expect, adopting some perspective at the far end of a room or a seated position which might to some extent blur the distinction, he comes right up to me and stands with the crown of his head aligned with my collar-bone: using sympathetic magic to steal my eminence.

Martin Amis is coming out of the main door of the house his work flat is situated in when I arrive at about midday. He's wearing a greenish suit in some lightweight fabric and an open-necked shirt. He's midway through his dental work and his face is all caved in at the cheeks and his nose appears to be pushed to one side. He looks a bit like my mother did after she died – when they had taken her dental plate out. I do a sort of double take, because Amis really doesn't look good . . . not at all *clever*, as he might say himself. He kind of shrugs, twists his deflated face in a moue, as if to say: Yeah, this is about the size of it, this is what *happens* when they remove all your *teeth*.

He goes off to post a letter and I head upstairs. The flat is messier than I remember. Ashtrays and glasses on unwiped surfaces, the former full, the latter half-empty. A shirt lies like a collapsed balloon on the divan. Most of the curtains are drawn. There isn't much light for the windows to admit anyway: it's a monochrome London day. I notice a few things: an invitation to the memorial service of Lucy Partington, Amis's second cousin who was murdered by the serial killer Frederick West in 1973, and to whom (along with his sons, Louis and Jacob) he has dedicated the new novel. On the fax machine rests a note to one of his publishers concerning some business. It's on A5 headed notepaper, typed and neatly signed.

The main room of the flat is unostentatious in the extreme: television and video module, sound system, wall of books, a few award citations from British and American press bodies. In *The Information* Richard Tull meditates on the 'shapelessness' of writers' lives. By which he means that writers – unlike, perhaps, visual artists, or musicians – are uninterested in the trappings of style, either personal or interior. And it is this that comes to my mind as I sit on the World of Leather-ish divan and await Amis's return.

At forty-five, Amis has for some years been at the peak of his profession. Whether it is a shibboleth or not, he is almost ceaselessly referred to as 'the leading writer of his generation'; 'the most talented contemporary English writer'; 'the writer who has had most influence . . .' and so on, and so on, each blurbacious formulation further gilding the lily of his achievement.

And in what does that achievement consist? To date he has written eight novels, including *The Information*, a collection of short stories, and three collections of journalism and occasional writings.

While the early quartet of novels, *The Rachel Papers*, *Dead Babies*, *Success* and *Other People*, can be viewed as of a piece, cruel but essentially local satirical dissections of the English class system, with Amis's fifth novel, *Money*, he seemed to go global – or at any rate transatlantic – producing a furious absurdist burlesque on the excesses of eighties materialism. Many people consider this novel to be his finest work. It was followed five years later by *London Fields*, a great doorstop of a book which reprised all of his preoccupations with the nature of the fictive art, the millennial condition of Western cities, the implosion of public space and the threat of a global pandemic.

The eighties also saw Amis focusing his attentions abroad and away from Amiscountry. In 1987 he published *Einstein's Monsters*, a collection of short stories that gave form to the writer's preoccupation with the imminence of nuclear holocaust.

In his journalism from this period, collected in two volumes, *The Moronic Inferno* (1986) and *Visiting Mrs Nabokov* (1993), Amis's acerbic *tour d'horizon* took in personalities (mostly fellow writers) as well as politics in the form of disquisitions on the Republican Party and the 'Megadeth Intellectuals' of Washington.

This strain in his writing and public pronouncements, towards the political, has always been characterized by a kind of bilious liberalism. Amis, one often feels reading his political pieces, is more than anything annoyed at being forced to venture beyond the confines of Amiscountry and tick these people off. In *The Information* Richard Tull muses: 'It often seemed to him, moving in the circles he moved in and reading what he read, that everyone in England was Labour, except the government.' And to me Amis says:

'There is nothing else to be, is there? The other stuff is *repulsive*.' Although he agrees the new Labour Party 'image' turns its leader into 'Bambi, a wuss'.

Interest in Jewish culture and in particular the enduring influence of the American-Jewish novel on his own work must have been part of what led him to a contemplation of the meaning and resonance of the Jewish Holocaust. But in particular it was a reading of the book *The Nazi Doctors*, by Robert Jay Lifton, that was the inspiration for the novel *Time's Arrow*. In this relatively short book, Amis married all of his technical skills as a writer to a subject-matter that not only was beyond the confines of Amiscountry but even antedated its establishment.

In the *Spectator*, James Buchan reviewed the book, saying: 'I find it creepy to see Primo Levi rearranged for literary fun and profit.' Amis considered it a hideous slur, and one that he felt incumbent to reply to (the first time he has ever broken the rule of not replying to public criticism, and he hopes the last). For a while it looked as if the controversy might catch fire, and that with the preternatural sensitivity of the Jewish community (particularly in the USA) to the idea of gentiles writing about the Holocaust, Amis might become a victim of what he himself terms 'literalism', that category mistake whereby a writer's work is treated 'in a phenomenal rather than a literary fashion'.

In the event this didn't transpire, and for good reasons. *Time's Arrow*, far from being a sensationalist or meretricious account of the Holocaust, is a wrenching, heartfelt plea against those who yoke themselves to the march of history or the destiny of nations. It is a book firmly of the Enlightenment, in the strongest sense.

Recently Amis has proved one of the staunchest public defenders of Salman Rushdie. At a *Sunday Times* literary dinner a couple of years ago, where Amis was the guest of honour, I found myself sitting next to a woman who turned to me and said: 'Bloody Martin Amis, he's a misogynist and a pain in the arse, what do you think?' I demurred, saying that he was a friend. We sat in silence throughout the meal. When Amis rose to speak he delivered a fearless and cleverly structured defence of Rushdie, which included a comprehensive attack on the media and political powers that were ignoring the writer's plight, including News International itself. As nice an example of biting the feeding hand as I can think of. When Amis sat down, to huge applause, the woman turned to me again and said she was humbled.

But now Amis has himself fallen victim to another kind of 'literalism'. Since the breakup of his marriage to Antonia Phillips eighteen months ago, there is a sense that the carrion-eaters circling the Amis encampment have begun to close in. A rash of tabloid-style articles covered the breakup, speculating on Amis's motivations and conduct. Photographs of Amis and his new girlfriend, Isabel Fonseca, appeared in the press, the latter usually insultingly termed 'a literary groupie'. Some hacks said that Amis was falling victim to the crime of hubris, and that having for so long critically dissected the morals of others, it was now his turn to be exposed for his peccadilloes.

It had been long known that Amis's new novel would be concerned with the notion of literary envy and achievement, and when an extract appeared in *Granta* last year, commentators and gossips were quick to pick up on the characterizations of Gwyn Barry, the successful but facile novelist, and Richard Tull, his failing friend, and cast round for real-life counterparts. Initially the word was (and I heard this at every gathering at which there were more than two 'litewawy' types present) that *The Information* contained a systematic character assassination of Amis's estranged wife, and that following the *Granta* extract there had been representations to him from friends and colleagues (in particular his agent Pat Kavanagh) to tone it down.

But however implausible this might seem – it is of course logical that those who can't imagine are also incapable of understanding the imagination – there was worse to come. Sooner or later we will know what went on in the meeting between Pat Kavanagh and representatives of Cape (Amis's then hardback publishers) and Penguin (Amis's then paperback publishers). Amis himself may be being slightly disingenuous when he implies that it wasn't he who was pushing for a £500,000 advance. Andrew Wylie, who has subsequently taken over Amis's global agenting, was already at that time in *de facto* control of Amis's American agenting, and the whisper in a writer's ear along the lines of: 'You're not being paid what you're worth', is the so-called Jackal's usual calling card when he goes out to poach a client.

Suffice to say, parties at the meeting were given the impression by Kavanagh that it was Amis who was pushing for the figure, and this in itself – the implication being that the relationship between agent and author was under stress – would have been sufficient to engender the leak.

From then on it was open season. The heady mixture of money and sex was mixed into a cake of pure literalism and pure 'trex'. People began to say that *The Information* was in fact about the rivalry between Amis and Julian Barnes (husband to Kavanagh and close friend of Amis), and that it was this that had precipitated the split between Amis and Kavanagh and resulted in him bringing in Andrew Wylie to secure the half-million advance.

The truth is there is a rich *mélange* of personal tensions here, some of them no doubt relating to the breakup of Amis's marriage, and to the presence of a new woman in his life. But wherever the onus of blame for the breakup in the agent–author relationship lies, it is the media reaction that has now overtaken all parties concerned and fractured friendships that had endured over many years.

This media reaction has been extreme, even by Amis's standards. When we had last 'formally' talked together (for an 'in conversation' piece for an American literary review) he had told me about a seminar in Boston on his work that he had attended. At the end he asked the academic convening the event why it was that given the respect his work was being shown in the USA he was still the repository of such odium in his native country. The academic told him succinctly: 'It isn't your work that they hate – it's *you*.'

In a way this 'hatred' for Amis is a paper tiger. For as many people who 'hate' him in the publishing world, you can find an equal number who have nothing but good things to say about him personally. But somewhere between the light source itself and what is projected on to the screen of public awareness a kind of distortion takes place in the image of the writer.

There's no question that Amis is being treated phenomenally. Not content with regarding his new novel as a phenomenon, the media have even zeroed in on a phenomenon that has been a source of pain and acute anxiety for him for many years. His teeth. He says: 'Not to be too self-pitying, but when you're *reeling around* outside some dentist's office in New York, coughing up blood like some terrible old *sap* who keeps getting into fights and always ends up yeurgh! – I thought, I knew this was going to happen but I didn't know I was going to get *shat* on for it. But that's because the voracious idiot of publicity, when it hears something like $20,000 in dental work, thinks I'm after a Liberace effect, that what I want is a *dazzling smile*. All I want to do is to be able to *eat*. But everything is taken negatively, so that is what happened.

'It's actually liberated me in lots of ways. I used to leave the room when people talked about teeth for the last fifteen years. If I'd known this was going to be in the paper . . .' And here his normally basso voice drops into a ravine of irony: '. . . I think I'd have *killed* myself a year ago. But within days of finishing the novel it was crunch in the dentist's chair.'

One of my central quibbles with *London Fields* was with Amis's characterization of Keith Talent, the darts-player and all-round yob. For me there was always a suggestion that lying behind Talent's awfulness was a doubly inverted form of snobbery, along the lines of: 'I'm not afraid to show what it is the middle class really think and fear about the working class, namely that they are a bunch of loutish, vicious thugs.'

In *The Information* the Talent role is taken by Steve Cousins, a criminal entrepreneur and *farouche-savant* who reads Canetti in his van while staking people out. Cousins's argot, and that of his accomplice, Thirteen, a black street kid, seems far more convincing than that of their counterparts in earlier novels. Had Amis, I wondered, been doing more than the usual research in this direction?

'No, it's made up really. I read up a bit, that wonderful book by Roger Graef, *Living Dangerously: Young Offenders in Their Own Words*, and what makes it great is that it is in their own words. Things like "They chief me out, they fucking chief me out" . . . but the thing about argot is that you have to generalize it, otherwise it's going to date.'

There is a whole aspect of *The Information* that is concerned with the idiocies of political correctness – Amis gets some of his best jokes from this Möbius strip of an ideology. But the smashing of these commandments is also connected to the brooding theme of physical violence in the book: Richard Tull plots to beat up Gwyn Barry, but there is also aggro in store for him: 'It's the dramatization of literary envy. There was a bit I was going to add this morning when I handed in the proofs saying violence is always a category mistake.'

But it's a category mistake that Amis must fear as well. It's the fear of not having *The Information* judged on its own merits, and it's the fear of the *ad hominem* and frankly odious criticism that must feel like being beaten up. And when you've made the protagonist of your novel a book reviewer, and *then* heaped all sorts of misfortune on him, and *then* introduced a gallimaufry of other litewawy types (some recognizably drawn from life) and shot them down with marvellously acidic darts, well, your anxiety levels would *have* to be fairly healthy.

Richard Tull is himself a fairly vicious reviewer: 'One doesn't soften up,' says Amis. 'I was like that myself. It *is* cruel. You know, everyone who writes a serious book puts a lot of pain into it, and ragging is to me like ragging is to *no one* else on this planet, in that I entered the house of someone who was making a living by his pen, and that has always been in my domestic landscape, and there is no other case of a writing son – *so I see it clearly*. Maybe not clearly in other ways, maybe too close to see some things about it.'

Amis realizes that it is a strange kind of *pas de deux* that he and the media are involved in: 'The relationship that I have with the media is different from before and it is not just to do with more shit and more attention. I am in the dance with them now.'

Talk turned – as it will – to impotence. Impotence is big in *The Information*. One of the finest comic riffs in the novel concerns Richard Tull's inability to make love to his beautiful wife, Gina: 'In the last month alone he had been impotent with her on the stairs, on the sofa in the sitting-room and on the kitchen table. Once, after a party outside Oxford, he had been impotent with her right there on the back seat of the Maestro.'

Tull's career as a high-speed book reviewer leads him to muse on impotence through the fictional ages, concluding with the memorable line: 'And as for Casaubon in *Middlemarch*, as for Casaubon and poor Dorothea: it must have been like trying to get a raw oyster into a parking meter.'

But why should impotence be such an obsession? Impotence and fellatio. In *The Information* there is even a riff that begins 'Whither fellatio?' And the principal McGuffin in the plot hinges on who has been sucking off whom. Amis obviously thinks that fellatio is the high-water mark of sexiness, the most profound form of ingress. I tackled him on it, but all his references to 'swallowers' and 'non-swallowers' are drawn from literature, rather than life: Amis keeps his penis close to his chest.

But the issue of fellatio relates to one of the wider charges against the writer, that of misogyny. This has stuck over the years to the extent that when a clique of women publishers in London were looking for someone to receive 'The Hooker Prize' (their spoof version of the Booker Prize, awarded for services to literary male chauvinism), Amis was the first candidate.

In *The Information* the female characters – the wives of the two writers – are better drawn than previous Amis females, but one still feels it's a depiction from the outside, that Amis can't really – in the metaphorical sense – get inside his women.

Of the character Richard Tull he says: 'He is averagely

fucked up along the usual male lines. He is not a woman-hater at all, but he is a bit fucked up, he is English and he is middle class.' I think that this is the key, if there is one, to understanding Amis's approach to women: it isn't that he hates them, it's that – as with class – there is a certain disarming quality to his admission of ignorance.

A certain disarming quality, but one that doesn't disarm altogether. It's partly to do with Amis's strengths as a writer in projecting a 'universal' voice, that one finds oneself disagreeing – as a man – with his pronouncements. No, Mart, not all of us wish for a notional 'brother' to substitute for us when we're having flop-on difficulties; no, Mart, not all of us are preoccupied with fellatio; no, Mart, not all men view their condition as one of being on a rickety stage in front of a lot of other men . . . and so on.

In *The Information* the penultimate nail in the coffin of Richard Tull's hatred of Gwyn Barry comes when the glib and successful writer wins something called a 'Profundity Requital', a vast, yearly sinecure with no strings attached. It doesn't take much imagination to see this concept as a reification of all of the author's concerns with the notion of posterity. I ventured heresy: had he ever considered jacking in the whole game of writing fiction?

'I worked through a big crisis when I was finishing this book. But it was just writer's midway-through-last-version pain, a kind I am used to.'

'The constipation grind . . .'

'. . . Yeah. And you recognize it and are ready for it, but like the mother of seven children, even the seventh time it happens you say, Jesus I didn't think it would be this bad. So it *flashed* across my mind to abandon the novel. And if I had known what was going to happen to it even before it came out I don't know what I would have done.'

The strongest elements in *The Information* are the satirical skits on the literary world itself. From the *Little Magazine* where Richard Tull grinds out critical essays to the depiction of Rory Plantagenet, the odious purveyor of literary tittle-tattle, Amis has the suffocatingly self-regarding book world to a T. But while journalists may go hunting for real-life counterparts to Richard Tull and Gwyn Barry it was always self-evident to me that the real-life model for both characters was Amis himself.

'Thank you. That is exactly what I was saying to one of the journalists who was trying to tee Julian up. I said, listen, that is one hundred per cent gossip . . . If you want the scoop on this book it is that both Gwyn and Richard are *me*. One is the over-rewarded side and the other is the whimper of neglect side.'

Lunch is over. We wander down to Holland Park Avenue, the border of his fiefdom. Amis is going to pick his kids up from school. After that he is off to the New World to pick up his new teeth.

'I can go anywhere I like,' he had said to me, with reference to the 'literalism' that has placed Salman Rushdie in internal exile. And while this may be practically true, psychically the world for Martin Amis has become an unpleasant place. The following day, a woman I was speaking to said to me, 'I saw Martin Amis yesterday – my son goes to the same school as his boys. I tried to get a look at his teeth . . .' Now that's all you need as a writer. You may be used to people trying to get inside your head, but your mouth, that's what I call true literalism.

Esquire, April 1995

Bret Easton Ellis: The Rules
of Repulsion

So, we're sitting in the Saloon Room of the Oyster Bar, underneath Grand Central Station having lunch with Will Self and Bret Ellis. Bret Ellis is wearing a plain, three-button, black, single-breasted suit which could be by Yves St Laurent, or could just be off the peg; a plain white shirt – which could be Thomas Pink or Marks & Spencer; and a tie with an exaggerated, swirly, paisley motif, which might well be Versace, or alternatively one he could have bought five minutes earlier, from one of the barrow boys outside the terminal. As for the black brogues, they might be Church's but they could just as well be Freeman, Hardy and Willis.

Will Self is a little bit more straightforward (after all, I dressed him this morning): Next three-button blazer, gone slightly to seed; black Levis: ditto; Rockport pigskin walking shoes, so stained they have acquired a sort of verdigris; and a Jasper Conran shirt in the slightest of charcoal checks, worn over a Wrangler T-shirt.

Bret Ellis is eating the crab salad entrée and, despite having made inroads into his Coca-Cola, is still glancing thirstily towards an iced tea which the waiter (some Hispanic in an asinine red uniform waistcoat which places him sartorially closer to Yogi Bear than any other biped)

314

is just bringing to the table. Will Self is ignoring this and tucking into the third of his Blue Point oysters on the half-shell, at the same time as he tucks into his third Brooklyn Lager.

The waiter sets down the iced tea by the elbow of the notorious writer. It has a section of the paper covering set on top of the straw like a miniature and ineffectual condom (and Christ knows why I notice this detail . . . surely it's only a function of the atrocity that subsequently occurs . . .), and Bret Ellis looks up from his crab salad entrée, actually looks directly at the waiter and says, very distinctly: 'Thank you.'

How macabre, how black . . . how disgusting! How can Bret Ellis just sit there and for three whole hours not once fail to thank the waiter for bringing something to the table (he later even declines a lobster bib with grace); not once say something arrogant or self-seeking; not once betray any sign of misogynism or contempt? Has he no respect!

And I know, because I taped the whole encounter on my Sanyo M1118 cassette tape recorder, with Voice Activated System and touch-pause capability. Taped it, and then listened back to the whole repulsive 'snuff' interview. An interview in which the received image of Bret Easton Ellis, the author of the reviled *American Psycho*, is put to death.

For a start he's both bigger and better-looking than his photographs. Funny how we're all victims of the media's attempts to slur people. How we actually believe that if someone has been labelled meretricious, adventitious and plain not nice, we imagine his physical attributes will conform.

Bret Easton Ellis is a tall, rangy, well-built man of thirty, who bears a distinct resemblance to the young Orson Welles (something he later tells me I am not the first to remark on). He has strong, fleshy features, warm brown eyes and, dare I say, a perceptible charisma, which emerges in his propensity to dissolve into shoulder-shaking guffaws with charming frequency.

But most of all there is his quality of embodiment. It has to be said that with people who are really creepy, really not nice, you always get those subliminal, yucky messages of physical unease. And with Bret Easton Ellis? None, *nada*, *rien du tout*. This is a man who I'd happily let bath my children – should he wish to engage in such an atrocity.

Or, to put it another way: a publicist in New York who both Bret and I know well, a woman in her thirties, the mother of two small children, said of the hated one: 'Oh, Bret? Well . . . he's so sweet!'

With the publication of his fourth book, *The Informers*, Bret Ellis isn't so much ready for rehabilitation, as habilitation. He may have sold many, many thousands of books (*American Psycho* has sold 150,000 copies in the UK alone and still steady-sells at 1,000 copies a month), but *The Informers* is his first work to receive a favourable review (in the *New York Times Book Review*) in any of the keynote American newspapers.

'I guess that's why I've found it easy to dismiss criticism,' he told me. 'If people had begun by saying nice things about me and my work and then got nasty I might have been upset. But they never said anything nice in the first place.'

Ellis wrote his first book, *Less Than Zero*, at the precocious age of nineteen, while still a student at Bennington College: 'I did it as part of my course credits. I was incapable of getting a job, so I did the book instead.' But it really wasn't a great act of precocity, because he'd already written two novels before this, the first when he was fourteen: 'No one's ever going to see them. Every writer has about a quarter of a million words of self-indulgence he has to get out. I was just fortunate to get mine out a little earlier than most.'

As for the filthy-rich, nihilistic Beverly Hills that forms the backdrop for both *Less Than Zero* and now *The Informers*, contrary to received opinion there was nothing particularly autobiographical about it: 'We lived further out in the suburbs when I was a kid, in a much more middle-class area; so, although I was aware of kids like those in the book, they weren't my closest friends or anything like that.'

His father, a real-estate man, did make a lot of money during the eighties, but this was a little too late to impact on the Bret Ellis lifestyle: 'When he died a couple of years ago, he left a disaster area behind him as far as tax is concerned. It's something we're still untangling, but I don't think the estate will have any value.'

In fact, if there's any flow of money the implication is that it goes the other way: from Ellis to his mother, whom he quite clearly adores: 'I would say she's the chief factor in why I became a writer. She was always tremendously encouraging of any creativity that I displayed.' Her house was hit quite badly in last year's earthquake and Bret has been out in California for three months helping her to get back on her feet.

The tension between paternal and maternal relationships is something that quite clearly underscores Ellis's work, and he admitted to me that he had 'an extremely difficult, possibly even abusive' relationship with his father. Critics have already remarked on the 'X' factor of poignancy which seems to inhabit the story 'In the Islands' from the new collection. A story which concerns the attempt by a distant and unloving father to build a spurious bridge to his nineteen-year-old son, by taking him on holiday to Hawaii. When I remark on this, Bret smiles ruefully: 'Well, I guess it is a far lighter, more Salinger-like story than some of the others, and that's why they find it easier to latch on to.'

As for the controversy that exploded around *American Psycho*: 'I really didn't see it coming . . . I mean, I just had no idea. I had thought there might be problems with the length of the manuscript – that's where my problems usually are, but not with the content.'

And I don't think he is being disingenuous about this – or even flip. Even now, only three years along the line, much of the brouhaha surrounding *Psycho* looks, quite simply, pathetic. Norman Mailer calling, in *Vanity Fair*, for a panel of 'twelve respected novelists' to judge the work before allowing it to be published; Fay Weldon defending the book's right to be published in the *Guardian*, but admonishing readers that they needn't actually go through the hell of the text, because good old Fay has already done it for them. And many, many other writers who really ought to have known better, shooting their mouths off in a most egregious fashion.

Ellis was accused of just about every crime in the production of this text, but the one of being mercenary seems just about the cruellest and least justified: 'I had no idea that the book would earn out its advance – I didn't expect it to earn out its advance. I had been more or less broke in the year before publication. I was doing journalistic assignments – which I'm not good at. And, as I say, I had no idea of the controversy the book would unleash.'

In 1991, Mark Lawson put Bret Easton Ellis in the dock in the *Independent Magazine*, the charge being how he could justify, in particular, the grossest and most sadistic scene of the novel, in which Patrick Bateman, the eponymous anti-hero 'offs' two prostitutes in an extravagantly sadistic fashion. Lawson looked at many possible defences, from art for art's sake, to the moral responsibility of the satirist, before concluding that the jury was still out. Well, the jury is now back in, and, with the publication of *The Informers*, I would say delivers a unanimous verdict of 'not guilty' on all charges. *The Informers* shows the work of a writer at the peak of his powers, deeply concerned with the moral decline of our society. The book takes us from the first to the seventh circles of hell, from Salinger to de Sade, and in doing so shows that *American Psycho* was no gratuitous exercise, but a keynote text in the development of a major writer's *oeuvre*.

Lunch is over. Will Self picks up the tab with his Mastercard, and the two writers head out of the Oyster Bar. Self is going to walk back downtown to where he's staying in TriBeCa, but Ellis, ever the cocaine-honking, money-spunking bratpacker, is going to take . . . the sub-way. But before that he has to find a post office. Obviously so he can do something vile, like send photographs of sexual atrocities to Gloria Steinem . . . er . . . actually no: 'I found this guy's wallet in the street yesterday, and I guess I oughta mail it back to him.' The sick, sick bastard.

Evening Standard, October 1994

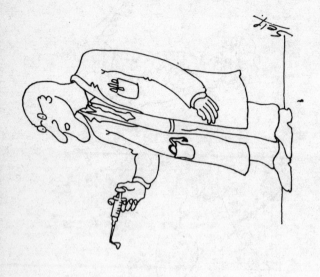

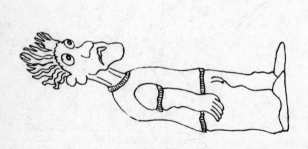

'I'M GOING TO COUNT TO THREE . . . AND THEN IF YOU WON'T COOPERATE I'LL TAKE THE MEDICATION MYSELF . . .'

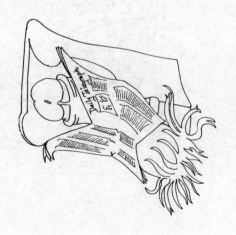

'AND OVER THERE SIR, IS THE CLUB'S OLDEST MEMBER . . .'

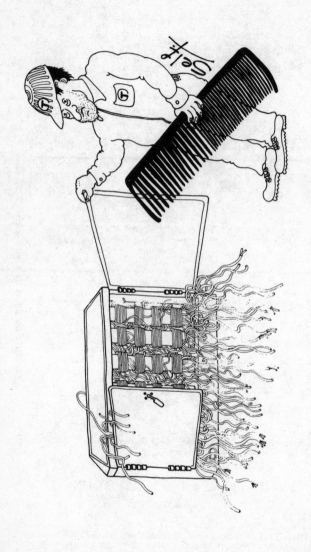

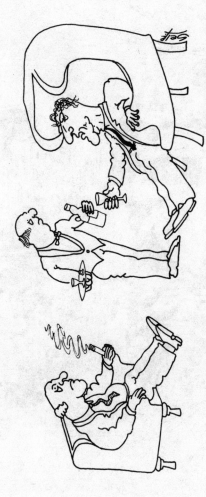

'APPARENTLY THE LORD CHANCELLOR HAS OVERRULED MY DECISION TO CUT THE BABY IN HALF......'

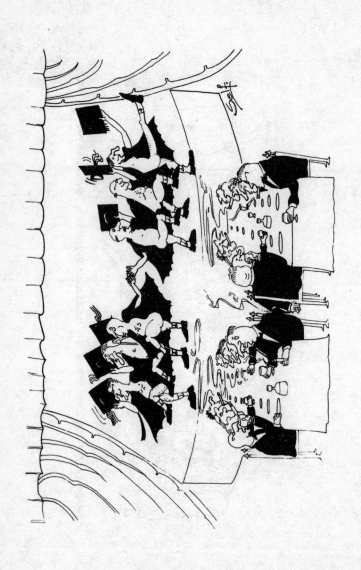

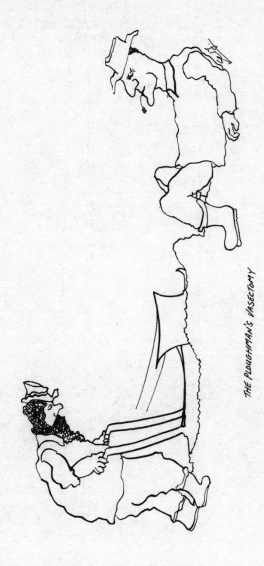

THE PLOUGHMAN'S VASECTOMY

CONVERSATIONS

J. G. Ballard

WILL SELF: Obviously the backlist got yanked up when Spielberg filmed *Empire of the Sun*, but my impression was that things were already starting to move again, there was a resurgence of interest.

J. G. BALLARD: Yes, it's hard to say. *Empire of the Sun*, the novel, helped enormously.

W.S.: But was anything actually out of print before *Empire of the Sun* won the Booker Prize?

J.G.B.: It didn't win the Booker Prize?

W.S.: Didn't it?

J.G.B.: No.

W.S.: Short-listed?

J.G.B.: Yes, it was short-listed. I have written a hell of a lot of short-story collections and some of those were going out of print. The novels were in print but the short-story collections were starting to go out.

W.S.: Whose idea was it to do the new Flamingo edition of *The Atrocity Exhibition* with the marginalia?

J.G.B.: It was suggested by the publishers of the *RE-Search* volume, Vail and Andrea Juno. They wanted to reissue *The Atrocity Exhibition*, which had long gone out of print in the States, and they had this large-page format, and I thought that there was going to be a sea of white paper because you can't have double columns; the readers' brains would start to frazzle. So I then thought that as this is a largely incomprehensible book it might help to have a few marginal notes. I thought it worked well.

W.S.: It works extremely well.

J.G.B.: So when Flamingo, HarperCollins, got around to reissuing it I suggested using the notes, which they did.

W.S.: And how's that gone, has it sold?

J.G.B.: I don't know. I wouldn't have thought it would have sold well. I have no idea, I never asked. The American edition has done well, which surprises me. I have always found that America is one nut I have never cracked.

W.S.: They have this expression in the States of being 'on the wall', which means that your sales have peaked so that you are always placed on a particular wall, a figurative wall in the bookshop.

J.G.B.: *Empire of the Sun* – thanks to the Spielberg movie – did well, but most of my other stuff is just tipped over there. Too pessimistic, too ironic. Everything has been published there but most of it is out of print, I would guess. It is a difficult market to crack, the Americans are so different from us, there is no question about that. There is a strangeness about America, it is not the pop–art aspect of the place, which of course most British visitors are struck by, and the huge advance that the American standard of living represents over ours, but their strange way of thinking. There is something very odd about the place.

W.S.: I wonder if I am missing out on something by not finding it as bizarre as perhaps I should. The other thing is that it is so polyglot now, and increasingly polyglot.

J.G.B.: I don't think it is bizarre, but their minds move in ways that one can't fathom all that easily. In a different way, the Japanese mind is a very difficult one to read. Whenever I go to the US, I love it, it is a marvellous place, so exhilarating and visually exciting. It is intensely in the present, which is wonderful. We barely touch the present here because of the dead weight of the past, but there the present envelops everything. It is like moving from a small TV screen to a huge cinema screen, you are conscious of a million little details that one can't find in the small-screen world. I am always aware there, after a while, of a missing dimension. I don't know what that missing dimension is – I have thought about it for years – but there is a missing dimension.

W.S.: Well, I think it is class, in a way. The dramatic irony of . . .

J.G.B.: Could be. Or maybe that they are all inherent optimists, that we are really very pessimistic people. We are in slow decline, and they are still confident.

W.S.: With no particularly good reason, it has to be said. On the face of it, they are in decline too.

J.G.B.: Yes, but the place still has such strength.

W.S.: I never feel like relocating there.

J.G.B.: How old are you, if I may ask?

W.S.: Thirty-two.

J.G.B.: You are certainly young enough to make a new life there if you wanted.

W.S.: But I think, what is the point? I am a writer who is very attached to the idea of place. I am concerned with the notion of topography, of visceral shape underlying the imaginative skin of the book.

J.G.B.: Yes, that comes through in your style.

W.S.: And once you are settled in that topography, uprooting yourself would be like pulling the tablecloth from under your imagination: you are not sure that everything would be left standing in the same place. Or whether you would wish it. Was there a certain point in your career where you knew that . . . I mean I know that for all sorts of practical reasons you were settled here, but was there a point in your emotional relation to your work where you thought, 'Yes, I am stuck here'?

J.G.B.: I am stuck here, and I realized that I was stuck here quite a few years ago, but I think that imaginatively I have always assumed I would be leaving England and settling somewhere abroad, somewhere in the Mediterranean. I have not actually drawn a lot of my fiction from the English landscape so it is rather different in my case. You have to remember I didn't come here until I was sixteen, and the brain is hard-wired by the time you are sixteen. You are constantly aware of what may seem trivial things: the density of light, the angle of light, the temperature, the cloud cover, a thousand and one social constructs, the shape of rooms and the way people furnish them, the way they furnish themselves. All these things, which a true native takes totally for granted and is unaware of, still seem . . . there is still an underlying strangeness for me about the English landscape and there is even about this little town of Shepperton where I have lived for thirty-four years. If you settle in a country after a certain age, after your early teens, then it will always seem slightly strange. In my case this has probably been a good thing, it has urged me to look beyond Little England for the source of what interested me as a writer.

W.S.: This is certainly what you have said, the proleptic quality of your fiction through the sixties and into the early seventies, that anticipation of England as a motorway-dominated culture. Do you think that is a function of that hard-wiring coming into this environment, that you simply didn't see England the way other people were seeing it at that time?

J.G.B.: I think that is true, absolutely.

W.S.: You said on the radio programme *Desert Island Discs*

that when you first arrived, and docked at Liverpool, you looked at the cars in the streets and they seemed like little prams to you, the sense of scale was wrong, you were used to an opulent and Americanized environment.

J.G.B.: Absolutely. There is nothing particularly unique in that. I think that any sixteen-year-old crossing the globe and going to a radically different environment, radically different culture, is going to be conscious of those differences for ever. But I think that in my case it has worked well because I have always been interested, keenly interested, in the next five minutes, where we are and what happens next. It has helped to have that distance. A lot of English fiction is too rooted. The writers are too comfortable, one feels. They are like people returning again and again to the same restaurant, they are comfortable with the flavours on offer, and the dishes on offer.

W.S.: You have fostered contradictions both in your self-presentation as a writer and in what you have allowed . . . well, you don't allow people to interpret you as they wish. On the one hand, I feel that you like to reject, as I do, the English image of the writer as a superior craftsman who wears a tweed jacket with leather arm patches and who stands up after a day's work and says 'There's another good coffee table I have sanded down today.' But on the other hand, you seem to embody the Magrittian idea of a very bourgeois lifestyle and a wild imagination. So there is a sort of contradiction there, isn't there?

J.G.B.: Magrittian? Bourgeois? I don't live a bourgeois lifestyle, none of my fellow residents in Shepperton considers this ménage bourgeois in the least. I live like a kind of student.

W.S.: I mean in terms of this *RE-Search* volume, which I read many years ago and am now looking over again: 'I live a solitary life. I get up in the morning. I type.' That sort of angle rather than 'I am wired up to sophisticated recording equipment, tripping on LSD in an upper bedroom.'

J.G.B.: Right. People are amazed by the low-tech state in which I live. I don't even own a hi-fi system. I don't have a PC. I write my stuff in longhand, which amazes Americans. My eye is fairly sharp, even at my age I am still interested in change.

W.S.: Do you go about much nowadays? I mean in the *RE-Search* volume you say in a scathing and deadpan way: 'In my youth I would drive many miles for small-talk.'

J.G.B.: No, I don't do that, but then no one does by the time they are sixty. I don't take part in English literary life in any way. That is partly age and it is . . . I have got to be careful what I say here . . . let's put it like this: when I was your age there wasn't anyone like Will Self around with whom I could speak freely. The typical writers of my youth were Angus Wilson and C. P. Snow.

W.S.: Aged and rather prissy queens.

J.G.B.: Well, the point is their whole intellectual outlook. I always felt much more at home with people from the visual arts like Paolozzi, who has been a long and close friend of mine. Or someone like Richard Hamilton. I felt that when I was talking to Hamilton I was on the same wavelength. I went to that epoch-making pop-art show at the Whitechapel Gallery in 1957, 'This Is Tomorrow'. There was a group of artists there, Paolozzi and Hamilton among them, who absolutely embraced the notion of the new and who were looking at subtexts and hidden agendas in the consumer landscape, in a way I was doing in my early science fiction. When I began to meet writers, mainstream writers, I didn't find that. I felt that – without naming any names – the mainstream writers I met in the sixties, even against the background of the space age, the youth explosion, the drug explosion, the burgeoning power of

TV in the communications landscape, most of the writers I met then were still mentally living in an England that hadn't changed since the 1930s. Maybe I met the wrong writers. Perhaps if I had been able to meet George Orwell before the war I would have found someone who shared my interest in the future. If I have not taken part in the English literary scene it is because I don't feel that I have much to talk about with A. S. Byatt or Karl Miller, with no disrespect to them.

W.S.: Isn't that also because when you read somebody, if you don't like what they write it is almost impossible to have any commerce of ideas with them? Whereas with visual images, if you're a writer, there is the business of translation which remains interesting.

J.G.B.: It is partly that, of course. I met writers whose work I did like, but I still felt – and this is going back thirty years – that we weren't on the same wavelength at all. Partly because of the tremendous retrospective bias of English fiction until very recently.

W.S.: When things seem to have opened up, if only through the agency of multiculturalism and the death of imperialism. Most of the interesting English-language writers domiciled here are writing now with a different slant, so perhaps with your background you were a fore-runner of that post-imperial and multicultural tendency.

J.G.B.: Perhaps. Certainly things have changed enor-mously. Younger writers of your generation are far more open to the world. Partly I think it is the literary culture which dominated English life since the mid-Victorian period and survived intact until the Second World War. It had laid down through generation after generation the blueprint of what was possible and what was not possible in one's work, one's writing, one's life and one's set of mental attitudes. I never met Graham Greene but I enormously admired him for all sorts of reasons. But I am pretty certain that had I met Greene during the sixties I would have found it difficult to . . . to have any sort of close rapport with him because he was so English really, even though he loved travelling abroad and all the rest of it.

w.s.: Did you know Anthony Burgess during the sixties?

J.G.B.: No, I never met him. I am sorry I didn't, because I admired him tremendously as a reviewer and critic. He had a wonderfully catholic and open mind.

w.s.: He would have been *simpatico*, surely, even at that time.

J.G.B.: He would have been. I am sorry that I never met him. It is unfortunate.

w.s.: You wrote that essay on William Burroughs in the late fifties, at a time when he was languishing and out of favour. Well, I suppose Girodias was just publishing *Naked Lunch* at that time. I was interested in your remarks upon Burroughs. Again, you said that you found it difficult to establish a rapport with him when you actually met him, though judging from the dates when you interviewed him, he was in the midst of a serious smack period.

J.G.B.: Have you met him yourself?

w.s.: No, I have never met him.

J.G.B.: I admire him enormously. I think he is the most important, innovative American writer, and possibly world writer, since the Second World War. But the man himself . . . the thing to remember about him is that he is a Midwesterner. He comes from an upper-class, provincial American family and he is not cosmopolitan, he doesn't have the natural cosmopolitanism of, say, a New York writer. He is very much a product of his Midwestern background, he has that built-in contempt for doctors, small-town politicos and policemen that a Bournemouth colonel might have, to use a counterpart from here. It is very difficult to penetrate that almost aristocratic mind-set of his.

w.s.: He has gone home to Kansas, he has gone home to die.

j.g.b.: Absolutely. We have met a number of times over the last thirty years and we always chat in a friendly way. Obviously I steer the conversation towards those things that I know interest him. But I have never been able to relax with him, partly because he is a homosexual . . . that is an important element, I think, because he comes from a generation which had to be careful. You could go to jail. This is true of Angus Wilson too, though he was a very different type, but you sense with older homosexuals that they have developed a system of private codes whereby they recognize one another and ease themselves into each other's company and friendship without endangering themselves in any way. Strangers can be dangerous. There is something of that in Burroughs, complicated of course because he had been a lifelong drug user, at a time when that too was extremely dangerous. It is difficult for an outsider like me who is not a drug user, not a homosexual, to penetrate. I regret that. What is so wonderful about the American literate class is that it produces unlimited quantities of young men and women, of your age group, who are so open to the world. But Burroughs is complicated.

w.s.: Did you read the Ted Morgan biography, *Literary Outlaw*?

j.g.b.: Yes, I did.

w.s.: Because in this *RE-Search* interview you said that you didn't really believe that Burroughs was as interested in the paranormal as some of his utterances and methodologies might lead one to believe. But he is, isn't he?

J.G.B.: Did I say that? Because I agree with you, he is. If I said that, I was wrong.

W.S.: Perhaps you didn't want to believe it because it smacks of table-turning. When you read in the Morgan biography of that business with Brion Gysin, propping their eyes open and scrying in mirrors, you begin to realize that they really did take it seriously.

J.G.B.: That is true. I remember going to see Burroughs when he was living in St James's, Piccadilly, way back in the late sixties. We had dinner together and he was distracted – he had this boyfriend who had 'hate' and 'love' tattooed on his knuckles and he was nervous about where this young man was going. The boyfriend cooked us a roast chicken, then slipped out, and I think Burroughs was unsettled by this. He had an obsession with handguns and how you kill somebody, where you stab them in the chest – all weird stuff out of popular magazines. Then he started talking about the CIA. He had to be careful when walking up and down the street, this little street in St James's, he said, 'because they are keeping a watch on me from a laundry van'. He wasn't that old then, about fifty, and I thought, 'This guy is paranoid.'

W.S.: He'd wigged.

J.G.B.: And all these images were coming from the trash magazines he'd read when he was young and from American movies, *noir* movies that he'd watched in the forties where police keep surveillance on Nazi spies who are trying to infiltrate the American dockyards – from laundry vans! Of course it flows seamlessly into his fiction.

W.S.: The impression I got – not so much from reading the Morgan biography, although that joined all the dots, more from the letters to Allen Ginsberg – was that there was a point at which Burroughs decided to live in the world of the imagination and take excursions into the world of observable fact, rather than the other way around. He went fully underground into his imaginative world.

J.G.B.: And that is probably why he is the great writer he is. That is the only way you can tackle life in the twentieth century and write a fiction about it.

W.S.: But you don't seem to have done that, yet you have produced an enormous amount of prescient work.

J.G.B.: Yes. Well, people are always saying that I have been strongly influenced by Burroughs, but it is not really true. I am much more influenced by the surrealists. They are the biggest influence on my stuff.

W.S.: You are certainly keen on the contemporary period. There is no air of disdain in your work, of 'I don't want to know what is going on now at all.'

J.G.B.: Oh, no, I am very interested in what is going on now. What I am not interested in is what happened twenty years ago. What happened twenty years ago, or thirty years ago, or even half an hour ago tends to be the subject-matter of most English fiction; it is profoundly retrospective. I wasn't interested in the English past – and the reason why, which I discovered when I first came here, was that the English past had led to the English present. One wanted to press the plunger and blow the whole thing up.

W.S.: Given your melioristic, if not optimistic, attitude towards the current period, I wonder if you find it difficult to look at how things have regressed in the last twenty years. There has been a move back towards a preoccupation with class, there has been more economic inequality, there has been a resurrection of Little England.

J.G.B.: I agree and I find it deplorable. I thought the sixties – which you didn't experience at first hand – were a wonderfully exhilarating and releasing period. All those energies, particularly of working-class youth, burst out;

class divisions, which had absolutely strangled and imprisoned the English, seemed to evaporate. Those divisions genuinely seemed to vanish or become as unimportant as they are in America, where there is a class system but one that doesn't serve a political function of controlling the population. Here the class system has always served a political function as an instrument or expression of political control. Everybody is segregated – *hoi polloi* at one end of the lifeboat and toffs sitting around the captain as he holds the tiller – and this prevents anyone from rocking the boat and sending us all to the bottom. In America the class system is not an instrument of political control. When the class system began to . . . well, it didn't disintegrate but it seemed irrelevant in the sixties, I thought, 'How wonderful, this country is about to join the twentieth century.' And then in 1971 – I think Heath had just got back into power – I heard someone use the phrase 'working class' and I thought, 'Oh, God, here we go again.' Now, of course, things are better than they were – I remember England in the late forties and fifties. Hopefully there will be another leap forward. Now we are in the grip of a much larger . . . well, we are not masters of our own fate any more.

w.s.: We probably weren't then; people were just under the impression that they were, which they aren't any longer.

J.G.B.: Now we are a northern turn-off, a slip-road off the northern end of the great European motorway.

w.s.: I remember Mike Petty – who, I believe, edited *Crash* – telling me that when he was working on the MS he'd lock it in a drawer at night for fear that young publishing colleagues might catch sight of it and be severely traumatized. And I only have to look at a few paragraphs of *Crash* to feel I am in the presence of an extreme mind, a mind at the limits of dark imagination. It imparts a sense of everything having been done.

J.G.B.: I haven't reread it since I read the proof so I can't . . .

w.s.: You haven't been back to it at all?

J.G.B.: No, too frightening.

w.s.: You dislike looking back in that way?

J.G.B.: I never read my own stuff, the mistakes come off the pages. Oh, God, all those infelicities of style. And one notices little stylistic tricks. Oh, God, no.

w.s.: You are never tempted to keep lists of things that must never be repeated or words that have been over-used?

J.G.B.: I try to do that mentally, because it is such a temptation.

w.s.: There is an American writer, Nicholson Baker, who must be the world's greatest anal-retentive, because when he writes a book he compares it with everything he has written before to check there is no repetition of imagery or vocabulary.

J.G.B.: I go in for a lot of deliberate repetition, I don't see why not. I like that. They are signifiers for the reader to cross-reference them.

w.s.: To go back to the idea of fictional topography, I was wondering if you felt there was a sense in which a writer's body of work, taken as a whole, is a kind of aerial shot of a foreign territory through which you are conducting the reader. And, further, a sense in which all these topographies join up into some other, numinous parallel world.

J.G.B.: They do.

w.s.: And the repetitions are, therefore, the switches directing the reader back into this other world.

J.G.B.: They are road signs. They point to possible destinations.

W.S.: In your most recent novel, *Rushing to Paradise*, the obvious transposition is that the Ballardian hero has become a heroine. Am I correct in saying that this is the first time you have used a female protagonist who has such an obvious affinity with your male protagonists of the past?

J.G.B.: Ah, I think that she is probably the first female protagonist. I wrote a number of short stories, a collection called *Vermilion Sands*, and in those stories – although they are all told in the first person by a male narrator – each story is dominated by an enchantress figure. They are the nearest I have come before to a dominant female protagonist. Dr Barbara Rafferty is my first naturalistic female protagonist.

W.S.: In a way, the protagonists in *Rushing to Paradise* play out the roles in *The Tempest*: you have a Prospero figure, a Caliban figure, an Ariel figure and a Miranda figure. This is also the case in *Concrete Island*; in fact, it is true of almost all your books. Were you aware of that as you were writing it, that it would be another island-based book?

J.G.B.: Yes, I was. I am aware of my current obsessions because as a writer I have always relied on my obsessions. I have always faithfully followed them. Barbara Rafferty is a new kind of figure for me, but I needed her simply because *Rushing to Paradise* is, in part, a satire on the extremist fringe of the feminist movement. I obviously need a female protagonist. I couldn't have used a lunatic male feminist. Also, the thesis this novel advances – that men are superfluous, there are too many of them, we don't need them any more, or we don't need more than a few – requires a female protagonist. A dominant female figure.

W.S.: I wondered if you were inspired by Jack Kevorkian, the American doctor who has been on trial for those euthanasia cases.

J.G.B.: I was aware of him, of course, Dr Death. The

satire on the animal rights movement – I mean the extremist fringes, because I am all for saving as many pandas, minke whales and dolphins as possible – is fairly straightforward. But the satire on the extremist fringes of the feminist movement is more ambiguous, because I actually take the side of Dr Barbara. That, I hope, gives the book more depth. As the writer, I am as in thrall to Dr Barbara as the boy, the teenager, Jim . . . Oh, what a slip of the tongue! . . . Neil Dempsey is. I can see that this is an immensely powerful, strong-willed woman who has all the ancient, ancestral power of women as creators, as controllers, as enchanters of men, as crones, as mothers – all those archetypal female images, which have so terrified and inspired men through the ages, are incarnated in a small way in this character. As a reader of my own book, I respond to her – although on a technical level she is a serial killer – as she is nonetheless immensely appealing. Leaving my book aside, people of that kind are immensely dangerous; they are the stuff of which charismatic leaders are made.

w.s.: But the link between extreme environmentalism and extreme feminism is a critique of arationality in political thinking, isn't it?

j.g.b.: Absolutely. It is something inherent in the fanatical personality. One of the dangers of these do-it-yourself environmental and similar movements is that they too easily become the vehicles for anyone who wants to get on board, turn the steering-wheel and drive off the edge of a cliff. Fanatics are constantly hijacking otherwise sensible political movements, taking control of them and then pushing them in some dangerous or absurd direction.

w.s.: Would that be your opinion of what happened when André Breton tried to link the original surrealist movement to Marxism?

j.g.b.: Yes, that was an absolute blunder. I don't think

Breton ever really understood or responded deeply to the painters who are now seen as the main exponents of surrealism, because he came from the literary side of surrealism, which was much more dominant in the early days. He saw it as a literary movement, and it was much easier to link a literary movement to Marxism than it was to yoke together this strange collection of painters – Magritte, Dali in particular. The whole point of surrealist painting is that it is answerable to nobody. It is unprogrammable because it all comes from the unconscious.

w.s.: If one were to derive a message from all this, it would be that arationality and the unfettered pursuit of what the imagination is prepared to throw up is fine as long as it is not coupled to some programmatic political aim.

J.G.B.: Absolutely. It is dangerous to follow anything to its logical end. The history of this century is the history of a few obsessives, some of the most dangerous men who have ever existed on this planet, being allowed to follow their obsessions to wherever they wanted to take them, as we saw in Nazi Germany, or Pol Pot's Cambodia or Mao's China. Millions were slaughtered on account of this notion of political cleansing that obsessed Mao. All the bourgeois elements had to be erased before the new Chinese Communists could emerge. The most bizarre things occurred during Mao's cultural revolution. Psychologically disturbed people with deep flaws in their make-up can climb aboard these carousels and start accelerating them until everything flies in all directions.

w.s.: In *Rushing to Paradise*, the fact that Dr Barbara has been convicted for euthanasia in the past seems to be a reprise of the Ballard preoccupation with the way the progress of technology is once again queering human destiny, whether or not it is mastered. And yet there are images in the book – the defunct camera towers and what they symbolize, for example – that suggest to me that we have arrived in a post-Ballard world which is not dominated by technology. That we have now reached a strange plateau where for a time human ideals and aspirations are mattering again. Am I wrong to see that in the book?

J.G.B.: No, I think that is fair enough. Saint-Esprit, the disused nuclear island in the novel, is loosely based on Mururoa, which is still a French nuclear test island. In fact the *Rainbow Warrior*, when it was sunk in Auckland harbour, was about to sail to Mururoa – the Greenpeace protesters later landed on Mururoa, not from the *Rainbow Warrior* but from other craft, and were thrown back into the surf by French soldiers. So I was referring to true-life attempts by animal rightists to defend the turtles. But beyond that, the point is that both the boy, who is myself, and Dr Barbara are, in their very different ways, obsessed with death. My depiction of the young boy, Neil, obviously draws on my own childhood experiences in Shanghai during the Second World War and my own personal obsession with nuclear weapons; these weapons represent a glamorous apocalypse, providing those great mushroom clouds over Eniwetok and Bikini Atoll. The idea that the human spirit might be somehow transfigured by an apocalyptic nuclear war, even at the cost of hundreds of millions of deaths, that this is a necessary step for mankind – this obsessed me for many years, and it comes through in a lot of my fiction; it informs the mind and imagination of my teenage hero. I provide him with a father who died as a result of cancer that he developed after observing a British nuclear test in Australia many years before. Dr Rafferty is not interested in the nuclear aspect of the island, she has her own agenda. She is obsessed with death but she sees it as some kind of minor detour that we will have to take at some point in our lives. Death for her is a door to safety.

w.s.: That is a running preoccupation of yours, this sidelining of death. In the conventional landscape of the novel, death has to be the end, but in your books it never is.

J.G.B.: That's right. In my imaginative life, death is a career move. But that is quite common, too.

w.s.: *Crash*, of course, starts with Vaughan's death and not with his birth. It is all cast in the form of an anticipation of death – as you say, a career move.

J.G.B.: Also, you can pre-empt death by anticipating all its terrors. That is a very old theme.

w.s.: In one sense, surrealists are the most orthodox Freudians there can be. Neil, for example, needs an extra shot of death instinct, and the fact that his father was killed by the nuclear test gives him that booster injection of thanatos which he needs to be a Ballard protagonist. To what extent do you view yourself as an orthodox Freudian?

J.G.B.: It depends on the perspective one takes. As a therapeutic process, psychoanalysis is a complete flop, it doesn't work. But Freud has enormous authority. He has the authority of a great imaginative writer. If you think of him as a novelist . . . Thomas Szasz, the anti-psychiatrist, refers to psychoanalysis as an ideology, and I think that is almost right. If you regard all the aspects of Freud's view of the psyche as symbolic structures, as metaphors, then they have enormous power. I don't think that there is such a thing as a death-wish wired into our brains, along with all the instinctive apparatus – the need to reproduce ourselves, the need for physical freedom, the need for food, water, light – I don't believe that there is a death instinct. It might have evolved as nature's way of . . . there may be an advantage to the gene pool as a whole if there are genes that predispose the sick and the dying to wander off to some elephant's graveyard to keep out of healthy people's way. Now, that could have evolved as a death instinct, a way in which the community cleansed itself of potentially dangerous toxins. But that hasn't happened. Nobody who is close to death wants to do anything but live. Very few people actually look forward to dying. Very few people will their own deaths. On the other hand, death has an enormous romantic appeal, there is no doubt about that. There would probably be more entries in a dictionary of quotations under death than under any other subject. Death has an enormous appeal for the romantic imagination. Obviously it stands for more than just physical dissolution of the body and the brain. It represents something else.

W.S.: Does it point up the notion of soul?

J.G.B.: Could be. Perhaps by visualizing our own death we are cocking a snook at the Creator, we are challenging the unseen powers of the universe with our own small but nonetheless real ability to destroy a portion of that universe. We have very little effect upon the world we live in, but we can catastrophically destroy a portion of it by visualizing our own death. By visualizing our own death we become godlike. Or, rather, we become satanic. That is part of the appeal. We are playing with ourselves, playing for the greatest possible stakes.

W.S.: We are not going to know the answer. But, in theory, if we extinguish ourselves we will know whether realism or idealism is true, whether solipsism is true; we are pushing ourselves to the place where metaphysical questions should be answered by imagining our own death.

J.G.B.: But within the safety of the novel or the film we are not really in danger. It is a form of game playing. The imagination takes strange forms. One can dream of dying, and some sort of powerful imaginative adventure is being undertaken by the sleeping mind. And by the waking mind in the large body of romantic poetry and fiction that celebrates or explores death. This huge metaphysical adventure is taking place inside the mind. Freud says, 'In the unconscious, every one of us is convinced that we are immortal.' Of course the unconscious is deluding itself. It is very difficult – at my age – to face the imminence of one's own death. I cannot visualize dying, or the notion that my mind will be switched off for ever. It is almost impossible to do so. Perhaps one can only do so by the back door, as it were, through works of the imagination. Cocteau's *Orphée* is an exploration of time and death in all its beguiling qualities. *Rushing to Paradise* is slightly off that particular beat.

W.S.: Just to pull you back to Freud, does not the characterization of him as one of the great twentieth-century novelists explain why the nineteenth-century novel is as dead as you have always said it is, particularly in your introduction to the French edition of *Crash*?

J.G.B.: I haven't read that introduction for a long time but, roughly speaking, as I remember it, yes. It probably said some absurd things.

W.S.: Not at all, it is something that I always urge people who show any interest in critical theory to read in the hope that it will cure them of the impulse.

J.G.B.: I went wrong in two ways in that introduction. First, in the final paragraph, which I have always regretted, I claimed that in *Crash* there is a moral indictment of the sinister marriage between sex and technology. Of course it isn't anything of the sort. *Crash* is not a cautionary tale. *Crash* is what it appears to be. It is a psychopathic hymn. But it is a psychopathic hymn which has a point. The other way in which I went wrong was in all my talk about science fiction. Of course *Crash* is not science fiction.

348

w.s.: You developed this concept of inner space, didn't you?

j.g.b.: I still had hopes in those days – the sixties had just ended, science fiction had at last begun to escape from its ghetto. A whole new raft of science fiction writers had come along who had read their Kafka, their James Joyce; they were aware of the larger world of the twentieth-century experimental novel, they were interested in surrealism – and they could see that science fiction needed to rejoin the mainstream, even if, as I claimed then and now, it wasn't the mainstream. There were hopes then, what with films like *Dr Strangelove* and *Alphaville*, and the imagery of the modern techno-media landscape starting to appear in dozens of films, and on TV too in series like *The Avengers*, which now looks quaintly folkloric. But in those days it seemed so chic and hard and gleaming, like a brand-new showroom radiator grille. There was a hope that science fiction could take a great leap forward and transform itself into a more sophisticated kind of fiction altogether. It didn't happen, sadly. By the mid-seventies the whole shebang had slammed into reverse, and science fiction entered its most commercial phase ever.

w.s.: When I read that piece I never pay any attention to that part of your thesis. Rather I was thinking of the decoupling of the literary enterprise from the relationship of individual characters to social change. In that piece you say that the nineteenth-century novelist could move in and out of the individual psyche to show its relationship to society. Coming back to Freud, he is the great deconstructive novelist because he made it impossible for other writers to undertake that project.

j.g.b.: The notion of the novelist as moral arbiter has gone for good. The idea that the novelist can sit like a magistrate above his characters, who are figures in the dark, or a collection of witnesses, or the accused in a shabby scandal – the notion of the novel as a moral structure in which the novelist can acquit some of his characters and sentence others, let others off with a stern warning – this Leavisite notion of the novel as a moral criticism of life doesn't belong in the present world. This was the world of the past. A world of static human values. We now live in a huge goulash of competing appetites and dreams and aspirations and activities. The novelist can't take a moral standpoint any more, he can't sit in judgement on his characters, he can't set in motion a series of divining machines which engage his characters and draw them out, and test them. The writer can rely only on his own obsessions.

W.S.: But that is always taken to be a lack of sympathy.

J.G.B.: This sort of fiction, your stuff, Burroughs's work, challenges all the perceived truths. It challenges the perceived securities of the present world.

W.S.: I was interested in your categorization of *Rushing to Paradise* as satire.

J.G.B.: Partly a satire, partly not.

W.S.: There is an essay I must send you by a young psychoanalytic thinker called Adam Phillips, who wrote a book called *On Kissing, Tickling and Being Bored*.

J.G.B.: I have its successor, *On Flirtation*.

W.S.: I thought you might like some of his apophthegms, such as 'An artist is a man who has the courage of his own perversions.'

J.G.B.: Very good point.

W.S.: If you remember, in his essay on Karl Kraus, Phillips says there is a fundamental instability in the satirical mentality. That the satirist, while seeking to locate the moral centre of the text outside the text itself, is at the same time endlessly in search of a moral certainty and dogma. That is the tension that produces a good satirical perspective. But of course it is very dodgy, because the satirist is drawn either towards dissolution or towards religion. So I was wondering if you had felt that tension, felt yourself being pulled in one direction or the other. I would agree with you that there is a strong tone of satire in *Rushing to Paradise*.

J.G.B.: I agree. I have written a lot of satire or skits, particularly in my short fiction. And in *The Atrocity Exhibition* with the pseudo-scientific papers at the end: 'Why I Want to Fuck Ronald Reagan' or 'Plan for the Assassination of Jacqueline Kennedy'. These are not satires exactly, although they contain satiric elements. I am satirizing the world of laboratory-obsessed researchers who are crashing pigs into concrete blocks, or showing pornographic imagery to disturbed housewives. Many of the things I invented subsequently happened. Atrocity footage has been shown to panels of disturbed housewives to see what the consequences are. There are satiric elements in those pieces, but at the same time, rather like in *Rushing to Paradise*, the frame in which the satiric elements are set works against the satire. The author seems to endorse what is being satirized. The obvious example is that I appear to lend my moral support to Dr Barbara and her activities. Maybe she is right. It may be horrible to think of a world run by Dr Barbara Rafferty and her ilk. This is what I hope the reader will feel when he or she comes to the end of the book.

W.S.: You are making a very precise point that the technologies of bio-engineering and contraception enable women to adopt all the necessary roles that men can adopt, so given a few cups of well-preserved semen, the need for men simply isn't there any more.

J.G.B.: And this is true, isn't it?

W.S.: It is.

J.G.B.: There have been news reports from China over the last week or so of a marked imbalance between the sexes. There are several million more men than there are women. When, in the next twenty or thirty years, parents are able to choose the gender of their children I assume most people will choose a boy first. But bearing in mind that a lot of women who have one child never have another for all sorts of gynaecological, social and personal reasons, that will lead inevitably to an imbalance between the sexes. Now if you have high unemployment and a huge army of young men who can't find wives, or even mates, or sexual partners, then that is a recipe for civil unrest on a vast scale.

W.S.: A lot of unnecessary testosterone flying around.

J.G.B.: Exactly, there are going to be problems. By the same token, in unexpected areas of western Europe or North America – those communities where parents have opted for more girls than boys – one may find havens of social ease, low crime rates, tolerance, a powerful sense of community. More and more people may realize that if you want all the things we ascribe to a civilized way of life, the best thing is to keep down the number of men. These tendencies made possible by the technology of bio-engineering touch upon extremely dangerous ground. These are ancient highways rolled through the human mind along which we have progressed for millennia, and when you begin to tinker with these archetypal forces a huge danger lies ahead. The human race is liable to drive off the edge of the motorway if it isn't careful.

W.S.: Given your personal experience, as someone who was denied the opportunity to exercise and define your male sexuality through manifest aggression, are you saying that that is all there is to masculinity? And further, that a lot of the traditional divisions between the public life and the private, intimate world were predicated upon men being allowed to go out and kick the shit out of each other somewhere else?

J.G.B.: That is true. Of course men, on account of their greater physical strength, were the dominant figures in most social activities: commerce, industry, agriculture, transportation. These activities no longer require man's great physical strength. A woman can just as easily fly a 747 across the Atlantic. A very small part of industry requires brute muscle. A woman computer programmer can control a machine tool that cuts out a car door. A large number of traditional masculine strengths, in both senses of the term, are no longer needed. The male sex is a rust bowl.

W.S.: And is in danger of becoming a genetic sport.

J.G.B.: Yes. There is another element in *Rushing to Paradise* that is equally important, and that is Dr Barbara's attitude towards sex. She represents the way that women have begun – thanks to the feminist movement in large part – to resexualize themselves. They have begun to resexualize their imaginations. I imagine that Dr Barbara would endorse the pro-pornography feminist lobbyists who believe that women have as much right to make, read and enjoy pornography, to express their own sexual imaginations, as men do. Dr Barbara has resexualized herself. Sex for her is as intense as it is for anyone else. She has not allowed herself to be stereotyped in a way that the traditional middle-class professional women would probably have been. She is a sexual predator.

W.S.: With this in mind, it seems significant to me that Neil is an adolescent.

J.G.B.: He would need to be from her point of view. A sixteen-year-old has the prime sperm.

W.S.: One has the sense that his musculature is merely a column of blood vessels. He is just a knob.

J.G.B.: Absolutely. She is interested in his genetic material and it is at its best at around the age of sixteen. Well, he could have been older . . .

W.S.: That would have introduced more complications.

J.G.B.: It would have introduced a romantic complication between him and Dr Barbara.

W.S.: Which you didn't want.

J.G.B.: Which she wouldn't have wanted. She has sex with the visiting yacht crew and anyone else who takes her fancy, but this boy is the stud bull, she wants to keep free of emotional involvement. She is just interested in him as the father of a new race of women. All the women in the book have resexualized themselves and this is very important because this is what women will do.

W.S.: But will they become more obviously mannish?

J.G.B.: Not necessarily. I don't think they will be mannish at all. Dr Barbara lists the qualities . . . she sees Saint-Esprit as a sanctuary for those qualities women possess that have been domesticated out of them. She says that women were the first domesticated animals: 'We domesticated ourselves.' So she wants to preserve all the qualities she admires in women: their passion, their cruelty, their fierceness, their danger, those archetypal qualities that impelled most of the matriarchal religions in the past. She wants a new kind of undomesticated woman who has resexualized her imagination and can take the stage now that men have become obsolescent as a species.

W.S.: But it is a little pessimistic, isn't it?

J.G.B.: Especially if you are a man. Yes, but I accept the emerging logic: women are going to become more dominant socially. The strides they have made in my lifetime are colossal. I see women emerging who are far stronger willed than their counterparts would have been thirty years ago.

J. G. BALLARD

W.S.: Do you think there is anything definitively masculine that is worth preserving aside from aggression?

J.G.B.: Well, of course.

W.S.: Well, what?

J.G.B.: This is a novel that presents an extreme hypothesis, it is not intended to be . . . no more than I am suggesting in *Crash* that we should go out and crash our cars.

W.S.: I know, but you speak to my condition. I feel genuinely pessimistic because if you look at the men's movement, the attempt to resexualize and recondition male sexuality, men are considered either effete or aggressive with nothing in between.

J.G.B.: Men are going to have to cope with the huge task of deciding who they are. And they are going to have intense competition from the world of women.

W.S.: Isn't it arguable that the wilder fringes of the gay movement are one of the phenomena that have sprung up because of the way in which avowedly heterosexual men are afflicted by a creeping sense of impotence?

J.G.B.: Could be. And other S & M practices, in particular among homosexuals, are the last survivals of true masculinity. I made the point years ago in *The Atrocity Exhibition* that the psychopathic should be preserved as a nature reserve, a last refuge for a certain kind of human freedom. This applies to the deviant imagination, too. It should be treasured because the imagination itself is an endangered species in this conformist world we live in. The whole planet is turning into a vast Switzerland. This is the other thing I dread; the suburbanization of the soul. I don't want to give the impression that *Rushing to Paradise*, any more than *Crash*, represents my last word on the subject.

W.S.: What we have been saying brings us neatly back

to Burroughs, who can be seen as the apostle of the male homosexual response to the feminist movement. I'm thinking of his avowed and essentially caricatured misogyny – I believe he once said that all women should be exterminated.

J.G.B.: His attitude to women is strange, there is no doubt about that.

W.S.: But any career homosexual tends to have strange ideas about women.

J.G.B.: My own contacts with male homosexuals have been rather limited. Most homosexuals I have known seem to have liked and enjoyed the company of women. I am thinking of masculine homosexuals, not effete homosexuals. Burroughs is odd because he clearly dislikes women in a visceral way.

W.S.: He is delighted now – and I think the Morgan book puts it very well – by the sight down Christopher Street in New York of all these very butch male homosexuals. He sees himself as an avatar of the male who is both homosexual and tough. But coming back to *Rushing to Paradise*, tough male homosexuals now exist because they have become this ghetto of male sexuality, and the rest of us heterosexual men are becoming increasingly feminized without really knowing it.

J.G.B.: My daughters have complained for years that most men are total wimps.

W.S.: Exactly. When you hear women talking about a man they always say, 'He's too nice.' Which means he is not sexy. Yet they hate the men they find sexy because they are dangerous and unstable. But you're not pessimistic?

J.G.B.: Me? No, I'm not. One can't speak collectively of human beings and discount sex roles. I am a great believer in the power of the human imagination to transcend almost anything, and the future is so unpredictable. When virtual reality comes on stream in twenty or thirty years' time, it could be the greatest transformation the human race has known since the invention of language, or the invention of consciousness.

W.S.: It is interesting that you should mention this, because last year I was commissioned to write a report on the potential of interactive video and virtual reality as an entertainment medium, and I was writing the report when that *New Nightmares* series was broadcast, in which you were talking about the same thing. I am not claiming any synchronicity, but I had just come to the same conclusion about the medium as you. That the medium will be pushed ahead when people are given the opportunity to commit murders or immoral acts in a 'virtual' way. That is what would make it a radically new entertainment medium.

J.G.B.: When one can start to play with one's psycho-pathology without any moral stigma attached. Some of us will be required to assume the roles, emotions and hatreds of a concentration camp killer in order to allow the virtual reality drama of the Second World War to unfold. Somebody has to play Iago, somebody has to play Lady Macbeth. The social constraints that we need on a day-to-day basis just to get along with each other will no longer be experienced.

W.S.: Unlike some of the other writers on the *New Nightmares* series, such as William Gibson, you don't seem to be enthralled by the technology. You forecast the possibility of major revolutions in social organization and collective thought, as a function of technological change.

J.G.B.: I do think that we are limited by our own central nervous systems. It is very difficult to say whether real evolution on the human brain is going to take place. It is possible that it will only take place at one remove, in those outer electronic shells . . . the externalizations of the central nervous system represented by computer systems.

W.S.: That is certainly what the Marvin Minskis of this world believe, that evolution in the strict Darwinian sense is going to occur in the human–computer interface.

J.G.B.: I wonder.

W.S.: I wonder too. It seems to be a good example of what Thomas Szasz would call professional closure: they have a vested interest in believing that it will be the case. I have been interested in Szasz for years because he wrote the definitive book in defence of free drug use, *Ceremonial Chemistry*, and he followed it up with *Our Right to Drugs*, so I went out to interview him at Syracuse.

J.G.B.: Who did you interview him for?

W.S.: *The Times*.

J.G.B.: I read *The Times*. Why didn't I read that? I have seen him on TV – this is going back twenty years or more when the anti-psychiatry movement was in full swing.

W.S.: He was described by Geoffrey Wheatcroft in the *Spectator* as a libertarian thinker, but he is archetypal Viennese.

J.G.B.: He is a psychiatrist himself?

W.S.: He is a psychiatrist himself and treats people. He is a very odd figure, very precise, very anal retentive. I wish I could meet a psychiatrist or psychoanalytic thinker who wasn't anal retentive. I wonder if Freud was anal retentive? Somehow I doubt he was.

J.G.B.: Well, he collected all those statuettes that look vaguely faecal. They look like coprolites, fossilized faeces.

W.S.: When I interviewed Szasz he said that R. D. Laing was guilty of hubris. Believing that schizophrenia was merely a different semiology, Laing had attempted to cure a schizophrenic who was of course incurable. Szasz wouldn't back-peddle from the idea that schizophrenia was merely a category error, which I found very strange.

J.G.B.: I was always very suspicious of Laing and his claims that schizophrenia was a social construct. Having known one or two people who were virtually schizophrenic, I believe the severe nature of the handicaps these people suffered from weren't in any way an adaptive response to a hostile reality. These people were crippled in a way that an autistic child is crippled. Something had gone wrong with the basic wiring.

W.S.: There is something about true madness that goes beyond mere eccentricity.

J.G.B.: Absolutely. These are people with sections of their skulls removed and their naked brains are flinching in the light. They are victims of circumstance, not proactive in the way that Laing suggested. But then he was a kind of novelist too.

W.S.: Certainly *The Divided Self* is a great work of fiction. But returning to your work, *The Kindness of Women* was published around the time of Burroughs's *Queer*. It is interesting that both of those books should have been published at that point, because both of them seemed retroactively to humanize your work. A lot of people came to your work through *Empire of the Sun* and I imagine, read it completely differently from the way, I did. I read it and, having known the earlier books, said, 'Ah, that is where all these images of empty swimming pools and people jammed into windscreens come from. This is the great repository of Ballard's imagery.' But it didn't really humanize the earliest books; there was nothing sentimental about *Empire of the Sun*. In fact, it was arguably one of your least sentimental books.

J.G.B.: It didn't need to be sentimental.

W.S.: It didn't need to be? Elaborate.

J.G.B.: Take the image of the drained swimming pool for example. Way back in the sixties, in some of my earliest short stories, abandoned apartment buildings and drained swimming pools and all the rest of it – these were images that were powerfully nostalgic. I used to set these drained swimming pools and so forth in a nominal future, in some nominal New Mexico, but they were powerfully nostalgic since they looked back to my own childhood. I wasn't aware of it at the time, at all. I had to clothe this rather wistful dream of Shanghai, which I knew I would never return to. I had to clothe these images in some sort of dramatic and emotional disguise to express the anguish I felt. But when I wrote about the real drained swimming pools in my life I could present them as they were. I have often thought that writers don't necessarily write their books in their real order. *Empire of the Sun* may well be my first novel, which I just happened to write when I was fifty-four. It may well be that *Vermilion Sands* is my last book.

W.S.: Or *Terminal Beach*.

J.G.B.: Yes, one doesn't necessarily write one's books in their chronological order.

W.S.: Similarly, there are no definitive texts, there are only versions of texts. But then we get to *The Kindness of Women*. One is conscious that it is an autobiographical novel. Everything that had been left out of the earlier books is plugged back into them. Was it a difficult book for you to write?

J.G.B.: *The Kindness of Women*? No. It is autobiographical, yes, but it is my life seen through the mirror of the fiction prompted by that life. It is not just an autobiographical novel; it is an autobiographical novel written with the full awareness of the fiction that that life generated during its three or four decades of adulthood.

W.S.: It is retroactively infusing the events with the

imagery they occasioned, plugging that imagery back into the *mise-en-scène*.

J.G.B.: It is the life reconstituted from the fictional footprints that I left behind me. It was no more difficult to write than anything else.

W.S.: I'd like to return to the subject of Burroughs's visceral hatred of women. When he was married to Joan Vollmer in the forties, he loved her very much – even though he found her physically very difficult to cope with. She said that he could function as a heterosexual.

J.G.B.: I find it hard to believe.

W.S.: Couldn't one say that the accidental killing of his wife triggered his misogyny?

J.G.B.: It is a retrospective justification of the act.

W.S.: Exactly. And it helps to explain the plunge that Burroughs makes into the magical world. He describes this brilliantly in the introduction to *Queer*. It's very easy to see how that experience would tip a man who was already living far too much within the purlieus of an exaggerated imagination into a full-blown magical obsession. The parallels with your own life and fictional existence are obvious, there is no need to recount them. Why, then, does one have the sense that you are an extremely rational and well-balanced person?

J.G.B.: That's true. It is something I have never understood about myself. Particularly in the years after *The Atrocity Exhibition* and *Crash* and *High-Rise* came out. People used to come to this little suburban house expecting a miasma of drug addiction and perversion of every conceivable kind. Instead they found this easy-going man playing with his golden retriever and bringing up a family of happy young children. I used to find this a mystery myself. I would sit down at my desk and start writing about mutilation and perversion. Going back to Burroughs, his imagination and mine – I recognize the similarities instantly whenever I read Burroughs. People say I have been heavily influenced by him, but I don't think I have at all. My fiction is highly structured, I know where I am going, I always plot my novels and short stories very carefully, I always write an extended synopsis. Burroughs doesn't do this at all. I don't think he starts a book with any sense of structure whatsoever. *Naked Lunch* in particular. I have a scientific imagination, my fiction is not generated by my emotions but by a natural inquisitiveness.

w.s.: A forensic imagination.

j.g.b.: Yes. I am in the position of someone performing an autopsy. Like all of us when we rent a strange apartment and find traces of the previous occupants – a medical journal, a douche bag, a videotape of an opera – and we begin to assemble from these apparently unrelated materials a hypothesis about who the previous occupants were. We carry out an investigation of our own. If we have fairly fluid and loose imaginations we can often come up with very striking visualizations of who our predecessors were. I operate in exactly that way. The environments both internal and external, the outer world of everyday reality and the inner one inside my head, are constantly offering me clues to what is going on. These clues secrete obsessional material around themselves. I then begin to explore various hypotheses: is it possible that car crashes are actually sexually fulfilling? It is a nightmare prospect but it could have a germ of truth – at least on a metaphorical level. I begin to explore the possibilities. How would this erotic frisson be achieved? Then I need to explore that. So let's explore a car crash as if it was an erotic experience. And so I push that out. I have a speculative imagination that is constantly exploring the interior, mythic possibilities of these ideas. Obviously there is an interiorized mythology that we all have, that gives our lives some sort of compass bearing; we dream that we will go out to New Zealand and become a sheep-farmer, or sail a yacht around the world, or open a nightclub in Marbella. We are sustained by these dreams. Now all these things come together in my fiction, but I think my approach is basically a speculative one. Therefore my emotions remain uncommitted to whatever my imagination happens to generate. This is not true of Burroughs. He believes everything he writes. He lives in a paranoid micro-climate of his own; the rain falls and the rain is the condensation of this paranoid climate. The rain is the material of his books.

w.s.: And he is in a frightening magical world, where malevolent spirits may destroy him psychically. But with your view of Freud as the great novelist of the twentieth century, you can write things like *Crash* and then experience a car accident without viewing your psyche as the toy of terrifying forces over which you have no control. Burroughs is the true Freudian. He believes in fate and thanatos and just about everything.

J.G.B.: I think that is true. As I said, I haven't looked at *Crash* since I read the proofs, but when I think of it, or when other people talk about it, I don't feel any emotional tie to the book. Which I do feel in the case of the straightforwardly autobiographical *Empire of the Sun*. When people say 'What was your camp like?' or describe scenes in the book, I feel a flood of emotional feelings of all sorts. Because I was directly involved. In a sense, *Empire of the Sun* is true. It represents a still-living body of experience that part of my mind is immersed in. That is not true of *Crash*. Had *Crash* been inspired by a real car crash, had I been lying drowsily, pumped full of morphine, and gazing at the nurses around me, feeling a strange, erotic merging of images of technological violence, the enticements of the flesh – had *Crash* emerged from that, it would be a completely different book from the one I wrote.

W.S.: *Rushing to Paradise* is classic Ballard, it has the Ballard elements that we have come to expect. Are you someone who thinks about the fictional project ahead? You may work forensically but do you think inspirationally about what you are going to work on next? Do you wait for ideas to come?

J.G.B.: Oh, yes, the images and ideas have a life of their own. They emerge through the topsoil of the mind, push forward and make their presence felt. And one then uses them as part of the larger inquiry which every novel or short story is.

W.S.: I feel that I am midway between you and Burroughs in this respect.

J.G.B: You have got Burroughs's manic humour. I am a little humourless.

W.S.: Sardonic humour. Gallows humour. Burroughs, to me, represents the last great avatar of modernism; he is like Beckett, he is like Joyce, he has been in exile. He is also a very dangerous person to look up to. Emotionally, he is a very tricky man, a blindingly selfish man, totally egotistic. Not nice.

J.G.B.: I am afraid that is true. I remember seeing a film portrait of him on television, with a strange heart-rending conversation between him and his son, who died of liver cancer. Burroughs had no feelings for his son whatsoever.

W.S.: I remember that scene in the film well; there is Grauerholz, his secretary, and Billy, his son. Burroughs and Grauerholz are behaving like bitchy queens . . .

J.G.B.: And the son wants some fatherly affection and reassurance. Burroughs is completely incapable of giving that. He may be an outrageous human being but he has produced some great fiction, and that is what counts, isn't it?

w.s.: Well, yes and no. I was going to ask you about that.

J.G.B.: We have to be grateful for what we have got. Take de Sade's novels. God knows, the man was reprehensible as a human being, as a father and as a husband, as an employer of young women whom he ruthlessly exploited. Yet he did leave his fiction. One has to leave all moral considerations aside. The imagination is not a moral structure. The imagination is totally free of any moral constraints or overtones. It is up to society as a whole to say whether the novels of de Sade should be available or not. Society has social needs that the individual imagination doesn't have. There is no reason why a mass murderer shouldn't write a beautiful poem.

w.s.: But don't you think that evil is incorrigibly banal? I am reading Shirer's *Rise and Fall of the Third Reich* at the moment and even in translation – I shudder to think what it is like in the German – Hitler's table talk is crushingly banal.

J.G.B.: Is that really true? I have read Hitler's table talk, *Mein Kampf* and speeches and so on. A totally evil man, of course . . . but there is something compelling about his diction.

w.s.: It is the compulsion of obviousness.

J.G.B.: He was a product of the self-improvement manual, the public library . . .

w.s.: Dale Carnegie Man.

J.G.B.: He was the product of the first popular newspapers, the first product of the era of mass literacy.

w.s.: The Great Autodidact.

J.G.B: His strange mix of Wagner, Darwin, Nietzsche, culled from newspapers and improvement manuals, culled from popular encyclopaedia accounts of Darwinism and Nietzsche, biology and race. There were an awful lot of race theories around in the last decades of the nineteenth century. He assembled these together in the way an autodidact does. It rather like a science fiction fantasy. But what he added was this tremendously compelling spin to it all. You can almost believe that what he writes and claims is true. There is an insane logic that you almost have to acknowledge. Almost, but you have got to be careful.

w.s.: What is fascinating about reading the *Rise and Fall of the Third Reich* is how damn modern it all was. It was right up to date.

j.g.b.: Absolutely, and that was a large part of its appeal. If you think of Hitler's contemporaries – Herbert Hoover and Balfour, men in frock-coats and wing collars who rode around in the world of hansom cabs. Whereas the Nazi order was the world of neon . . .

w.s.: New drugs . . .

j.g.b.: . . . New drugs, fast aeroplanes, fast cars, uniforms worn for their theatrical effect, the whole society conceived as a dramatic and imaginative statement. This was absolutely new, it had never been done before except in the heyday of ancient Rome or ancient Egypt or Babylonia. They brought technology into it all. You have technology at the service of madness.

w.s.: Technology is the key. What are your feelings on the role of technology today, when things seem so undefined? I am not asking you to play the Seer of Shepperton . . .

j.g.b.: The nightmare marriage of sex and technology that I wrote about in *Crash* may not have taken place. Still, I would maintain that the thesis advanced by *Crash* may be just beginning, if not literally at least imaginatively: with video arcade games, a culture of violence in the cinema, the first hints of virtual reality systems, a culture of sensation for its own sake. We are walking through the shallows of a great, deep sea of possibility; at any moment we are going to feel the seabed drop away beneath our feet. I think we are in a lull before a momentous change that you will see but I won't.

W.S.: I'd rather not see it, personally.

J.G.B.: I think it will come.

W.S.: Not that I wish to be a reactionary but I don't share your melioristic temperament. I am a pessimist by nature. Surely it is the climb-down of the Soviet Union that has given us this sense of a false lull? But you are horrified, as I am, by the prospect of a future of boredom, a Switzerland of the soul.

J.G.B.: Not just a planetary suburbia, a future of utter boredom, lit by totally unpredictable acts of violence. The forces of social cohesion will ensure we get the drab city of the plain again. These unpredictable acts of sudden violence may take all sorts of forms, not necessarily physical violence. There could be weird consumer trends or bizarre vacation schemes, financial scams. All sorts of strange diseases may well flare up, and they will be welcomed by the bored inhabitants of the super-Switzerland of the future. More like a Düsseldorf suburb actually. They will be welcomed in the way that people like reading about serial killers, or rent videos about psychopaths, because these deviant acts provide some sort of compass bearing. I think what we are seeing now in the post-Soviet Union breakdown is the consumer culture finally settling globally into place. In Russia there is the equivalent of a land rush, they are all charging forward trying to get their piece of the consumer society – of course it is a total cock-up. Sooner or later eastern Europe and the Soviet Union will embrace suburbanization, and the global consumer economy will finally have wrapped itself around the planet, leaving tragic sections of the Third World out in the cold for ever. Then we will get this Kafkaesque prospect – you can already see it in place. How dull it all is.

W.S.: In conclusion, I'd like to talk about your long-standing interest in visual imagery. What is your view on what contemporary visuals have to offer? Are you stimulated by any of the work that is going on in contemporary art?

J.G.B.: The contemporary visual arts are in a parlous condition.

W.S.: Aren't they just!

J.G.B.: I agree with almost everything Brian Sewell says. I have been to many diploma shows at the Royal College and elsewhere. I went to the show where Damien Hirst exhibited his sheep in the tank. All the installation art was very badly put together. My girlfriend and I compared it to an exhibition at the Hayward Gallery twenty years ago. At the Hayward exhibition there was a lot of installation art – Kienholz's Vietnam War memorial, a huge silver thing with a built-in café; there was even a Coke machine there, and I bought a Coke from it. That's the first time I ever bought a Coke from a piece of sculpture. The Kienholz piece was a beautifully constructed thing. I remember an Oldenburg tableau, a tacky motel room with zebra-striped bedspreads and zebra-striped furniture; it was the American vernacular at its most popular.

W.S.: Kitsch.

J.G.B.: Verging on kitsch. But this installation was very carefully constructed to make its points all the more telling. Had it been casually flung together it would have undercut its own strange magic. Judging the visual arts by the Turner Prize and the sort of things that the Saatchis collect, I think they are in a deplorable state. But to some extent, just as we don't need any more novels, we don't need the visual arts any more.

W.S.: It is all very well for you to say that with so many novels under your belt.

J.G.B.: It may be that the imaginative stimulus provided by the easel painting and the free-standing sculpture is now provided by different sources altogether. In the old days a sculptor would look at a 747 and think 'What a magnificent flying machine this is!' and he would create a sculpture that embodied the magic of flight. Nowadays the people who design the engine of a 747 themselves put the imaginative dimension into the construction. As American car designs have always done – there are remarkably few images of cars in the visual arts of the last hundred years simply because the cars have been providing the imaginative dimensions themselves. So many consumer goods are built to such a high standard of design that the aesthetic dimension is almost as strong as the functional dimension. So the role of the artist may be unnecessary. Or it may be that modernism has just run out of gas. Concept art and installation art can be regarded as the fag-ends of modernism.

W.S.: It is amazing that we should be treated to such an appalling derogation. Mind you, I interviewed Hirst for that show. His description of what he was doing was much better than the thing itself.

J.G.B.: He is a great novelist, it is his titles that are so brilliant. The shark in the tank isn't a particularly telling image, it is the caption that was a poetic statement. But you have got to bear in mind the question of commodification. Put a sheep in a tank and you can sell it to the Saatchis for twenty-five thousand pounds. Just write the idea down on a piece of paper and you won't get anything.

W.S.: The interesting thing about the car is that the car windscreen has been more influential in making us all cinéastes than film has itself. The experience of continually driving around confronting a seventy-millimetre frame observing the world like that.

J.G.B.: That is a very good point. Recently, I went on Sky TV's books programme, and they sent a car for me. Usually I don't like it when they send cars because it is so boring and they play the radio for hours. But this was a short ride. So I was sitting in the back seat of this Vauxhall Senator, which is about the same size as my car – I have never sat in the back of my car – and it was like watching a movie. The sensation of sitting down at the wheel is slightly different, but I agree with you.

W.S.: The way in which we have interiorized the cinematic view has something to do with our dramatic rehearsal of our death, doesn't it? Having internalized the cameraman's perspective, we are then free notionally to annihilate figures on our screen. People of my generation are afflicted with this as if it were a virus; they are not aware of the extent to which their view of their own identity has been compromised by film and the car windscreen.

J.G.B.: I absolutely agree with you.

W.S.: Which could be another explanation of why the contemporary visual arts seem so sterile.

J.G.B.: You are right. The way we see the world, thanks to movies and TV, the car, the presentation of a commodified landscape through thousands of mini-film dramas – I mean, so many advertisements in magazines look like stills from films. It has changed the way we see the world, and the world of the imagination as well. The biggest disappointment for me is the experimental video film. They are so crushingly boring, aren't they? In a way that the experimental cinema fifty years ago never was.

W.S.: You just have to go back to early Buñuel.

J.G.B.: The video technology is too easy to master.

w.s.: There is a facile quality to it. You were talking in *RE-Search* about one of the early Bowie videos, the video to 'Ashes to Ashes', which is superb.

J.G.B.: Yes, that was marvellous.

w.s.: It was very simple, they weren't exploiting the technology.

J.G.B.: There are too many special effects now.

August 1994

*In July of this year (1995), the incoming French President, Jacques Chirac, announced the resumption of nuclear testing on Mururoa. As I write a flotilla of environmentalists is setting sail to protest. W. W. S.

Martin Amis

WILL SELF: What struck me about the reversal of time and causality in *Time's Arrow* was this idea that once you have reached a certain plateau, death starts to suck you in.

MARTIN AMIS: Who knows when it happens – it happens in your late thirties – but it happens. Suddenly you realize, both as a person and as a writer, that you are switching from saying 'Hi' to saying 'Bye'. And, as I said in *London Fields*, it is a full-time job: death. You really have to wrench your head around to look in the other direction, because it's so apparent, and it wasn't apparent before. You were intellectually persuaded that you were going to die, but it wasn't a reality.

W.S.: That's the trope about suicide, isn't it? Tod's soul can't commit suicide.

M.A.: You can't do that. It's La Rochefoucault's line: 'No man can stare at the sun or at death, with unshielded eyes.' It's interesting to think that a child has no idea of death. They talk about it as something you can return from. Until they're about six or seven, and then death arrives as an idea. Maybe from then on in, it arrives in instalments. The thirty-five-year-old, or thirty-six-year-old, doesn't get it. It's what being young is – almost by definition.

W.S.: So I'm fucked. Because that's what I got from the book. Perhaps I just read it at the right point.

M.A.: I did think it would be wonderfully comic to have

somebody getting younger, and the inner voice continually exulting about feeling better. Because you never really do exult in your health. It's tragic.

W.S.: That's Dostoevsky's idea of the reprieve from execution, isn't it? That you never really appreciate the very quiddity – one of your favourite words – the ordinariness of your existence, until it's under threat.

M.A.: The thing is that if you're going the other way, you know exactly how long you've got. When Anthony Burgess was told that he had only a year to live – and he wrote fifteen novels to give his wife something to live on – he said he had a sense of luxury. Because he'd never been sure before that he was going to live . . .

W.S.: . . . That he wouldn't be knocked down by a car . . . About the critical reaction to *Time's Arrow*. I felt it was monstrously unfair.

M.A.: Among my writer friends I'm known as a sort of tyrant of cool. That I don't mind reviews. Some of my writer friends will assume the foetal position for eight hours after receiving a lukewarm review. And I always used to josh them along about this. I was thick-skinned – I am thick-skinned about this – simply because I'm the son of a writer. I do think that by various complicated processes this does thicken your skin. Being a writer is being someone whose solitary thoughts turn out to have some general interest. Which is an extraordinary thing, but it's never struck me that way because my dad did it. So I'm not as fragile as people who got there by themselves. When I was pissed off by some of the reviews for this book, my writer friends said: 'Well, there you are. Now you know.' And I said: 'Look, come on. You've never been accused of profiting from the slaughtered of Auschwitz, as I was. You haven't had your basic integrity questioned – more than questioned – mocked.' So I did think that it went beyond what one considers to be normal criticism. To be called 'talentless', one would brush it off like a midge on a summer evening. But I was told that I was blasphemously intruding with the motive of profit. Sure, you wake up furious at three in the morning. You wake up feeling, 'son of a bitch'. I even entered into a correspondence – which I've never done before – with the reviewer on the *Spectator*, who had put all these points. Really, just as a way of letting off steam. Funnily enough, it didn't have that reaction in America, where you expect them to be more protective of the subject. In fact, my rough impression is that the more someone knows about the Holocaust, the more they like the book.

W.S.: Yes, I wondered, because I've read Fest and Levi. I knew all that material. I wasn't coming to it fresh. And in a way that made the book more exciting for me, because I knew what was coming. I knew just how horrible it was. And I felt myself sucked through the book in this way.

M.A.: That's right, you can't get off the train – and the image of the train is significant, because it's so resonant in this story. But you're taken the other way; and it's harder to resist that journey when you're taken the other way. Jeremy Treglowan taught a class at Princeton where he compared the American and English reviews. I sat in on the class and gave the reason that I've just given you. Which is that in America the Holocaust is much more present, much more visited, and therefore not hedged in what we might call 'good taste'.

W.S.: Do you think that's anything to do with the different status of the Jewish communities? By this I mean that here – apart from the frumahs – the Jewish *modus vivendi* is to submerge itself in the English culture. There's a strange complicity between the English and the Jews, that the Jews shouldn't exist, in quite an important way. I'm half American Jewish, and I have a very prickly sensitivity for any gentile dealing with these matters, and I didn't find the book remotely offensive. I couldn't even conceive of how it could be perceived that way. I didn't actually look back at the criticism, but my hunch is that it didn't come from Jews, it came from the English.

M.A.: It came from the sort of philistine journalistic end of the market. Apart from this James Buchan guy in the *Spectator*. But I looked for all those sorts of explanations: how the Jews are much more intellectually prominent in America. In fact when Dan Quayle talks about the 'cultural élite', that's code for 'Jew'. It means Hollywood and New York, basically. But Jeremy Treglowan looked at all these things and said, 'It's nothing to do with that, it's just that people hate you.'

W.S.: What you're talking about here is the urge of the critic to elide the writer's moral being with his work. And although you talk about this business of inheriting the family trade, it does seem to me that this tendency in criticism washes right over that. Perhaps it's because I'm a writer myself, but I do feel that the novelist puts himself out on the line to a far greater degree than perhaps any other artist. It is a risky business in that way.

M.A.: In an age of growing literalism . . . there's also the vulgar interest in the writer himself – or herself. Because personalities are much more accessible than a corpus of work. Everyone can understand a person, you can see them on *Wogan*, and you've got a handle on them. In TV age terms, it's pretty onerous to have to wade through a body of work, when all you're interested in is personalities.

W.S.: Do you think that's a reaction against structuralism? Against the idea that literary works are separate, parallel worlds, that need to be considered in isolation, solely in terms of themselves?

M.A.: No, I think that that's over-sophisticated. The people out there aren't reacting to structuralism; I think it's a TV age thing. They want it simple. They want it explained: how do you do it? It's really a sort of sub-*Time Out* investigation. They want to know how you make money by doing this thing – that's basically it.

W.S.: The question you are most frequently asked by non-writers is, 'How do you get your ideas? Where do they come from?' To them, imagination seems to be this separate faculty in the mind that just spews out ideas, doesn't it? I don't know if you would agree with me, but I don't see my imagination in that way at all. I'm not sure I even believe in the idea of imagination conceived in that way.

M.A.: I agree. I think the real mystery is talent. Because all writers have had those days when it doesn't feel like endeavour, when it feels like you're just clearing away stuff to get at what's there. Auden described writing as scraping away on a dusty stone to see what the inscription is.

W.S.: There's the alternative idea though, isn't there? There's Hemingway's concept of being 'juiced', or Simenon's view of himself as just watching an internal film, and copying down the dialogue as it's spoken. A sense of automatic writing and production, do you ever have that?

M.A.: Kerouac took writing off the top of the head as far as it would go; where you just write down what occurs to you, and trust to a kind of inner mumble. But the nearest I get to that is a kind of comic flow, a flow of comic invention. Then ideas suggest themselves and seem to come very naturally, the comedy starts to impact and become more like itself, more ridiculous.

W.S.: That's like being a stand-up comic, isn't it? The timing of each gag suggesting the timing for the next. Presumably when that's happening you bifurcate, forming an internal audience that's giggling at what's coming out.

M.A.: Yes, I think that's true. And I'm very fond of the notion, which is summed up by the anecdote that there was a writer – in the days when you still had to put your occupation on your passport – who was going to Amin's Uganda. And on the plane he thought that he would change his passport, just to be on the safe side. So he made a little squiggle and transformed 'writer' into 'waiter'. I do think writing is waiting a lot of the time. Not waiting on table, but a vigil. When it isn't flowing, when there isn't an internal voice dictating what you ought to say, then it's better just to sit and wait.

W.S.: There's a crucial need for indolence, isn't there?

M.A.: It's a sort of dream state. It's amazing that that should be so, that that's how you earn your living. You enter a hypnagogic realm that's to do with words, and you hang out there until they're ready. It's Auden again: he spoke of poems 'wanting to be written', and him saying, 'not yet my precious'. He also had the congruent thing of scrapping poems, like Graves whose collected poems got shorter every year. Auden said of that poem 'September 1939', 'it's probably a good poem, but I shouldn't have written it'.

W.S.: It's a very revealing poem, a raw poem. It's interesting that you should talk about Auden. I wonder, what does he represent to you? Do you bring him us because of the question of 'Englishness' and exile?

M.A.: The common view is that Auden committed literary suicide when he left England. And there's a lot in that. To me Auden represents the last of the poet-legislators; an enormous figure who spoke with enormous authority. It's that authority – in the Shelleyan sense of speaking for the whole species – that seduces all the poets who are influenced by him. That's vanished from poetry now, and as we were saying the other night, it's the novelists who have moved in.

But there was something inimitable and forbidding about Auden's high style.

W.S.: So it's that that attracts you to him?

M.A.: It's the voice . . .

W.S.: It's not the idea of literary suicide?

M.A.: But that's very much the received wisdom, it's not my conclusion. I wouldn't suggest, as Larkin did and as my father does, that it was the cowardice, the desertion, that destroyed his talent. I don't think it works like that.

W.S.: Coming back to *Time's Arrow*, just a small thing, but I particularly liked Tod Friendly's assonant perfecto. Perhaps it's because I'm writing a book at the moment in which the protagonist always smokes a cigar, and often it's a Partaga perfecto. Where did you get it from? It's an unusual cigar. Did you get it from Donald Duck? Or is it the bomb shape of the cigar? Or is it serendipitous?

M.A.: It's serendipitous. Anything that hangs around in my mind for a while gets in, purely on the strength of that. I think, 'What's this doing in my mind? It must resonate with some experience.' I think the appeal was that it was a kind of comment on his morality.

W.S.: But smoking is another continuum, isn't it? Like all habits it's a very powerful expression of the idea of temporal continua, that's what I got off it . . .

M.A.: . . . Was it?

W.S.: It's interesting that you didn't use that gag. There's a short Woody Allen piece called 'Conversations with Helmholtz', in which Helmholtz – who was a contemporary of Freud – is smoking a cigar; and despite the fact that he hasn't lit it, he's drawing on it so strongly that it actually decreases in length. You didn't put in a reversal gag on smoking.

M.A.: No, except for preparing the girlfriend's butts . . .

W.S.: Yeah, but no actual smoking. Perhaps that's because it's too central a continuum?

M.A.: Maybe, but there are some things you just decline to elaborate on.

W.S.: Moving on. I wondered, particularly with *London Fields*, whether you felt under pressure to produce 'movement' fiction. And by that I mean a book where you work consciously to unite your individual voice – in some way – with the *Zeitgeist*?

M.A.: No, I don't think I've ever felt conscious of a pressure to write this or that. *London Fields* began life as a novella. It was going to be a sixty-page story called 'The Murderee'. There was going to be a Keith figure and a Nicola figure, just moving towards each other and then the deed would occur. But then, what opened the novel up was this third character, Guy, which enlarged the social ambit; and then there was the narrator, who became a kind of actor.

W.S.: So that came later? Because in some ways it seemed to me to be a reworking of the ideas in the back-end of *Money*.

M.A.: From *The Rachel Papers* on, I've never really written a naïve novel in the sense that the action is presented as actually happening, there's always a playful element and there's always a kind of writer figure hovering around, or a more than usually animated narrator. And then – in *Money* – there is the writer figure, me, who, having hovered round on the outskirts of previous novels, decides to come in, to actually enter the book. *London Fields* is a kind of post-modernist joke in that the narrator is taking something down that's actually happening, he's incapable of making anything up.

W.S.: And there's this Mark Asprey figure who you can heap opprobrium on . . .

M.A.: . . . Exactly. He's an anti-writer.

W.S.: Is that self-hatred?

M.A.: No. It's really a deflected parody of hatred I feel aimed at me.

W.S.: He's drawing fire?

M.A.: In a sense. But this is what a *really* hateful writer would be like. And now there's the novel which I'm doing at the moment, which is about – well, sometimes you have a dry run for a novel in its predecessor – and this novel is completely realistic, set in London, with a trip to America in the middle of it. This was going to happen in *London Fields*, and I wrote a whole middle section that took place in America, which I just didn't use.

W.S.: It was all impacted into the Departure Lounge.

M.A.: He never gets there. I was writing the American section and wondering why I felt ill. After a few weeks it dawned on me that the reason I was feeling ill was that these pages shouldn't be in the book. So that was a dry run for this one, which is about two writers; one is hideously successful – and undeservedly so. And the other is undeservedly neglected. Deservedly in the sense that what he writes is unreadable, but he is talented and he is a genuine artist in the way that the successful writer is not. And I imagine this book will have a lot of what *Money* and *London Fields* had, which is just what it's like to live in this city, now . . .

W.S.: . . . And 'Madame Bovary, c'est moi', have you split yourself in two?

M.A.: Yeah, as usual. I think this is to do with my essential comic crudeness as a writer. Most writers, if they were writing a novel like *London Fields*, would have used only one .male character, who would sometimes be romantic, and sometimes he would be lustful, sometimes have generous and beautiful thoughts, sometimes have mean and ugly thoughts. Most writers would have only had one child, sometimes nice and sometimes horrible. Comedy seems to flow from me when I can divide these traits. Many writers would be interested in the subtle shifts between these two moods. I'm much more interested in plastering them on to the walls.

W.S.: I would say that that's because, at root, you are a satirist. And satire is a form that depends on comic exaggeration, and on stereotyping.

M.A.: Do you feel *you* are a satirist?

W.S.: Unquestionably, yes. I mean, when critics say – well, one critic said about *Quantity Theory*: I don't think Self is interested in character, or in narrative, he's interested in conceits and language – and I took this on the chin. I read this when I was writing *Cock & Bull*, which is, of course, an elaborate joke about the failure of narrative. It's true, I'm not really interested in character at all. Indeed, I don't even really believe in the whole idea of psychological realism. I see it as dying with the nineteenth-century novel.

M.A.: Yes, I think a whole set of notions, of character and motivation, and fatal flaws and so on, are nostalgic creations . . .

W.S.: . . . It's sort of sentimentality . . .

M.A.: . . . Yes. Would that character were still like that – if indeed it ever was. It's much more jumbled and incoherent now.

W.S.: Kundera's point that people do construct elaborate motifs to grace their lives, to explain their lives to themselves. Perhaps in the nineteenth century people were much happier to do that, they had the sense that it was legitimate. Perhaps we don't feel that way any more?

M.A.: Think of the raw material that they had, and the raw material people have for this shaping now. What people are up to now is post-modernist, in the sense that they are loose beings in search of a form. And the art that they bring to this now, to shape their lives, is TV. In the nineteenth century, whatever it was, it wasn't TV. It might have been a penny dreadful, but it wouldn't have been a soap.

W.S.: Yes, that seems to be entirely legitimate. And I can't understand why people have difficulty with this philosophically, because it's obvious that something which is more commonly perceived just does have more ontological validity. Television is the new substratum in that sense.

M.A.: What is the urge to give your life shape? It's a muted artistic urge – is it not? But instead of doing it on the page, you do it to your life, or the way you think about your life.

W.S.: But isn't that the paradox: that the people who are given the job of describing what non-writers' lives are like actually don't – in quite a crucial way – understand what those lives are like?

M.A.: It is. Because I think, to writers, non-writing life actually appears appallingly thin; sort of one-dimensional, because nothing is being done with it. You're like a slave in your own life.

W.S.: That's the point about Tod's soul, his homunculus, his inner being, isn't it?

M.A.: That was a kind of instant decision, because I knew the novel couldn't be written any other way, except with an innocent narrator. But it also comments on the idea that one is just obeying orders, that one has no free will. And of course, later on, this was the most commonly grasped-for excuse: we were only obeying orders.

W.S.: This makes the 'moral' thrust of the criticism against you even more disturbing. Because it's quite clear that that's what you are commenting on, given your credits at the end of the book. And especially Levi's *If This Is a Man*; because his suicide occurred during, and some say it was predicated on, the growing tide of German revanchism, and their desire to abandon the notion of collective guilt – which they are. I was grilling a twenty-four-year-old Swabian about this the other night. And it's true, the new generation don't see themselves – as Germans – as having any responsibility for this. But I think the Germans committed a crime against the idea of nationhood that was so profound that they must be denied the opportunity to become a nation – in that sense – perhaps ever again.

M.A.: Yes, I think the Germans should have a few centuries more to meditate on what they did in the Second World War. But what seems to be happening now is a kind of punk notion, that there's no future. And another notion that there's no past. Except for the imagery that's helpful for nationalism: you can always loot the past for a few flags and badges. There is a new breed of people who are absolutely concentrated in the present and have a kind of contextless view. This seems to liberate them from any kind of morality. They are fixed in time, with no present and no future.

W.S.: But I would say that one of the things which characterizes Nazism is a kind of exaggerated sentimentality. You get that very well in *Time's Arrow*. And, of course, there's something mordant, if you look at late romantic German culture, which presaged the Holocaust. This kind of sickly carping on emotion, a kitschness about it. But the irony is – and you got this as well – that the Jews were very much involved in that late romantic phase of German culture. It's very odd.

Do you have any ideas on the relation between drugs and creative inspiration, the *machine à penser*?

M.A.: I'm a very habitual, but timorous, user of drugs. I think it's good for making notes, but not for the executive side of it. Good for ideas, but not for getting on with it.

ON OTHER THINGS

W.S.: It's what you could say about Burroughs: that he abandoned the control tower.

M.A.: Yes. I think if you're seriously into drugs, then drugs are going to become your subject, and you have to look around for a method, a way of writing about drugs, that has to do with drugs as well.

W.S.: I suppose that's true of me. I am a drug addict-writer in that way. But what I think is remarkable about marijuana is that it does produce this kind of conceptual synaesthesia: you 'hear smells' on the level of ideas. It produces these conceptual involutes. And I do think they're interesting. I've written on dope and off it, and I do think there's a certain 'X' factor.

M.A.: What's the difference? Is the whole operation different? Because when I'm actually writing a finished paragraph, I want to be straight. Even drink is no good . . .

W.S.: No, liquor isn't a working drug. Well, I wrote *Cock* entirely on hash. But that was smoking all day, every day, in Morocco, and that's a very different ambience. In England – I agree with you – I wouldn't finish a paragraph on dope.

M.A.: All day, every day, for how many days?

W.S.: Well, I wrote most of the first draft in about ten days. But although you say 'I'm a habitual but timorous user', in *Dead Babies* your evocation of the drug-saturated consciousness is very exact. There's a point where one of the characters lights a joint, and you say: 'hash smoke had become like air to him'.

M.A.: Yes, well that did reflect the terror engendered by my four encounters with LSD, and one with MDA, during my last year at Oxford. Two of the trips were nice and two were not nice.

W.S.: Ego death?

M.A.: Well, I don't quite know what it was, just the horrors. But I do know what Hunter Thompson means at the beginning of *Fear and Loathing*, when there are these two old heads drinking cocktails and tripping at the bar, and they've become so habituated to the horrors that he says: an old head will look down and see a miniature of his granny crawling up his thigh with a knife between her teeth, and won't think much of it. There they are – these two heads – seeing all these people in this awful Las Vegas bar, as dinosaurs eating each other. They're drinking and smoking, and saying to each other: 'Jesus, did you see that pterodactyl, have you ever seen so much blood in your life?' But they're completely calm. I never got to anything like that point.

W.S.: You say that, but in *London Fields* you say that addiction is 'easy to understand'. What do you mean by that?

M.A.: My sister is an alcoholic, and my oldest friend is an alcoholic. Both of them are partially reformed, but still alcoholics, as they'll be the first to tell you. I don't know, I think it's got to do with waking up and knowing that you're going to do it that day. And it's a deep physiological decision – if it's a decision in any sense – the body has made. And there's this great luxury – for a few hours – before you actually do it, of knowing that the debate is shelved, that you're just going to do it.

I increasingly find that once one has taken a drug, the next few hours have to be about *you*. And if you're a writer, it will either have to be planning something, or gloating over something. But you have to be the centre. And, as you get older, that begins to look like a steep price. You think, 'Look, I don't want it all to be about me this evening.' You don't want the self-communion.

W.S.: Yes, I agree. But – and there's an element of

self-pity – I feel trapped in that self-communion, because I grew up on drugs. By the time I was fifteen I was a daily drug user.

M.A.: Which drugs?

W.S.: Speed and dope; and then heroin when I was seventeen. So, I feel sort of protective of my younger self. I don't really think I stood a chance. But I also thought that if you were a hard drug addict, you were an underground writer, of necessity. It was horse and carriage. I felt very cheated when I woke up at the age of twenty-one with a bad heroin habit, in complete obscurity.

M.A.: You thought you were working all that time.

W.S.: But I do think that the Beat trinity of artist, hipster and spade was only the last in a long line of self-obsessed, thanatos-driven images of the creative sensibility. You do feel the pull of that, don't you?

M.A.: I don't know, *Novel with Cocaine* is something I might like to have written.

W.S.: It was a fraud, wasn't it?

M.A.: Yes. A lot people thought that Nabokov might have written it.

W.S.: I wanted to talk a bit about your willingness, and your freedom – which I envy – to acknowledge your mentors within your own work. Something I would find very hard to do – particularly with Nabokov. I'm thinking of a couple of passages in *London Fields*, where you explicitly draw out how you feel Nabokov might have dealt with, or reacted to, a situation. Are your spectral, ghostly mentors a bulwark against the late romantic, self-destructive image of the writer?

M.A.: I feel much happier about acknowledging them in my books now that they aren't influences, but rather inspirations. And that's a definite rite of passage: when they cease to be one thing and start to be the other.

W.S.: Is that – I'm skating on thin ice here – a feeling that they're your peers now?

M.A.: No. Absolutely not. It's just taking Nabokov and Bellow as examples – the feeling that I would no longer steal a phrase of theirs to get me out of a tight corner. The basis of all plagiarism is to feel the security of another writer's presence in your work, because everybody knows that *they're* good. So if I can get a bit of them in my work, it will give it a bit of strength. But, of course, it isn't; it's a bit of weakness. But now it's much more a feeling that when I address a particular scene or description, I think not so much: how would they do it? as just thinking that they've done it, and it can be done and it can be made new. So it's just a feeling of a kind of friendly presence.

W.S.: Maybe you can comment on this: for a lot of writers, the extent to which they feel their work is universal is predicated upon how they deal with cultural markers in their work. It's interesting that on the one hand you are very inventive – particularly with satirizing cultural semiology, signage is one of your preoccupations – and on the other hand you have this freedom about name-checking. Do you think about it in those terms? Do you think about things being more or less universal?

M.A.: Increasingly I've come to equate talent with the universal. Nabokov said, when asked to distinguish between various schools of writers, there was only one school of writers, that of talent.

W.S.: Is that in the *Lectures on Literature*?

M.A.: No, I think it's in *Strong Opinions*. And it's a very peculiar idea – talent. When I create a character who I think people aren't going to like, and I proceed without worrying about it, it's almost axiomatic that the more I think the character is hateful, the more it will be liked by readers. This is largely true of literature: we do like rogues and villains. And as Updike has said, the reason for this is that what we like is life. And if the character is alive, we will like it. If it is vigorous, we won't care about the morality of liking it, we'll just respond. But I think it's a universality question in that there's enough, as it were, John Self or Keith Talent in everyone – it may only be half a per cent, but it's enough. We all are that person sometimes.

When invoking these writers in my mind, it ties in with the dissipation question. In that they both happen to be very good examples of dedication. Fierce dedication. You can see the trouble with drugs in the history of American literature. After the Vietnam War, writers didn't actually have to be junkies, but they became identified with the drug counter-culture; the stately progress of the American novel actually disintegrated. And the writer became not an establishment intellectual figure, but a marginal one, with a sort of bandanna tied around his head. Robert Stone, Don DeLillo, etc. But I said to Robert Stone: 'What's your relationship with hard drugs?' And he said: 'I admire them from afar.' Mailer said that drugs were a form of spiritual gambling. What he meant by this was that when you take a drug, you call in quite a lot of future time and condense it in the experience. You are making a kind of raid on the future. And you have the intense experience – which lasts however long it lasts – but then you have depleted your future.

W.S.: That's why I'm so fucked. I've called it all in, far too early.

M.A.: It's a measurable deal. The time you've spent high, you have to spend at least that much time straight, to repay the debt.

W.S.: Nabokov, in the *Lectures on Literature*, is very preoccupied with the idea of topography in fiction as a means of understanding it. In his lecture on *Northanger Abbey*, he draws a diagram of the house . . .

M.A.: . . . And for Joyce, he draws a map of his Dublin.

W.S.: Now, in your writing on London – and this relates to the question of cultural markers – I wonder, how much do you want your readers to feel that they are in an actual London? And how much do you assume that if they don't know where they are, then they don't need to know where they are?

M.A.: Yes. Well, I don't know why Nabokov was so preoccupied by this. I think it's a kind of corrective literalism that he applies. He wants to cut through the haze that people feel when they read. That's why he always says: don't identify with the hero or heroine of the novel, identify with the author. See what the author is trying to do. Remember that debate that got going after *The Bonfire of the Vanities*. When Tom Wolfe wrote a piece saying the great subjects are all out there. The writer should be more journalistic, should do more research. And I think he even had a ratio between inspiration and research, which went something like: 20 per cent inspiration to 80 per cent research. I think that's fine for some writers, him for example. But for me it's the other way round, I don't want to do too much research. And this is what I try to do with London: I don't want to know too much about it. Of course, I soak it up willy-nilly, but I have to push it through my psyche and transform it. So it isn't, in the end, London any more. It's London in the patterning of my cerebellum.

W.S.: I must say, I do find your London a bit Saul Steinberg. There's a lot of signs, there are a lot of clouds – you seem very much concerned with cloudscape and stars – and in a sense not a lot else.

M.A.: Sure, that's true. It is the same old street that they walk up and down.

W.S.: And the sky is a real obsession . . .

M.A.: Well, Bellow talks about transcendentalism as being an aspect of the ghetto. Because, if in looking round you see everything there is to see in the form of the master mounds of human turpitude – by the time he was ten, he said he'd seen everything, murder etc. – so the head goes up, it has to. So, if you live in a city, the head goes up. It's a kind of physical imperative. And the sky mocks this arrangement. I mean, I feel more and more writers are always looking for first principles. And when I look around at the city I think, what's this doing here? Nobody said there had to be cities. It's just a direction we took and went along with. When I'm walking the streets, I'm thinking: why cars? Why parking meters? Why walls? Why bricks? Who said? It doesn't have to be this way.

W.S.: You get this through your gag in *Time's Arrow*, where Tod's soul thinks about the arbitrary way in which the city will become country . . .

M.A.: . . . That's right, and he wonders how cities arrive. Just in a sort of gasp of soot and men.

W.S.: My London is, I think, much more literal.

M.A.: Well, your London is your world. It's this place that nobody knows, that's unwritten. A kind of shadowy super-suburb, beyond the 'burbs, where everybody has peculiar jobs that no one knew about before.

W.S.: But also, I can draw an A–Z of my London. A schizophrenic once knocked on my door in Shepherd's Bush and said, 'Can you drive me to Leytonstone and give me £17.37', and I did. As we were driving to Leytonstone he was ranting, completely incoherent. And I said, 'Look, you're mad. I want to check in the A–Z exactly where you want me to take you before I go further.' And he said: 'But you and I know that the A–Z is a plan of what's going to be built.' That's how I conceive my London. But – and it's not a criticism of you in any way, our perceptions are different – in my London there is a lot between the signs and the sky. I'm very concerned with the physical reality of the buildings, the landscape. I'm harping on this, I suppose, because of what you said about Nabokov. About geography just being a critical corrective for him, because when you look at his own work it isn't really there. With a book like *Pnin*, it's a very odd New England, isn't it?

M.A.: Yes, it is. And the train conceit expresses this very nicely. In that when the book begins, he's on the wrong train.

W.S.: And it's the same for Berlin in *King, Queen, Knave*. So it's odd . . .

M.A.: Yes, and in *King, Queen, Knave* our sense of Berlin comes from Karl. From seeing it through Karl's myopic eyes. That's the beauty of it. His vision is not good. That's what the novel is about – his myopia. And the journey across America in *Lolita*: while it's given the motel bookmatch, the tourist guide treatment, it remains as nebulous as this sinuous trail of slime he talks about leaving in his wake.

W.S.: It's interesting that in your introduction to the new edition of *Lolita*, you champion the book on moral grounds. Are you being a bit perverse?

M.A.: There's something Oedipal in this. In that my father wrote a piece on the book, attacking it on moral grounds. He made the preposterous claim that there was no distance between Nabokov and Humbert Humbert. He said, you know, you look at *Pnin*, and it's the same style, so there's no question that this is Nabokov all over, this is Nabokov's unadorned voice.

W.S.: So it is very Oedipal?

M.A.: . . . Yes, it is. I must give my father this piece and say, 'Take that!' But what also pricked me was something I read that a friend of mine wrote recently. A very intelligent and good, close reader, Craig Raine. Who said that the end was tacked on to justify this priapic riot that's been going on for two hundred and fifty pages. And I thought, no, no, no. It's there all along. I think it is the truth of the novel, that he is in wonderfully subtle moral control throughout. He outsoaringly anticipates every possible moral objection from page one.

W.S.: The book is an enormous confirmation of that aphorism: God created sex in order to humiliate man, by forcing him to adopt ridiculous postures, isn't it?

M.A.: Yes. There's a link passage that happens both twenty pages into the novel and twenty pages from the end. The first instance is when Humbert is in Paris, and he's looking across a crowded bedsit, and in the half-light he sees what he thinks is a nymphet getting undressed. He watches, fascinated, and then as his climax is arriving, the image resolves itself into a repulsively fat man, sitting at a table in a vest reading a newspaper.

W.S.: But you're ambivalent about sex in your work, aren't you? There's a certain strain there.

M.A.: No, I don't think so. I mean, the world I write about, that invented world, presents very few opportunities for healthy Lawrentian sex. It's just not going to happen in your world . . .

W.S.: . . . No, indeed. I only have the one sex scene in *Quantity Theory*.

M.A.: The one with the fat blonde with the post-coital sweats . . .

W.S.: . . . That's right. And my narrator describes the sensation of his penetration of her as being that of 'a rubberized claw, torn from a laboratory retort and thrust into the side of a putrefying animal'. That's why, when I wrote *Cock*, I was pissed off, because some of the criticism seemed to imply that they didn't expect this sort of thing of me. Whereas . . .

M.A.: . . . It was ready to go.

W.S.: That's right. But perhaps it's just projection on my part, because I do have this ability to actually feel disgusted with sex.

M.A.: I would say that there is a strain of youthful sexual disgust, and that comes from the fastidious end of things.

W.S.: That's the skid mark in *The Rachel Papers*.

M.A.: There's a lot of it in that. Sometimes I'll pick it up, and I'll be skimming along, thinking 'Hum, there's a lot of vigour in this . . .' and then I'll reel back from the page. It's partly a kind of jelly-kneed fear of the political thought police. But that book is so pre-feminist anyway. Once I'm into my stride, I don't think that sort of thing crops up. But anyway, I reckon I can spot an actual misogynist at a hundred yards, and you're not one. I mean, there's that aside in *London Fields* where I describe some type who fixes your eyes with his, and then tells you some ghastly tale about a purulent mackerel in some unfortunate lady's knickers. Now that kind of guy I can see coming a mile off, and I know I'm not one.

W.S.: A critic described this – in my work – as the 'standard nail-paring prose of the callow male writer'. But when we get to *Money*, there's the flip side of this. There are the unfettered delights of Selena's knicker drawer.

M.A.: I've got into terrible trouble over underwear.

W.S.: But underwear just is sexy, isn't it?

M.A.: Well, statistically it is the case. Hugh Hefner's targeting people sorted this out many years ago. We all know that the difference between male and female sexuality is that men like pictures and women like words. There's a visual stimulus to do with the female shape, particularly when it's emphasized, or defined, by the standard underwear, that goes straight into the eye, then straight down the central nervous system to the penis. And that's the end of it: bingo.

W.S.: Yes. I wrote *Cock* out of rage at the involuntary character of my own sexual arousal. And I feel that in your work as well.

M.A.: I would say that the only aggressive feeling that I actually have towards women is to do with their power over me. That I've spent a big chunk of the last thirty years thinking about them, following them around, wanting to get off with them, absolutely enthralled. And that's bound to produce a slave's whinny for mercy every now and then. Tod, according to the narrator of *Time's Arrow*, is an insatiable chaser. He actually gets out of his chair to look at a passing shape, just because it might be a woman. The narrator says, 'Women are great', and I pretty much go along with him there.

W.S.: Would you like to be Jewish?

M.A.: I'm a very definite philosemite. My first love was Jewish. That's as formative as things get. I do like this kind of heightened intelligence, this tendency towards transcendentalism, which one associates with Jews. Because they are homeless, they're always looking upward.

W.S.: But isn't it also a corrective to the anti-intellectualism of Little England. It's a culture in which it's acceptable for men to be both effete and scholarly.

M.A.: Yes. I do think of the modern American Jewish experience as being to do with living in a ghetto and going, aged thirteen, to the library to read, say, Spengler. And then you went back to this house which you shared with eight families of Poles, who are killing each other all day long. The other thing I like is the promiscuity of verbal and social registers. So that the high and the low mix easily together. That's very attractive to me.

W.S.: Yes, as I see it one of the great achievements of your fiction is to mix high and low: the demotic and the mandarin.

M.A.: That's why the middle classes are underrepresented in my books.

W.S.: You don't like their language.

M.A.: There's nothing going on there.

W.S.: You want the proletarian cock to penetrate the bourgeois lexicon. You want it to push in there and spunk it up a bit.

M.A.: That's right. The novel I'm writing at the moment opens with a longish scene in which two writers are jockeying for position around each other. Then, suddenly, we cut to two bruisers who are watching these writers, for reasons that become apparent, and the injection of energy almost had me reeling back from the typewriter.

W.S.: That's Lawrentian, isn't it?

M.A.: There is a parody of *The Rainbow* in the early pages of *London Fields*. You know, 'Brangwen felt the wind on his chest, and how should this cease . . .' This is all done in Keith's terms: 'He had the Saudi Arabian Granny in the back of the cab, and how should this cease. He felt the tug of the pub . . .' You see it's a thwarted energy. It's an energy that has nothing to do, especially in a modern, post-industrial city.

W.S.: But you feel betrayed by the working class, don't you? You feel that they're decadent as well?

M.A.: I think it is an absolutely exhausted culture. But that's kind of great from my point of view. I try to get that in *London Fields*, where Keith goes into the television studio for the darts final and says, 'Where's the pub?' And they say, 'Well, we have enough trouble as it is without having to wheel two hundred pissers in and out of here every week.' And they use these outtakes of grannies having a knees-up when they have dead time to fill, and they have a machine that snorts cigarette smoke on to the oche.

w.s.: Is there also a fear there of tough guys, of people who really know how to fight?

M.A.: Non-civilians. I think that evaporates as you get older. I don't sense that much on the street any more. Because I think it has to do with gangs. I was a mod in the mod and rocker days. I had a scooter. And I was a hippy in the hippy and skinhead days, when one was obsessed with the idea of being beaten up. But it didn't stop you having long hair or wearing flowered shirts. It was part of the deal. I think it's a kind of mob-testosterone-territory thing. I like talking to working-class people, I like what they say. There's often something very beautiful about it.

w.s.: And that's your other life, isn't it? Down the club. It's also where the games make their appearance, isn't it? Which play a large part in your fiction. Chess, tennis . . .

M.A.: . . . Darts.

w.s.: Darts. But that's really a gag, isn't it?

M.A.: Yes, I suppose so, although I did get very deeply into darts culture, such as it is.

w.s.: But the gag about darts is really a gag about sports in general. You're really taking the piss out of your own interest in games, aren't you?

M.A.: Yes, that's right.

w.s.: I'm intrigued, because I don't have any interest in games, and I know why that is; it's because I can't stand to lose. I think you can't stand to lose either, but you're still prepared to play.

M.A.: I obviously can bear to lose, because I do a lot of it. I even set myself up to lose by playing people who are far better than me. I hate it every time, as if it's a fresh experience. But although the ludic element in writing is strong, games still feel like a relaxation from it. A therapeutic relaxation.

MARTIN AMIS

w.s.: I want all my playing to be in literature. Perhaps it's as Cocteau said, that up until the age of about thirty-five he simply couldn't bear his experience, in the sense that he wanted to transmute it into art so much that he could hardly get on with it. Is that something you feel you've gotten over?

M.A.: I increasingly wonder whether writers experience anything.

w.s.: Is this what's coming up in the new book?

M.A.: Yeah, some of this. The Wordsworth phrase, 'emotion recollected in tranquillity'. I think more and more of as 'emotion *invented* in tranquillity'. You're always on duty. It's like being a terrific snob. You're always looking for the writerly angle. When you're in the high-intensity phase of writing, you go home and you're not there at all. You're not there for your wife, or for your children. You are an impostor in your own life while you're living elsewhere. One definition of a writer is: 'He who is most alive when he is alone.' I don't know how that sounds to you, but it has a lot of pathos in it.

w.s.: Yes, well, Wittgenstein observed that, paradoxically, if you view the world from a completely solipsistic viewpoint, then since you are the universe, the universe must be real. I see that as being the writerly consciousness.

M.A.: And you're in a thoroughly godlike position vis-à-vis what you create.

w.s.: On this new book, it's being put about that it's concerned with literary rivalry. That's a telling phrase, 'put about . . .'

M.A.: If people think it's going to be about what I think of Will Boyd, then they're in for a big disappointment.

w.s.: That's what they want, isn't it?

M.A.: Yes, and really this book is a way of answering all the curiosity I feel directed at me.

W.S.: This age of literal-mindedness?

M.A.: Exactly. You'll get so used to hearing these questions when you do interviews, or readings, or signings. And they all reflect the same central question, which is: how's it done? My book is a kind of a joke, in that I say: you want to know about me, about writers, well here it is. But, of course, nothing would happen in the book, if it were about a writer. He would just get up and go to work. So, in a way I've had to pander to vulgar curiosity by making these writers great schemers in their careers. And I've had to put in a sub-plot, to give myself something to write about. So, it's a self-defeating exercise from the off.

W.S.: You like to kick ass though, don't you?

M.A.: Whose ass?

W.S.: Well, the people in the philistine journalistic culture, who are scheming their careers, using the medium of tomorrow's fish and chip paper.

M.A.: I'd like to kick ass in a very particular sense. I'll give you an example. In the correspondence I had with James Buchan, who reviewed *Time's Arrow* for the *Spectator*: he had said in his review that the whole thing came down to a question of taste. Well, I'm glad it comes down to that, because, if I come to your house, then I'm going to behave with good taste. But if you're going to enter the experience of reading me, it's so intimate, there's so much at stake, that really good taste is something that we're not going to bother with. It has no bearing upon art at all.

W.S.: Do you think there's something essentially phoney about aestheticism?

M.A.: Aesthetics as a field is fine, but good taste is just borrowing some social more and trying to plaster it all over literature.

w.s.: It's like Mill on money: you start off pursuing it for what it can get you, and end up pursuing it for itself. Isn't that true of aesthetics? You start off pursuing beauty for truth, and end up pursuing it for World of Interiors.

m.a.: Yes, we don't like that. It's an extra-literary consideration. It means, could you talk about it with your aunt in a salon? I don't want to write the sort of novels that people feel comfortable with.

w.s.: In that sense *Time's Arrow* was a definite advance on your earlier work.

m.a.: I don't know. It's too early to say. We won't know until it's been around for a few years. But in some ways I do view it as a bit of a diversion, in that what I feel I'm here for is to write about this city and what it's like to be alive in it now. That's the main thing. But I'm delighted to see any novel that comes along, asking to be written.

w.s.: Have you ever entertained this comparison between yourself and Evelyn Waugh? In the sense that you are both operating in a consciously postlapsarian world. A world in which we've fallen from grace. And while, of course, there are satirical elements in your books which suggest criticism from an ethical point of view, there is also a strong sense of amorality. Actually, I would also, contrary to yourself, view that as the congruence between your work and Nabokov's; it's amorality of tone. And an acceptance of the loss of objective moral correlatives.

m.a.: I am very interested in where my characters stand morally. And in that sense I'm not in a moral vacuum. But on the other hand, I don't feel any urge to convert them, or punish them, or bring them round. Or even to make them see what they're doing. Because that doesn't square with how I see the world.

w.s.: With the truth?

m.a.: Yes, with the truth. Also, whatever I inherit from

my father, I inherit from my mother a deep reluctance to judge. If you said to my mother, 'I'm a junkie, nymphomaniac, kleptomaniac', she'd say, 'Of course, dear.' 'I was in Spain with her once, and we were walking down the street when the local spastic came past. He walked very oddly, like a marionette, with one eye here and one eye there. And he's very kindly treated by everyone in the street. My mother said as he walked past, 'I love living in Spain. I now regard that as *completely* normal.' There's a paragraph in *London Fields* where I tried to express this – about Keith: 'I try to imagine him as a child, being slapped by his dad for getting the score wrong . . .' And then I say: but hold on a minute, if you go that far back in anyone's life – you can't judge them. Because it's all there, it's all intelligible, it's all written. There's nothing they can do about it.

W.S.: And now, as Camus says, 'Every man is responsible for the nature of his own countenance.'

M.A.: I don't agree. The forty-year-old in the new novel quotes that line, not exactly, but, 'By the age of forty every man has the face he deserves.' And he's looking in the mirror thinking, 'But no one deserves the face I've got. Not even Caligula or Mengele deserves this face.' And, in fact, that's true. You know, the grinning porn star, the handsome child-dismemberer, they all exist.

W.S.: But maybe not true of writers?

M.A.: Not true of people. Period.

W.S.: I don't know. I look in the mirror and think, 'You've got everything you deserve. It's written there.'

M.A.: I think it's a great remark because it describes the suspicion of the truth.

W.S.: There's a great *New Yorker* cartoon with the caption 'The T-shirt of Dorian Gray', which shows a sort of grinning, nerdish, Alfred E. Neuman figure with his face hideously distorted on the T-shirt he's wearing.

We've skirted round this, and I feel a reticence on your part to pin down this business of being a stranger in a strange land. Englishness specifically. And your generation of writers have been accused of attaching themselves to other countries. Barnes to France, yourself to America. Is this true? Are you English?

M.A.: Oh yes, inescapably. But sure, I do need the North Atlantic, just for air as much as anything else.

W.S.: And what about monoglotism? Again, I don't think it's something you say in your introduction to *Lolita*, but there is a penetration into the English language, from outside, that gives Nabokov's narrative voice a peculiarly distanced feeling.

M.A.: There are very odd Russianisms: 'She had the cheek of taking my photograph.' But then again, for page upon page, startling intimacy with the English language, and terrific ear as well. They say the great twentieth-century writers are Conrad and Nabokov, because they had to come to the language from outside. I do suffer from monoglotism, and sometimes think that it would be nice to take a step out of the language and look back at it. But Nabokov made all these super-articulate laments for the beautiful plasticity of the Russian language he had abandoned; and yet, when he came to translate *Lolita* into Russian, he found it terribly limited.

W.S.: One knows intellectually that one's lexical palette is a lot bigger in English. In fact Russian is the only other language with as large a vocabulary.

M.A.: Whereas in Spanish they have only one word for walk. There's no slouch, or amble, or wander.

W.S.: In a way that's a problem for English writers now; there's no incentive to get out of the language.

It's like being a child in a room full of sweeties; you needn't leave.

M.A.: Yes, I'm much more interested in how my novels go down in New Zealand than in France . . .

W.S.: Really?

M.A.: Oh yes. Because once it's translated, it's only half me. The historical accident of Americans speaking English is what's made it so encompassing. They were only two votes away from making it German.

W.S.: Is what attracts you to America the English view of it as being raunchy, emotionally immediate, lacking side? Lacking class in that way, is that the appeal?

M.A.: The appeal is of another vast language centre, really. But I think the greatest American export has really been one notion, and that is 'the cool'. That's an American idea – it's certainly not an English one.

W.S.: Perhaps Afro-American?

M.A.: I think just American.

W.S.: But I think there is a very powerful synergy between black and white. The modern popular song is an elision between traditional English ballad form and the 4/4 rhythm of Africa. It's a great myth that soul is black music; it's black/white music. And maybe 'cool' is black/white as well?

M.A.: Well, wherever it comes from, all Americans are capable of it – and the English aren't.

Mississippi Review, Summer 1993